W9-BLE-014

UNION PUBLIC LIBRARY
TIVERTON, R. I.

May 1977

The Encyclopedia of Household Plumbing Installation and Repair

by Martin Clifford

N. F. 3099

BONANZA BOOKS • NEW YORK

The Encyclopedia of Household Plumbing Installation and Repair

by Martin Clifford

DRAKE PUBLISHERS INC.

NEW YORK • LONDON

Copyright © MCMLXXVI by Martin Clifford
Library of Congress Catalog Card Number: 75-10777
All rights reserved.
This edition is published by Bonanza Books
a division of Crown Publishers, Inc.
by arrangement with Drake Publishers Inc.
a b c d e f g h
Manufactured in the United States of America

CONTENTS

THE ENCYCLOPEDIA OF HOUSEHOLD

PLUMBING

Chapter *I*

The Plumbing System in Your Home

Basically, a plumbing system is simple. Fresh water comes into your home, is used for various purposes, and then exits into a drainage arrangement. Water just doesn't flow into your house; it is pushed. It is water pressure, the force exerted on water by machines, that sends the water to the upper floor of your home. You don't need to push the water for the return trip, for gravity takes care of that. When you open a faucet, water doesn't fall out; it is pushed. But the water going down the sink drain does fall in response to the pull of the earth.

All plumbing systems have three main sections, or divisions: the fresh water supply, drainage, and a vent or air system.

The Fresh Water System

If a plumbing system looks complicated, it is simply because you aren't familiar with it. The water is conveyed to various fixtures—your sinks, your bathtub and shower, your toilet—by means of pipes. To get to these fixtures the pipes must make various bends and turns. A single pipe conceivably could be designed to extend from the point where the water supply enters your home to a fixture, but it just isn't practical to do so. Instead, various straight lengths of pipe are used, together with various sections of pipe which make right angles. The pipes are often joined by a thread arrangement at their ends.

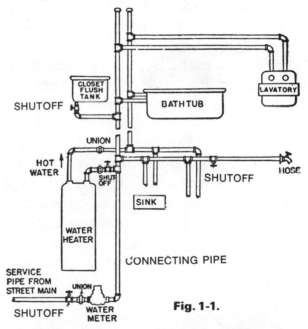

Fig. 1-1.

Part of the water piping arrangement in a home.

Fig. 1-1 shows one possible piping arrangement. The lower left of the drawing shows that water comes into a house from a service pipe connected to the street main. There is a shutoff valve connected to the service pipe, a union, and then a water meter. There is usually another shutoff valve following the water meter. The valve preceding the meter is called the meter shutoff; that following it is the main shutoff. When you need to close off the total water supply to your home, and you can be sure there will be such times, always use the main shutoff valve. As a start toward becoming acquainted with your plumbing system, you should locate the water meter and the main shutoff valve. Some meters come equipped with a hinged face cover to protect them against dirt and damage. To see the meter, just lift the meter cover.

Locate, in Fig. 1-1, the part labeled "union," positioned between the meter shutoff valve and the water meter. A union is simply a threaded connecting link, in this case between the water shutoff valve and the meter. It is more practical to use a union than to try to connect the meter shutoff valve directly to the meter.

After it flows through the water meter, the water goes through the main shutoff valve (not shown in the drawing) and then passes through a connecting pipe. Although this connecting pipe is shown as verticial in the illustration, it may be a combination of vertical and horizontal pipes.

At the top end of the connecting pipe the water is able to follow several paths. It may pass through the water heater shutoff valve, shown to the left of the connecting pipe. If it does so, it will enter the water heater, where its temperature will be raised to an amount depending on the setting of some sort of gauge or thermostat on the water heater.

The water may also flow to the right to a sink, or continue on to to a tub, or, finally, to an outside hose connection, shown at the far right. And it may do all these things simultaneously. Thus, you may have the sink faucet turned on, the outside hose turned on, and also water replenishing the supply in the water heater. If the water pressure is low—that is, the water pressure maintained by your local water company or government—then the water may emerge as a trickle. If the pressure is adequate, the water will flow quite strongly.

From the connecting pipe the water also may continue up to a closet flush tank, or toilet tank, to a bathtub, and to a lavatory sink. Note that some of the fixtures, such as the closet flush tank, the outside hose, and the hot water heater, have separate shutoff valves. This means you can discontinue the flow of water to these fixtures when they are in need of repair. If the plumbing system did not contain such valves, the only alternative would be to close the main shutoff valve. The effect would be the same as turning off the individual shutoff valves, but closing the main shutoff valve means having the inconvenience of no water in the household.

Hot and Cold Water Supplies

The hot and cold water arrangements are part of the fresh water supply system. In Fig. 1-2, the white pipes are the cold water pipes; the black are for hot water. At the lower right of the drawing, you will see that all water arrives through the pipe connected to the water meter. There is a connection between the

their respective faucets or, more simply, by touching. Turn on the hot water faucet and let the water flow for a while, long enough to warm the pipe.

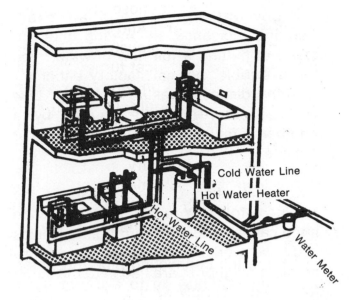

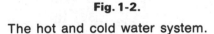

Fig. 1-2.

The hot and cold water system.

hot water heater and the cold water line, but this is simply so that the heater can get water. From the heater the cold water line connects to various fixtures on the lower and upper floors.

All hot water comes from a pipe connected to the hot water heater. Whether hot water or cold comes out of left or right faucets depends on the plumbing contractor. Actually, it makes very little difference. Fig. 1-2, indicates it is the right faucets that control the hot water. It could just as easily have been the left. In some cases a faucet is designed to handle both hot and cold water, with the temperature of the water determined by the handle position.

You can learn which are the hot or the cold pipes either by tracing them to

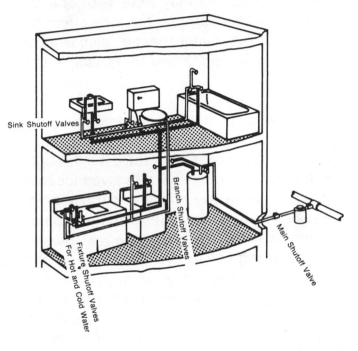

Fig. 1-3.

Shutoff valves in a home plumbing system.

Shutoff Valves

You have at least one shutoff valve, most probably more. The main shutoff valve, located close to the water meter (Fig. 1-3), closes water flow throughout the entire fresh water system. Indirectly, it also turns off the drain system as well, for without a supply of fresh water, any water remaining in the system can soon be removed. There are various reservoirs of water in your home. The water heater is one; the toilet tank is another. But unless these receive a replenishing supply, they soon run dry.

It has become good plumbing practice in newly built homes to install individual shutoff valves for each fixture. The toilet may have one such valve, since it uses cold water only, but a sink or washing machine may have two: one for the cold water supply, the other for the hot. The hot water heater also has a shutoff valve connected in its cold water line.

The most convenient and certainly the most logical place for individual shutoff valves is at the fixture itself. Thus, a sink will have its shutoff valves located directly below it, usually not too visible, but certainly accessible. In some cases, however, the shutoff valve is located some distance away, possibly in the basement of the house. In any home, it is a good idea to locate the shutoff valves before trouble starts, so you will know where they are when you need them.

The purpose of an individual shutoff valve is to let you close the water flow to a fixture. You can turn off the main shutoff valve to make plumbing repairs, but this can be inconvenient. It is much easier and better to work with an individual valve. And if a fixture, possibly because of age, does not have one, installing one is a worthwhile project.

In addition to the main shutoff valve and the various fixtures shutoff valves, a fresh water supply system may have branch valves. Such valves control water flow through a branch network of pipes going to various fixtures. They are useful when it becomes necessary to close the flow of water to a certain section of the house. Fig. 1-3 shows the location of the three types of shutoff valves in the home.

What You Can Do about Low Water Pressure

Low water pressure is an exasperating nuisance. It means that instead of getting a full flow of water, you get a dribble, not satisfactory either for washing dishes or taking a shower. Low water pressure can be caused by a number of factors, either in your home or outside it.

Locatization of the problem is the routine to follow. You must first determine if the cause is outside your home. Unless you have a private well, you and your immediate neighbors are tied in to the same fresh water supply system. Get in touch with these neighbors and determine if they too are plagued with low water pressure. If they are, then the fault is outside your home and now becomes the province of your local water company or government. A phone call or two should get you the information as to why water pressure is low and when pressure will be restored.

If the problem is one that has lasted a long time, possibly a month or several months, then you can be fairly sure you have an in-house plumbing difficulty. You can be absolutely sure of this if some of your faucets have normal pressure while others are weak.

Sometimes the problem is due to nothing more than the busy fingers of children who have located shutoff valves beneath sinks and have turned them a bit—not enough to close off the water supply but enough to make it dribble weakly. So your first step is to go to every fixture you have and determine that all shutoff valves are turned on. To make sure of this, turn their handles counterclockwise. This will open them to maximum. And in your inspection tour, be sure to include *all* valves. This means not only fixture valves but branch valves, and also the main valve in your basement or wherever your fresh water supply enters your home.

If your faucets, shower heads, and washing machine are equipped with aerators, remove them and examine them. They use fine mesh screening that can easily become partially clogged. While it is unlikely that all the aerators will become clogged at the same time, it is still a possibility. Sediment accumulating in the aerators will not turn off the water flow, but will diminish it considerably. The solution is simple: Either clean out the aerators or replace them. After you remove the aerators, turn the faucets full on. If at that time the water supply comes full on, your problem is solved.

If that has not eliminated the problem, your next step is to compare the hot water flow with the cold. Do they flow with unequal force? Does the hot water flow much more slowly than the cold? If you have already checked the hot water shutoff valve and have made sure it is fully open, then you have a clogged water heater.

Turn the heater off and let the water cool for several hours. Then, using a bucket, flush the heater by opening its drain valve. This may remove any clog that exists in the exit pipe of the heater. If

not, then you may have a heater that is badly corroded. In that case you have no choice but to replace it. At this point you will need a plumber to advise you. He will be able to tell you if your conclusion is correct.

The best hot water heater to buy is one having a large capacity. If you are going to use gas heat, install at least a 40-gallon unit. Use a 60-gallon unit for an electrically operated hot water heater. This will save you the aggravation of having the hot water run cold when you least expect—or want—it, and it will permit the simultaneous use of a number of hot water faucets. It's a nuisance to postpone shaving become someone else is taking a shower or washing dishes, and vice versa.

If you have a problem of low water pressure and none of your sinks has leaking faucets, that's the time to become suspicious. If water pressure is extremely low, it may not be enough to cause a faucet drip.

If just one faucet gives symptoms of low water pressure, but there is adequate pressure at all the other faucets, you have obviously located the trouble. Located it, but not cured it. The difficulty may very well be inside the faucet. Remove the handle and then the stem of the faucet. Detailed instructions for doing this are given in a later chapter. The faucet valve seat may be corroded or the washer may be twisted up and bent out of shape. Sometimes pieces of the washer fall off and manage to clog the flow of water. Sometimes the valve seat bends inward because of corrosion. This has the effect of narrowing the channel through which the water flows. You can repair the seat with a suitable tool or replace the entire faucet.

Take a tour of areas in your home that have exposed piping. If the pipes are deeply pitted, if they show white spots, if they have pinhole leaks which you repaired at one time, it may be that your pipes are gradually filling with the results of metal corrosion. Still another problem is mineral buildup inside the pipes. If the pipes are not too far gone, a water softener may help. There are water softener powders you can use, or permanent water softening devices you can have installed.

Clogging due to mineral buildup takes place in horizontal piping. You may need the services of a plumber to open the joints (where the pipe connects with some other pipe) for a visual inspection.

Water pressure is a function of your fresh water supply system. It has nothing to do with the other part of your plumbing setup—drainage and venting. So don't bother taking traps apart, or tapping on drain pipes or trying to examine air vents. That would just be a waste of your time.

Water Costs and How to Cut Them

In many areas, water coming into your home is metered, particularly if you have a house. If a faucet leaks at the rate of 60 drops a minute, not at all an unusual situation, you will be allowing a total of 2,-299 gallons a year to go running down the drain. Look at your water bill to determine how much this costs you, or else phone your water company. They'll be glad to give you the good news.

The cost of water varies depending on where you live. In some cities neither private houses nor apartment buildings are metered. Bills are sent to property owners based on average use. But in other areas many private homes do have meters with the cost of water ranging from about 30 to 85 cents per 1,000 gallons.

An average family uses about 60 gallons per day per person; more in the summer, less in the winter. For a family of four this will be about 18,000 to 20,000 gallons every three months. If your water rate is 50 cents per 1,000 gallons, your quarterly cost is $10. Of course, in some areas, where water is rather scarce, the price is much higher.

Fig. 1-4.

Water meter measures water in gallons or cubic feet.

Your water meter, Fig. 1-4, measures water in gallons or in cubic feet. If you want to know how much water you are using, just read the meter and make a record of the numbers, and repeat the process a week later. Subtract

6

the first reading from the second to get your water consumption for that week.

You can easily convert cubic feet of water to gallons. There are approximately 7½ gallons of water per cubic foot. If your meter registers 14,105 cubic feet at the first reading and 21,797 at the second reading, you have used 21,797 minus 14,-105, or 7,692 cubic feet of water. Multiply by 7½ to get the volume in gallons: 7,692 x 7½ = 5,769 gallons. At a cost of 40 cents per 1,000 gallons, this would be $2.30. Of course, if your meter reads directly in gallons the arthmetic becomes much easier. If your water bills seem unusually high and the water meter is an old one, have your water company run a test on it. As meters get older, they lose their accuracy.

Water Leaks

You can lose water in your home without being aware of it. As the water dribbles down the drain, so does the money you pay for it. To determine if you are losing water somewhere in your plumbing system, turn off all faucets and all appliances that use water. Check your water meter and take note of the reading. An hour later, the meter reading should be identical to your first one. If the leak is more than just a small one, you will be able to see one of the pointers on the meter moving.

To locate a water leak, first check all your faucets. With the handles turned to their off position, there should be no dripping of water, not even drops. If you have water spots on a ceiling or wall, you have evidence of a leak. Touch the spots. If

they feel slightly damp, you've located a leak. Examine all toilets. If the water shutoff mechanism in the toilet tank isn't working properly, it will let water dribble into the tank. This water must go somewhere, and so it will run down the overflow tube in the tank. If you examine the water in the toilet bowl, you may see evidence of bubbling— tiny air bubbles beneath the surface. This indicates an overflow condition in the tank.

Check all exposed pipes. Unexplained drops of water on the floor may be caused by a leak. If it is produced by condensation on the outside wall of the pipe, it will not result in a single wet area but will show wetness all along the floor, in a line following the pipe. Check radiator valves for leakage. Also check all pipe joints, that is, sections where one pipe joins another.

How to Save Water

The first step in saving water is to make sure you have no leaks anywhere. A periodic check will not only save money on water bills, but may save on painting and other repairs.

If you have had your plumbing fixtures for a long time and they are due to be replaced, consider installing some new ones designed to be water savers. You can, for example, get a toilet that uses about half as much water as older models installed years ago.

If your present toilet is working well and does not give you any trouble, you can get a kit that changes it into a dual flush cycle type. These units have two flushes: one for a liquid waste, the other for solid. Because liquid waste is easier to flush away, the liquid waste flush works with less water. The standard toilet has only one flush, which is designed for flushing solids. Thus, it uses the same amount of water for liquid or solid waste. This means that for liquid waste only, it uses a lot of water unnecessarily.

There are many other ways you can conserve water, but they take some alert thinking. Don't let the faucet run full on while you brush your teeth. Don't let your lawn sprinklers come on automatically during a rain or shortly thereafter. You can save both water and fuel charges by using the right amount of water for cooking or making coffee. A shower takes much less water than a tub. Use the right amount of water in your clothes-washing machine.

Hard Water

Water containing dissolved lime, or calcium, is called "hard." You can't smell, taste, or see it, but you'll know you have hard water when clothing comes out of your washer looking sort of grayish, or when stains and spots begin to form on your plumbing fixture plating. Hard water forms scale inside boiler pipes, and it will do so inside a teakettle as well. As a final check, call your local water company. They will tell you all about the water hardness of your fresh water supply. You may need to install a water softener.

Plumbing Drawings

Figure 1-5 is called a pictorial. The great advantage of this type of drawing is that it supplies a good picture of how pipes are connected and their relation-

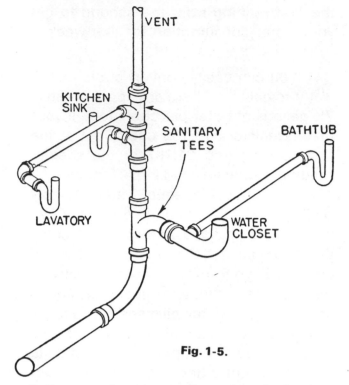

Fig. 1-5.

Bathroom pipe connections for single-story house.

ship to each other. Dimensions aren't ordinarily used in a pictorial. Don't expect your plumber to show you a drawing of this kind. Through experience he knows just what the pipe setup looks like. Instead, he may show you a drawing like Fig. 1-6. This is much easier to draw, and the plumber need not be an artist to do it.

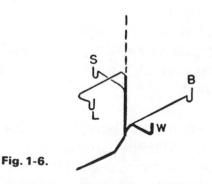

Fig. 1-6.

Drawing of plumbing arrangement using plumbing symbols. This represents the same arrangement shown in Fig. 1-5.

In Fig.1-6 the vent portion is shown by a dashed line; the soil stack by a rather thick solid line. Letters represent the fixtures: *B* stands for bathtub, *S* for sink, and so on. Vertical lines indicate vertical piping; horizontal lines horizontal piping. A bend in any line represents a corresponding bend in the pipe. Traps look somewhat like the letter *U,* but with one of the straight lines of the *U* longer than the other.

Of course, Figs. 1-5 and 1-6 represent the same plumbing installation. Both types of drawings will be used throughout this book.

Drainage and Venting Systems

Of the three sections of the plumbing system in your home, the fresh water supply is and must be independent of the other two—the drainage and venting systems. Drainage and venting are inseparable, and a drainage pipe can serve both for the removal of waste and also as a vent, to supply air.

The purpose of a draining system is to carry away water which has been used. This includes water from kitchen, bathroom, and laundry sinks; bathtubs; showers; utility tubs; clothes and dish washing machines; and toilets. After the water has been used in any of these fixtures, it is no longer fit for human consumption and must be removed. Such water often contains disease producing bacteria.

While the water supply system and the drainage system are completely separated, and must be completely separated, to prevent contamination of the fresh water supply, there are times when a cross connection occurs. This is an undesirable condition under which the water in the drainage system can get across and into the fresh water system.

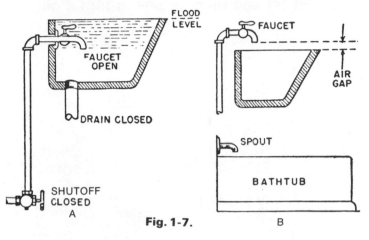

Fig. 1-7.

Drawing A shows a possible cross connection between drainage and fresh water supply systems. Air gap between faucet and spout (B) prevents this condition.

Cross Connection

Fig. 1-7 illustrates how a cross connection can exist between the fresh water supply and the drainage system. Here we have a sink with an open faucet and a closed drain. Dirt from the drain can now mix with water in the sink or tub and enter through the faucet. The dirt can diffuse through the fresh water supply and then exit through other faucets in the house.

There are several ways of preventing this situation. One is to mount the faucet so an air space exists between the topmost level of the sink or tub and the faucet or spout. In this way there is no possibility that waste water will get into the fresh water supply.

A more modern arrangement is to have an overflow relief, an opening in the sink or tub that will drain excess water when it reaches a certain height. The overflow drain is also a protection against flooding in the event someone turns on the faucet and then forgets to turn it off.

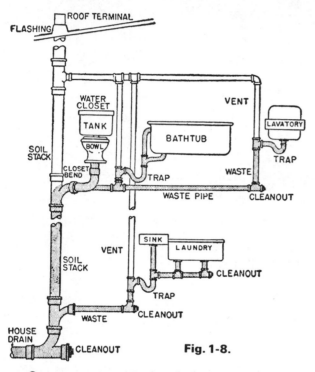

Fig. 1-8.

One arrangement of a drainage system.

A Drainage System

Fig. 1-8 shows one arrangement of a drainage system. Note that while there are traps, there are, unlike the fresh water system, no shutoff valves. The purpose of the traps is to prevent gases which develop in the waste pipes from working their way through the pipes and into the home. The traps also help prevent the crossover of waste water into the fresh water supply.

The drainage system is made up of two parts: The first consists of pipes and

fittings which carry water, waste, and food particles; the second consists of pipes and fittings which carry only air. The pipes which carry liquid and other matter include drain pipes, waste pipes, and a part of a pipe known as the soil stack. In Fig. 1-8 the liquid-carrying pipes are colored gray.

The pipes that carry air are vent pipes, vent stacks, and the upper part of the soil stack. The vent pipes are shown as white in Fig. 1-8. A vent is any pipe which allows the flow of air to and from a drainage pipe, or any pipe which allows air to circulate in the drainage system.

Air vents keep water from being forced out of the traps. Note that each of the vent pipes in Fig. 1-8 terminates in a union that connects to a trap. The laundry tub doesn't have its own trap but shares one with a nearby sink. In more modern installations the laundry tub is either omitted or is equipped with a trap of its own.

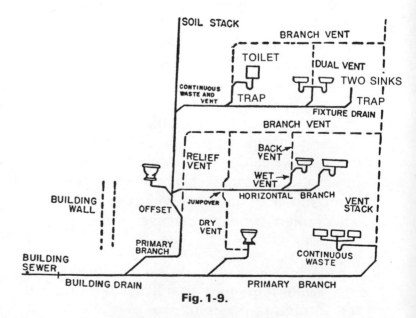

Fig. 1-9.

Pipes in the drainage system.

The Names of Drainage Pipes

Pipes used in the water supply and drainage systems in your home have names which often define the work they do. Fig. 1-9 shows a representative drainage system and the names of the pipes used in that system.

The general name "drain pipe" is given to any pipe which carries away water waste in the drainage system. The words "drain pipe" are used to distinguish pipes in the drainage system from those in the fresh water system.

A fixture drain is that part of a drain line between the fixture trap and the point where it joins any other drain pipe. You can get a clearer understanding by looking at the upper part of Fig. 1-9 and locating the two adjoining sinks. Each of these sinks has a trap. The toilet shown to the left of the double sink also has a trap. The traps of these fixtures empty into a fixture drain which carries the waste liquid to a pipe called the soil stack. The drawing shows representative traps and the beginning of the fixture drain.

A waste pipe is a drain connected to any fixture that supplies nonhuman liquid waste. This includes pipes connected to kitchen sinks, laundry tubs, and bathroom tubs but excludes urinals and toilets, since these carry human waste.

The largest pipe in the plumbing drainage system is the building drain, or the house drain. You can see the beginning of this pipe in the lower left part of Fig. 1-8, shown earlier. This is the pipe which leads to the outside house sewer

pipe, which, in turn, runs to a sewer. All of the drain pipes in the drainage system ultimately reach the house drain.

Drain pipes and waste pipes do not run directly to the house drain. Instead, they form branches which lead to a larger pipe, called a main. Thus, as shown in Fig. 1-8, the soil stack is a main, accepting waste from a number of pipes. The word "stack" is used to identify any vertical main in the drainage system.

Figs. 1-8 and 1-9 also show the various vents, which, of course, are also pipes. A branch vent, as shown in the upper part of the drawings, means a pair of fixtures have vents which join and which then lead to a main vent or vent stack. A dual vent connects to the point at which two fixture drains come together and provides a vent for both drains. A continuous waste and vent is a vent pipe and a waste pipe in a straight line.

The same illustrations also show relief vents. A relief vent is connected between a branch from the vent stack and the soil stack or a waste stack. The branch and relief vents let air circulate between the two stacks to which they are connected.

A back vent is any vent that lets air enter a waste pipe to prevent water from being drawn out of fixture traps by siphoning action. A wet vent is any section of a waste pipe that also acts as a vent for other fixtures on the same line.

A horizontal branch, or lateral, is a drain pipe that receives the discharge from one or more fixtures and extends to the soil stack.

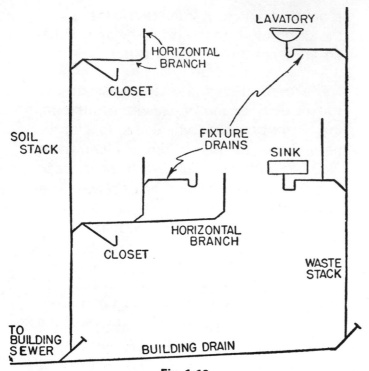

Fig. 1-10.

Alternative arrangement of a drainage system.

Arrangement of Drainage

Because drainage pipes can often cause serious problems in a plumbing installation, it is a good idea to get a general overall view of the piping arrangement. Fig. 1-10 is a line drawing that should give you a good perspective.

The building drain shown at the bottom of the drawing is the lowest pipe in the drainage system. Consider it as a sort of pipe reservoir which receives all waste products produced in your home. Note that the line representing the building drain slopes downward, because the actual pipe does so. The waste feed arrangement is a gravity system. Waste exits from the building drain to a sewer, also by gravity. Actually, all horizontal branches, or laterals, have a downward slope as well.

Fig. 1-10 shows just one possible arrangement of the drain and waste pipes. In some installations, a fixture or group of fixtures may exit into a common pipe which makes a junction somewhere with the building drain. This common pipe will supplement the soil stack and waste stack.

Drain pipes up to 2 inches in diameter are made of galvanized wrought iron or galvanized steel. In larger sizes, pipes are made of cast iron. Underground drain piping is cast iron, not wrought iron or steel.

Drain Pipe Sizes

Drain pipe sizes are often determined by local plumbing codes. If you plan to have a pipe replaced, your plumber can advise you of the pipe size he intends using. As a general rule, you can install pipe having a larger diameter but may not have smaller pipe replacements. The larger the diameter of the pipe, the more it costs. While a larger diameter pipe may have certain benefits—it will handle a larger volume of waste—there is also the practical problem of connecting the pipe into an existing system.

The following table will give you some indication of the minimum diameter, in inches, of representative fixture drains. You should regard these as average, not mandatory. Your local plumbing code may specify other sizes, but you will probably find they are very close to those in the table.

Fixture Drains

Fixture	Minimum Diameter in Inches
Bathtub, foot bath, sitz bath, or bidet	1½
Shower head	1½
Shower stall	2
with multiple sprays	3
Lavatory, one (1½-inch preferred)	1¼
two	1½
three	2
Water closet (direct to stack)	3
Urinal, wall hung or stall type	2
pedestal and blowout types	3
Slop sink	2
Kitchen sink	1½
Pantry sink	1½
Two sinks	2
Laundry trays: 1-, 2- or 3-section, one trap	1½
combination with one sink, one trap	1½
Floor drain, plain	2
Rainwater leaders	3
Areaway drains	3
Semipublic or public bathtub	2
Semipublic or public shower head	2
Semipublic or public multiple spray shower stall	3
Restaurant or hotel glass, silver, or dishwasher sink	1½
Restaurant or hotel pot sink	3
Restaurant or hotel vegetable sink	2
Bar sink, large (lunch counter, etc.)	2
Bar sink, small (soda fountain, etc.)	1¼
Service sink, plain	2
Slop sink with jet or flushing rim	3
Drinking fountain	1¼

The reason for having drains of sufficient size is to enable the pipe to carry away normal discharges from the fixtures in your home. You cannot assume just one fixture will used at a time. Ideally, your drain pipes should be able to handle the waste product of every fixture in your home working simultaneously. While this is unlikely to happen, at least it eastablishes a maximum working limit.

Operating on the theory that if a little is good, then a lot must be better, it is possible to go to extremes. Oddly, pipes that are too large are undesirable. While you don't want the drain pipe to be so small as to interfere with the passage of waste, a pipe having too large a diameter will reduce the velocity of movement of the waste. A rapid movement of waste helps keep the interior of the pipe free of clogs and deposits. And so, piping size is a matter of compromise and experience.

However, this doesn't actually leave you up in the air with no place to go. If you are planning to have piping replaced, take the experience you have had with your in-home plumbing into consideration. If you have constant clogging of the drains, if there is a tendency for waste to back up into your sinks, then there is a possibility that pipes of the wrong size were installed originally.

Sometimes this situation arises when you add more fixtures to a house without taking into consider that the waste from such additional fixtures must be handled by the drain pipes in your home. But at least, an understanding of the problem will enable you to discuss it more intelligently with your plumber, who can then advise you of what your local plumbing code will or will not permit you to do.

Joining Pipes of Different Sizes

It is possible, through suitable connectors, to join pipes of different sizes. Thus, the drains that feed into the building drain usually have a smaller diameter than the building drain. So this situation isn't at all uncommon.

There are three possibilities: pipes

of the same size joining; a small pipe joining a larger pipe; a larger pipe joining a smaller pipe. With pipes of the same size there is no problem, assuming, of course, that the pipe has the right diameter for the job it is supposed to do.

When a large pipe feeds into a smaller one, there is always the possibility of blockage and backup. The larger pipe can handle so much more waste so much more quickly that it may easily overwhelm the capacity of the smaller pipe. And so, as a rule, we don't want to feed from a larger pipe to a smaller one.

It would seem that feeding from a smaller pipe to a larger should present no problems, and yet it does. It all depends on the ratio of the two sizes. If you have a very small pipe—that is, a pipe with a small diameter connected to one having a much larger diameter—you can get a rapid drop in the temperature of the waste liquid. The velocity in the large pipe will be much less than in the smaller one.

Consider also that this piping may be in an unheated area, such as a basement. The reduced temperature may help cause the formation of greases, which in turn could represent the beginning of a clog. There are so many factors involved it is impossible to make a positive prediction. But a clog *is* a possibility.

Slope of Drain Pipes

There are two ways in which you can increase the velocity of waste in a drain pipe. One method is to use pipe with a small diameter. There is a practical limitation, of course, for if the diameter is too small, the waste will just pile up inside the pipe. Another method is to give the drain pipe a downward pitch or slope. Pitches vary from 1/16 to 1/2 inch per foot of horizontal length, but a pitch of 1/4 inch per foot of pipe is commonly used.

The pitch must not be so great that the outlet from an unvented part of the pipe is lower than the bottom part of the trap on the fixture. If this is the case, there is the possibility of water siphoning out of the trap.

One of the problems with drain pipes that are of considerable length is that they may have an inadequate downward pitch. This, coupled with the fact that the pipe diameter may be somewhat too large, will permit the accumulation of grease and waste matter in the pipe.

The process just described is an accumulative one. Not only is there the buildup of a possible clog, but the inside walls of the pipe also become coated with grease and waste. The net result is as though you had replaced the pipe with one having a smaller diameter. This, in turn, can cause siphoning of the traps of various fixtures in your home. But with this water siphoned out, sewer gases would have an opportunity to discharge into your home through your fixture drains. Whether this will happen depends on the amount of venting your plumbing system has. Of course, if the drain pipes in which this is happening *originally* had a small diameter, you will have the backup of waste right into your fixtures.

How to Determine the Slope of Horizontal Fixture Drains

You can calculate the slope of horizontal fixture drains by keeping this in mind: The total drop from the trap wire to the fitting at which the the vent pipe is attached should be no more than one pipe diameter. As an example, for a 1¼-inch drain pipe, the fall should be no more than 1¼ inches; for a 2-inch pipe, no more than 2 inches; and so on. The developed length (length along center lines) from the trap weir to the vent fitting must be at least two pipe diameters but not more than 48 pipe diameters. If we take a 1½-inch pipe as an example, the length must be at least 2 x 1½ inches, or 3 inches, but may be no more than 48 x 1½, or 72 inches (6 feet).

The slope of a horizontal drain pipe should be no less than ¼ inch per foot for pipes having up to and including a 2-inch diameter, no less than ⅛ inch per foot for pipes 2½ to 4 inches in diameter, and no less than 1/16 inch per foot for sizes of 5 to 8 inches. The table of horizontal drain pipe length and slope, which follows, is based on these rules.

1¼	2½	5	1¼	1¼
1½	3	6	1½	1¼
2	4	8	2	2
2½	5	10	1¼	2½
3	6	12	1½	3
3½	7	14	1¾	3½
4	8	16	2	4
5	10	20	1¼	5
6	12	24	1½	6
8	16	32	2	8

Features of Drainage Fittings For Waste Lines

There is a slight, but important difference between the joints used in the drainage system and those used in the fresh water system. This difference is in the threaded ends of the pipes.

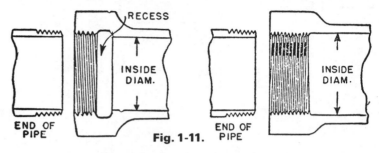

Fig. 1-11.

Drainage fitting (left) compared with a fitting used in fresh water supply.

Fig. 1-11 shows a pair of pipes, one for drainage and the other for fresh water. The inside diameter of the drainage fitting is the same as the inside diameter of the pipe which screws into it. The effect is as though we had a single pipe whose diameter is unchanged throughout. The inside diameter of a water supply fitting is larger than that of the pipe, the difference being about 1/3 inch in a 1½-inch pipe size. There is less length of thread in a drainage fitting than in a water fitting, but in back of the thread in the drainage fitting there is a recess which receives the end of the pipe. The ends of the threads may have a slight bevel or may be straight.

Drainage Fittings

Since horizontal drain pipes have a downward slant, the fittings used to connect one horizontal drain with another must be designed so that the overall effect is that of one continuous pipe with the same slant. By using a wrong fitting, it is possible to have one horizontal drain pipe that has a slant connected to another pipe that is completely level. The result would be an accumulation of waste in the second pipe.

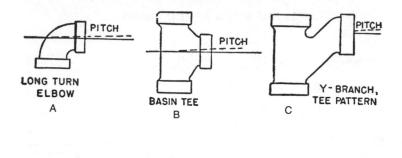

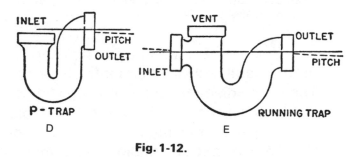

Fig. 1-12.

Various fittings used in drainage systems.

Note the pitch of the fitting in drawing A in Fig. 1-12. This fitting is used to connect a horizontal pipe to a vertical one. The pitch, or slope, is the angle formed by the dashed line and the horizontal line. The horizontal pipe, then, comes into the fitting at a downward slant. This means that the fitting must be designed to receive a downward slanted horizontal pipe. Fitting A is used to let the pipes make a right angle turn.

The fitting in drawing B is the same as that in A except that it will accommodate two pipes. The horizontal pipe to come in from the right will have a

downward slope. The pipe coming from the top will be straight, for in the vertical position a pipe has the maximum slope it can achieve.

The fitting shown in drawing C is the same as that in B, except it is designed to allow a more gradual change in velocity of the waste. In drawing B the fitting is such that the pitch goes from a small amount to maximum since the vertical section of the fitting has maximum slope. In drawing C the pitch changes from a small angle to one of 45° and then to 90°.

Drawing D shows a typical trap, such as that used with a single sink. The part marked "inlet" is connected to a vertical pipe which extends up to the sink. The "outlet" is connected to a horizontal drain. Note that the horizontal drain has a horizontal pitch.

Drawing E shows a running trap. Two pipes are to be connected to this trap—one a vent that will connect at the top, and the other a horizontal drain that will connect at the left. Note that the trap itself is not pitched; that is, it is not mounted at an angle. However, the threaded inlet and outlet are designed to receive pitched drain pipes, which will be mounted at the angle formed by the dashed lines with the solid horizontal line.

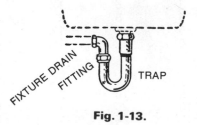

Fig. 1-13.

Connection of a fixture drain to a sink trap.

16

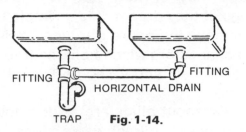

FITTING ──── FITTING
HORIZONTAL DRAIN
TRAP **Fig. 1-14.**

Two sinks connected by a single horizontal drain. The drain must be pitched downward from right to left.

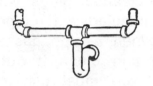

Fig. 1-15.

Alternative arrangement for connecting two sinks to a common trap.

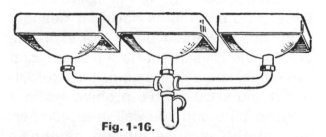

Fig. 1-16.

Three sinks joined by a fitting to a single trap. This is the sort of setup that might be used in the washroom of an office building or department store.

Fig. 1-13 shows the relationships among a fixture drain, a fitting, and a sink trap.

Continuous Waste Fixtures

In some plumbing installations a pair of sinks may be mounted adjacent to each other (Fig. 1-14). This could be a double sink in a kitchen, or a pair of sinks in a bathroom. The situation is quite common. It is possible that each of the sinks

will have its own drain, a vertical pipe leading down from the sink to a trap. In some cases, though, the two downward drains will be connected by a horizontal drain. The horizontal drain pipe joining the two sinks must have a downward slope, from the sink at the right to the one at the left.

Such an installation is an economy move, or else it may have been physically difficult to have separate drains for each of the sinks. And, since the trap is handling the waste from two sinks, instead of just one, it has a greater opportunity to become clogged.

Fig. 1-15 is an alternative arrangement for connecting two sinks to a single trap. In this installation the horizontal drains at the left and the right of the central fitting must both slope downward toward it.

Taken together, Figs. 1-14 and 1-15 indicate two options open to plumbers. Which a plumber uses depends on the materials he has on hand and the way he is accustomed to work. The installation of Fig. 1-14 is simpler, but both work the same way.

It is uncommon for three sinks to be connected to the same trap, and theoretically you should be able to attach as many as you want—theoretically, not practically. Fig. 1-16 shows three sinks using a pair of horizontal drains and one vertical drain that comes down from the central sink, joined by a common fitting. Again, both horizontal drains must have a downward pitch to the fitting. While sinks may be connected this way, no sink or

17

similar fixture may be joined this way to a toilet. If the waste in connected sinks backs up through the drain into the sinks themselves, there is the possibility that such waste will not be contaminated. However, if a sink used a trap in common with a toilet, toilet waste could back up into the sink. This would be more than disgusting; it would be unhealthy and dangerous.

Indirect Wastes

The soil stack was shown earlier, in Fig. 1-8. It is a vertical pipe that leads to the house drain, which, in turn, empties into the sewer pipe. Because of their proximity to the soil stack, some fixtures, such as toilets, drain directly into it. However, because rooms are spaced out, it is physically impossible to do so with all fixtures, unless several soil stacks are used. Even then, there will always be a number of fixtures that must have horizontal drains leading to the soil stack.

Fig. 1-8 shows one possible arrangement. The horizontal pipes in the center and lower parts of the drawing are called *waste pipes,* or just *wastes.*

Each of the fixtures in this drawing has its own trap. Coming from each trap is a drain pipe, which in turn connects to the waste pipes. Such connections are sometimes referred to as indirect wastes, a way of indicating that the fixture is somewhat removed physically from the soil stack.

Cleanout Plugs

Also shown in Fig. 1-8 is a cleanout plug associated with the house drain.

Traps may or may not have cleanout plugs. If they do not, it is a simple matter to remove the entire trap unscrewing the two connectors which hold the trap to the vertical drain and to the horizontal drain.

Cleanout plugs are seldom found in drain pipes, indirect waste pipes, or any other pipes in the drainage system, since every part of the interior of a pipe can be reached by some kind of auger. But if you don't have cleanout plugs, you will wish you did, particularly when pipes become clogged. When a pipe has a cleanout plug, you can clean it out yourself. Otherwise, you must call in either a plumber or a company specializing in the cleanout of pipes.

Of course, if a pipe is inside a wall, there is no point in its having a cleanout plug. But basement pipes are exposed, unless the basement is finished—and even then, some of the pipes may be visible. If you should have problems with a clogged pipe and you call in a plumber, you might inquire about having a cleanout plug installed. He will, at least, advise you as to its feasibility.

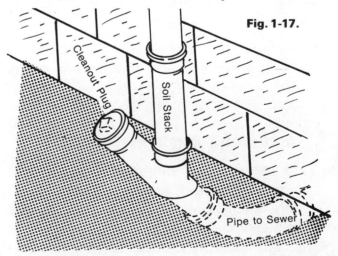

Fig. 1-17.

Cleanout plug at bottom of soil stack.

As Fig. 1-8 illustrates, a cleanout plug gives you access to the bottom of the soil stack. The soil stack is vertical and may make a rather sharp angle with the connecting sewer pipe (see Fig. 1-17). Because of this bend and because the soil stack carries all the waste produced in the home, you may get an accumulation at the bottom of the soil stack large enough to block passage—or at least large enough to result in very slow drainage of waste. In a severe blockage there will be a backup of waste water into the fixtures, resulting in a crossover of the drainage system into the fresh water system.

Note the way in which the pipe holding the cleanout plug in Fig. 1-17 is positioned. It comes up at about a 45° angle. This means that when you remove the plug, no water should drip out. It will drip out only if there is a blockage at the bottom of the soil stack.

Before trying to turn the cleanout plug, put a pan or basin beneath it to catch any water that may have collected. If, when you open the plug, water does come out, you can take this as an indication that there is a clog. The clog will be further down in the pipe, possibly at the point where it bends to join the sewer pipe.

Remember, when you are checking for clogs, that in some homes there is more than one drain leading to the sewer. If that describes your plumbing installation, locate those drains and remove their cleanout plugs.

Because the cleanout plug is opened so seldom, it may very well be rusted into position and you may need to use a large wrench. There are also various liquids you can buy which can penetrate the rust and remove enough of it to enable you to loosen the plug.

If the cleanout plug or plugs are so rusted that you can't budge them, you have several alternatives. One is to use a liquid chemical that will open the clog. Pour the liquid drain opener into the drain of the fixture that is closest to the cleanout plug. This could be a utility sink in your basement.

If the chemical does work, follow up by turning on the hot water faucet of the same fixture. The hot water will act as a cleaning agent. Let it run for a half hour, preferably longer. In flowing through the pipe, the hot water will heat it, and in the process the water will cool somewhat and thereby lose some of its effectiveness as a cleaning agent. The less pipe that will be heated, the hotter the water will remain. For that reason, it is best to select a nearby fixture to provide the hot water.

If the chemical process doesn't work, and you still have a stubborn plug, another choice is to select a plumbing service that specializes in clearing blocked drains. They use a power driven tool, inserting it in the nearest convenient drain opening. The tool will cut through the clog, putting your drainage system back to work again.

If, instead, you prefer to have a regular plumber do this for you, ask him to put in a new plug. Make sure the threads are covered with piping compound or any other substance that will protect the threads against rust. Thus, if you should need to remove the plug again, you will be able to do so without calling in outside help.

If you have a relatively new home, it would be a good precaution to remove the plug immediately and coat the threads with piping compound. This may not have been done by the contracting plumber when your house was built.

Preventive Maintenance

Whenever you do plumbing work the usual objective is to repair a fault. But as long as you have taken a fixture apart, or have removed a trap or a plung of some kind, make a thorough inspection to make sure that the pipe has no cracks or that it isn't about to rust through at some spot.

When you replace any connector that is threaded, and many of them are, put pipe compound or its equivalent on the threads to help prevent the formation of rust. If the threads of a connector are practically rusted away, don't try to salvage the connector. You'll save yourself a lot of work and time by getting an exact replacement.

Some connectors require washers. If so, take a good look at them and replace them if necessary, even if, at the moment, they aren't causing trouble. They will. If you are cleaning the inside of a pipe, possibly with an auger, try to remove as much material clinging to those inside walls as you possibly can. You can make

a homemade scraper out of a length of wood and a bit of scrap tin.

How to Clear the Main Drain Yourself

Using Water Pressure. Once you have removed the cleanout plug, you have a number of ways of clearing the clog out of the drain. Which method will succeed depends on just how firmly the clog is in position, and on its overall mass. One method, shown in Fig. 1-18, is to clear the clog by using water pressure.

Remove the spray nozzle from your garden hose and insert that end of the hose into the cleanout pipe. Push the hose in until you feel the resistance of the clog. Take a number of rags and pack them around the hose where it enters the drain. The idea here is to form as effective a seal as possible against water backup.

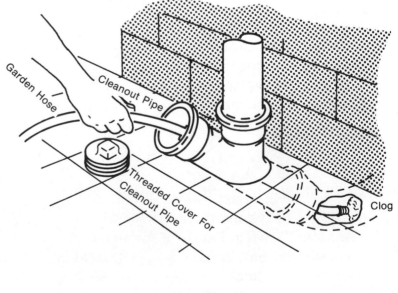

Fig. 1-18.

Water pressure method of clearing sewer drain.

To make sure no contaminated water backs up into the hose, connect it to a water source that is as far above the cleanout pipe as possible.

You'll need someone to turn on the hose while you keep watch at the cleanout. If the clog is stubborn, the water pressure may force the rags out of position and so flood your basement. Your assistant should be within hearing and should understand that he or she is to follow shouted instructions of "on" and "off" as quickly as possible.

If this technique does eliminate the clog, turn off and remove the hose. Coat the threads of the cleanout plug with pipe joint compound or any other substance that helps threads resist rusting, and then tighten the plug back into position. Turn on hot water in the nearest fixture and let the water flow for at least a half hour.

Meanwhile, let clear water run through the hose to clean it. Also, wash the end of the hose that made contact with the plug thoroughly. It is a good idea, after washing the hose end, to soak it in a pail of clear water containing some disinfectant for an hour or so. Also, make sure you wash your hands thoroughly.,

Using a Hand Auger. Some clogs are easy to dispose of, while others are stubborn and will resist the water treatment. You can use a hand auger on the tougher clogs, as shown in Fig. 1-19. Because the pipe at this point is so wide and because the bend is such a gradual one, you shouldn't have any difficulty in getting the auger to "snake" through the pipe until it reaches the clog. You will know it has done so by the resistance you will feel to

any further forward movement of the auger.

Turn the handle clockwise, but do not reverse it. At the same time, push the handle back and forth. The fact that you will be able to push the auger forward to its maximum length will let you know that the clog is being cleared.

After the clog is removed, use your garden hose to rinse the drain (Fig. 1-20). This will help remove any waste that may still be clinging to the inner wall of the drain and that may form the beginning of a new clog. After you have finished and have replaced the cleanout plug, you might also try the hot water treatment described earlier. Wash the auger thoroughly, and you hands as well.

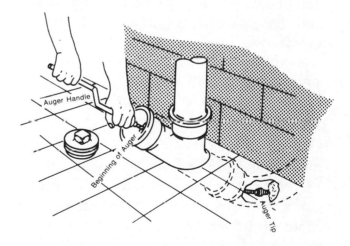

Fig. 1-19.

How to use a hand auger to clear the main drain.

Using an Electric Auger. The obstruction inside the drain may be caused by something that is pushing hard against the inner walls of the pipe. It is

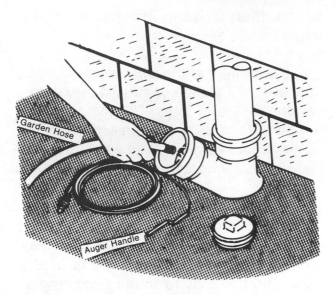

Fig. 1-20.

After using hand auger, clear drain by flushing it with water from garden hose.

Fig. 1-21.

Use electric auger for stubborn clogs.

also possible that any attempt to clear the clog by using a hand auger has only aggravated the situation, making the clog even more compact and even harder to remove. These things happen. For such severe clogs you will need to use an electric auger.

At this time you need to make a decision. Electric augers aren't cheap. If you are a determined "do-it-yourselfer," it might be better to rent one. Clogs in the main drain aren't all that common, but your plumbing setup could be an exception. To buy an electric auger so you can use it once every ten years or so doesn't make economic sense. Sometimes a group of neighbors will join in, contribute, and own an electric auger in common. But that can sometimes lead to a hassle. As a last resort, you can always use the services of a plumber or a company that specializes in clearing clogged drains.

Generally, use an electric auger for clogs you can't get rid of by any other method. The electric auger (Fig. 1-21) has sharp teeth which are turned by the auger, which acts as a shaft. Be careful not to touch the rotating blades, and hold the flexible support which houses the auger with your hands well away from either the motor portion or the blades. If the basement floor in and around the drain is wet, mop it dry before using the device. Water and electricity don't mix, and when they do, the results can be dangerous. It is also a good safety idea to wear work gloves when using the electric auger, but make sure the gloves are dry.

The fact that you have the services of an electric auger does not mean you should use brute force to clear the clog. Whenever you use an auger of any type you must work by feel. If the auger should jam inside the pipe there is always the possibility of a motor burnout.

After removing the clog, flush the drain with a garden hose. Another technique you can use is to operate the nearest toilet several times. Water from the toilet tank will flush away any metal filings or debris remaining in the drain pipe.

As a final precaution, whenever you work with an electrically operated rotating device—and that's just what an electric auger is—do not wear a necktie or a long-sleeve shirt. The idea here is not to get any part of your clothing entangled in the auger. Granted that the likelihood of this happening is small, but a few simple precautions will put all the odds in your favor.

And now that you have some idea of the fresh water supply system and also of drainage, there is one more plumbing section that needs attention—the venting system.

The Venting System

Venting systems have a double function. The air inside the venting system maintains a pressure on the water in all the traps, preventing this water from being siphoned out when a fixture is in use.

Consider, for example, what happens when you turn on a kitchen faucet. Water flows down through the sink drain, down the drain pipe, into the trap. The movement of the water out of the trap into and through the drain pipe produces a siphoning action. After you turn off the

faucet, the flow of the remainder of the water through the drain results in a partial vacuum. Water that has remained in the trap will be pulled, or siphoned, into the drain pipe, with the result that little or no water will remain in the trap.

It is to prevent this from happening that we use a venting system as part of the plumbing. The pressure of the air, the weight of the air, exerts a force on the trap, preventing the water in the trap from being siphoned away. In short, the air pressure of the venting system counteracts the vacuum effect produced in the drain pipe connected to the trap.

There is still another reason for having a venting system. If there were no air vents, the drainage system would need to be a closed system. This would mean that gases, which are formed as a result of fermentation and decomposition of wastes, would remain in the drain pipes. Ultimately, the pressure generated by these gases would be strong enough to force the gases through the traps, up through the vertical drains, and out of the sinks and toilets. Aside from the odor, it would be an unhealthy situation.

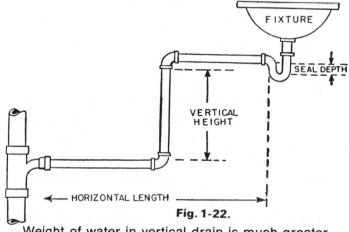

Fig. 1-22.

Weight of water in vertical drain is much greater than in the trap.

23

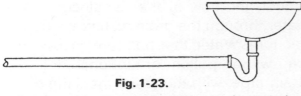

Fig. 1-23.

Momentum of water through long horizontal pipe in unvented system can pull water out of the trap.

Fig. 1-22 is an example of a closed plumbing system. At the right is the "seal depth," which represents the water in the trap. The height of this water column indicates the amount of pressure it can exert, which is relatively small. If the faucet in the fixture is turned on, both the trap seal and the vertical drain pipe will fill with water. But the water in the vertical pipe is much greater in amount than that in the trap, and so it weighs more. The excess weight of water in the vertical drain, in moving out of the drain, will siphon most of the water out of the trap.

The purpose in showing you such a drawing is to illustrate the point that installing an extra fixture as a do-it-yourself project can involve unexpected problems. Even if your local plumbing code permits you to do your own installation, this doesn't guarantee that such an installation will be done properly. Gravity does initiate the action when water flows out of a faucet and then down a drain. But the movement of water down the piping system also produces a siphoning action, and this action must be considered.

Siphoning action results when a vertical pipe is part of a plumbing system, and vertical pipes must be included since we want the wastes to go down and out. However, we can also get trap emptying when the trap is connected to a long

horizontal pipe, as shown in Fig. 1-23. Note, in this illustration, that the horizontal pipe will have very little pressure, and so we cannot blame siphoning action for emptying the trap. The downward slope of the horizontal pipe, however, results in waste flowing through it at a fairly substantial velocity. It is the momentum of this pipeful of water that pulls all the water out of the trap at the end of the discharge.

Water momentum exists in all pipes in the drainage system, to a smaller or greater degree, depending on the pitch of the pipe, its diameter, and water volume. And it exists whether the pipe is vertical or horizontal. In vertically arranged pipes, water momentum works together with the siphoning action to remove water from traps; in horizontal pipes, that momentum works alone but can have the same effect.

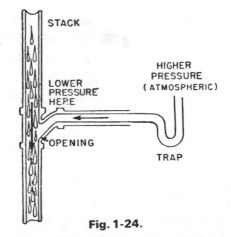

Fig. 1-24.

Condition in which water flowing through a stack can empty a trap.

Effect of Water in Vertical Pipes

Fig. 1-24 shows a trap connected to a horizontal drain. The end of the horizontal drain terminates in a fitting which opens into the soil stack and has a downward slope of about 45°. The horizontal drain itself has a slight downward slope from the trap to the fitting.

At the present time, as indicated in the drawing, water is falling through the stack. As it moves past the opening of the fitting, it pulls some of the air away, thus lowering the air pressure in and near the fitting. However, the air in the drain pipe between the sink exit and the trap hasn't been disturbed, and so it has maintained its normal pressure. Because of this difference in pressure, the higher pressure of air in the drain between the trap and the sink will push the water out of the trap into the horizontal drain.

It isn't easy to visualize the air doing this since air is invisible. But if you have ever tried to walk against a strong wind, you have some idea of the force air can exert.

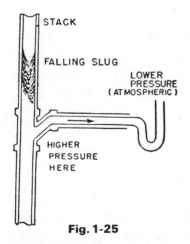

Fig. 1-25

Stack condition that can cause waste backup.

Effect of Back Pressure in the Stack

Sometimes an effect that is exactly opposite can take place. Fig. 1-25 is basically the same drawing as Fig. 1-24.

Only the conditions have changed. We now have a falling slug, consisting of waste and water, which fills the interior of the stack, compressing the air in the stack. Think of the stack as containing a column of air. It is true that the bottom of the stack isn't closed, yet consider that the stack is a vertical pipe and that it connects to a house drain that is horizontal. The two pipes, then, form a right angle, and so the air, in moving, must make a sharp turn. But with such a sharp turn, it can't move so freely.

We now have a falling slug which literally compresses the air in the stack. But when air is compressed its pressure rises. In effect, we have more air per unit volume. You get a similar compression when you force air into a tire. The air inside the tire exerts more and more pressure because with the help of an air hose you are pushing more and more air in. The falling slug in the stack works somewhat like an air pump.

We now have a higher air pressure at the fitting, higher than the air pressure above the liquid in the trap. But when air is under pressure, it will try to escape, and so the air will move through the horizontal drain connected to the trap. When it reaches the trap, it will push the water out of the trap, up the vertical drain connecting the trap to the sink, and then up into the sink itself. But since the stack not only receives sink, shower, and tub waste, but toilet waste as well, you can understand that this sort of backup does represent a bad situation.

It is also possible—but improbable—that we could get back pressure of this sort by a gust of wind blowing down the roof vent connected to the stack.

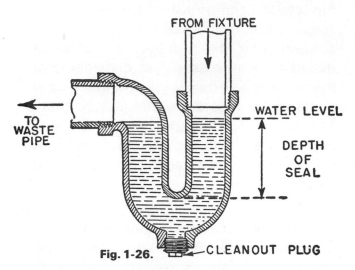

FROM FIXTURE

TO WASTE PIPE

WATER LEVEL

DEPTH OF SEAL

Fig. 1-26.

CLEANOUT PLUG

Air pressure exists on both surfaces of the water in the trap.

Importance of Vents

There must always be a continuous open connection through the vents to the upper part of the soil stack or the vent stack and through the tops of the stacks to the open air. The purpose of the vent pipes is to equalize the air pressure on both sides of the water in the traps.

Examine the trap shown in Fig. 1-26 and you will get an idea of the effect of air pressure on the liquid in the trap. On the right side of the trap there is a column of air resting on the water in the trap. This column of air is the air in the pipe leading down from the sink to the trap. The air is confined in the pipe, but it has weight and so presses down on the water in the trap. It could push the water through the fixture drain, except that there is a counterbalancing weight of air in that drain, which prevents the water in the trap from being siphoned off.

Water in the trap acts as a seal, and it is the purpose of the vent pipes to maintain that seal. When you open a trap by removing a plug at its base, or by turning the pair of connectors which hold it in place, you can logically expect the water in the trap to drip out of it.

When the drainage pipes aren't at work, that is, when no fixtures are being used, there is a circulation of air from the building drain through the soil or vent stack, to the terminal pipe on the roof. This air movement has a number of advantages. It prevents the buildup of sewer gas and the gases formed in your various waste pipes. If such gases were allowed to accumulate, their pressure might enable them to force their way through the traps and into your home. Aside from any unhealthy aspect, sewer gas has a particularly bad odor.

The air motion also has a drying effect on the interior of the vent pipes, which reduces the possibility of slime formation on the walls of the pipe. Thus, the moving air helps prevent corrosion.

Need for More Vents

When two fixtures are connected by a common drain pipe, it is possible for them to use a single vent. But if the fixtures are widely separated, as they would be if they were placed in different rooms, another vent might be needed.

Fig. 1-27 illustrates this need. In the center right of the drawing we have a basin and a sink. There is a trap beneath each of these, and those traps are connected to a common drain which exits into a soil stack. The upper part of the soil stack is vented, and so the stack acts as the vent for the basin and the sink.

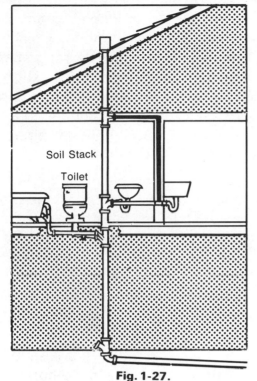

Fig. 1-27.

When installing an additional fixture, you may also need to put in an extra vent.

Since the sink and the basin are widely separated, an extra vent is included for the sink. (While the sink is shown adjacent to the basin in the drawing this is simply to show the relationship of the different fixtures and pipes.) Note how this vent is connected. One end is joined to the drain pipe leading away from the sink trap. The other end exits into the soil stack.

On the roof, above the roof flashing, the soil stack ends in an increaser. As its name implies, an increaser is a section of pipe with a larger diameter than the soil vent pipe to which it is connected. If the vent pipe exit from the roof is too narrow,

accumulation of moisture inside the pipe might freeze and result in blocking of the vent. This is much less likely to happen when the exit pipe is rather wide.

Not all installations use an increaser. In warm climates, where winters are mild, the stack exit can be a rather narrow pipe. Apartment houses often use increasers since they must vent a large number of fixtures compared to private homes. In some installations, whether private houses or apartment buildings, there may be several roof vents so that clogging of any one of them will not block the free passage of air through vent pipes.

Note also the location of the cleanout plug at the bottom of the soil stack.

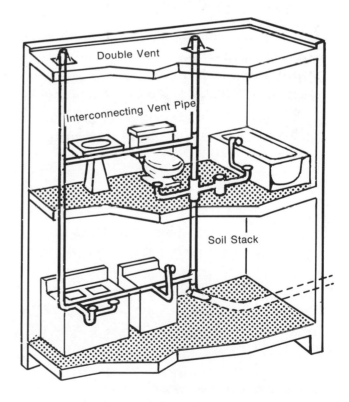

Fig. 1-28.

Double venting system.

27

Double Venting

Modern plumbing systems are usually double vented, or may have more vents if needed. Fig. 1-28 shows a double venting arrangement. The venting pipes aren't isolated from each other, but, as shown in the drawing, are inter-connected. Double venting is a greater assurance of the free flow of air in the venting system. Generally, in the construction of a new home, the plumbing contractor will try to distribute the venting arrangement so that the venting pipes carry an equal number of fixtures. However, if a single fixture is off somewhere by itself, remote from all the other fixtures, it isn't uncommon for it to have its own venting arrangement.

In a double venting system, both vent pipes exit through the roof. The vents are usually placed sufficiently high above the roof top, especially on flat roofs, so that roof debris cannot accidentally fall into the open pipes. This is less of a problem with slant roofs, and so such vents are often closer to the roof surface.

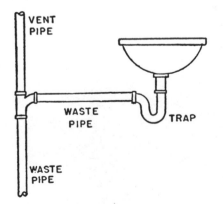

Fig. 1-29.

Vent pipe for sink.

Venting Arrangements

The buildup of air pressure extremes can be avoided by correct venting of the pipes in the drainage system. Fig. 1-29 shows a plumbing setup in which we have a sink and a venting arrangement. The trap is connected to a slightly downard-slanted section of waste pipe. The waste pipe, in turn, attaches to a fitting which holds a vertical vent pipe.

Now suppose you turn on the faucet in the sink. Water will flow down the drain pipe attached to the sink and the trap, through the trap and the horizontal waste pipe, and then down the vertical waste pipe. We now have an excellent setup technique for producing a siphoning effect, and as a matter of fact, a siphoning effect will take place. But this siphoning will act on the air in the vertical vent pipe, rather than on the water in the horizontal waste pipe. It is easier to draw a large volume of air through the vent than a small volume of water out of the trap.

The vent pipe in Fig. 1-29 may go direct to a vent on the roof. Or it may connect with another vent which is already connected to a roof vent. Just as the free flow of fresh water into your home requires a pipe large enough to accommodate the volume of water needed, so too must the vent pipe be able to supply as much air as required.

The next drawing, Fig. 1-30, shows a long horizontal waste pipe with the vent pipe connected to it through a fitting. Water momentum through the waste pipe will pull air down through the vertical vent.

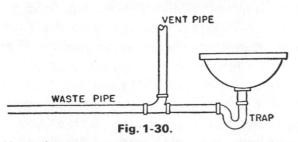

Fig. 1-30.

Vent pipe connected to horizontal waste pipe.

Vent Pipe Positioning

Compare the length of the horizontal waste pipe in Fig. 1-29 with that of the corresponding pipe in Fig. 1-30. In Fig. 1-29 there is a much longer section of horizontal waste pipe before the vent pipe is reached. In Fig. 1-30 the vent pipe is located much closer to the sink trap. Since it is the function of the vent to help the trap maintain its water seal, it is preferable to have the vent pipe as near as possible to the trap. While it is not always physically possible to have the vent near the trap, it is a consideration to keep in mind when building a new home or installing a new sink.

The Single Vent

Fig. 1-31 shows a number of fixtures using traps that are connected to the soil stack through very short lengths of horizontal waste pipe. In this case the soil stack acts as the vent for all of these fixtures and no other venting pipes are used. This is an economical setup since it minimizes the amount of pipe required and also means there is less physical labor involved for installation.

However, it isn't the best setup. It may mean, for example, that the fixtures aren't in the most desirable locations in

the home. And, with this arrangement there is always the possibility of backup from one fixture to another. This type of plumbing connection is called stack venting. The soil stack must have a diameter sufficiently large to allow the passage of enough air for adequate venting. Any clog in the soil stack will affect all the fixtures connected to it.

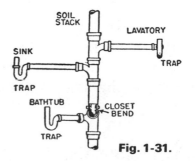

Fig. 1-31.

Arrangement in which the soil stack acts as a vent for several nearby fixtures.

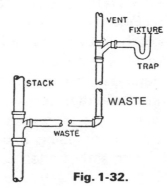

Fig. 1-32.

When a vertical waste pipe is relatively close to the trap, it is better to have a vent placed near the trap as well.

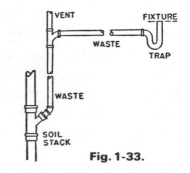

Fig. 1-33.

When the waste pipe connected to the trap is horizontal, the vent can be positioned further away.

Fixture Vents

A fixture vent is one which is used with only a single fixture, as shown in Figs. 1-32 and 1-33. In these examples the fixture is too far from the soil stack to be connected directly to it. Instead, the fixture drain is connected to the vent through a fitting. From the fitting, waste pipes lead down and then across to the stack.

Fig. 1-34 shows the venting arrangement for a toilet. The arrangement is made as close to the soil stack as possible.

Combined Fixture Venting

A vent can be used to supply air for a bathroom sink (lavatory) and a toilet, as illustrated in Fig. 1-35. But note the relative sizes of the pipes. The sink uses a smaller waste pipe than the toilet since the sink will handle liquid waste only. The vent pipe is narrow in diameter compared to the soil stack or the pipe used for the toilet. This method of using a common vent for a toilet and sink is often used on a lower floor.

Fig. 1-36 is a plumbing arrangement for a complete bathroom, consisting of a toilet, bathtub, and sink. Since these are all grouped in a single room, they can all vent to the soil stack. The toilet is positioned closest to the soil stack. The bathtub and sink are connected to the soil stack by waste pipes in the lower half of the drawing and by vent pipes in the upper half.

Figs. 1-35 and 1-36 are alternative arrangements in the same bathroom for the same set of fixtures. In Fig. 1-35 the bathtub is positioned more to the right. You can use either arrangement. The whole idea here is to show that fixture positioning isn't all that rigid and that you may conveniently move fixtures about, provided you supply them with adequate vent lines and adequate waste piping.

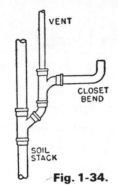

Fig. 1-34.

Vent for a toilet (water closet).

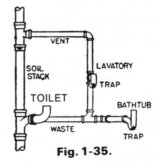

Fig. 1-35.

Alternate arrangement to one in Fig. 1-34.

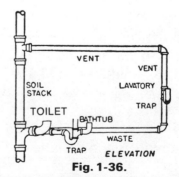

Fig. 1-36.

One possible arrangement of fixtures in a single bathroom. Vent pipes that connect to the sink also vent the bathtub. Although the toilet is linked to the tub through a waste line, the toilet itself is vented through the soil stack.

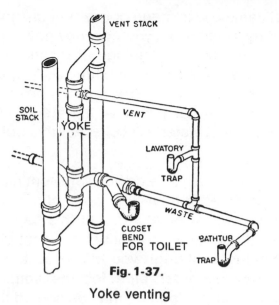

Fig. 1-37.

Yoke venting

Yoke Venting

Fig. 1-37 shows this method of venting. Here we have a soil stack and a separate vent stack, parallel to each other and physically close. Over at the right side of the drawing we have the waste and vent connections to a toilet, bathtub and lavatory.

Note the pipe, called a yoke, located between the vent stack and the soil stack. As the drawing shows, both the vent and waste pipe connections from the bathroom fixtures are connected to the yoke. The yoke is connected to the vent stack through a pipe which slopes downward from the vent stack. At the lower end of the yoke vent, there is another downward slope, but this time to the soil stack.

The arrangement you see in Fig. 1-37 is for the fixtures on a single floor. You can follow the same piping arrangement on a floor or floors either above or below the one represented by the drawing. The

vent stack and the soil stack can continue vertically upstairs or down. However, on each floor you would have a separate yoke.

The yoke arrangement means that venting can be supplied to the soil stack at a number of different floor levels. This is a better arrangement than having a soil stack to which all waste pipes are connected and which also functions as a vent stack. In the yoke arrangement, not only are the vent and soil stacks separated, but there is much less risk of choked off venting due to some clog in the soil stack. The drainage system is also better since there is greater opportunity for air circulation.

You could modify the yoke arrangement, if you wish, by adding another vent line to the tub. This would consist of a vertical pipe connected to the bathtub's waste line, and then a horizontal vent pipe connecting to the existing horizontal vent, presently connected to the lavatory.

This additional vent pipe would eliminate one potential problem that exists with the yoke venting setup in the drawing. Assume that the vertical drain leading from the lavatory trap to the waste line below it becomes clogged, with the clog also existing in the waste line. Without the additional vent, this would mean that the bathtub would have no venting at all.

Other Vent Arrangements

There are many ways in which you can arrange venting for fixtures. Normally, this is not a problem unless you are having a new home built and want to get involved in the plumbing, or if you are adding a room that will contain plumbing fixtures, or if you just want to have another fixture installed. If you know the need for venting, you can at least discuss the various venting methods—and there are many—so as to get maximum venting at the lowest possible cost. Have your plumber or contractor draw the proposed venting arrangement for you so you know just what is involved. It is also helpful to have a drawing showing pipe locations inside walls.

Vent Pipe Connections

Although a vent pipe is a sort of air pipe, it is possible for liquid to collect in it. On a humid day, for example, moisture may condense on the inside walls of vent pipes. Or a rainstorm may send some small amount of water down through the roof vent, particularly if that vent has a large diameter. This is not problem if the vent pipe is placed so that liquid collecting in it will drain down either into some pipe that ultimately connects with the soil stack or directly into the soil stack. This is no problem so far as vertical vent stacks are concerned, but with horizontal vent stacks it means they must be slanted slightly downward to give gravity a chance to move collected liquid toward the soil stack.

If you are using a horizontal pipe for venting and if the pipe is one piece and slants toward a vertical vent or the soil stack, there is little or no possibility of water collecting in the pipe. But suppose the available pipe just wasn't long enough, so that the pipe used for horizon-

tal venting was made of two sections joined by a fitting. As you know by now, pipe can be joined by fittings. But the fitting that was used may provide a slight dip where the two pipes join, possibly because of the shape of the fitting. This means that water will collect at this point.

Obviously, we do not want vent pipes clogging at or near their point of connection to waste pipes. Should this happen, the effect will be to constrict the vent pipe opening as though you had used a very narrow diameter pipe for the vent. In some cases, clogging may be so bad that the vent opening is closed and then, of course, the effect is as though no vent pipe existed.

The reason why a vent pipe may clog can be understood with the help of the two drawings in Fig. 1-38. Suppose that the fixture in each drawing, a sink, becomes full of water and begins to drain. The water will move from point A to point B, not in a straight line, but through the pipes. The effect, though, is as if we had a pipe going from point A to point B. If you will examine the drawing at the left, you will see that the dashed line between points A and B is below the vent. In fact, it is below the fitting connecting the vent to the waste pipe.

Now compare it with the drawing at the right. In this case the dashed line, A-B, is not only above the fitting, but actually cuts across the vent pipe. As a result, waste water from the sink can rise to point C in the drawing at the right, thus partially flooding the vent pipe at its lower end.

Point A in both drawings is a center point on the top of the water collected in the sink. As the water level goes down, point A will go down with it. In both drawings, the line connecting A and B will also go down. What it means in the drawing at the right is that the vent will empty the water it collected into the waste line and so the vent will once again be clear.

However, the water from the sink is waste. It may contain bits of soap, hair, and food particles. If these get into the vent pipe and if the vent pipe is sufficiently narrow—and some vent pipes are quite narrow—there is always the possibility of a clog. It doesn't look that serious in a drawing, but if the vent is in a wall, then getting at the vent pipe to remove the clog can not only be a nuisance, it can be expensive.

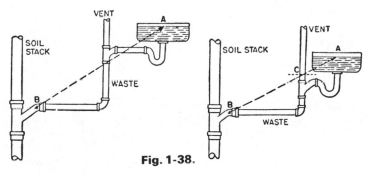

Fig. 1-38.

Possible cause of clogging in a vent pipe.

Garbage Disposal Units

A garbage disposal, a motor-operated device for shredding sink wastes, can be part of your drainage system. The unit can be installed directly below the kitchen sink in the drain pipe between the sink and the trap.

In some areas, garbage disposal fixtures are prohibited by local plumbing laws. Despite that, such units do have a number of advantages. They grind all kitchen waste, including soft bones, paper, and large food particles, into tiny pieces. Since the garbage disposal must always be used with water flowing through, that is, with a faucet turned on, the waste is contained in liquid. Because of the ground-up condition of the waste, it has a scouring action on the inner walls of the trap and waste pipe, preventing or minimizing greasy buildup on those walls, thus working against the formation of clogs.

Garbage disposals come equipped with a quick-opening fuse which can be easily reset. Items which cannot be ground, such as spoons, jam the motor, causing it to stop and the fuse to open. After the item is removed, the motor can be easily unjammed with a special tool supplied with the garbage disposal. After the reset fuse button is depressed, the disposal is ready for work once again.

In a way, the garbage disposal acts as a strainer for it limits the size of food particles which can go through it and on to the trap.

Chapter II

Become Familiar with Plumbing Tools

A plumbing tool is any tool that will help repair your plumbing or that may help in preventative maintenance. With this liberal definition, a screwdriver becomes a plumbing tool, and so does a hammer, a wrench, or any of the other tools you may already have around your home.

But there are also a number of others which are specifically intended for plumbing use. For the most part they are very convenient, if not actually indispensable and have a relatively modest cost. All sorts of tools, powders, soaps, scouring pads, paints and paintbrushes, mops, vacuum cleaners, and brooms are used to maintain the home. You should regard plumbing tools as fitting right into that category.

Quite often a plumbing tool will more than pay for itself by saving the cost of an expensive plumbing repair. And there's no gainsaying the fact that you can get some satisfaction out of being able to do a job yourself, and relying less on others. You will also find it easier to get a plumbing tool that is designed for a specific job rather than trying to make do with usual household tools, which are not intended for such purposes. Repairing plumbing isn't the easiest job in the world. It can be messey or dirty or both, and you should welcome anything that will make your work easier.

What Tools Should You Buy?

There are some plumbing tools you may never need, so obviously there is no point in buying them. But you should at least know that such tools exist. If you home develops an uncommon plumbing problem, it wouid be helpful to know that an uncommon tool is available. There are certain tools you should have—such as wrenches and screwdrivers—but as for the others, it would be just as well to buy or rent them when the need arises.

Drain Pipe Cleaning Tools

Various devices can be used for cleaning drain pipes, a few of which are shown in Fig. 2-1. You can attach them to rods of various lengths and then work the rods back and forth with an action calculated to scrape the inside walls of the pipe.

The problem in cleaning a drain pipe isn't the cleaning action so much as being

UNION PUBLIC LIBRARY
TIVERTON, R. I.

able to get into the pipe. Drain pipes, particularly those located in the walls of your home, are generally in accessible. There are a number of companies that offer their services. They use power operated tools which can "snake" their way down to the drain with a rotating action that cleans the interior walls.

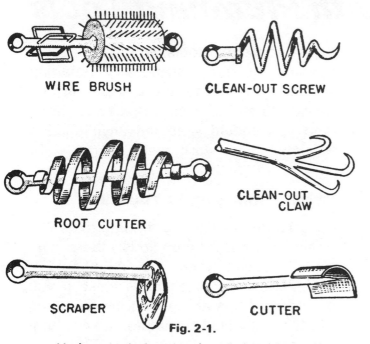

WIRE BRUSH   CLEAN-OUT SCREW

ROOT CUTTER   CLEAN-OUT CLAW

SCRAPER   CUTTER

Fig. 2-1.
Various tools for cleaning drain pipes.

However, some drain pipes can be reached and opened by you. For example, suppose your kitchen sink is clogged and you have already removed and cleaned the trap and cleaned the pipe connecting the sink drain with the trap—with no results. This means that the clog is in the drain pipe leading away from the trap.

This drain pipe generally consists of two parts: a vertical section of pipe going down to the basement, and a horizontal section which may have a slight vertical slant and which connects with a main

drain pipe. The horizontal section of pipe, after being in use for a number of years, can very well become clogged.

One way of removing the clog is to drill a hole in the pipe, enlarge it to about ½ inch with a tapered reamer, and then insert a cleaning tool. Instead of a cleaning tool, you can try using a metal clothes hanger. Straighten the hanger, make a U hook at one end, and insert the U hook into the pipe. Rotate the wire, and the hook will catch on to portions of the clog. Pull the clog material out of the hole and deposit it in a pail or on a newspaper.

A cleaning tool will be helpful if it is of a size that will fit through the hole. If it is possible to open one end of the pipe, a tool such as an auger will be much more effective and certainly faster than the makeshift wire tool.

The Auger

The auger is one of the most effective of the drain cleaning tools. Basically, it consists of bright galvanized spring wire with a spiral gimlet head. Fig. 2-2 shows a typical auger, with the circle enclosing a magnified view of the head. The head is inserted into the drain pipe and is made to rotate by means of a handle or wheel at the other end of the auger. The gimlet head pushes against and through the clog forcing some of it into the coiled spring which forms the head. The auger is then removed, the head is washed, and the process is repeated until the clog is removed.

Augers are available in various lengths, beginning at about 6 feet. And they come equipped with all sorts of handles for turning the head, from a simple wooden handle or some sort of wheel to the more complex gear-driven device. The more elaborate the auger, the more it costs.

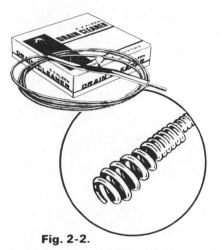

Fig. 2-2.

Typical auger circle. Circle shows an enlarged view of the "business end" of an auger, a gimlet head. (Chicago Specialty)

Fig. 2-3.

Gear-driven auger. Gear drive supplies the torque, or turning power, often needed to get the auger past the trap and bends in the drain pipe. (Chicago Specialty)

The Gear-Driven Auger

As Fig. 2-3 shows, there are actually two handles in the gear-driven auger. The one at the top is used to withdraw the auger and cable from the pipe and to wind them for storage, and also for releasing the auger from its storage position (in the canister). The other handle,

when rotated, turns some gears which rotate the entire length of the auger.

The advantage of an auger with a gear drive over a more simple auger is that the gear drive produces a high torque action which takes the full length of the auger easily around corners and bends to clear clogged traps and drains.

There are two actions you can take in clearing clogs. One of these is to work the auger back and forth. The other is to rotate it so that the gimlet head will rub against the interior wall of the pipe. Getting the auger to move forward is sometimes difficult, especially if the drain pipe makes a right-angle bend.

The Drum Auger

Fig. 2-4 shows another type of auger, known as a drum auger. The drum is a canister mounted by a handle. When not in use, the auger, made of high-tensile spring wire, is stored in the drum. Feed the auger out to use; feed it back when finished. When using the auger, hold the pistol grip with one hand, and rotate the canister handle with the other. This action will whip the auger around in the pipe. However, you cannot get as much torque, or turning power, with the drum auger as you can with the gear-drive type.

Fig. 2-4.

Drum auger has pistol grip. (Chicago Specialty)

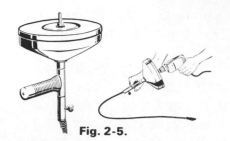

Fig. 2-5.

Power drum auger. (Chicago Specialty)

The Power Drum Auger

If you have a variable speed portable drill, you can use it with a power drum auger to supply all the turning power you need. Connect your drill to the auger as shown in Fig. 2-5. When working with the auger you will need the use of both hands. Hold the auger handle with one hand, and the electric drill with the other (see the drawing).

Do not try to use the power drum auger with drills which do not have a variable speed control. With variable speed drills you get the greatest turning power at the slowest speeds, and that is just what you want. The whole idea is to get the auger to rotate inside the drain pipe—slowly, not rapidly. Power drum augers usually contain about 25 feet of cable.

Fig. 2-6.

Auger designed for use with toilet bowls. (Chicago Specialty)

The Toilet Bowl Auger

All of the augers discussed so far are intended for use on drain pipes, quite often those connected to sinks. While an auger for a clogged toilet bowl follows the same general principles, the clog is much more accessible and so a lot of turning power isn't needed. Fig. 2-6 shows a toilet bowl auger, which has a handle for turning the auger. The part near the handle fits through a tube which holds it in position yet permits it to rotate. Because of its construction, this auger will not kink.

Toilet bowl augers, also known as closet augers, are generally either 3 or 6 feet long—not so long as augers used for cleaning pipe drains. All closet augers are hand operated; power augers aren't used for toilets.

The covering over the length of auger connected to the handle, usually about half the total auger, is called a vinyl bowl guard. Its purpose is to keep the auger from thrashing about inside the toilet bowl and possibly scratching or cracking the vitreous china construction. Closet augers are made of plated wire, while the tube portion is often plated steel, or brass.

Wrenches

Wrenches are among the more widely used tools in household plumbing. Since piping and fixtures are joined by connectors of various sizes, loosening and removing these connectors are often a necessary first step to a repair. When the connectors are readily accessible, as in the case of a packing nut used on a faucet, wrenches such as the money wrench or crescent wrench are adequate.

Monkey and Crescent Wrenches

Advantage. The advantage of either the monkey or crescent wrench (Fig. 2-7) is that it has adjustable jaws. In other words, the jaws can be moved, by means of thumbscrew adjustments, to accommodate a wide variety of connectors.

Sizes. These adjustable wrenches are available in sizes ranging from 4 to 24 inches long. The wrench size to use depends on the size of the nut, bolt, or connector to be turned. The maximum opening of the jaws of the wrench is related to the length of the wrench—that is, small wrenches have small jaw openings and larger ones larger openings.

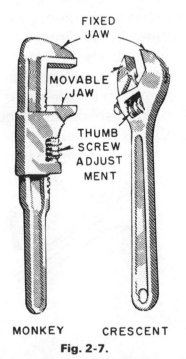

Fig. 2-7.

The monkey wrench and crescent wrench are suitable for plumbing repairs where the connector is easy to reach.

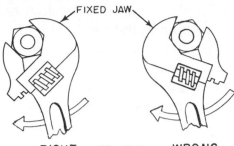

RIGHT   **Fig. 2-8.**   WRONG

Correct and incorrect methods of pulling an adjustable wrench.

How to Use an Adjustable Wrench. Wrenches rank high among a long list of tools that aren't used properly. Adjustable wrenches are sometimes called "knuckle busters" because of the accidents which sometimes happen when these tools are used. You can avoid trouble by following these steps:

1. Pick a wrench of the correct size. If you must open the wrench jaws to their utmost limit to fit a nut or other connector, then the wrench size is too small. A 50 percent jaw opening is just about right.

2. Make sure the jaws of the wrench fit the connector smoothly and securely. Tighten the thumbscrew so that even if you remove your hand the wrench will remain securely fastened in place. Make sure the wrench jaws are across the flat portion of the connector, and not on the apex or joining line of any two flat surfaces of the connector.

3. Position the wrench so that the nut is all the way into the jaws of the wrench. If not, then the wrench is likely to slip when used, which can result in a severe case of finger and knuckle scraping.

4. Finally, place the wrench so that you will be pulling the handle in the direction of the side having the adjustable jaw, as shown in Fig. 2-8. This will keep the adjustable jaw from springing open and slipping off the connector.

The Pipe Wrench

Sometimes it is necessary to turn a pipe instead of a connector. For this, use a pipe wrench, also known as a stillson wrench (see Fig. 2-9). The movable jaw is pivoted, enabling the serrated jaws to get a firm grip on a round surface. The gripping action of the jaws will leave a mark on the pipe, but if the pipe is one that is hidden from view you need not be concerned. However, if it is an exposed and possibly a plated pipe, put a small piece of rag around the area before using the wrench. Always adjust the jaws so that the bit on the work will be from about the center of the jaws.

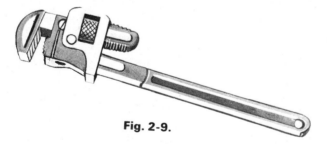

Fig. 2-9.

Adjustable pipe wrench, or stillson wrench.

The Chain Pipe Wrench

It is unlikely that you will ever need to use a chain pipe wrench but you may find it helpful to know that this is the type used mostly on large sizes of pipe. The tool, Fig. 2-10, works in one direction only, but you can back it around the work and take a fresh grip on it without freeing the chain.

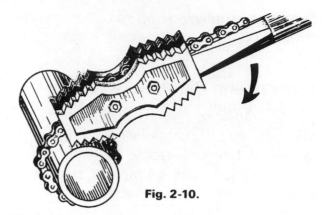

Fig. 2-10.

Chain pipe wrench, used for turning pipe. Arrow indicates the direction of motion of the tool.

The Strap Wrench

A modification of the chain pipe wrench is the strap wrench (Fig. 2-11). This wrench can also be used for turning pipe and is much less expensive than the chain pipe wrench. One end of the metal braid forming the strap is fixed to the handle. The other end is free and can be wrapped around the pipe. The tool can then be turned in the direction shown by the arrow in the drawing. When using the tool, hold it at the end opposite to the strap to get maximum leverage. This tool is unsuited for use on nuts, bolts, and connectors.

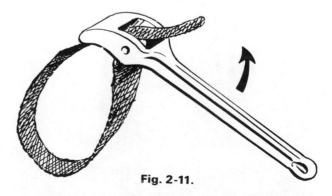

Fig. 2-11.

Strap wrench is inexpensive tool for turning pipe. Arrow indicates the direction in which to turn wrench.

The Spanner Wrench

It is unlikely that you will buy a spanner wrench, more commonly known as a spanner, any more than you would buy a chain pipe wrench, but, again, you may be able to borrow or rent such a tool should you need one.

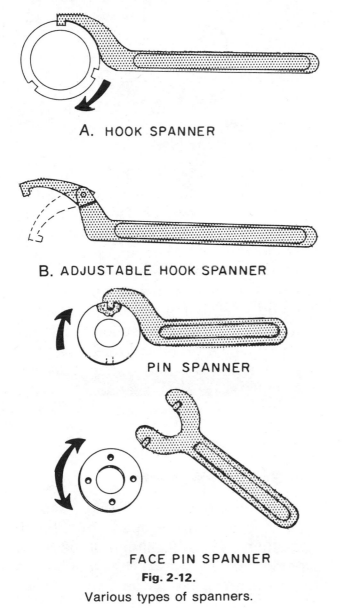

A. HOOK SPANNER

B. ADJUSTABLE HOOK SPANNER

PIN SPANNER

FACE PIN SPANNER
Fig. 2-12.
Various types of spanners.

Some connectors and nuts are made with notches cut into their outer circumference. These connectors and nuts are specifically designed to be turned by

a spanner. The wrench comes equipped with one or two curved arms and a long handle (see Fig. 2-12). The curved arm fits into one of the notches on the connector, and force exerted on the spanner handle will then either lock or open the connector.

Drawing A in Fig. 2-12 shows the hook spanner, one of the simplest types in this family of tools. The arrow shows the direction to be taken for opening the connector. For tightening it, reverse the connection of the spanner and push it in the opposite direction.

The hook spanner's limitation is that it will fit only one size of connector. The adjustable hook spanner (drawing B) is designed for use with a number of different sizes. It has a hooked arm and so in this sense is adjustable.

Instead of a notch in their outer edge, some connectors have holes in the face or in the circumference. For use with such connectors we have the pin spanner and also the face pin spanner.

When using a spanner, make sure that the pins, lugs, or hooks of the spanner fit securely into the connectors. It takes quite a bit of force to turn some connectors, and so good contact between the tool and the connector is important. It will make it easier to turn the connector and will keep you from getting bruised fingers.

The Open End Wrench

Open end wrenches are solid, nonadjustable tools, with openings at both ends. They usually come in sets of from six to ten wrenches, with sizes ranging from 5/16 to 1 inch. Wrenches with small openings are usually shorter than wrenches with larger openings.

Open end wrenches can have their jaws parallel to the handle, at a 15 angle to it, or any other angle up to 90° (see Fig. 2-13). The wrench with a 90° angle is called a right-angle wrench, but the average angle of open end wrenches is 15°. This angular displacement makes it easier to use a wrench where there isn't room enough to make a complete turn of a nut or bolt.

The handles of open end wrenches are ordinarily straight, but some may be curved. Those with curved handles are known as S wrenches. Some open end wrenches have offset handles. This allows the head to reach nut or bolt heads that are below surface level.

The open end wrench must fit the nut or bolt it is to turn. If there is too much play between the tool and the nut or bolt, tool slipping or damage can result. Fig. 2-14 shows how to use an open end wrench in a confined space.

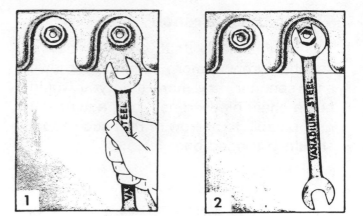
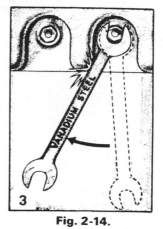

Fig. 2-14.

Open end wrench is convenient tool to use in enclosed spaces.

Fig. 2-15.

A 12-point box end wrench.

The Box End Wrench

The box end wrench (Fig. 2-15) is safer to use than the open end wrench since there is less likelihood of the tool's slipping off the work. The wrench fits completely over the nut or bolt.

The most frequently used box wrench has 12 points or notches arranged in a circle in the head and can be used with a minimum swing angle of 30°. Six-

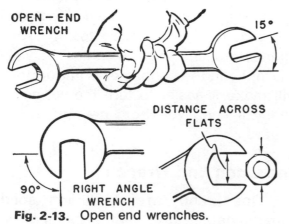

Fig. 2-13. Open end wrenches.

and eight-point wrenches are for heavy duty, 12- for medium duty, and 16- for light work only.

The Combination Wrench

The combination wrench (Fig. 2-16) has a box-style wrench at one end and an open end at the other. The box end is sometimes offset, as shown in the illustration, to let the tool clear other nuts and bolts that might interfere with movement of the tool.

When you use a fixed wrench, whether open end or box end, don't push on the wrench. Always pull. Pushing a wrench is a good way to take a layer of skin right off the top of your knuckles.

The Allen Wrench

The allen wrench (Fig. 2-17) is also known as a hex (hexagonal) wrench because it has six sides. It is a rather small tool and quite inexpensive. Some faucet handles are held in by small hex screws, so if you have faucet handles of this kind, the allen wrench will come in handy. They are available in various sizes, generally in kit form. Faucet handles, of course, may be force-fit types, in which case they use no screw at all, or the screw may be a small set screw that can be removed with a flat blade screwdriver.

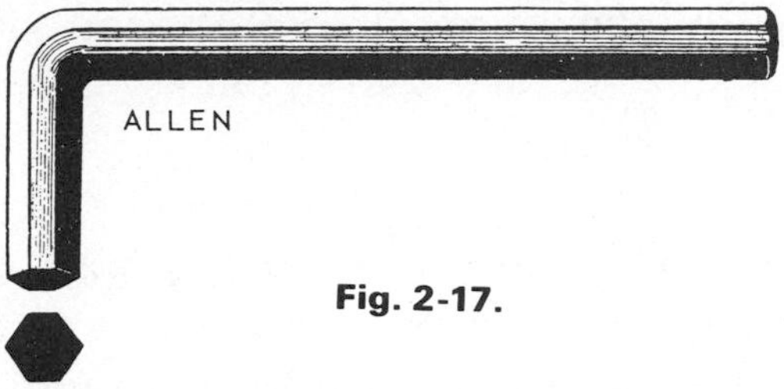

Fig. 2-17.

Allen wrench.

Hacksaws

Hacksaws are fairly inexpensive tools and you can use them in a number of different ways in plumbing chores around the home. You can use them for cutting: (1) rusted nuts and connectors that can't be removed otherwise, (2) pipe, (3) bolts, (4) metal stock.

There are two types: those with an adjustable frame and those with a solid frame (see Fig. 2-18). Either saw consists of two parts: the frame and the blade. The adjustable type is more suitable for plumbing work, since you can use blades of different lengths for different jobs. In either case, whether adjustable or fixed, the saw blade is replaceable.

The blades range in length from 10 to 12 inches for the adjustable type. The fixed type can use only the blade for which it is designed. If you examine the blade, you will see it has two holes—one at either end. These holes are for fitting the blade into the saw, generally by means of a pair of pins mounted on the frame. The length of the blade is the distance between the blade holes.

Hacksaw Blades

Hacksaw blades have either 10-inch or 12-inch lengths, and are made of

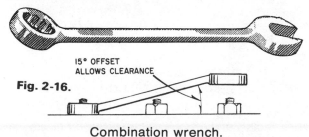

Fig. 2-16.

15° OFFSET ALLOWS CLEARANCE

Combination wrench.

tungsten alloy steel or high-speed steel. Blades are usually sold in packs of five or ten.

Since you will be using just one blade at any one time, you will need to store the others. They will rust if you do nothing to prevent it. Give them a light coating of machine oil, sold in just about all hardware stores and department stores. Put some of the oil on the blade and rub lightly with a cloth to spread the oil all over the blade surface. Coat both sides in this way and then wrap the blades in a newspaper. Put rubber bands around the paper to hold it in place and then keep the blades in some area where you can find them readily. Don't try to use a hacksaw blade whose teeth are worn, even if they are worn in just one section of the blade.

Hacksaw blades are about ½ inch wide and have from 14 to 32 teeth per inch. For cutting through angle iron, heavy pipe, brass, or copper, use a blade having 24 teeth per inch. For thin tubing try a blade with 32 teeth per inch (Fig. 2-19).

To put in a blade, follow the technique illustrated in Fig. 2-20. Hold the blade so that the teeth point away from the handle of the hacksaw and also face upward. Arrange the blade so that its holes fit into the corresponding pins of the frame.

At the end of the frame, near the handle, you will find a wing nut arrangement that will let you tighten the blade in place. When you do so, make sure the blade is straight and does not tilt to either left or right along its length. Do not try to

tighten the wing nut with a tool. Just make the blade finger tight.

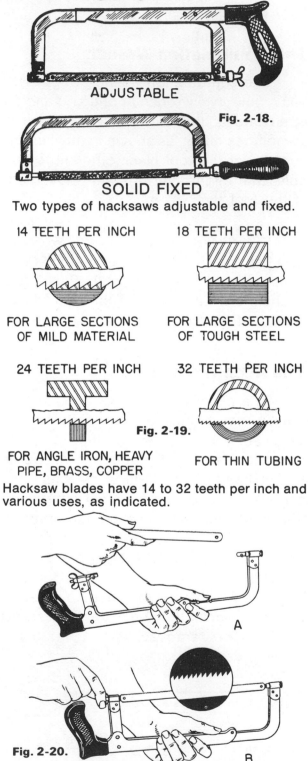

ADJUSTABLE

Fig. 2-18.

SOLID FIXED

Two types of hacksaws adjustable and fixed.

14 TEETH PER INCH

18 TEETH PER INCH

FOR LARGE SECTIONS OF MILD MATERIAL

FOR LARGE SECTIONS OF TOUGH STEEL

24 TEETH PER INCH

32 TEETH PER INCH

Fig. 2-19.

FOR ANGLE IRON, HEAVY PIPE, BRASS, COPPER

FOR THIN TUBING

Hacksaw blades have 14 to 32 teeth per inch and various uses, as indicated.

A

Fig. 2-20.

B

How to insert a hacksaw blade. Hold blade with teeth facing upward and with teeth pointing away from handle (A). Turn wing nut near handle in clockwise direction to tighten blade (B).

How to Use the Hacksaw

Of all tools, the hacksaw is probably the one most often used incorrectly. If the blade is mounted askew, that is, at some angle however slight, or if the hacksaw frame isn't held vertically, it is quite possible for the blade to snap. The first step in using a hacksaw is to select the correct blade.

Coarse blades having fewer teeth per inch cut faster and are less likely to become clogged with metal chips. However, the fewer the teeth, the coarser the cut and the harder you must drive the blade to make the cut. For cutting thin sections, such as thin-walled copper pipe used in plumbing, work with a finer blade.

When you cut, remember that the cutting action takes place only on the push stroke. And so, you may find the work a bit easier if you lift the saw just slightly on the return stroke. This will raise the teeth a bit above the metal, reducing friction and making the return stroke less work.

Fig. 2-21 shows the right way to hold and use the hacksaw. Extend a finger as shown in the drawing to guide and support the frame. Hold the pistol grip of the hacksaw securely with the remaining fingers. Use your other hand to support the opposite end of the frame. Not only does this use of two hands help keep the saw steady in its forward cutting action, but it also keeps the hands away from the cutting teeth.

Cut with long, steady strokes, trying to use as much of the blade as possible. If you use short, choppy strokes, you may finish with a rough, gouged cut instead of one having smooth edges. Further, with this incorrect sort of cutting, the cut will be uneven—wide in some parts, narrow in others. Always mount the work in a vise, as shown in Fig. 2-21. Mount the work so that the cut to be made is close to the edges of the vise.

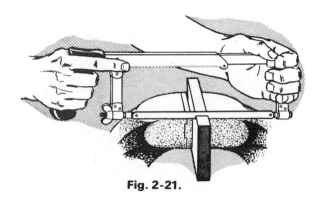

Fig. 2-21.

Proper way to hold and use hacksaw.

Fig. 2-22.

Sometimes it is convenient to mount the hacksaw blade at right angles to the frame.

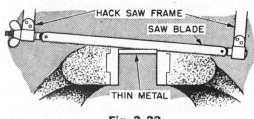

Fig. 2-23.

One method of cutting thin metal.

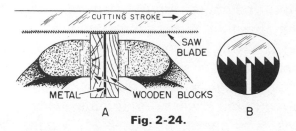

Fig. 2-24.

When cutting thin metal, support it between a pair of wooden blocks (A). Drawing B shows why it is necessary to use a hacksaw blade having a large number of teeth per inch when cutting thin metal.

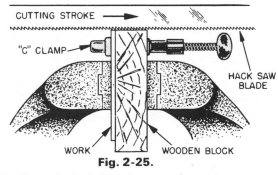

Fig. 2-25.

C-clamp is helpful when cutting thin metal.

The adjustable hacksaw is made so that the blade can be put at right angles to the frame. (Fig. 2-22). The advantage here is that you can saw through long sections without having the frame interfere with the work. The metal being cut, of course, must be mounted in a vise. Be sure to hold the hacksaw just as though the blade was in its normal position. It is also a good idea to move the work up in the vise after cutting through a section of the metal so as to keep the cutting section always above the top level of the vise.

When cutting thin metal (Fig. 2-23) hold the frame of the saw at a slight downward angle. The trouble with cutting thin metal, though, is that the sawing action can bend the metal out of shape. This not only may spoil the metal for the use you have in mind, but makes it difficult or impossible to continue with the sawing. To prevent deforming, you can mount the metal between two blocks of wood, as shown in Fig. 2-24. The blocks hold the metal in place and keep it from vibrating while being cut.

The reason for using that technique is illustrated in Fig. 2-24B. Here the teeth of the saw and the metal have been magnified. Note that the metal fits between two sawteeth. As a result, the trailing tooth tends to catch the metal and push it forward, possibly bending or breaking the metal.

Another technique for cutting thin metal requires only one wood block (Fig. 2-25). However, you will need a C-clamp, a type of hand vise, to help hold the work.

Removing a Frozen Nut

Sometimes a nut or connector will become frozen. The word "frozen" as used here means that the nut or connector has become so rusted that its threads have merged with the threads of the bolt to which it is fastened. Various liquids are made which will help "dissolve" the rust, but with connectors having many threads it is often difficult for such liquids to get in and attack the rust. The problem is that turning the frozen connector with a wrench may also result in turning the bolt to which the connector is fastened, and therefore the nut will not come loose.

You can remove a frozen nut with a hacksaw, as shown in Fig. 2-26. The drawing shows a top view, A, and a side view, B. Using the hacksaw, position the blade as close to the threads of the bolt or stud as you can get. The blade will then be parallel to the bolt, as indicated in drawing B. Cut parallel to the bolt until you are almost through it. If there is a lock washer under the nut, don't try to saw through it but stop at this point. Lock washers are sometimes made of hardened steel and so, instead of cutting through the washer, you may wear out or dull the teeth of the hacksaw blade.

Instead, use a cold chisel and insert the sharp end into the cut you have just made. Hold the chisel with one hand and tap its top with a hammer. If you have cut through most of the nut or connector you will find that just a few taps on the chisel will be enough to split the connector.

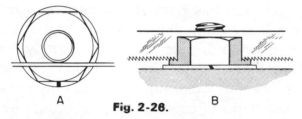

A   **Fig. 2-26.**   B

How to use hacksaw to remove frozen connector.

Preparing a Bolt for Plumbing Use

One of the toughest problems in plumbing is working in confined, restricted areas where it is difficult to reach in with a tool, or where it is difficult to handle a tool or to use it. If you need to mount a bolt in a place where turning the bolt with a wrench is difficult or impossible, you can try cutting a notch across the head of the bolt. For doing this, you'll find it easier to use a hacksaw blade having a larger number of teeth. Mount the bolt in a vise so that the head of the bolt clears

the upper part of the vise. Try to saw so that the cut divides the top portion of the head of the bolt into two equal parts. The cut should be deep enough and wide enough to accommodate a large screwdriver. *Don't make the cut too deep, as this will weaken the nut.*

Chisels

Ordinarily, a chisel is a tool for chipping or cutting metal. But in plumbing you can use a chisel for forcing threading into a connector to help prevent leaks, for notching connectors, and for helping to shear or cut away rusted connectors. Since chisels are made of tool steel and have a hardened cutting head, you can use them on softer metals such as iron or copper pipe.

There are various kinds of chisels, as illustrated in Fig. 2-27, but the one you will find most helpful for plumbing is the flat cold chisel shown at the top. As the drawings show, chisels differ in the shapes of their points.

As with all other tools, there is a correct method for using chisels. For large work use a large chisel. Conversely, for small work, select a smaller chisel. These are rather rough guidelines, but it is all a matter of experience. Also, since you will be using a hammer for hitting the head of the chisel, you will need a hammer capable of delivering sufficiently strong blows. Again, a heavier hammer for a heavier chisel. If you use a light hammer on a heavy chisel, the chisel will absorb the blows of the hammer and will transfer little of the energy to the metal being worked on. You'll know something is wrong when you realize that the chisel is doing practically no cutting.

There are two fundamental ideas in using chisels, just as there are in using any other tools. The first is to keep from damaging yourself, and the other is to do the job. Hold the chisel in your left hand using just your thumb and first finger, about one inch from the top. Relax. If your fingers are tense and tight, an accidental blow by the hammer means your digits will resist the force of the strike and take more punishments. If your fingers are relaxed, they will move with the blow and you will reduce its effect.

A safer method is to hold the chisel with a pair of slip-joint pliers. Slip-joint pliers are designed to have a wider jaw opening than ordinary pliers. Since your fingers will be out of the way of the hammer blow, any miscalculation will result only in the blow being received by the pliers. Much better for you; possibly not so good for the pliers. You may fracture the pliers if they are made of cast metal, as they often are, but that is still much better than a smashed digit.

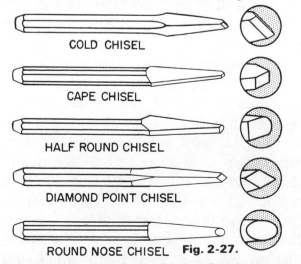

COLD CHISEL

CAPE CHISEL

HALF ROUND CHISEL

DIAMOND POINT CHISEL

ROUND NOSE CHISEL   **Fig. 2-27.**

Various types of chisels. Cold chisel is the one most commonly used in plumbing.

Keep your eyes on the work and your mind on the job. Also wear safety goggles. Metal chips flying away from the work can travel astonishing distainces with equally astonishing velocity. Goggles are uncomfortable: You can't see so well, and they may make you perspire. *So wear them.* Better discomfort than a damaged eye.

Faucet Seat Dressers

In time, the movement of water, the chemicals contained in it, and the rubbing action of the washer will cause the faucet seat to wear away. When it does so, it will wear irregularly, with tiny cracks forming in the seat or with the seat becoming uneven.

When this happens, it becomes impossible to turn the water off. Water will continue to drip no matter how tightly the faucet handle is turned. Replacing the washer may help but will do so only for a short time. Possibly putting in a new washer will be of no help at all. There are two cures: (1) Dress the seat, that is, grind it down until it once again has a smooth even surface, or (2) replace the entire faucet. Tools for dressing the seat cost much less.

The basic idea behind all faucet seat dressers is the same. A grinding tool is mounted at one end of a rod, and a handle at the other. The grinding tool fits against the seat and cuts the upper surface of the seat, in effect providing a new surface. It is important to mount the dressing tool so that it is truly vertical and does not move from side to side in use.

Fig. 2-28 shows a number of different faucet dressers. The device in drawing A has a wheel at the top and a cutter at the other end. The cone in the center of the tool is a reversible double cone guide. It is used to hold the tool in position and fits into the inner threads of the faucet.

The size of the grinding tool depends on the faucet. Cutter sizes are 1/2 inch to 11/16 inch, and 3/4 inch. The cutter in drawing B is similar to that in A. It has a double reversible guide made of brass. The cutter in drawing C is somewhat simpler than the others, but works in the same way.

Fig. 2-29 illustrates another type of faucet seat grinder. When using a seat grinder it is important to keep the tool from gouging or leaving burrs. This means you should turn the handle steadily, smoothly and easily, and try to use uniform pressure. The special handle on the grinder in Drawing A is designed to let you do this. As shown in drawings B and C, you can use the grinder with an electric drill which has a speed control or with a hand drill. However, for home use where you may have just one leaky faucet to contend with at a time, turning the faucet seat grinder by hand is best.

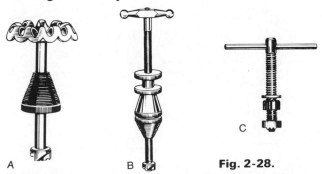

Fig. 2-28.

Various styles of faucet seat dressers. (Chicago Specialty)

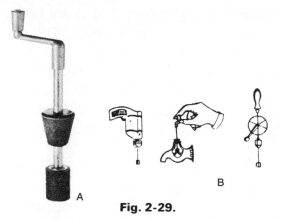

Fig. 2-29.

Faucet seating tool with swing handle (A). You can grind faucet seat (B) with speed-controlled drill, by hand, or with hand drill. (Hancock-Gross)

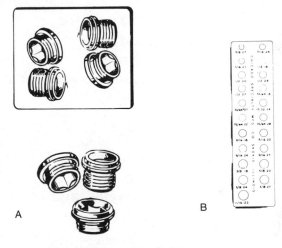

Fig. 2-30.

Various types of faucet seats (A), and faucet seat gauge (B). (Chicago Specialty)

Removing Faucet Seats

When a seat can no longer be ground to make it watertight when sealed with a washer, you must replace either the seat or the faucet. The hole in the seat may be round, square, or hexagonal and it may be threaded if the faucet contains a removable seat. Fig. 2-30A shows various types of faucet seats. Since such seats come in a variety of sizes, it is important to replace the seat with an exact duplicate.

One way of doing this is by using a facuet seat gauge (drawing B). The other is to remove the seat using a tool such as a six-step seat wrench. It has three hex sizes on one end and three square sizes on the other. Made of hardened steel, bright plated, it fits most seats in general use.

To remove the seat, remove the faucet stem and insert the faucet seat wrench. After the wrench fits into position, turn the handle counterclockwise. As you do, the seat will turn and will gradually come loose, at which time you will be able to remove it with the wrench. To install the new seat, follow the reverse procedure. Insert the seat in the faucet and tighten it with the faucet seat wrench.

Pipe Cutters

The most economical way of buying pipe is to buy it in the length you need, having the correct diameter, and threaded at both ends. But that isn't always possible; you may need to get pipe longer than you need and then cut it to size. Whether it is worthwhile buying a pipe cutter depends on how much use you expect to get out of it.

You can use a pipe cutter to cut pipe made of steel, brass, copper, wrought iron, or lead. There is a difference between pipe and tubing, although they may do the same work. Tubing has much thinner walls, and so it may be more convenient and practical to flare its ends rather than cut grooves in it.

Fig. 2-31 shows a variety of pipe and tube cutters. A No. 1 pipe cutter can cut pipe having diameters ranging from ⅛ inch to 2 inches, while the No. 2 has a cutting capability of 2 inches to 4 inches. The cutting element is a special steel alloy cutting wheel plus a pair of pressure rollers which can be made to tighten against the pipe by turning the handle of the tool.

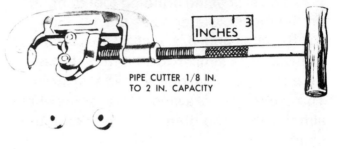

PIPE CUTTER 1/8 IN.
TO 2 IN. CAPACITY

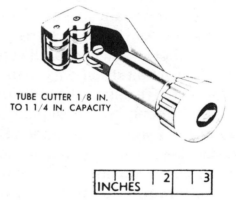

TUBE CUTTER 1/8 IN.
TO 1 1/4 IN. CAPACITY

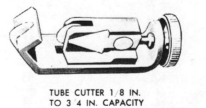

TUBE CUTTER 1/8 IN.
TO 3/4 IN. CAPACITY

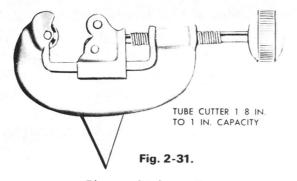

TUBE CUTTER 1 8 IN.
TO 1 IN. CAPACITY

Fig. 2-31.

Pipe and tube cutters.

How to Use a Pipe Cutter

A pipe cutter produces a clean 90° angle cut. You can use a hacksaw for cutting pipe, but with a hacksaw it is difficult to get a clean right-angle cut. It is not easy to thread pipe that has been cut with a saw, so use a hacksaw only if you don't plan to thread the end you have cut.

Before cutting the pipe with a pipe cutter, mark the precise position where you want the cut. You can use your hacksaw to produce a starting line, or a pen or pencil if the pipe is clean and the mark will be readily visible. Put the pipe cutter on the pipe and make sure the cutting wheel rests on the mark you have made. Tighten the handle of the tool so the cutting wheel bites into the starting mark. If you haven't already done so, put the free end of the pipe into a vise. If the pipe is plated and you do not want to damage the finish, put a pair of wood blocks between the jaws of the vise, or use any other material, such as leather or rubber, that will keep the jaws of the vise away from the pipe.

Give the pipe cutter one full turn. If you examine the work, you will see that you have now made a line completely around the pipe. It will actually be a rather shallow cut. Now apply some pipe cutting oil around the cut you have just made. This will make it easier for you to cut the pipe and will also prolong the life of the cutting wheel. Make another complete turn and then another. Examine the work to make sure that the cutting wheel is following the original groove. Now keep turning slowly until the pipe is completely cut through.

After the pipe is cut, use a cloth to wipe the cut end. Be careful. There may be some sharp metal burrs, and these can be painful. You may need to dress the cut end with a file to remove any burrs or rough edges.

You will find cutting pipe easier if you can mount the pipe between two vises. The reason for this is that the action of turning the cutter sometimes moves the pipe up or down out of position, even if it is held tightly in the vise. While the vise may be tight, it is making contact with the pipe at only a pair of horizontal lines along its length and not with the entire surface area of the pipe.

Pipe Threaders

Pipe threads can be internal or external. An internal thrread is one that is cut along the inside surface area of the ends of the pipe. An external thread is cut around the outside surface areas, also along the pipe ends. Taps are used for cutting internal threads; dies for cutting external threads.

Threads are cut not only on new pipe, but on old pipe as well. The threads of a used pipe may be in poor condition, and the pipe can sometimes be salvaged by rethreading. Fig. 2-32 shows two types of dies. The name of the one at the right, "square pipe die," is a reference to the shape of the die, not the pipe it cuts.

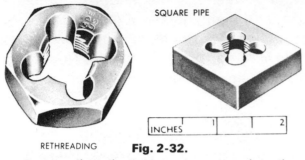

SQUARE PIPE

INCHES 1 2

RETHREADING **Fig. 2-32.**

Rethreading die (left), and square pipe die.

Parts of a Thread-Cutting Tool

Essentially, a thread-cutting tool consists of two parts—the die and the die holder. Fig. 2-33 shows a die (left) and its holder (right). A pair of pipe handles known as die stock, form part of the tool and are used to supply the turning force needed for cutting threads into pipe. Die stock is threaded at one end, so the tool can be disassembled and stored after use. The tool is also supplied with guides to enable it to form a perfect right angle when it is mounted on the end of the pipe that is to be threaded.

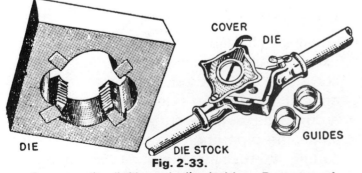

COVER
DIE
DIE
DIE STOCK
GUIDES

Fig. 2-33.

Square die (left) and die holder. Purpose of guides is to make sure tool fits on pipe correctly, making a precise 90° angle with it. Cover fits over die and holds it in place. Handle used for turning tool is called die stock.

How to Use a Pipe Threader

Prior to using the die, it is inserted in the holder, which clamps the die and holds it in position. Push the die onto the end of the pipe to be cut. The pipe, of course, must first be securely fastened in a vise. Mount the pipe vertically in the vise (Fig. 2-34). The advantage of doing so is that the total weight of the tool will then bear down on the pipe and so you will not need to exert very much pressure. It also means you will be in a position to look down on the work and will be able to guide the cutting tool more easily.

Some vises, such as the one shown in Fig. 2-35, are made specifically for holding pipe. The advantage of such a vise is that it will hold the pipe more securely since the heads of the vise are shaped to conform to the round shape of the pipe. This gives the vise a greater gripping surface, so there is less opportunity for the pipe to move. However, unless you plan to do a considerable amount of pipe threading there isn't much point in investing in this tool.

Turn the handle of the thread-cutting tool clockwise. Turn slowly and after you have cut a single complete thread, move the die back part of a turn. Then continue turning the tool clockwise to cut still another thread. After cutting the next complete thread, turn the tool counterclockwise for about a half turn. In effect, you will be taking a quarter to half step backward for every complete forward step. The purpose here is to remove any metal chips or burrs that may form while you are using the die. While using the die, apply cutting oil. This will make the job easier and will prolong the cutting edge of the die threads.

After you have made as many threads as you deem necessary, turn the tool counterclockwise, but hold it with both hands so as not to damage any of the threads you have formed. The first thread, that is, the thread at the very edge of the pipe, is susceptible to damage. It is probably the most important of all the threads, for if it is damaged you will be unable to mount a connector on the pipe.

After you have removed the pipe threader, wipe the threads with a cloth containing some cutting oil. Then take a connector of the appropriate size and mount it on the threads, turning the connector until it reaches the final thread. It should do so easily and smoothly. This will also help clear the threads of any burrs or sharp edges.

If you find, however, that the connector tends to jam before it reaches the last thread, one of the threads may be incompletely formed or may be damaged. Don't try to force the connector further. Actually, you should be able to move the connector back and forth with your fingers. Do not use a wrench as you may damage the threads by cross threading, a condition in which the threads aren't uniformly spaced. Instead, put the die back on the pipe, and work the die back and forth on those threads that seemed to block the passage of the connector. After you have removed the die, try the connector once again. When you are finished, lubricate the threads with a light coating of machine oil.

The purpose of threading pipe is to join one pipe to another by means of connectors having internal threading. If there is too much play between the external threads of the pipe and the internal threads of the connector, water will find its way along the threads, which can result in leaks. This can happen if the die you used for cutting the threads isn't sharp or if the threads have become worn. To stop the leak you can wrap the threads with Teflon all-purpose thread dope, with a compound called pipe seal, or with pipe joint compound.

Pipe joint compound is available in tubes or cans. You can wrap thread dope around the threads, as shown in Fig. 2-36. This will not only permanently seal threaded pipe joints and valves, but it also supplies lubrication for easy assembly and disassembly. Teflon all-purpose thread dope is not affected by acids, gases, or organic solvents, and it will tolerate any temperature in the home. It will not harden with age, will not drip or run. One of its great advantages, however, is that it prevents pipe or bolt threads from corroding or rusting together. And so, for that reason alone, it is advisable to use it when joining a connector to a threaded pipe.

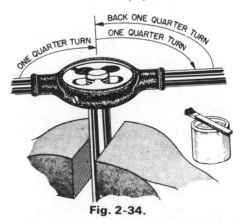

Fig. 2-34.

Using a die to cut threads on pipe.

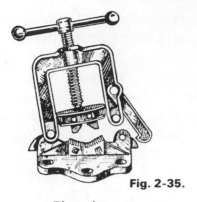

Fig. 2-35.

Pipe vise.

Fig. 2-36.

Method of applying Teflon all-purpose thread dope. (Hancock-Gross)

Tool Summary

Here are the tools you should have on hand to make simple plumbing repairs:

Wrenches, including pipe wrenches, in a range of sizes to fit the pipe, fixtures, equipment, and appliances in your home plumbing system.

Screwdrivers in a range of sizes to fit the faucets, valves, and other parts of the system.

Hammer.
Sink plunger and toilet plunger. Do not interchange the two.
Cold chisel and center punch.
Cleanout auger. Get two types: one for kitchen and bathroom fixtures, and another designed for use on a toilet.

Friction tape. You can use friction tape to protect the chrome finish on your fixtures when you must use tools on them. The advantage of friction tape over rags is that the tape will stay in position.
Adjustable pliers.

The tools listed above are basic. This doesn't mean you must use them exclusively for plumbing repairs, for most of them, with the exception of the auger and plungers, can be used for other household jobs as well. If you want to have a more extensive set of tools, here are some you can include:

Pipe vise.
Set of pipe-threading dies and stocks.
Hacksaw and blades. Be sure to include blades that have 32 teeth to the inch for cutting thin-wall pipe.
Tapered reamer or half-round file.
Copper tube cutter with reamer, if your plumbing system uses copper tubing. Most new homes do include such tubing.

Some Precautions in Using Tools

Always use the proper size wrench or screwdriver. Don't use pipe wrenches on nuts with flat surfaces. Instead, use an adjustable or open end wrench.

Don't use pipe wrenches on polished surface tubing or fittings, such as those found on fixtures.

Tight nuts or fittings can sometimes be loosened by tapping lightly with a hammer or mallet.

Never use an electrically operated

tool while standing on a wet floor. Always use tools only for the purpose for which they were designed. Thus, do not use a screwdriver as a chisel, or a wrench as a hammer.

Always use pipe joint compound, pipe seal, or Teflon all-purpose thread dope when joining threaded pipe or fixtures.

Some tools, such as open end wrenches, may be made of cast metal. Tapping them with a hammer can cause them to fracture.

Always remember to shut off the water supply before you start working on a fixture.

Plumbing Emergencies

Working on household plumbing on a do-it-yourself basis is fine, but there will be times when it will be necessary to call in a plumber. It is better to have a plumber available who is willing to supply 24-hour service, or who will at least come to your home as soon as possible.

Burst Pipe or Tank

The first thing you should do is to close the shutoff valve to the fixture that is in trouble. If you don't know where the shutoff valve is, don't waste time trying to look for it. Instead turn off the main water valve. You should know where that is. If not, take a few minutes out to locate it, not during an emergency, but now.

Toilet Tank Overflows

Immediately turn off the water valve

to the toilet. It is right below the tank, generally at the left side. If the valve is out of order, remove the top of the tank, and reach in and pull the tank float rod up toward you. This will force the inlet valve to close more tightly. Yell for help. If you are alone, hold the tank float rod up toward you and reach in and remove the tank ball. This will let the water out of the tank and will flush the toilet.

Do not use the toilet again until it is back in working order.

Rumbling Noise in Hot Water Tank

This is sometimes an indicationg of overheating. Another symptom of overheating is hot water backing up into the cold water supply line. Turn off the hot water heater immediately. Call a plumber.

Protecting Your Piping

If you must leave your home during winter months and if you live in an area where below-freezing temperatures are common, do one of two things. Either keep your house heating system turned on, but with the temperature gauges set to at least 40° F, or else drain your water pipes. A drain valve is usually provided at the low point of the water supply piping for this purpose. Also drain any water storage tank, hot water tank, toilet tanks, water treatment apparatus, and any other water system appliances or accessories.

After you have drained the plumbing system of water, pour antifreeze into all sinks, and that includes kitchen and bathroom sinks. Pour antifreeze into the bathtub and stall shower drains. Also all toilets. The intent here is to fill the traps with antifreeze.

When water freezes, it expands. The pressure of expansion can be enormous and is capable of bursting pipes. Then, when the ice in the pipes changes back to water again, you will have a flooded home.

Also be sure to drain your hot water and steam heating system. When you return home and decide to use your plumbing system once again, turn the main water supply valve on slowly. It will take a little time for all the pipes to fill. Also turn faucets on slowly. They may spit or hammer at first, but as soon as the piping system is filled with water, this show of temperament will stop.

Chapter *III*

Pipes and Fittings for the Home Plumber

The water supply section of your plumbing system contains water throughout its entire length. When you turn on a faucet, the water doesn't make a mad rush from some point near the water meter. Instead, the water is right there, just waiting for you to turn the handle. Water pipes are always filled, right up to the point of exit. The water is under pressure and so opening a pipe or removing a fixture anywhere in the water supply line means you will have a flood on your hands unless you first turn off the appropriate valves.

And that is why the water supply system contains (or should contain) so many valves. It is to give you the opportunity to turn off a selected part of the water supply system without interfering with the rest of it. Pipes containing fresh water form a sort of reservoir, with the water pushing somewhat forcefully against every valve.

The drain system contains very little water, and actually the only water it does have is that contained in the various traps. Sinks, bathtubs, and showers have traps that are separate from the fixtures.

The toilet, however, has a built-in trap. The water in the toilet tank is not part of the drain system and does not become part of it until you flush the toilet. The tank contains water that is part of the fresh water system. Your water heater is also part of the fresh supply, and not of the drain system.

For the most part, then, fresh water pipes are filled; drain pipes are empty. Drain pipes carry liquid only when some fixture is being used. Vent pipes, of course, are always empty.

Pipe Construction

Pipes can be made of steel, wrought iron, copper, chrome-plated brass, cadmium-plated steel, stainless steel, nickel-plated brass, cast iron, fiber, and plastic. Drain and vent pipes are often made of cast iron, although rigid copper is being used in newer installations. Water supply pipes are usually iron in older homes; copper in newer ones. Pipes associated with fixtures are often chrome-plated.

Copper Pipe

At one time galvanized steel pipe was the most commonly used for home plumbing, but in newer homes you will find it being replaced in some or all parts of the plumbing system with copper pipe and copper tubing.

Copper pipe has quite a number of advantages for plumbing work. It is lightweight. You can solder it. It resists corrosion and is not as subject to scaling, a condition in which mineral deposits form a stonelike deposit on the interior of the pipe. Unlike iron pipe, the interior of copper pipe is quite smooth, and so copper pipe, for a given diameter, has much less resistance to water flow.

Resistance to water flow, or any partial clog for that matter, has an effect equivalent to that of reducing water pressure. The decreased resistance that results from the use of copper means you can use a pipe having a smaller diameter, reducing the cost of the installation. The disadvantage of copper pipe, however, is its cost in comparison with other types.

Copper Pipe Specifications

Copper pipe is specified by its inside diameter (ID). If you want to know the approximate outside diameter (OD), add 1/8 inch to the ID. Since the outside diameter includes two walls, this means the wall thickness is 1/16 inch. This is just an estimate since wall thickness depends on the type. ID's of certain types of copper pipe for a fresh water supply system are 1/4, 3/8, 1/2, 3/4, and 1 inch.

ID (Type K-l) (in inches)	OD (in inches)
1/4	3/8
3/8	1/2
1/2	5/8
3/4	7/8
1	1 1/8

Copper pipe for drainage is generally sold in ID's of either 1 1/2 or 3 inches, and in lengths of 10 or 20 feet. You can use the wider diameter for a soil stack, and the narrower for connecting waste lines or vents. While copper can be used for drainage and venting, not all plumbing codes permit it.

Temper of Copper Pipe

The "temper" of pipe refers to its hardness. In the case of cast iron or steel we aren't concerned with temper, but copper can be rigid or flexible. For copper pipe having a hard temper, the pipe is always straight, just like iron pipe. Soft-temper copper pipe is flexible. Hard-temper pipe resists damage more than soft-temper and so is better suited for use where the pipe will be visible.

Types of Copper Pipe

Copper pipe is available for plumbing in four different thicknesses: K, L, M, and DKV. Type K is the thickest, L is regarded as a medium weight, M is still lighter, while DKV is the thinnest. You will need to consult your local plumbing code to learn which type is permitted in your area.

Since the water in your fresh water supply is under pressure, the pipe must be able to withstand it and, further, must be able to tolerate variations in pressure. However, as mentioned earlier, only the fresh water supply is under pressure, not the drainage system, and so a copper pipe that would be prohibited for the fresh water supply might be suitable for drainage. Types K and L are available in both hard and soft tempers.

How to Handle Copper Pipe

Copper pipe, whether the rigid or flexible type, is much softer than iron or steel and so is more easily damaged. If you drop a heavy tool on a length of iron pipe, nothing will happen, but under similar circumstances the copper pipe may be dented, nicked, cut, or pushed in. Since this would constrict water flow, the only solution is to replace the entire pipe or cut out the damaged section.

You must also be careful about the kind of tools you use with copper pipe and how you use them. Exerting too much pressure on copper pipe can deform it, depending in part on wall thickness.

How to Cut Copper Pipe

You can cut copper pipe with a special copper cutting tool or a hacksaw, but when using a hacksaw be sure to select a fine-toothed blade having either 24 or 32 teeth per inch. You will probably find that a blade with 24 teeth per inch is just about right. The fine teeth will give you a smoother cut with a sharper edge and there will be fewer metal burrs. You can cut copper much more easily than iron pipe. However, while you can use a hacksaw, it is still preferable to use a copper pipe cutter, a tool designed especially for such work.

You can put copper pipe in a vise to hold the pipe while you saw it, but don't use a vise with serrated jaws unless you modify them somewhat. Cover the jaws with leather, or use a pair of wood blocks, or else use a vise with smooth jaws. If you can cut a V notch lengthwise in the wood

blocks, you will find it easier to clamp the pipe more securely.

Another pipe holding technique is to use a miter box. Try a pair of C-clamps to hold the pipe at both ends so you can concentrate on the cutting. Put a strip of wood above the pipe so the clamp presses against the wood, not the pipe. This will distribute the pressure of the clamp and will keep it from deforming the pipe. The intent here is not to crush the pipe but just to keep it in place, so don't use excessive force.

The advantage of using a miter box is that it will let you cut at a 90° angle across the pipe. Copper pipe cuts quite easily, so there is no need to use cutting oil. After you have finished the cut, use a flat file to deburr the outside cut edge of the pipe. File gently. You don't want to make a chamfer—just to smooth the edges. Then, with the help of a round file or a tapered reamer, clean out the inside edge of the cut. Burrs on the inside, or a not completely smooth inside surface will interfere with water flow; burrs on the outside may mean difficulty in making pipe connections.

The Pipe Vise

The difficulty with the average vise is that it can clamp and hold pipe only at two lines along the length of the pipe. But since a strong turning force must sometimes be used on the pipe, it is difficult to keep the pipe from turning. With copper pipe and tubing, since the force exerted by the vise along the length is so considerable, it is easy for the pipe or tubing to become deformed.

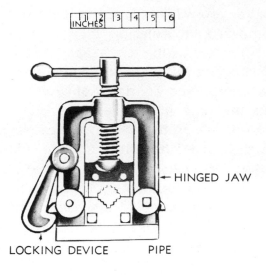

Fig. 3-1.

Vise for holding pipe or tubing.

The pipe vise shown in Fig. 3-1 is especially designed to hold round stock. The vise in this drawing has a capacity of 1 to 3 inches. For pipe and tubing having smaller diameters you can use any soft material to fill the space. A scrap bit of canvas or flexible rubber or soft leather will do. Alternatively, you may be able to get a vise having a smaller capacity.

One of the jaws of the vise is hinged so you can position the work and can then bring the hinged jaw down. A locking device on the other side of the vise is then used to lock the hinged jaw in place.

IPS

The abbreviation IPS means "iron pipe sizes." Brass and copper pipe tables list the outside and inside diameters and weights per foot of copper pipe, and also brass pipe, in iron pipe sizes. The advantage here is that you can make a direct comparison between pipes of different metallic structure.

In the accompanying table the figures given for brass and copper pipe are the same as for corresponding nominal sizes of steel or wrought iron pipe. There may be some variations in wall thicknesses and inside diameters, but not significantly so. Both brass and copper pipe are threaded with the same tapered threads and the same number of threads per inch as iron and steel pipe.

⅜	.675	.494	.421	.61	.64	.81	.85
½	.840	.625	.542	.91	.96	1.19	1.25
¾	1.050	.822	.736	1.24	1.30	1.62	1.71
1	1.315	1.062	.951	.1.74	1.83	2.39	2.51
1¼	1.660	1.368	1.272	2.56	2.69	3.30	3.46
1½	1.900	1.600	1.494	3.04	3.20	3.99	4.19
2	2.375	2.062	1.933	4.02	4.23	5.51	5.79
2½	2.875	2.500	2.315	5.83	6.14	8.41	8.84
3	3.500	3.062	2.892	8.31	8.75	11.24	11.82
3½	4.000	3.500	3.358	10.85	11.41	13.67	14.37
4	4.500	4.000	3.818	12.29	12.94	16.41	17.25
5	5.563	5.062	4.813	15.40	16.21	22.52	23.67
6	6.625	6.125	5.751	18.44	19.41	31.32	32.93
8	8.625	8.000	7.625	30.05	31.63	47.02	49.42
10	10.750	10.019	9.750	43.91	46.22	59.32	62.40

Copper Tubing

One of the big disadvantages of pipe, no matter the material of which it is made, is that various fittings must be used to enable the pipe to change its direction. Also, because of its weight, iron and steel pipe become very difficult to handle and so there is a practical limit on pipe length. Copper pipe cuts down on the weight problem a bit, but unusual lengths become unwieldy.

Flexible copper tubing eliminates many of the difficulties of steel, iron, and copper pipe. It is available in K and L types. Because it is flexible, you can bend it around corners. When making plumbing repairs in a house you can manipulate the tubing through the walls, avoiding obstructions. Copper pipe must follow a straight line; copper tubing need not do so and can bend out of the way of a physical interference.

Cutting Copper Tubing

A method of cutting copper tubing that is cleaner and better than using a hacksaw is provided through the use of the tubing cutting tool shown in Fig. 3-2. The tool consists of an extremely hard circular cutting blade and a pair of circular jaws for holding the tubing in place. The pair of circular jaws holds the tubing in place.

Fig. 3-2.

Tool for cutting copper tubing. (Chicago Specialty)

To cut tubing, open the jaws by turning the knob counterclockwise. Mark the tubing where it is to be cut and insert it into the tool between the cutting wheel and the circular jaws. Turn the knob clockwise until you feel the tubing securely in place. Do not exert too much pressure, for you will only bend in the walls of the tubing.

Before you rotate the tool, make sure the edge of the cutting blade is directly on the mark you have made. Turn the tool once and you should see a thin

mark on the tubing. If there is no mark, the tool hasn't been tightened enough. If the cut made by the tool is too deep, you may see the formation of a burr. In that case, loosen the handle slightly.

After you have made on complete turn, tighten the handle slightly and make another turn. After every turn, tighten the handle until the tool cuts completely through the tubing. Then remove the tool and wipe the cut edges of the tubing with a cloth to remove any copper "hairs." The cut edge of the tubing should be completely circular and not squeezed out of shape or deformed in any way.

As a protection for the tool, never keep the handle so tightly closed that the cutting blade rests against the circular jaws. Never leave the tool mounted on a section of tubing. And when you finish cutting, make sure no bits of copper cling to the cutting wheel or circular jaws. Use a cloth to wipe the tool.

How to Connect Copper Pipe and Tubing

You can connect copper pipe in the same way as pipe made of iron or steel. The ends of the copper pipe are threaded and the copper pipe is joined by a fitting. By using special fittings you can connect copper pipe or tubing to steel or iron pipe having threaded ends.

Fig. 3-3 shows two ways to connect copper tubing. The tubing can be soldered to a coupling, or if the tubing is threaded, the ends of the pipe can be connected by a flange nut. However, the easiest way is to eliminate both threading and soldering by slipping a flange nut over the end of the tubing and then flaring that end. The flared end prevents the flange nut from sliding off.

Fig. 3-4 illustrates a preliminary step in using flared copper tubing. The flange nut is on the tubing and now a threaded fitting is inserted into the open end of the tubing. You can then move the flange nut forward and screw it onto the thread fitting. This will force the fitting tightly against the end of the tubing. If you have another section of copper tubing you can attach it to the other end of the fitting in the same manner.

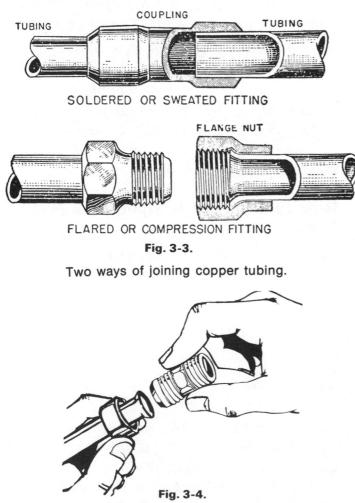

TUBING   COUPLING   TUBING

SOLDERED OR SWEATED FITTING

FLANGE NUT

FLARED OR COMPRESSION FITTING

Fig. 3-3.

Two ways of joining copper tubing.

Fig. 3-4.

How to connect flared copper tubing to a fitting.

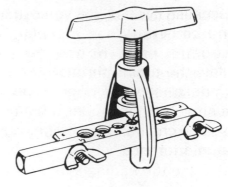

Fig. 3-5.

Flaring tool for copper tubing. (Chicago Specialty)

How to Use the Flaring Tool

Flaring copper tubing is easy, but you must have the right tool to be able to do it. Fig. 3-5 shows a flaring tool. The lower portion of the tool is an adjustable clamp held in place by a pair of wing nuts at both ends. The clamp contains a number of holes for the most common sizes of tubing.

The upper part of the tool consists of a handle at one end and the flaring section at the other. Turning the handle clockwise pushes the flaring tool into the copper tubing, forcing the tubing end to assume a bent-out shape having a lip. The lip bends outward.

The lip has a double purpose. It acts as a stop for a flange nut that is mounted on the tubing before flaring it. And the wider opening caused by using the flaring tool means you have provided an entrance for a fitting.

To use the flaring tool, turn the wing nuts so that the two clamps separate a bit. Select the opening corresponding to the size of the tubing you are using and insert the end of the tubing through this opening until the tubing touches the flaring section of the tool. Tighten both wing nuts securely. Turn the handle of the flaring tool so it enters the end of the tubing. If the tubing tries to move down because of the pressure of the flaring tool, tighten the wing nuts more securely. Keep turning the handle in a clockwise direction until the end of the tubing has flared outward.

When using this tool, exert pressure on the tubing by turning the handle slowly and smoothly. If this is not done properly, it is possible for the end of the tubing to split. In that case your only alternative is to cut off that end, either with a hacksaw or a tubing cutting tool, and then to start over again. If you have had no prior experience with a flaring tool, it would be helpful to practice on a few scrap bits of tubing.

You can save the cost of buying a flaring tool by getting the individual flaring tool shown in Fig. 3-6. You can order this tool by specifying the ID of the copper tubing you want to flare. The tool has a tapered edge and a knurled handle to supply a good gripping surface. Just insert the tapered edge into the tubing as shown in the illustration, and rotate the tool. The lip of the copper tubing will then flare out, following the shape of the flare on the tool.

Fig. 3-6.

Individual flaring tool. (Chicago Specialty)

How to Bend Tubing

One great disadvantage of iron pipe is that you must use a fitting if the pipe is to make a bend or turn. This means the end of the pipe must be threaded and turned tightly into the fitting to prevent any leaks.

If copper tubing is sufficiently soft you can bend it and avoid the expense and time and work involved in using a fitting. Do not try to bend tubing by hand. The only result will be a bend with a crimp. This will not only reduce the total amount of water flow but is a potential trouble spot for leaks. Instead, use the tube-bending spring illustrated in Fig. 3-7. The spring is flared at one end so you can insert copper tubing easily. Bend the spring with the buting in place as shown in the drawing. Because of the flexibility of the tube-bending spring, you will be able to remove it easily after you have completed the bend.

Tube-bending springs are available in different diameters, and you must use one having the correct diameter for your copper tubing. The springs are identified by the outside diameter of the copper tubing and are available in these sizes: ¼, 5/16, ⅜, 7/16, ½, ⅝, and ¾ inch.

While the tube-bending spring can let you bend tubing into just about any angle, try to avoid extremes. If you must make a 90° turn, make the bend as wide and as gradual as you can. A sharp turn restricts not the amount of water, but the rate of flow. You slow down when you maneuver your car around a turn, but the mass of the car, its bulk, doesn't stop and continues on its travels.

You can avoid buying a bending tool, if you like, by bending the tubing around something with a circular shape.

Thus, you can bend copper tubing around a scrap section of metal pipe. However, you will find it easier to bend copper tubing having a smaller diameter. And the larger the diameter of the copper tubing, the easier it will be to dent it.

Kinds of Copper Tubing

You can get tubing in K, L, and M types, with K and L available in hard or soft temper and type M in hard temper only. Hard-temper copper tubing is difficult to bend unless you soften it first by heating. The following chart supplies specifications of K, L, and M copper tubing.

⅜	.500	.402	.430	.450	.27	.20	.14
½	.625	.527	.545	.569	.34	.28	.20
¾	.875	.745	.785	.811	.64	.45	.33
1	1.125	.995	1.025	1.055	.84	.65	46
1¼	1.375	1.245	1.265	1.291	1.04	.88	.68
1½	1.625	1.481	1.505	1.527	1.36	1.14	.94
2	2.125	1.959	1.985	2.009	2.06	1.75	1.46
2½	2.625	2.435	2.465	2.495	2.92	2.48	2.03
3	3.125	2.907	2.945	2.981	4.00	3.33	2.68
3½	3.625	3.385	3.425	3.459	5.12	4.29	3.58
4	4.125	3.857	3.905	3.935	6.51	5.38	4.66
5	5.125	4.805	4.875	4.907	9.67	7.61	6.66
6	6.125	5.741	5.845	5.881	13.87	10.20	8.91

You can use Type L for horizontal or vertical runs of pipe, open or concealed, but type K is often preferred because it is stronger. One of the problems involved in using soft-temper tubing for drainage is that the tubing may have a tendency to sag and so you won't get a uniform downward slope, or pitch. For drainage it is better to use hard-temper tubing.

If you will compare the inside diameters of copper tubing with the equivalent sizes of steel or iron pipe, you will see that the bore of the copper tubing is smaller. Generally, however, because of the greater wall smoothness of copper, there is no noticeable difference in water flow.

Stainless Steel Pipe

One of the problems of plumbing codes is that they can lag behind technology. You can, for example, get stainless steel pipe for use in the water supply system, but whether your local plumbing code will permit it is another matter.

Copper pipe and tubing is relatively expensive, but stainless steel is much less so. Stainless steel resists corrosion and like copper isn't as subject to mineral deposits on the inner walls as iron. It is much more difficult to bend than copper.

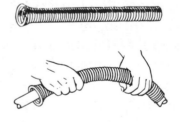

Fig. 3-7.

Spring for bending copper tubing.

Galvanized Steel Pipe

At one time galvanized pipe was the most widely used form for plumbing, but it has largely been replaced by copper. Galvanized steel pipe (steel coated with zinc) does have some advantages: it is strong, can take much more abuse and punishment than copper, does not dent or crimp as easily, and is less expensive than copper. However, it is much easier to join copper than galvanized steel. You can use a flaring tool with copper, but steel requires threading. Cutting steel is also more difficult. If you are going to work on a do-it-yourself basis then you need not worry about labor charges, but if you ask your plumber to use galvanized steel your labor costs will rise simply because it takes longer to work with steel than copper.

Galvanized pipe can corrode, and the corrosion can be caused by either acidic or alkaline liquids. Further, it is quite possible for scale to build up inside the pipe. Finally, the interior surface of galvanized steel pipe isn't as smooth as that of either copper pipe or tubing, a factor that increases resistance to water flow.

Galvanized pipe is suitable for water supply, waste, or vent. The pipe is available as standard weight, extra strong, and double extra strong. Standard weight is most often used in the home, for it has ample strength. Not only are the extra-strong and double-extra-strong pipes more costly, but the bore becomes smaller. Thus, size 1 (1 inch) steel pipe has an inside diameter of 1.04 inches, but the same size in extra strong is 0.957 inch and drops to 0.599 inch for the double extra strong. And so wall thickness is achieved at the expense of the inside diameter.

Cast Iron Pipe

Cast iron pipe is widely used for soil stacks and waste. Even in newly built homes you will commonly see cast iron installed for drainage and venting, with copper used for fresh water supply.

Cast iron pipe has a number of advantages. It is extremely durable, is substantially free of corrosion, and can also be used underground.

Cast Iron soil pipe is available in two weights: standard (or service) and extra heavy. Fig. 3-8 shows the construction of soil pipe made of cast iron. One end is known as the bell or hub end, the other the spigot end. For this reason, cast iron soil pipe is sometimes referred to as bell and spigot pipe, or hub and spigot pipe. The bell end is enlarged, so it loosely fits the spigot end of the next section of pipe. Fig. 3-9 illustrates the way in which the spigot end fits into the hub end.

Fig. 3-8.

Single section of cast iron soil pipe.

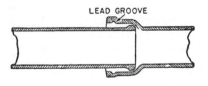

Fig. 3-9.

Cross section showing how two sections of cast-iron soil pipe are joined.

Plastic Pipe

Plastic pipe is still prohibited by many plumbing codes in the sense that use of such pipe has not as yet been approved. However, there seems to be little question that in time plastic pipe will be widely adopted for in-home plumbing. It is light in weight and, size for size, is less heavy than the metallic pipes. It will not corrode, scale, or rust. It is easy to clean—just wipe it with a cloth. It does not add a metallic taste to water. For finished basements where piping must be exposed, plastic pipe in various colors is less offensive looking. Further, plastic pipe usually does not condense water on its outside surface and so eliminates "pipe dripping" in humid areas. Plastic pipe isn't so unyielding as metallic pipe and so can tolerate the expansion of water that is freezing somewhat better than other types of pipe. Costwise, it is competitive with metallic pipe, but its price has gone up dramatically compared with other pipes.

Water Hammer

Plastic pipe does have its drawbacks. You cannot, for example, use it as a ground connection for your electrical wiring system. It is much more susceptible to damage than iron or steel pipes. It can be damaged by the internal pressures crated by fast-opening and closing faucets, or by quick-acting valves in dish and clothes washing machines.

However, you can eliminate this problem by installing air chambers, such as those shown in Fig. 3-10, near any fixture that has a fast water shutoff feature. Without the air chambers you will get a pipe condition known as hammer or water hammer. There will be a tremendous knocking sound in the pipes. Copper, iron, and steel pipe can tolerate the effects of water hammer much more than plastic. You can use the method shown in Fig. 3-10 with any type of pipe.

Fig. 3-10.

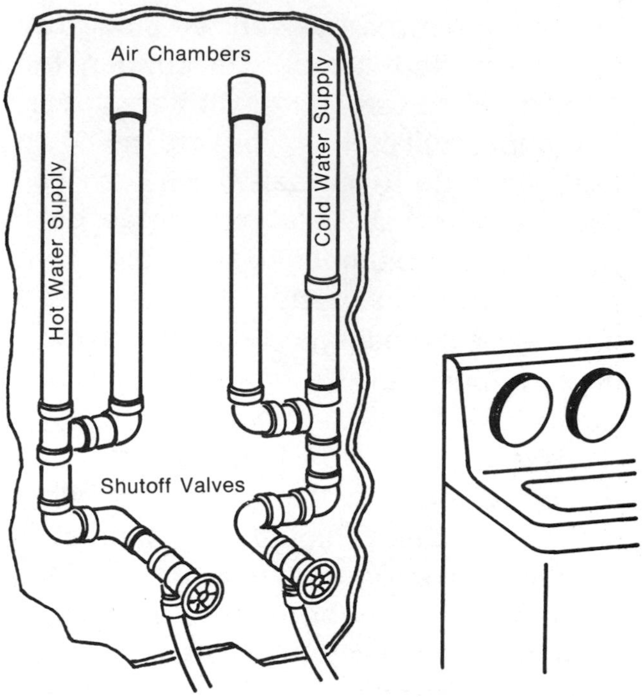

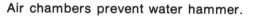

Air chambers prevent water hammer.

The air chambers are simply tubes, about a foot and a half long, that are capped at one end, the other end is connected to the water supply pipes, both hot and cold, through a coupling.

Expansion of Plastic Pipe

Plastic pipe can expand as much as 0.4 percent when the water flowing through it is extremely hot. When installing the pipe, then, use hangers made especially for plastic which will let it change its length without putting undue stress on it.

Types of Plastic Pipe

There are various kinds of plastic pipe that are comparable to rigid copper, and there is also one type that could be referred to as tubing. The most commonly used plastic pipes are polyvinyl chloride, better known as PVC pipe; acrylonitrile-butadiene-styrene, or ABS pipe; and chlorinated polyvinyl chloride, which you can ask for as CPVC. Of these three, only CPVC will handle both hot and cold water. Use PVC and ABS for cold water piping only. CPVC pipe is quite a bit more expensive than the other two types.

Plastic pipes generally are available in 10-foot lengths and you can get fittings for them just as you can for other types of pipe.

PVC, ABS, and CPVC are rigid types, but you can get polyethylene pipe. This flexible, black plastic pipe is equivalent to tubing. It is sold in 100-foot rolls and is intended for cold water use only. Its flexibility has definite advantages. You can snake it through walls, going around obstructions.

Not all poly pipe is the same; some brands cost more than others. The more expensive types are stronger and can tolerate greater amounts of water pressure. Your local water company can supply you with information about water pressure in your area and so you can be guided accordingly. It is always best, however, to give yourself the benefit of a generous safety margin. Poly is excellent for use in underground installations, such as a buried watering system for a lawn.

Fittings

The purpose of a fitting is to join two or more pipes. Fittings are used to extend the total length of pipe or to let the pipe change its direction. Fittings are used when you want to change from one type of pipe to another, such as joining rigid copper pipe to copper tubing. Fittings can be threaded or unthreaded. There are fittings for joining copper to steel or for connecting threaded pipe to tubing. Fittings are identified by the work they do or by their shape. A vent increaser is a fitting that increases the diameter of a vent pipe. All traps are fittings that trap sewer gases. A cleanout is a fitting that lets you get at the interior of a pipe to clean it. A tee is a fitting that presumably resembles the letter T. We also have wye fittings (Y).

Finally, there are special fittings for every type of pipe and tubing, for every kind of metal or plastic. Many of these fittings resemble each other. You can have a tee fitting for iron, and still another tee fitting for copper. So you must specify the kind of fitting you need not only by name, but also by the kind of pipe or tubing for which it is designed.

Metal Fittings

Metal fittings are usually, but not always, threaded. The threading can be internal or external, or both. In some instances, the pipe comes equipped with its fitting as part of the pipe structure. Soil pipe, for example, is actually constructed so that one section can fit in and be joined to another section. The joined end of the pipe, then, can be regarded as a fitting.

Nipples

A nipple is a short length of pipe that is either completely threaded or is threaded at both ends. The threading is external. Nipples are available in iron, brass or chrome-plated brass, and galvanized iron.

Nipples are available in three general types: close, short, and long. Close nipples are completely threaded. You can use a close nipple to join a pair of fixtures when you want the fixtures to be immediately adjacent. On a short nipple the threads do not meet. There is a space of about ½ to ¾ inch near the center of the nipple that is unthreaded. Use such nipples when you want fixtures relatively close, but not butting, or touching, each other. A long nipple, such as the one shown in Fig. 3-11, is a pipe about 3 inches to 6 inches long, with external threads on the ends.

Fig. 3-11.

Long nipple. (Hancock-Gross)

A tapered nipple, such as the plain brass type in Fig. 3-12, has a combination of straight and tapered threads. The tapered end is useful for fitting into almost any kind of fixture and is helpful when you want to connect pipe and fixtures when these items have different diameters.

Couplings

Couplings are internally threaded fittings used to join two lengths of pipe having threaded ends. There are two types of couplings: sight and reducing. A straight coupling connects a pair of iden-

tical pipes. A reducing coupling, also known as a reducer, joins a pair of pipes having different diameters. The two basic types of couplings are illustrated in Fig. 3-13.

Elbows

The couplings shown in Fig. 3-14 are intended for several runs of pipe. You can use elbows when the pipe is to change its direction. Elbows are internally threaded or internally/externally threaded, at both ends. Internal threads are sometimes called females; external threads, male. The angle indicated beneath the elbows in the drawings refers to the angle that will exist between the lengths of pipe when joined by the elbow. Thus a 90° elbow means the two pipes will form a right angle.

The reducing elbow in the drawing lets you join two pipes having different diameters. The reducing coupling in Fig. 3-14 is a 90° type, but such elbows are also available to supply different angles.

The two pieces of plumbing hardware shown at the right in Fig. 3-14 are street elbows. They have external threading at one end and internal threading at the other. You can use them for connecting pipe to fixtures. First, rotate the externally threaded end into the fixture. You can then connect a pipe to the other end of the street elbow. The externally threaded end of the pipe will mesh with the internally threaded end of the street elbow.

Fig. 3-12.

Tapered nipple. (Chicago Specialty)

COUPLINGS

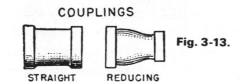

Fig. 3-13.

STRAIGHT   REDUCING

Straight and reducing couplings.

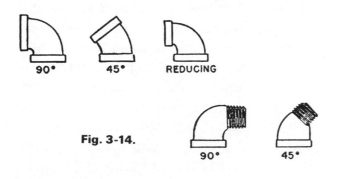

90°   45°   REDUCING

Fig. 3-14.

90°   45°

Various types of elbows. The two shown at the right are street elbows.

90° ELBOWS

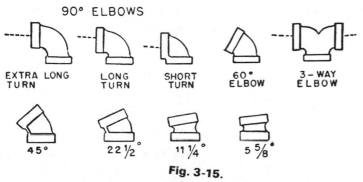

EXTRA LONG TURN   LONG TURN   SHORT TURN   60° ELBOW   3-WAY ELBOW

45°   22½°   11¼°   5⅝°

Fig. 3-15.

Elbows for drainage pipes and fixtures.

Drainage Elbows

When an elbow is used in a fresh water system, the pitch of the elbow is of no consequence, for the water is under pressure. An elbow that joins a pair of horizontal pipes, for example, is so designed that both sections of pipe joined by the elbow will be reasonably horizontal.

However, for drainage, as explained earlier, we depend on gravity to carry the waste to the soil stack and so drainage piping must have a downward pitch.

Fig. 3-15 illustrates some of the more widely used drainage fittings. The dashed line represents the pitch of the threaded opening. The pitch is such that it will not interfere with the pitch of the drain pipes. Elbows are made so you can have an extra long turn, a long turn or a short turn. The purpose of the extra long turn is to avoid the possibility of a clog. The shorter turns are used where the waste is liquid. The 5 ⅝° elbow is used where the connecting pipes are practically in line with each other. It can also be used to supply a pitch or slope of about 1⅛ inches per foot of pipe.

Tees

A tee is a coupling that has three openings. The openings may all be internally threaded or have a combination of internal and external threads.

Three types are shown in Fig. 3-16. The one at the left is a straight tee. You can use it when you want to join three lengths of pipe, two in a straight line and a third at right angles to them.

The tee shown in the center is a reducing tee. Use it to join one length of horizontal pipe with another length of horizontal pipe, which has a smaller diameter. As with the straight tee, it accommodates a third pipe which makes a right angle with the original tee.

The tee at the right is a street, or service, tee. It works in the same way as the street elbows previously described but has provision for a third pipe.

Elbows, tees, and nipples can be mounted in any position. If the pipes to be

69

joined are vertical, then the coupling hardware can be mounted so as to accommodate the pipe. If we assume that the pipe is horizontal, then the pipe entering from the left is known as the first run and the opening in the tee is called the first run opening. The first run is usually the pipe that is closest to the sewer drain. The second run opening in the tee is directly opposite the first run opening. The outlet opening is the one that permits connecting the pipe at right angles to the other two sections of pipe.

Fig. 3-16.
Various types of tees.

You can buy tees in which the openings are all of the same size, or with size variations among the different openings. All the openings, of course, must mesh with the pipes and fixtures with which they will connect. The following table supplies some indication of the various opening sizes that can be used in combination with a first run opening of 1 inch. This is not intended as a complete table, for you can find a much greater variation than the opening sizes listed here.

First Run Opening	Second Run Opening	Outlet Opening
1	1	1½
1	1	1¼
1	1	¾
1	1	½
1	1	⅜
1	¾	1
1	¾	¾
1	¾	½
1	½	1
1	½	⅜
1	½	½

As with elbows, you can buy tees that have a pitch to accommodate the downward slope of pipes, or that fit pipes which are completely horizontal or vertical. Fig. 3-17 shows a pair of tees to be used in a drainage system, with the dashed lines representing the slope of the threads. The tee connections here have the side outlet pitched upward so that the tees can be attached to pipes having an upward slope toward a fixture. For example, you could have the 5⅝° elbow attached to the drain pipe of a sink. The pipe in the elbow would lead downward and connect to the right side of the basin tee. The two other openings of the basin tee would connect to a pair of vertical drain pipes, one coming down into the upper opening of the basin tee, and the other leading down from the lower opening.

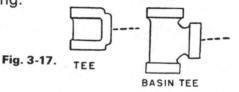

Fig. 3-17. TEE   BASIN TEE

Tees for use in a drainage system.

The Y-Branch

The Y-branch shown in Fig. 3-18 is a coupling for joining three pipes, two of which are in the same straight line and the third entering at an angle of 45°. Couplings of this kind are often used for connecting waste pipes to the soil stack.

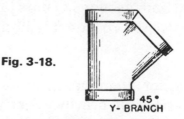

Fig. 3-18.

45°
Y-BRANCH

Y-branch accommodates pipe entering the coupling at a 45° angle.

Crosses

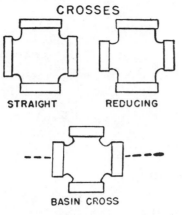

Fig. 3-19.

Crosses are couplings for four pipes. The basin cross is pitched for use in drainage systems.

Still another type of coupling is the cross; two examples of which are shown in Fig. 3-19. Crosses come in two types: straight or reducing. The straight cross is used for connecting four pipes having identical diameters. The reducing cross is used when one pair of pipes has a smaller diameter than the other. For example, the openings for the first and second runs can be the same; while the two oultlets openings can also have matched diameters; but somewhat different from those for the first and second runs.

Crosses are mainly used in drainage and venting systems. Thus, three of the openings can be used for joining drain pipes, and the fourth as the opening for a vent.

Caps

Fig. 3-20. CAP

Cap is used to close open-ended pipe or in connection with an air chamber.

A cap (Fig. 3-20) is hardware used for closing the end of a pipe. Air chambers (see Fig. 3-10) are sections of pipe about 1½ feet long, closed at one end with a cap. You can also use a cap if you have a section of pipe which you wish to close off when the pipe openings is not to be used. The advantage of a cap under these circumstances is that it keeps unwanted debris from falling into the pipe. It also keeps the open section of pipe from being used as a nest by insects.

Bushings

Fig. 3-21.

Outside head bushing (A); flared face bushing (B); straight face bushing (C).

Bushings (Fig. 3-21) are threaded inside and out. Assume you have two pipes, both with threaded ends but with different diameters. You can insert the smaller-diameter pipe into the inside threaded portion of the bushing and the larger diameter pipe to the outside threaded portion. You can also use this technique to connect fittings, faucets, or values. Thus, by using a suitable bushing, you can connect 1-inch pipe to pipe of a smaller or larger diameter. Bushings have heads which are hexagonal or octagonal so you can tighten them with a wrench. These are known as outside head bushings, but you can also get straight face bushings which do not have the outside head feature. The straight face bushing may be flared at one end; or it may resemble a short nippe which, unlike a nipple, is threaded both inside and out.

Return Bends

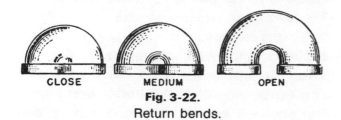

CLOSE   MEDIUM   OPEN

Fig. 3-22.
Return bends.

A return bend (Fig. 3-22) is used when a pipe must double back on itself. Various types of return bends are available, giving you some control over the positioning of the pipes relative to each other. With a close return bend the pipes will be almost touching; with the medium they will be further away; while with an open return bend you will get maximum separation. Return bends are used for very special applications in plumbing and it would be unusual to find them in a home plumbing system.

Use of Fittings in Piping Assembly

The purpose of fittings is to let you connect piping so that water can be delivered to various fixtures; or to connect piping so as to remove waste. There are some precautions; however. For the water supply system the fittings must not leak, something they can do rather easily, since the water is under pressure. For the drain system; the fittings must not interfere with the downward flow of waste; and so they must have the correct pitch for horizontal piping. And since water also flows through drain pipes, the fittings must be watertight.

Fig. 3-23 shows the order in which we would assemble piping so as to connect a fixutre to a waste pipe. The waste

pipe could; in turn, be connected to the soil stack or, more probably, to more fixtures.

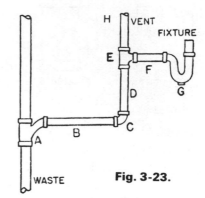

Fig. 3-23.

Use of fittings in connecting piping from a waste line to a fixture. Y branch (A); horizontal drain pipe (B); 90° elbow (C); vertical drain pipe (D); tee (E); horizontal drain pipe (F); trap (G).

The letters used in the drawing are arranged in the order of assembly. We would start with Y-branch A, screw threaded pipe B into the Y-branch, and then attach elbow C to the threaded end of pipe B. Next, we would screw in pipe D and thread tee E onto pipe D. With the addition of pipe F, trap G, and vent H, the job would be done.

This doesn't mean you must always follow this procedure. You may find it convenient or necessary to alter the assembly routine. However; if you are using threaded rigid piping, Fig. 3-23 is a good pictorial of the completed work.

There *is* one serious drawback to the plumbing setup shown in this drawing; although it will work well. As an example, suppose pipe B has developed such a serious leak that replacement is the only solution. Consider the difficulty of removing that pipe. If you try to turn it with a pipe wrench; you will only succeed in forcing it more tightly into fittings A or C, depending on which way you turn. The only way to get at Pipe B is to remove the trap G, then pipe F, then fitting E, then pipe D, and finally fitting C.

And not only do you have all the work of disassembling this section of the plumbing system, but when the replacement for pipe B is in position, you must first start putting the system back into working order again. All of this means quite a bit of work if you do it yourself, and a rather steep bill if you decide to have your plumber do it.

Unions

The piping situation just described indicates that plumbing is more than just a matter of connecting pipes. You must consider that you may need to replace some part, whether a pipe, a fitting, or a fixture.

A union is a fitting that will let you disconnect pipes with the least amount of trouble. The piping leading from your hot water system, for example, is a potential troublemaker. Essentially; a union is a three-part device. One part of the union threads onto the run-in pipe while another part threads onto the run-out pipe. The third part, a specially designed nut, holds the first two parts together and can be made to pull them together.

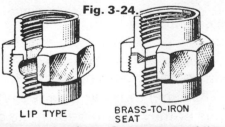

Fig. 3-24.

LIP TYPE   BRASS-TO-IRON SEAT

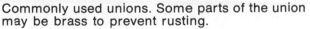
Commonly used unions. Some parts of the union may be brass to prevent rusting.

The most commonly used union is the lip type, shown in a cutaway view in Fig. 3-24 along with another type that works the same way and is almost identical in construction. The upper half and the lower half of each is threaded internally. One pipe fits into the upper half, another pipe into the lower half. All you need do now is to tighten the nut to make a secure, tight joint. However, you can get water leakage at a union, so use piping compound, or Teflon all-purpose pipe dope to get a watertight connection.

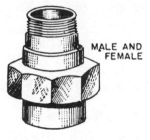

MALE AND FEMALE

Fig. 3-25.

Union that will accommodate internally and externally threaded pipe.

The two pipes that would be used in connection with the unions in Fig. 3-24 are externally, or male, threaded at their ends. However; you can use the union shown in Fig. 3-25 if one of the pipes is internally threaded at its end and the other pipe is externally threaded. Other than that; the union in Fig. 3-25 is used in exactly the same way as the previous two unions. Connect the pipes and then use a wrench to tighten the nut. If, at some time in the figure, you want to remove the connecting pipes, just turn the nut in a counterclockwise direction.

Some unions are equipped with a nut made of brass or may have a brass seat. This makes it easier to loosen the union since brass will not rust.

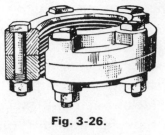

Fig. 3-26.

Nut union.

Fig. 3-26 shows still another type of union, one which is rarely used in home plumbing systems. The union is internally threaded and consists of two halves which can come apart. Each half is threaded onto the pipes to be connected. The union is held together and tightened by means of nuts and bolts.

Symbolic Drawings for Fittings

Drawings using plumbing symbols were described earlier. Such drawings are quite simple, and when you get accustomed to them; it will be easier for you to plan your plumbing system on paper. And if your plumber shows you such a drawing, you will at least know what he is talking about.

Fig. 3-27 shows how to use plumbing symbols for fittings. Drawing A is that of a tee. For tees and Y-branches, the larger run size is given first, then the smaller run, and finally the outlet. In drawing A we have a 2-inch pipe that is joined to another 2-inch pipe with both connected to a 1½-inch pipe through a tee fitting. Drawing B shows a 2½-inch pipe connected to a 2-inch pipe, joined to a 1-inch pipe through a tee. Note that except for labeled dimensions, drawings A and B are identical.

Drawing C is a Y-branch. Here we have a 3-inch pipe connected to a 4-inch pipe while the branch pipe is 2-inch. Drawings D and E use cross fittings, while drawing F has a side outlet tee. A side outlet tee is one having an opening for an additional pipe coming in at an angle.

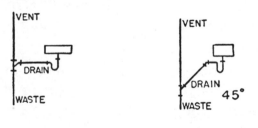

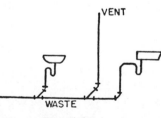

Fig. 3-28.

Symbolic drawings showing use of fixture, pipe, and fitting symbols.

Fitting symbols are used in conjunction with other plumbing symbols. as in Fig. 3-28. Dimenions can be used on such drawings or may be omitted. In the center drawing; for example; the only dimenion

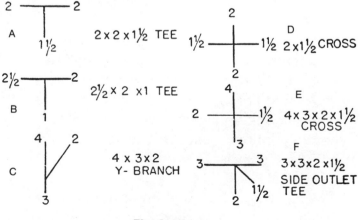

Fig. 3-27.

Symbolic drawings for some fittings.

information supplied is that the Y-branch has a 45° angle.

Cast Iron Drainage Fittings

The purpose of a drainage fitting is to join two sections of drainage pipe, while permitting entry by one or more pipes. The entering pipes may make a 90° angle with the drainage pipes and so the entering pipes look horizontal. However, they are not, for they must have a pitch to permit the flow of waste into the drainage pipe.

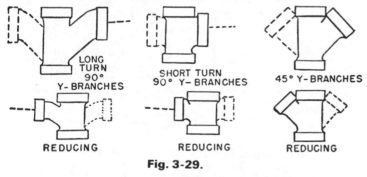

Fig. 3-29.

Cast iron Y-branches for drainage.

Fig. 3-29 illustrates some cast iron drainage Y-branches. The single horizonnal dashed line indicates the pitch of the entering pipe. The dashed outlines show the possibility of having two entering pipes instead of just one. Y-branches may be long turn or short. A long turn simply means that the extension of the Y-branch arm is longer than that of a short turn.

Although the Y-branches shown in the drawings are 45° or 90°, they are also available as long sweep quarter bends; or sixth; eighth, or sixteenth bends.

Soil Pipe Fittings

Just as in the case of iron pipe

described earlier, soil pipe fixtures can also have a hub and spigot end. In effect, then, you can regard the soil pipe fixture as a very short length of soil pipe, but with a bend in it ranging up to 90°.

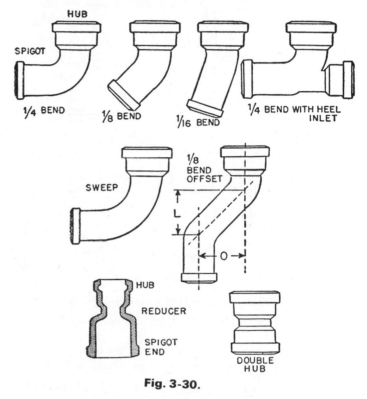

Fig. 3-30.

Fittings for soil pipes.

Fig. 3-30 shows various types of fittings that can be used with soil pipe. The ¼ bend is just another way of describing a fitting to join pipes that are at right (90°) angles to each other. The ⅛ bend fitting is for pipes that are at an angle of 45°, and the 1/16 bend for pipes at an angle of 22½°. Note that the ¼ bend fitting also has provision for the entry of another pipe, an arrangement that is sometimes called a heel inlet.

In Fig. 3-30 the ⅛ bend offset fitting has two dimensions indicated as L and O. The offset, O, is the same distance as

L, with both specified in inches. The offset may be as little as 2 inches to as much as 24 inches. Pipe diameters range between 2 and 6 inches.

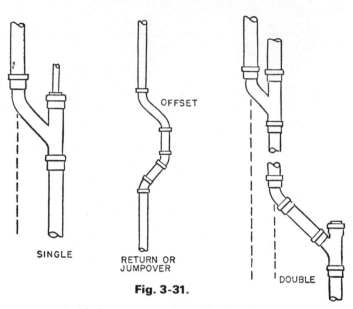

Fig. 3-31.

Fittings used with soil stacks.

Fig. 3-31 shows how offsets are used with soil stacks. The offset fittings in the center drawing may be used to avoid some obstruction in the building.

Increasers

An increaser is a fitting that is used on top of a vent stack. The vent stack, or main vent, lets air circulate to and from the other pipes in the drainage system. Sometimes the vent stack extends through the roof without any change in its diameter. At its lower end; the vent stack must connect full size to the soil stack. At its upper and, it should always be at least 1 foot above the roof. If the roof is a slanted one and is not used for any other purpose but protection, then a 1-foot extension above the roof is sufficient. But if

the roof is a flat area, which may be used as a place for hanging wash, the vent should extend at least 5 feet above the surface.

One of the possible causes of a vent clog is the formation of frost in and across the top of the stack. One way of reducing this risk is to use a stack increaser, a fitting designed to fit on the end of the stack. It is available in various heights.

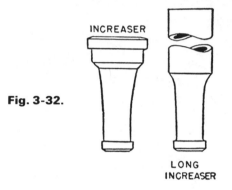

Fig. 3-32.

Increasers for use with roof vents.

Fig. 3-32 shows two types. The one at the left is simply called an increaser; the one at the right a long increaser. These are just relative terms.

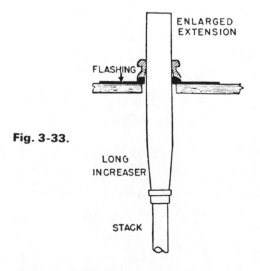

Fig. 3-33.

Long increaser mounted on top end of soil stack.

Fig. 3-33 shows the use of a long increaser at the end of the soil stack. The increaser is joined to the stack below the roof, and the extension portion of the fitting extends above the roof.

In very cold areas it may be necessary to insulate the vent extension. You can do this by packing insultation—such as rock wool, hair felt, or similar materials—around the pipe, as show in Fig. 3-34. The roof flashing is then brought up and around the insulated pipe and turned in at the top. The turned-in portion of the flashing can be held in securely by a ring which is forced into position.

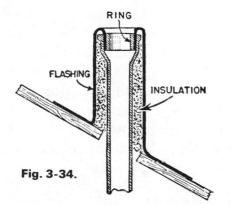

Fig. 3-34.

Method of protecting roof vent against frost.

How to Connect Vent Extensions

There are various ways of connecting roof extensions to the vent stack. Fig. 3-35 shows just two of the possible methods used. In drawing A, the roof flashing is brought up and into the hub end of the stack. The extension is then fitted into the hub, and the joint is calked. The calking material can be oakum, which is stranded hemp such as used in ropes, or else lead wool. There

are also various compounds available which can be used.

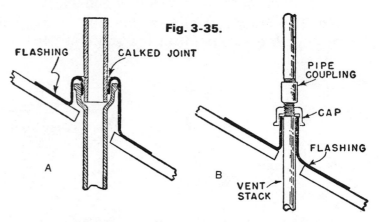

Two methods of adding vent extenders to the vent stack.

In the method shown in drawing B, the top of the vent stack is covered with a cap which has an internally threaded central opening. With the help of a pipe coupling, a length of open pipe can be connected to the vent stack.

There are several points to keep in mind when installing vent extenders. Since you have one or more pipes coming through the roof, there must be no possibility of rain following the drain down into the house. Since the drain is hidden in the walls, not only can the damage be extensive, but it requires an expensive repair job if the walls must be removed to get at the pipe. Another point is that the vent above the roof must be able to withstand wind pressure and not tilt. These pipes are sometimes hit by falling branches, another reason for making sure yours cannot be moved accidentally.

Plugs for Fittings

It is sometimes helpful to use a plug in a pipe, or to cover the end of a pipe.

The purpose of the plug can be to allow relatively easy access to the pipe. The plug at the bottom of a trap is one example. The cleancup plug at the bottom of or near the exit point of the soil stack is another.

Fig. 3-36.

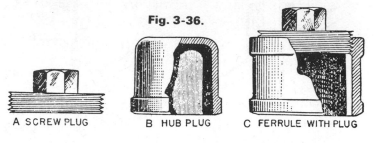

Various types of plugs used with pipes or fittings.

Fig. 3-36 shows three types of plugs used in fittings. The one in drawing A is a screw plug. This plug has external threads which fit into the internal threads at the end of a pipe or on some part of a fitting. The plug shown in drawing B is a hub type. The hub plug is threaded internally so it can screw on to the threaded end of a pipe. The ferrule type shown in C allows putting a brass screw plug into the hub end of a fitting.

Slip Couplings

Slip couplings are fittings with slip nuts at each end. The nuts are threaded so that externally threaded pipe can be connected. All you need do is to insert the pipe ends into the coupling, tighten the slip nuts that come with the coupling, and the two pipes are effectively joined.

Fig. 3-37 shows a few of the more commonly used slip couplings. That in drawing A is available in 1¼ x 1¼ inch or 1½ x 1½ inch sizes. Drawing B shows a coupling known as a 45° slip ell. When joined by this coupling, the two pipes will have an angle of separation of 45°. Drawing C shows a slip joint tee. Three pipes with threaded ends can be joined by this fitting. Finally, D is a 90° slip ell.

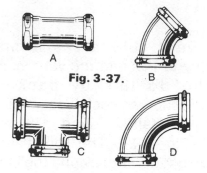

Fig. 3-37.

Some commonly used slip couplings: (A) slip coupling, (B) 45° slip ell, (C) slip joint tee (also known as 3-way slip tee), (D) 90° slip ell. (Chicago Specialty)

Since the couplings have two nuts; one at each end, they are sometimes called double slips. They are generally equipped with washers. Slips couplings are often used where piping is visible, and so they are crome plated, but you can also get them in rough brass, unplated cast metal, or PVC vinyl.

Fig. 3-38.

Ordinary coupling. Coupling is threaded internally and pipes of the same diameter fit in both ends.

You can also get an ordinary coupling, without the slip nut feature. Fig. 3-38 shows such a unit. It is internally threaded to accommodate threaded pipe at both ends. This coupling, available in ⅜- and ½-inch sizes, is used to join pipes having identical dimensions. It is not as convenient as the slip type of coupling. To use this coupling, insert one pipe at one end and tighten and then insert the other pipe at the opposite end and tighten. Tightening, in this case, means using a wrench on the pipe.

Bushings

You can use a bushing when you have a pipe end; a fitting, a faucet, or a valve which you want to connect to a threaded opening of a larger size. Bushings are both internally and externawly threaded. Thus, by using a suitable bushing you can connect a pipe having a 1-inch threaded opening into a piece whose thread size is ⅜, ½, or ¾ inch. The bushing head has either a hexagonal or octagonal shape so that you can tighten it with a wrench.

Fig. 3-39.

Bushings can be used to connect two pipes of different diameters. (Chicago Specialty)

Fig. 3-39 shows a representative bushing. If you were going to connect a pair of pipes with the help of this bushing, the pipe having the smaller diameter would be threaded into the center hole of the busying. The externally threaded portion of the bushing would then be inserted into the internal threaded portion of the larger-diameter pipe. The bushing could then be tightened by using a wrench.

Slip Nuts

The slip nuts shown earlier in conjunction with slip couplings are also available separately. (see Fig. 3-40). You can, for example, place a slip nut over a pipe whose end is to be flared. You would, in effect, be making your own slip coupling. Slip nuts are often brass or chrome plated and come equipped with washers, as shown in the drawing. Make sure to use the washer, or a water leak will develop around the slip nut. When you buy slip nuts you will probably get washers at the same time. Slip nuts are available in a variety of sizes, commonly from ½ to 2 inches.

Fig. 3-40.

Slip nut with washer. (Chicago Specialty)

How to Specify Fittings

The size of a fitting is the nominal inside diameter of the pipe to which you connect it. The dimension of the main run is mentioned first, and then the size of the branch. For reducers; increasers, and offsets, give the size of the main run first, then the outlet size or the amount of offset, and finally the length of the fitting if it is available in more than one.

How to Join Cast Iron Pipe (Hub Type)

You can buy cast iron pipe in standard 5-foot and 10-foot lengths, so with some planning you may be able to avoid the chore of cutting it. Since the spigot end of one section of cast iron pipe is designed to fit into the bell or hub end of the next section, you must make allowance for that part of the pipe which will fit into the hub. In effect, when you join cast iron pipe, you lose a bit of the overall length because one pipe fits into the next. For 2-inch pipe allow 1½ inches; for 3-inch pipe, 2¾ inches; and for 4-inch pipe, 3 inches.

Cast iron pipe is heavy and awkward to handle, and although one person can do it, the job is easier and faster with two.

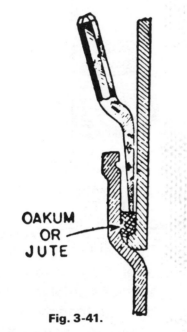

Fig. 3-41.

First step in joining cast iron pipe. Pack oakum or jute with help of calking tool.

Insert the spigot end of one length of pipe into the hub end of the other pipe. As a first step, use a calking tool to pack in oakum or jute tightly so it makes a snug fit in the region where the two pipes meet. Fig. 3-41 shows the calking tool in position with the oakum or jute beneath it.

Fill the remaining space with molten lead. The lead should occupy about one full inch above the oakum or jute. The

lead must fill with a single pouring, so you can't do this on a two- or three-step basis. The reason for this is that the lead fill must be a uniform mass when it cools. It will require anywhere between a half to a full pound of lead per inch diameter of the pipe. You can buy pig lead in bars weighing about 5 pounds.

Working with hot lead is dangerous, so it is much better to let your plumber handle this job. But you should at least know what is involved, to have some idea of what it is all about when he does his work.

Your local plumbing regulations may call for the use of hot lead when calking cast iron pipe. However, if the plumbing rules in your area permit, you may be able to use lead wool. This is in fibrous or shredded form, somewhat in the shape of a loose rope. You don't need to heat it. Just pack it into the space between the two pipes, right above the jute or oakum, and pound it into position with a calking tool and hammer as shown in Fig. 3-42.

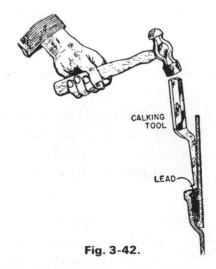

Fig. 3-42.

After packing lead wool in place, force it into position with hammer and calking tool.

How to Join Hubless Cast Iron Pipe

In some areas, local plumbing codes permit the use of hubless cast iron pipe. This is straight pipe and does not have either a spigot or a hub. When joining pipe of this type, simply butt the ends against each other, and since this pipe does not dovetail, measure the actual length you require. Fig. 3-43 compares hubless pipe with pipe having a hub and spigot.

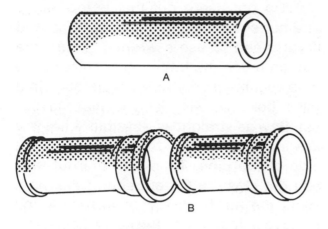

Fig. 3-43.

Hubless cast iron pipe (A) and cast iron pipe with hub and spigot (B).

How to Cut Cast Iron Pipe (Both Types)

After measuring the length of pipe you want, mark a circle around the proposed cut and then, with a hacksaw, cut the circle into the pipe to a depth of about 1/16 inch. Put the pipe on a block of wood as shown in Fig. 3-44, and with a cold chisel and a hammer, notch the pipe completely around. After you have gone around several times, the pipe will break off. You can use this technique with both types of cast iron pipe: straight and hub-spigot. If the pipe does not break off by

itself, tap it with a hammer at the end that is farther from the cut and up in the air.

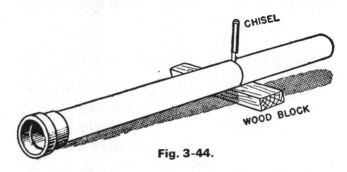

Fig. 3-44.

How to cut cast iron pipe.

How to Join Hubless Pipe

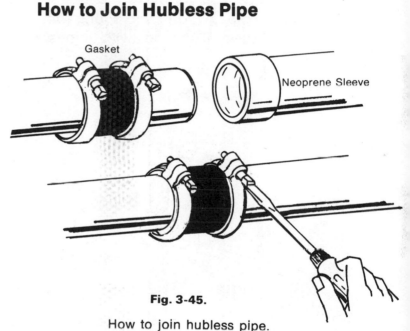

Fig. 3-45.

How to join hubless pipe.

To join hubless pipe you will need a special gasket made for this purpose. It is available complete with a neoprene sleeve and a pair of clamps, each of which has a large machine screw. To join hubless pipe, first slip the neoprene sleeve over the end of one of the pipes, and the gasket and its clamps over the end of the other pipe (see Fig. 3-45). Bring the two pipe ends tightly together. Slide the sleeve so that it covers both pipes equally and then slide the gasket and its clamps over the sleeve. All you need do then is tighten the machine screws with a screwdriver.

How to Measure Threaded Pipe

Any of the rigid metals can be threaded and that includes steel, iron, brass, and copper. To determine how much pipe you need, measure the distance D (Fig. 3-46) between the face of each fitting and then measure the amount of pipe thread that will enter each fitting. Add these and you will have the overall length of the pipe. If you need a long run, you can join several sections with unions.

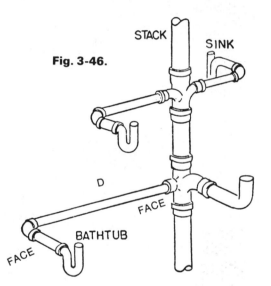

Fig. 3-46.

STACK
SINK
D
FACE
BATHTUB
FACE

To measure threaded pipe, determine the distance D between the faces of each fitting and then add the distance that both ends of the pipe will move into the fittings.

There is one thing to keep in mind: just because a pipe is threaded to a depth of 1 inch on each end does not mean that the fitting is also threaded for this distance. Quite often, when joining pipe to a fitting, a number of the threads on the pipe will be external to the fitting.

How to Cut Threaded Ends

Cutting pipe is one thing; cutting the threaded end of pipe is quite another. If you try to hacksaw your way across a threaded section you may well find yourself unable to put a fitting on the end of it. The threads will simply not engage.

To avoid this difficulty, always put a nut on the threaded end and turn the nut onto the end until it can go no further.

Do not use a nut that is too loose. The nut should make a firm, tight fit, and if you need to use a wrench to turn the nut, so much the better. Next, mount the pipe securely in a vise or, preferably, in a miter box that will let you make a 90° cut. Saw as straight as possible. After you are finished, deburr the outside and inside of the pipe. Then turn the nut until you get close to the cut end of the pipe. Work the nut back and forth before you remove it. In that way the nut will be working as a die and will straighten any threads that may have become bent from the action of the hacksaw.

How to Remove a Fitting

You will need two wrenches to remove a fitting from a pipe (see Fig. 3-47). Use one wrench to hold the pipe, the other to turn the fitting. Always be sure to move the wrench in the direction of the open jaws. If you want to tighten a fitting, just reverse the position of both wrenches.

Loosening a fitting is sometimes a two-person job, for you may need to use both hands on a single wrench to exert enough pressure on its handle. The wrench holding the pipe should not be more than a few inches away from the wrench turing the fitting. If the end of the fitting resembles a hexagonal or octa-gonal nut, make sure the jaws of the wrench fit firmly on the flat surfaces of the nut. If, for any reason, the nut end of the fitting is dirty, oily, or greasy, clean it thoroughly first to give the jaws of the wrench a chance to get a good grip. If the fitting and the pipe are plated, cover them with friction tape to keep the wrench jaws from scratching or cutting the finish. Always make sure the wrenches are tight. They should be tight enough so they can remain in position without being held.

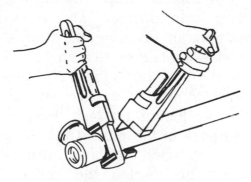

Fig. 3-47.
How to remove a fitting from a pipe.

Use the right-size wrench. If the jaws of either wrench must be opened to about maximum, the wrench is too small.

Painting Pipe

Chrome-plated pipes can be quite attractive, particularly if it is kept clean and polished. Copper pipe and plastic both manage to retain a relatively clean, smooth surface. Iron pipe, though, tends to rust, and this can happen even to new pipe. You can paint iron pipe, but if you paint the threads on the pipe that are out-side a fitting, you may find it impossible to remove the pipe at a later date should you need to do so.

Never paint valves, even though you do not use them. The purpose of valves is to give you control over the water supply, and while you may not use them often, the time will come when it will be necessary to do so. Shutoff valves on steam radiators are commonly painted—and should not be. Never paint air valves that are mounted on the sides of a radiator. The small hole on the top of the air valve has a purpose: to permit the escape of air from the radiator. If that small hole becomes filled with paint, the radiator either will become only moderately warm or will re-main completely cold.

Repairing Pipes

Iron or steel pipe can develop cracks or small holes. When this happens, shut off the water supply, clean the opening with emery paper, and wipe the entire area around the crack with a cloth so it becomes cclean and dry. You can then fill the crack with iron cement. Pack the ce-ment in as tightly as possible and let it dry thoroughly and harden before you turn on the water supply. You can also use epoxy cement, first following the same suggestions about cleaning and drying the opening.

Leaks frequently develop around the threads at the end of a pipe where the pipe enters a fitting. The leak is due to corrosion of the threads, forming a tiny channel through which water can escape. Remember that the water isn't just flowing out, it is being pushed. If the pipe does not have a union anywhere along its length, tightening the pipe at the leaking end will loosen it at its opposite end. Thus, you may not only fail to repair the existing leak, you may possibly start a new one.

If the pipe is an old one, it may be impossible to tighten it. Corrosion of threads usually is a condition that has existed for years, and the threads of the fitting and the pipe likely have "frozen." An alternative method is to apply epoxy cement all around the edges of the fitting. Before doing this, however, examine the fitting carefully and see if you can determine the exact spot from which water is leaking. It is unlikely that the entire circumference of the joint is causing the trouble, so it is better for you to concentrate on the exact location of the leak. Turn off the water supply and dry the area around the leak thoroughly. Cover the section with epoxy cement, and with a flat blade screwdriver, try to force some of the epoxy into the region of the leak. Let the cement dry for the number of hours specified in the instructions before turning on the water supply.

You may find that the epoxy cement technique doesn't work. Or it may work only partially, cutting the leak down to just a few drops. This is no cause for satisfaction, for there is no question that the tiny drip will work its way into a larger one. You can make a repair using the technique shown in Fig. 3-48. Here a sheet of brass or copper has been formed into a slightly tapered tube or collar. The flanged end fits over the end of the fitting. Pack the entire area around the end of the fitting with iron cement or liquid iron, making sure you cover all the threads of the pipe. However, before you do so, clean the area of any dirt or rust.

Put a metal strap around the collar, holding it in position with a machine screw and nut. However, the strap around the collar must do more than just hold the collar. It must exert a force on it. You can do this by making the circumference of the collar just a bit less than the circumference of the pipe. Then, when you tighten the machine screw on the strap, you will be forcing the collar tightly against the pipe.

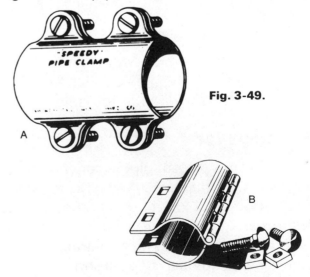

Fig. 3-49.

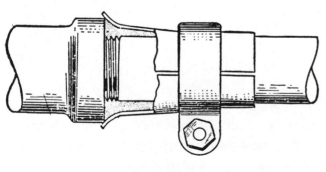

Fig. 3-48.

How to repair a leak where a pipe joins a fitting.

Pipe repair clamps. (Chicago Specialty)

You can also get pipe clamps of the type shown in Fig. 3-49A in a plumbing supply house or home supply center. This unit is cadmium-plated steel, and you can use it for ⅜-, ½-, or ¾-inch pipe. The interior portion of the clamp has asbestos and rubber gaskets. The clamp has four threaded ears to hold four bolts. When the bolts are removed, the clamp is in two sections. Put the two sections around the pipe, insert the screws, and tighten them.

Still another clamp is the hinged type shown in drawing B. This unit is made of extra heavy-duty steel and is cadmium plated. The inside part of the clamp has a neoprene gasket. You can use this clamp on pipe ranging from ½ to 2 inches. The clamp is held in position by a pair of machine screws and nuts.

Fig. 3-50.

Clamp for soil pipe. (Chicago Specialty)

Cast iron soil pipe isn't subjected to the strong pressures of the fresh water supply. However, because it is iron it can corrode and develop a leak. Removing and replacing cast iron soil pipe is a troublesome job and can be expensive. Instead, you can get a large clamp that will accommodate 2-inch to 4-inch pipe. Fig. 3-50 shows such a clamp. The U bolt fits around the pipe, and the clamp portion fits over the leaky section of the pipe.

Another method of repairing a leak where a pipe joins a fitting is shown in Fig. 3-51. Wrap strong cotton thread around

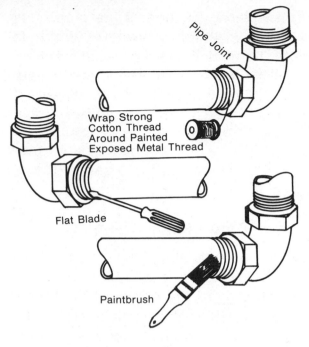

Fig. 3-51.

Alternate method of repairing a leak at a pipe joint.

the exposed metal threads, and then, using a flat blade screwdriver, push as much of the cotton as you can into any available space between the fitting and the pipe. Concentrate on the area of the leak. Use a hammer to tape the handle end of the screwdriver to supply more driving force.

After you have pushed in as much cotton thread as possible, coat the entire area with epoxy cement, going completely around all the threads. You can spread the epoxy with an old paint brush that is ready for the junk heap or with your screwdriver. Give the cement a chance to dry thoroughly before turning the valve that controls water flow through the pipe. Don't bother trying to put epoxy on damp threads or a damp joint.

Sometimes you will find joints that are soldered, usually where copper tubing is used as piping. The leak is sometimes caused by vibration in the home, causing the soldered joint to crack and then leak. It requires a rather large soldering iron or a torch to be able to supply enough heat to make a repair. This is a job best done by a plumber, unless you have the equipment and know enough about soldering to handle the job yourself.

How to Plug Leaks in Tanks

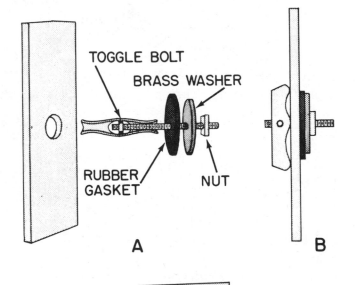

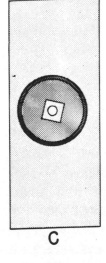

Fig. 3-52.
Technique for making a temporary repair in a tank.

Generally, a tank leak is caused by corrosion. The fact that a tank leaks at one place only is no cause for rejoicing, for once corrosion makes itself known, it frequently exists at other places in the tank as well. So once a tank starts to leak, the best procedure, and the most expensive, is to have it replaced.

But you can easily do a temporary repair, using a toggle bolt technique to close holes in the tank, until such time that you can get a new tank. Fig. 3-52 shows the setup. Ream the hole in the tank until it is as round as you can make it and so the hole edges are smooth. (You may find it helpful to use a round file.) Insert a toggle bolt through the hole, as shown in drawing A. After the bolt is through the hole, it will assume its expanded position, as shown in drawing B. Make sure the nut is as tight as you can make it. Drawing C shows an outside view of the completed repair.

The water level in the tank must be below the point at which you make the repair. If not, you will be working under very difficult circumstances. Shut off the water to the tank, and if it's possible to empty the tank, do so. If not, put a pail beneath the hole after you have shut off the water supply to the tank, and let the water drip out until it stops.

While the toggle bolt repair can be used for either pipes or tanks, it is easier and more effective with a tank, especially if the tank has flat walls. If a pipe has a small diameter, its curvature may be so severe that this sort of repair will have a high risk of faulure. Even when a tank is curved, the amount of curvature is ordinarily not so pronounced as it is with pipes.

How to Plug a Pipe

You can easily repair a hole in a pipe. First, shut off any water source that results in water flowing through the pipe. It's enough of a nuisance having to repair a pipe without having water squirting in your face. Use a tapered reamer and enlarge the hole. There are two reasons for doing this. The first is to make the hole round and to remove any rough edges. The second is to remove the rust that has accumulated around the edges of the hole. You'll know you're finished when you can see the bright edge of the pipe metal all around the circumference of the hole. Measure the diameter of the hole and buy a plug (Fig. 3-53) at your local plumbing/hardware store. The plug diameter should be a bit larger than the hole diameter.

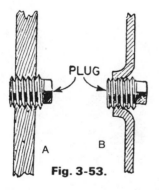

PLUG

A   B

Fig. 3-53.

Use plug for closing hole in pipe.

If the hole is of the correct size, inserting the plug and turning it will cut threads in the pipe. After you have inserted the plug, try the water supply to see if the plug is watertight. If you get a few drops of water around the outer edges of the plug, shut off the water supply and thoroughly dry the area around the plug with a cloth. Then apply some cement around the plug and let it dry for about 24 hours.

If the pipe you are repairing has thin walls, you will need to do some preparatory work first. Insert the end of a tapered punch in the hole, and tap the punch so that the walls forming the hole turn inward. This will supply the surface necessary to hold plug. After you insert the plug, a cross section will look something like drawing B in Fig. 3-53. Once again, if you get drops of water collecting around the plug, finish it off with some cement.

If the walls of the pipe are fairly thick, you can do a more professional job by cutting threads into the hole. For this you will need a plumber's tap of the correct size and also a tap holder. It may not be worth your while to buy a tap and tap holder for you may not have occasion to use these tools again. But if they are available, there is no question but that this is the preferred technique.

Vibrating Pipes

Pipes of all types, whether rigid or not, must be supported. If there aren't enough supports, or if they have worked their way loose or have fallen off, tighten them and possibly add more. Tube straps of the type shown in Fig. 3-54 are made for copper, but you can get straps for any other kind of metal or plastic. Copper tube straps are available in ⅜-, ½-, and ¾-inch sizes.

Fig. 3-54.

Copper tube strap. (Chicago Specialty)

You can also use perforated pipe strap when the pipe has a wide diameter or is too far from a support to use a regular strap. The advantage of perforated pipe strap is that it lets you make your own straps. The type shown in Fig. 3-55 is ¾ inch x 10 feet long and is made of 20-gauge steel, with a copper finish.

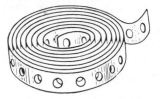

Fig. 3-55.

Perforated pipe strap. (Chicago Specialty)

Troubles with Shutoff Valves

A valve is very much like a faucet, and its general design follows the same plumbing principles. Like a faucet, a valve is a plumbing fixture intended to give you control over the flow of water. You may very well have shutoff valves located in the water supply line going to your kitchen faucets, and to your lavatory faucets as well. You have a main shutoff valve in the basement of your home, and probably a shutoff valve to your water heater. Some oil burners come equipped with shutoff valves. Your clothes washing machine has valves in both the hot and cold water lines.

Shutoff valves aren't used as often as your facuets. You rarely need turn off the main shutoff valve in your basement. The only time you may close the shutoff valve connected to your kitchen faucet is when you replace a kitchen faucet washer or the faucet itself.

However, because of the corrosive action of water, valve washers may need replacement. To replace the washers in any valve around the home, you will need to shut off the main water valve. If the main water valve requires repair, it would be best to get the help of a plumber.

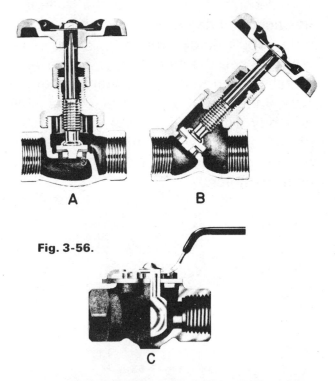

Fig. 3-56.

Different types of valves. (A) globe valve is designed to let large amount of water pass; (B) Y-pattern globe valve permits a more straightforward flow of water; (C) ball valve is designed for straight flow.

You can easily recognize a water valve by its location in the water supply line and by the fact that most valves come equipped with a round handle, or wheel. Fig. 3-56 shows several types. Like facuets, valves come in a variety of sizes, shapes and styles.

Valves are ordinarily operated in their open position. It is when you try to close a valve that you may first begin to note some difficulties. Thus, if you are repairing a leaky faucet, and you have taken the precaution of closing the valve, a continual flow of water from the facuet indicates that the associated valve isn't working. You can replace the valve washer following the same procedures as in replacing a faucet washer.

To put in a new valve washer, shut off the main water supply. Also do this when replacing a faucet washer and closing the associated valve does not shut off the flow of water sufficiently to let you work on the faucet.

In some cases, ball valves (drawing C) will deliver more water than globe valves. Some globe valves deliver more flow than others for ideftical pipe sizes. Y-pattern globe valves, in straight runs of pipe, have better flow characteristics than straight stop valves.

When replacing a valve, shut off the main water supply and, using a wrench or wrenches, remove the valve from the water supply line. If you have been satisfied with the amount of water coming out of your faucet, then get an exact replacement. If not, take the valve to your local plumbing supply house, show it to them, and find out if you can replace it with one that will let you have a greater water flow.

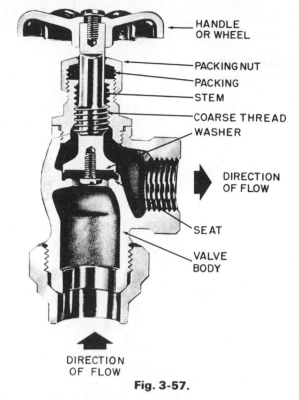

DIRECTION OF FLOW

Fig. 3-57.

Cross section of valve. It works in the same way as a faucet.

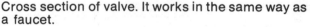

A valve will sometimes drip from its packing nut (Fig. 3-57). What is happening is that the packing around the inside of the packing nut has worked Its way loose and is permitting water to escape. The problem is identical with similar leakage from a faucet. Turn off the main water supply. Rotate the handle or wheel of the valve to its full counterclockwise position. Loosen the packing nut with a wrench, and then remove the entire assembly, consisting of the handles or wheel and the valve stem. Buy new packing if you have none available.

Chapter *IV*

Plumbing Jobs You Can Do

This is one thing you can be absolutely sure about and that is, sooner or later—and generally sooner rather than later—some part of your plumbing system will break down. It will not be at a convenient time, and it will undoubtedly happen when you are harassed by a houseful of children, a packet of unpaid bills, and assorted other worries. And to make your day complete, your favorite plumber has a phone that's always busy, or he is unavailable or has moved or for any one of a number of valid reasons can't help you with your problem.

Now what?

So do it yourself.

Many plumbing jobs around the home are quite simple. It's very easy to define a simple job—it is one *you* can handle. And if you can do one plumbing job, you can do two. And if you can do two, four isn't such an impossible number. Some of the jobs may be a bit on the messy side, but so what? You can get the water running again, both hot and cold, and that plus a bit of soap puts you back in condition again. What you get when you do a plumbing repair is not only a functioning plumbing system, but something that's equally valuable,

possibly more so: self-confidence and self-respect.

Plumbing jobs fall into three categories. Plumbing is often considered *repair*. Something goes wrong and you fix it, or the plumber does. But *preventive maintenance* is also important; so when you do preventive maintenance, you are really doing plumbing. Finally, *cleaning* is part of plumbing. Cleaning here doesn't mean the mess that must be handled after a repair is done, although that is obviously essential. Cleaning means not only the day-to-day cleaning that goes on around a household, but correct cleaning so as not to damage plumbing appliances and accessories.

How to Prepare For Leaking Faucet Repair

Fig. 4-1.
The time to repair a leaky faucet is when the drip continues no matter how tightly you turn the handle.

Every home has a leaking faucet (Fig. 4-1). If not now, then soon. Don't be smug if you hear no dripping now. Just wait. There's a leaking faucet in your future. Your first step is to buy a box of assorted washers and brass machine screws. As a matter of fact buy several boxes, for a number of reasons. The first is that faucet washers come in various shapes and sizes. Further, you have no assurance that all the faucets in your home all use the same washer size. Such consistency and logic would be too much to expect from your house builder. Some washers are black, some brown, others white. Some are made of plastic such as urethane, or synthetic rubber such as neoprene, or some other kind of rubber substitute, or natural rubber or Buna rubber. Hardware stores sometimes carry rubber or other washers, but neoprene is more commonly used, and with good reason. It will outlast rubber by a factor of about 5 or 10 to 1. This means that the time between faucet drips is that much longer.

But since a leaking faucet is such a little thing, wouldn't it be better to postpone the repair? Perhaps the dripping will stop by itself.

But the dripping will not stop by itself, it never does. It will get worse. In many areas there is a water charge, based on usage, so a dripping faucet means it is your money that's going down the drain. Aside from the fact that the constant dripping is annoying, those tiny drops will produce a spot or blemished area in your sink, and rubbing with steel wool or cleanser will only aggravate the existing damage; it won't repair or cure it.

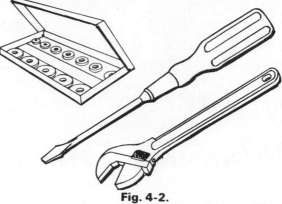

Fig. 4-2.
You will need an assortment of washers and brass machine screws, one or more screwdrivers, and an adjustable wrench.

You will also need some tools (Fig. 4-2). You will need the right size Phillips screwdriver and a flat blade type. Screwdrivers are inexpensive, so it's nice to have a variety around. You'll need them. You'll also need a small monkey wrench or an adjustable open end wrench.

How to Repair a Leaking Faucet

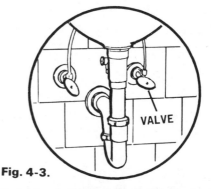

Fig. 4-3.

You will find a pair of shutoff valves—one for hot water and the other for cold—somewhere beneath the sink, in the cabinet enclosing the sink. This is the setup used in apartments and more modern homes. Some older homes lack this convenience, so you must close the main water valve in the basement.

Turn off the water. Before you rush down to the basement, examine the pipes beneath the sink (Fig. 4-3). In some homes and apartments there is a shutoff valve right below the fixture. If not, then you must turn off the main water valve, in the basement. But before you do that, rotate the handle controlling the leaking faucet so that the water comes out moderately strong. Now listen to the sound of the water. Familiarize yourself with it. Then, when you turn the shutoff valve, the absence of this sound will assure you the water is indeed turned off.

This isn't as silly as it may sound. If your shutoff valve is in the basement, and the leaky sink is on the first floor, you may be able to hear the sound. Also, you can verify by looking at the faucet. This is your assurance that the water is really off. If you do try to repair a leaky faucet without being certain the water is off, you will regret it when you slosh through the puddle on your floor, and while looking at soaked walls and possibly the ceiling as well. You see, the water doesn't fall from your faucet, pulled by gravity. It is pushed, and the force of that push can be astonishingly strong.

If the shutoff valve is beneath the sink, you will find you have two of them, one for the hot water and the other for the cold. It is only necessary to shut off the value for the faucet that is leaking, but there is no harm done if you turn off both valves. If you have an electric hot water heater, but no valves under the sink, shutting off the valve in the hot water line going from your electric heater to the hot water faucet that is dripping.

If you are not sure you have turned the right shutoff valve, you can check quite easily. If the water out of the defec-tive faucet pours out full strength, you haven't turned the right valve. If, however, you do get some water out of the leaky faucet even after you have closed the shutoff valve, don't worry about it. All it means is that your shutoff valve is leaky, and that's a repair job you can post-pone—at least for a while.

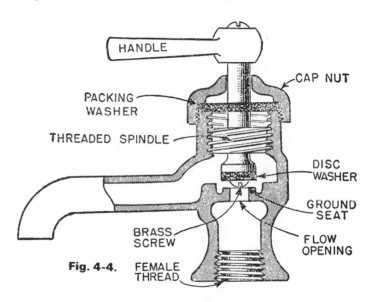

Fig. 4-4.

Basic type of compression faucet.

Before you move ahead, take a look at Fig. 4-4. This is a cross section of a compression-type faucet, not the only one by any means, but one commonly in use. The female thread down at the bottom represents the end attached to water-carrying pipe. The water is forced up through the pipe, filling the entire opening above the female threaded area. The water then passes through the flow opening and then out of the faucet.

Immediately above the flow opening is a disc washer. When the handle is turned clockwise, the disc washer presses against the ground seat, effectively seal-ing the water in the lower chamber so that the water is prevented from coming out.

Examine the part identified as "brass screw." The head of this screw must be smaller than the flow opening. If it is larger, no amount of turning the handle will shut off the water, since the screwhead's size will prevent the disc washer from making firm contact with the ground seat. Further, forcing the screwhead into the ground seat by applying too much pressure to the handle may damage the seat.

Note that the only function of the brass screw is to hold the disc washer in place. The disc washer, of course, must be large enough—that is, it must have a sufficient surface area—to cover the flow opening.

Fig. 4-5.

Loosen the packing nut with a wrench. Put a rag between the wrench and the packing nut to protect the finish of the nut.

Now that you have the water shut off, loosen the packing nut (also known as a cap nut) with a wrench (Fig. 4-5). Turn the wrench counterclockwise. Since your faucet is chrome or nickel plated, you will want to protect the finish. Do this by wrapping the packing nut with an old cloth before using the wrench. Hold the wrench close to its end (the end furthest

from the faucet) and apply force gently until you feel the nut loosening. After it is loose enough to rotate by hand, turn it until it comes completely off the faucet (Fig. 4-6). Now turn the handle of the faucet counterclockwise and you will see the threaded faucet stem emerging from the faucet.

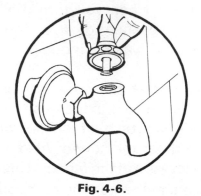

Fig. 4-6.

After the packing nut is off, turn the handle of the faucet counterclockwise and the entire assembly will come out.

You now have the handle assembly removed and should be able to see the washer. The washer may have completely disintegrated, or else it will be quite worn. Using a flat blade screwdriver, turn the brass screw holding the washer in place counterclockwise until the screw plus its washer comes off (Fig. 4-7). Examine the screw. If it is still in good condition, use it again. If it is corrodoed or the screwhead is damaged, out it goes. But before you throw it away, use it as a guide to help you select a replacement screw from your stock of new ones. Look for a screw that has these three things: (1) the same size head, (2) the same length, and (3) the same screw diameter.

Your only problem now is to select the right washer. If the old one is in reasonable shape, try to match it for size

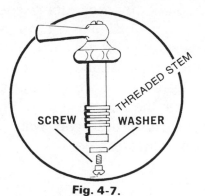

Fig. 4-7.
This is the part you have removed. The handle is at the top. Right below it is the packing nut. Down at the bottom is the washer and its holding screw.

and appearance. Pick a washer whose diameter is the same as the old one. If not, select one that will just about fit in the space occupied by the old one (Fig. 4-8).

Fig. 4-8.

After the new washer is in position, insert the screw and fasten it into position with the screwdriver. The screw should be a brass machine, round head type.

Washers are available in different sizes: 00, ¼s, ¼, ¼L, ⅜, ⅜M, ⅜L and ½. The letters *S, L,* and *M* represents "small," "large," and "medium."

There are two general washer shapes. One is completely flat; the other looks somewhat like a cone (Fig. 4-9). The advantage of the cone type is that it will enter the ground seat of the faucet

and is more likely to result in a successful washer replacement job than the flat kind. Some plumbers may disagree with this. But in reality, the best washer is the one that stops the leak and keeps it stopped.

Fig. 4-9.
Washers for compression type faucets: beveled type (A), flat (B), and screwless (C). (Hancock-Gross)

Sometimes the screw used for holding the washer in place can't do so because the internal threads of the stem are too worn. In that case you can replace the stem or you can use the screwless-type neoprene washer shown in drawing C in Fig. 4-9. The washer just snaps into position, and no screw is needed.

One of the nice things about plumbing—if that is the way to describe it—is that for every step you take forward, you always take one step backward. In other words, replacing the faucet is just the reverse procedure of removing it.

Fig. 4-10.

To replace the part you removed, insert it in the faucet. Make sure the faucet handle is in its counterclockwise position. Tighten the packing nut. Use a cloth around the packing nut to keep it from getting scratched by the wrench.

Put the threaded spindle back into the faucet and turn it a bit. Push the cap nut back on and turn it, using your fingers. Tighten the packing nut with a wrench (Fig. 4-10), but before you do, turn the handle counterclockwise. The intention here is to keep the washer up and away from the ground seat inside the faucet until the packing nut is completely tight. Once it is tight, you can close the faucet, just as though you were shutting off the water.

Now is the time to test.

Have someone watch the faucet while you slowly turn on the water valve. If, after you have done so, no water drips out of the faucet—congratulations! When you do decide to use the faucet again, turn it on slowly. You may hear some pipe banging, or the water may flow out of the faucet in spasmodic jerks. Don't let it bother you. As soon as the pipe leading to the faucet is filled with water again, water flow will be smooth.

Preventive Maintenance

If the faucet doesn't bother you, why should you bother the faucet? The trouble is that corrosion—like death and taxes—is always with us. The solution is preventive maintenance. About once a year, replace all the washers and reassemble the faucet. In so doing you will make sure that you will never be bothered with dripping.

Faucet Types

Faucets come in a variety of sizes; shapes, and styles, but the basic idea of replacing a washer remains the same. Usually it is the washer for the hot water faucet that deteriorates first, for it is subjected to heat as well as the wear of the moving water and the chemicals contained in it. It is easy to determine which faucet is leaking; just put your fingers under the drip. If the water feels warm, then it is the hot water washer that needs replacement. Your hot and cold water faucets may be separate units or may consist of two faucets sharing a single spout, usually a swinging type. (Fig. 4-11).

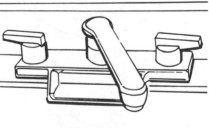

Fig. 4-11.

Faucets come in a variety of shapes and styles. Mixing faucets—used on kitchen sinks, laundry tubs, and bathtubs—are two faucets sharing the same spout.

When Washer Replacement Doesn't Work

After you replace a washer and put the assembly back together again, you may be shocked to see that the water still drips, and may even drip worse than before. Don't be shocked. It happens to all of us.

There are several possibilities. You may have used the wrong size washer, may not have tightened the washer holding screw, or may not have tightened the assembly enough when you replaced it. Retrace your steps and do the job over again. Begin by shutting off the water, and then remove the faucet assembly.

Sometimes the seat inside the faucet is worn or cut or jagged. This is the part against which the washer rests. If the washer cannot make good contact with the seat, water can leak through between the washer and seat. It will do this every chance it gets, for the water is under pressure. If, no matter what you do, water persists in dripping, you can buy an inexpensive tool in your local hardware or discount store for "dressing" the seat. The tool is easy to use and is supplied with instructions. Its function is to remove any burrs or nicks from the seat and to make it round and smooth once again. But don't jump to the conclusion that this is what you need. It's more likely that you did something wrong when replacing the washer. It usually takes many years for the cavitation of the water—the effects of its motion—to do any damage to the seat.

How to Stop Packing Nut Drips

After you replace the washer, you may find that the faucet doesn't drip any more—an indication that you have done a good repair job—but that water now leaks from around the packing nut. The packing nut is right beneath the handle of the faucet. If you turn the faucet handle so that water comes out of the faucet, the leakage around the packing nut will diminish or stop. However, the problem isn't solved, for the water is simply going where it's easiest for it to go. Water, like human begins, follows the path of least resistance.

In this example the packing around the packing nut isn't doing its job. As a first step, take a wrench and try tightening the packing nut. If this doesn't stop the leak, turn off the appropriate shutoff valve. Keep the faucet turned to its off position. Remove the faucet handle, and then loosen the packing nut and remove it.

You now have two possibilities. There may be a washer inside the packing nut or Teflon-coated faucet packing. Whatever you have needs replacement. If you need a new packing nut washer, take the packing nut to a hardware store or a plumbing supply store and ask for a washer for that particular packing nut. Buy a number of washers since you may need them for other faucets around the house.

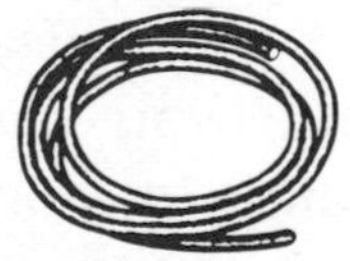

Fig. 4-12.

Composition packing is available in 2-foot rolls. (Chicago Specialty)

As an alternative, you can use wicking of the kind shown in Fig. 4-12. This composition packing is self-forming, self-lubricating acd self-sealing. It forms its own washer under compression. Simply wind it around the stem and tighten the packing nut. You can also use it to fix leaky shower heads, radiators, and slip joints.

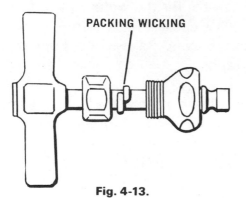

PACKING WICKING

Fig. 4-13.

Insert the wicking (or washer) into the packing nut.

When you have the washer or wicking, insert it into the open end of the packing nut (Fig. 4-13) and then replace the nut on the stem of the faucet. Move the nut down until it engages the threads of the faucet. Finger tighten the nut and then use a wrench to fasten it more securely.

When replacing the packing nut make sure it engages the threads of the faucet properly. You should be able to feel the nut engaging the threads, and to turn it with your fingers. If you use brute force on the nut, you may get cross threading, a situation in which the threads do not mesh properly but ride roughshod over each other. When that happens you may need to replace the entire faucet.

Temporary Repairs

If you do not have the correct washer or wicking for the packing nut, you can make a temporary repair by winding

some string around the stem directly beneath the packing nut. After you have finished tightening the packing nut, you may find that some of the string sticks out of it. Trim the string off with a razor blade.

The trick is to turn the packing nut tightly enough so no water leaks from it and yet not so tightly that it interferes with the rotation of the stem. What you need now is some sort of compromise. If, after you have tightened the packing nut, you note that the faucet handle is very hard to turn, loosen the packing nut just a bit, and then try the handle again. As the string inside the packing nut becomes saturated with water, it will work as a more effective seal. However, the string is just a temporary measure, meaning you will probably ignore it for as long as you can get away with it.

Plating

When your plumbing fixtures and fittings are new, they are nice and shiny. Nickel was used as a plating material at one time, but the best fixtures now have chromium-plated brass. The advantage of chromium over nickel is that it is shinier, requires little or no polishing, and is very hard.

To keep your fixtures looking bright, wash them occasionally with soap and water, but don't let it go at that or you'll have water spot stains on the metal. Dry and rub the fixtures with a soft, absorbent cloth. This will remove any surface film and should make the unit look like new. If the fixtures have been neglected, you may need to use some cleanser. But bear in mind that the abrasive action of scouring powders removes the plating and may get you down to the bare metal.

How often you must clean plated fixtures—and this applies to plumbing fixtures all through your house—depends partly on where you live. If you live in a city and the air has a high sulfur content, or if you are in a seacoast town and the air has a high amount of salt, you then have factors at work corroding the plating. Here you will need to clean more often. To protect the metal plating, put a very thin wax coating on it after cleaning. Use the same liquid polish you reserve for your furniture. You'll find liquid much easier to work with than paste. Don't just smear on the wax and let it go at that. Use a soft, clean cloth to burnish the fixture. You will be removing some of the wax, of course, but don't worry about it. What will be left will be a fine, invisible film of wax that will protect the fixture against the effects of the air.

Sometimes you may notice green spots appearing on the fixtures. If you do nothing about them, they will spread and ultimately you will not be able to get rid of them without getting rid of the plating as well. When such spots do appear, rub vigorously with a dry cloth. If that doesn't dispose of them, use cleanser. Visit your local hardware or plumbing supply store and see if you can get a cleanser that will remove such spots without damaging the plating. If not, use your household cleanser, but sparingly. After the spots are off, wash the fixture with soap and water, dry it thoroughly, and then apply a thin coating of wax.

If you have older-type nickel-plated fittings, wash them with soap and water. Get some whiting from your local hardware store and then moisten the whiting with household ammonia. Ammonia, even the household type, packs a wallop, so keep your nose away from it. Polish the nickel fittings with the whiting using one cloth, and then rub them down with a new, clean cloth to remove the polishing material.

The Short-Lasting Repair

It is possible that a week or so after replacing a faucet washer correctly, you find you must tighten the faucet handle forecefully to prevent dripping, and that a day or two later not even this expedient helps. The drip is back with you.

The solution is not to replace the washer. You've already done that, and the faucet has notified you that you've just done a temporary, not a permanent, repair.

The problem is that the ground seat of your compression faucet has become grooved, pitted, or notched. Turning the faucet handle tighter pushes the washer into the grooves in the seat. This has the effect of making the washer surface rough and sooner or later—generally sooner—the washer develops a groove through which water will course. And run it will.

The solution here is to dress the seat using a tool such as one of those shown in Fig. 4-14. There are several variations, but they all work along the same lines. The tool has a small wheel on handle at-

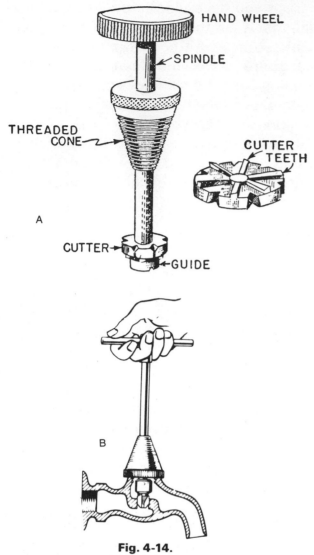

HAND WHEEL

SPINDLE

THREADED CONE

CUTTER TEETH

A

CUTTER

GUIDE

B

Fig. 4-14.
Two types of tools for dressing faucet seats. The tool in drawing A uses a hand wheel; that in drawing B uses a sliding type T handle. (Chicago Specialty)

tached to a spindle. The tool is also equipped with a threaded cone, which slides right onto the spindle. Mount the cone so that the threads point down and away from the wheel at the top of the spindle. Another part you will get is a cutter. Mount this on the bottom end of the spindle so that the teeth of the cutter also point down. Finally, you will also have a guide for holding the cutter in place.

When you buy the tool, you may get a set of tool assembly instructions, printed on a separate sheet of paper or on the outside of the box containing the tool. Read the instructions, since tool assembly methods may vary from one manufacturer to the next.

After you have the faucet seat dresser assembled, proceed just as though you were going to change the faucet washer, which is precisely what you are going to do, but with one added step—dressing the faucet seat.

Insert the dressing tool into the faucet after you have removed the faucet assembly holding the washer. Adjust the tool so the brass guide at the bottom enters the flow opening in the faucet. Turn the threaded cone so it engages the inside threads of the faucet. Just make it finger tight and it should hold properly. Now turn the hand wheel or T handle. Try to turn it with the longest possible movement, rather than a series of short, choppy strokes.

You may find, when you first turn the tool, that it has a rough feel. However, after a few turns, the turning action will be smooth. What has happened is that the cutter has smoothed the rough spots of the seat.

Now remove the cutting tool and put it aside. Take a small brush of the type used by schoolchildren in their painting classes. The cutting action has produced brass metal filings, and what you want to do now is to sweep them away from the area around the seat. If allowed to remain, they will cut into the washer. A better method is to put a dab of glue on the flat rubber end of a pencil and use it to extract the filings.

Replace the washer and then put the washer assembly back into position. After you have turned on the water, you will find the water will shut off with much less handle pressure than before.

There is always the possibility that no amount of seat dressing will cure this problem. If the water dripping has persisted over a long period of time, and if the problem has been neglected, the seat of the faucet may be damaged beyond repair. In that case the only solution is to replace the seat or the entire faucet.

Using the Right Washer

Sometimes the problem of a dripping faucet is due to nothing more complicated than using the wrong washer. After you have shut off the water and removed the handle, packing nut, packing, and faucet stem, use a flashlight to look inside the faucet. Examine the faucet seat. If it has a crown or round ridge, you should use a flat washer. If the seat is tapered, that is, if it has a sort of V-shaped downward slope, use a tapered washer.

Fig. 4-15.
Hex seat wrench for removing faucet seats. (Chicago Specialty)

If a new washer doesn't do the trick, remember that some faucet seats are replaceable. You can recognize them by their square or hexagonal shape. You can remove them with a seat removing tool (Fig. 4-15). For non-replaceable seats you will need to use the seat dressing tool shown in Fig. 4-14. Of course, in that case, if dressing the seat doesn't work, you will have to replace the entire faucet.

Washers are inexpensive, so don't go looking for bargains. Yes, you can buy cheap ones, but they have a tendency to swell when used with a hot water faucet.

Noisy Faucet

After you have replaced washer and the water no longer drips, you may find that the faucet has become noisy, chattering away when water flows through it. This can happen if you do not tighten the replacement washer adequately. The washer is held in place by a small machine screw. Be sure to tighten this screw with a flat blade screwdriver. The worst thing you can do is to try to tighten this screw while holding the part with one hand and the screwdriver with the other. The safest procedure is to mount the part in a small vise with just enough vise pressure to hold it firmly, but not to deform it.

If you don't have a vise, use a heavy glove to hold the part while you tighten the screw with the screwdriver. Then; when the screwdriver slips, as it very well may, the glove gets punished, not you. It all depends on how careful you are with tools, how mechanically inclined you are, plus a bit of experience. Some professional plumbers may not follow these suggestions, *and they have the scarred fingers to prove it.*

If the faucet still rattles after you have tightened the washer screw, press down on the faucet handle while water flows out of the faucet. If your hand pressure stops the noise, the trouble is due to a loose stem. Remove the stem assembly, take it to your local hardware or plumbing store and ask for an exact replacement. Don't wander into the store without it, for stems come in all sizes and shapes. Just any stem will not do (Fig. 4-16).

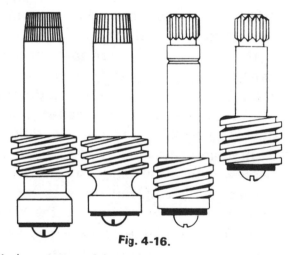

Fig. 4-16.
Various types of faucet stems. (Hancock-Gross)

A lot depends on the kind of faucets you have. With some, you can replace all the parts. With others the only solution is a new faucet. If you do get a replacement faucet, though, find out if it is a replacement-part type first. After you get a new faucet, disassemble it. Examine the seat and note what type it is. Examine the washer, and then buy a box of replacement washers that are identical to it.

Learn what type or plating the faucet has, and get some advice about cleaning it.

Replacing Compression Faucets

Thoretically, replacing a faucet should be easy. If the faucet is connected to a water supply pipe by a nut, the only question is loosening this nut. The nut screws onto male threads at one end of the faucet. These threads may come out of the faucet horizontally, as illustrated in Fig. 4-17, or may join the faucet vertically.

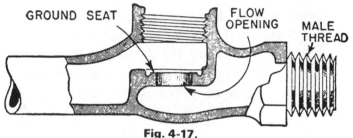

Fig. 4-17.
Male thread portion is held on to water supply pipe by a threaded nut.

Since this part of the faucet is beneath the sink, you will need to work in a small, dark space. Sometimes the curvature of the sink will make it very difficult to get a tool into position for loosening the nut. Plumbers have a special tool for such situations. Explain the problem to your local hardware or plumbing supply house and you will soon have this relatively inexpensive tool in your possession.

Fig. 4-18.

Pipe joint compound is an antiseize compound with lubrication characteristics. It permits tighter joints, remains in the threads, and prevents water from flowing through the threads. (Chicago Specialty)

When replacing the faucet, smear the male threads with pipe joint compound (Fig. 4-18). This paste will fill any open spaces between the male threads and the holding nut, which, of course, is also threaded. As a matter of fact, it's a good idea to use pipe joint compound whenever you mate two threaded parts.

After you have removed the faucet, take it with you when you go shopping for a replacement. The holes cut into your sink may limit your choice.

Kitchen Faucets

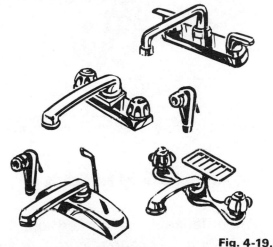

Fig. 4-19.

Kitchen faucets are mounted on 8-inch centers. The unit at the bottom is a singlelever type. You can use it to control both the volume of water and its temperature. (Melard Mfg. Co.)

Modern kitchen faucets (Fig. 4-19) may have separate handles for the hot and cold water supply, using a common spout that can swing left or right. Such faucets are mounted on 8-inch centers—that is, there is a distance of 8 inches from the center point of the cold water faucet to the center point of the hot water faucet.

The two faucets may come mounted on a frame known as a deck, and so the full name is "deck faucet with tubular spout." Some deck faucets are equipped with a separate spray, useful in dishwashing. However, if your sink doesn't have a hole cut out for the spray, forget about it.

If the faucet doesn't have a deck, it may have a metal dish for holding soap. Finally, you can get a single-lever faucet for controlling both cold and hot water. These are available with or without a spray.

How to Save on a Faucet

The easiest procedure to follow when replacing a faucet is to have your plumber do the job and also to get the faucet. If the plumber furnishes the faucet, he will charge you its full list price, plus possibly a bit extra. If you supply the faucet yourself, you can shop and get the most for what you spend. But when you do buy a faucet, make sure you do so on an "I can return it without any nonsense" arrangement.

How to Replace Faucet Handles

If the plating on the handle of your faucet has worn off, or if the handle is loose and cannot be tightened, you can easily replace it. The handle is kept in position by a single screw, either a Phillips head or regular single-spot type. The screw may be located just about anywhere in the handle. It may be recessed and reached through a hole on the side. On some faucet handles the screw is located beneath a plastic insert on the top of the handle. The insert may be a snap in type or threaded. Remove the insert by

103

pulling on it or by turning it **counter-clockwise** and you'll then expose the screwhead. Turn the screw with a screw-driver, and you'll be able to take the handle off easily.

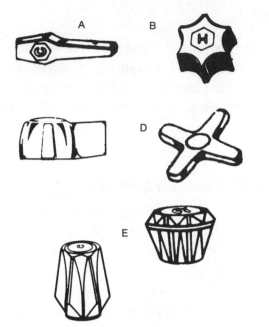

Fig. 4-20.

Representative faucet handles: (A) lever type handle, (B) canopy handle, (C) canopy lever handle (combination of canopy and lever), (D) cross handle, (E) Lucite handles. (Melard Mfg. Co.)

Handles for faucets are either metal or Lucite (Fig. 4-20). The advantage of Lucite is that it is much easier to clean and doesn't corrode. Handles come in various shapes, sizes, and styles, so what you pick is a matter of personal choice. Some are identified by the letters *H,* for hot, and *C,* for cold. The faucet will work just as well if the *H* and *C* handles are interchanged. The left handle is generally the hot handle.

Laundry and Pantry Faucets

Mechanically, laundry and pantry faucets work the same way as kitchen faucets, but one isn't a substitute for the other. Laundry and pantry faucets are built on a 4-inch centers, and while they have a tube spout, the spout can be arched differently, as shown in Fig. 4-21. Laundry and pantry faucets are generally less expensive than those used in the kitchen. They are, however, subject to the same ills.

Fig. 4-21.

Laundry and pantry faucets. The spout is shaped differently from those used in kitchen faucets. (Melard Mfg. Co.)

How to Align Faucet Handles

When faucets are turned off, the handles should occupy mirror-image positions. Thus, if the handle for the hot faucet points in a straight horizontal line to the left, the handle for the cold faucet should point in exactly the opposite direction, in a straight horizontal line to the right.

This has nothing to do with the functioning of the plumbing. A faucet will work just as well with the handles pointing in any direction. However, you will fund it easier to turn off the water fully if the final stop position of the handle is almost, but not quite horizontal, as shown in Fig. 4-22.

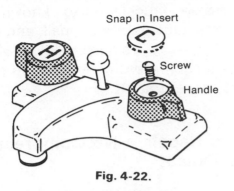

Fig. 4-22.

How to align faucet handles.

As a preliminary step, turn the water off by adjusting the handles to their off position. To get at the handles, remove the snap-in plastic insert (if there is one) and loosen and remove the screw beneath it. (In faucet handles that don't use snap-in plastic inserts, the screwhead is clearly visible.) Rock the handle back and forth until you feel it coming loose. Repeat with the other handle and then replace both in their correct position. You may need to tap them into place. Put a small section of solid cardboard on top of the handle and tap with a hammer. Before you proceed further, turn both faucets to their on position and then off again. If you are now satisfied with the way the handles look, tighten the screw, and replace any plastic inserts.

Some faucet handles never need alignment. One such type, for example, wguld be the Lucite handle shown in Fig. 4-20E.

The Modern Compression Faucet

The compression faucet shown earlier in (fig. 4-4) is an old-fashioned type, but it is still being sold, installed, and used. Newer faucets look somewhat different but still work on exactly the same principles. The faucet may be a single unit, or it may be a double type, with one faucet for hot water, the other for cold, and a common spout. The spout may be fixed or movable.

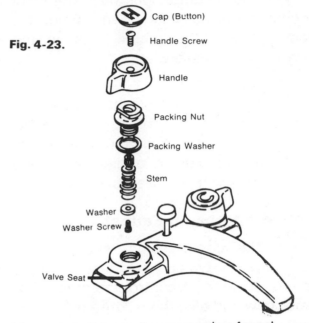

Fig. 4-23.

More modern type of compression faucet.

Fig. 4-23 shows the various parts of one of these newer faucets. At the top of the faucet you will see a little plastic button identified by the letter *C,* for cold, or *H,* for hot. You caf lift this button out with your fingernails or by using a screwdriver with a fine blade. Immediately beneath this button is the handle screw.

Before you proceed further, make sure the valve controlling water flow to this faucet is turned off. Turn the handle of the faucet slightly counterclockwise. You will be doing this for two reasons: first, if no water comes out of the faucet you can be sure you have turned off the water control valve correctly. Second, you want to relieve any pressure on the washer inside the faucet. When the faucet is tightly closed, this washer is pressed against the seat below it.

Remove the handle screw and you will be able to lift the handle off. Now remove the packing nut with pliers. Turn the packing nut counterclockwise. The stem should come out at the same time. If it doesn't, screw the handle back on and turn it counterclockwise.

As soon as you have the stem in your hands, you will be able to replace the washer following exactly the same directions as those given earlier. After you make the repair, reassemble the faucet.

Noncompression Faucets

Unlike compression faucets, noncompression types have just a single handle or knob to control the amount of water flow and also the mixture of hot and cold water. With a compression type you must adjust two faucet handles to get lukewarm water, and at the same time you must turn them to get the amount of water you want.

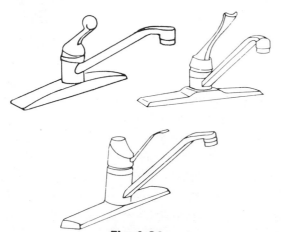

Fig. 4-24.
Noncompression, or single-lever, faucets. (Hancock-Gross)

You'll find three basic types of noncompression faucets (also known as single lever faucets): valve, ball, and cartridge (Fig. 4-24). It's hard to know which type of noncompression faucet you have until you take it apart.

How to Repair a Noncompression Valve Faucet

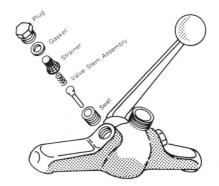

Fig. 4-25.
Water control assembly for valve faucet.

Fig. 4-25 shows a single-lever valve faucet with the spout removed. On the side of the fixture is a plug. Remove the plug, and right beneath the head of the plug you will see a gasket. Replace the gasket if it seems worn. Beneath the gasket is a strainer and then a valve stem assembly. The valve stem assembly is designed to slide into a valve seat. To remove the valve seat, you will need a special valve seat remover.

Problems in this type of faucet are usually due to the gasket, the strainer, or the value stem assembly. The best thing to do is to get a kit of replacement parts for your particular faucet.

The purpose of the strainer, a small mesh screen, is to protect the valve stem assembly parts from damage. As preventive maintenance, you should clean the screens regularly and replace them if and when they become damaged.

How to Remove the Valve Faucet Spout

You can remove a valve faucet spout with a leaky base by loosening the connecting ring with a wrench. Rotate counterclockwise. You will then be able to lift the spout out of the base (see Fig. 4-26). Put a coating of a heat-resistant grease over a replacement O-ring and then reassemble the spout assembly. After you have finished, check for leaks by turning on the water.

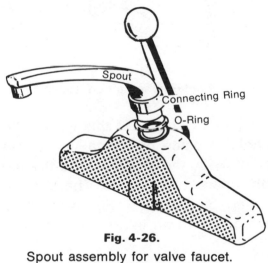

Fig. 4-26.
Spout assembly for valve faucet.

How to Repair a Leaky Ball Faucet

The ball faucet, as its name implies, controls the amount of water flow by the position of a ball inside the faucet. It also controls the mixture of cold and hot water.

Troubles in this type of faucet are due to the cam assembly, the ball, a pair

of seat assemblies, and O-rings if the unit has them.

Unlike the valve faucet, which has its lever behind the spout, the ball faucet sits on a support that also holds one end of the spout.

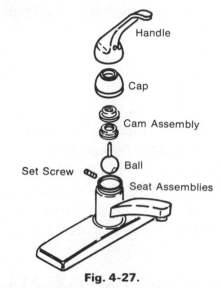

Fig. 4-27.
Water control and mixing assembly for ball faucet.

Fig. 4-27 shows one arrangement of a ball faucet. After you have closed the water valve to this faucet and have opened the faucet to let all water drain, look for a set screw in the base of the handle. It is a screw with a recessed head known as an allen set screw. To remove the screw you will need an allen wrench of the correct size. Allen wrenches are inexpensive, and you can get a complete set at low cost.

Insert the allen wrench and turn it counterclockwise. You won't need to exert much force since this screw is quite small. Don't remove the screw, just loosen it. Getting the screw back into position again can be a nuisance, plus the fact that the screw is easy to drop and lose.

After you have loosened the set screw, wiggle the handle back and forth a bit and you should be able to work it loose readily. Beneath the handle you will find a circular type of cap. Wrap the cap with a bit of dry cloth to protect its finish and then, using a wrench and turning counterclockwise, loosen the cap and remove it.

You will now be able to take off the cam and ball assemblies. A kit of parts for such faucets is a good way to make repairs, even if some of the parts are still in working order. Replace the ball, both seat assemblies, and the O-ring if your faucet has one. (Fig. 4-27 doesn't show an O-ring.) When reassembling the ball faucet, make sure you put the cap on tightly.

How to Repair a Cartridge Faucet

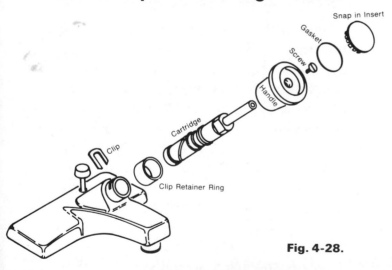

Fig. 4-28.

Cartridge faucet assembly.

The cartridge faucet (Fig. 4-28) controls both the mixture of hot and cold water and the amount of water flow by a ported cartridge. The cartridge faucet is probably the most complicated of all the faucet types.

A good technique to follow when you must disassemble any plumbing fixture with which you have no experience, is to remove a part and then put it back into position again. Then disassemble this part and move on to the next part, disassembling and assembling as you go along. This does take some time, but so does any learning process. The most aggravating feeling in plumbing, as in anything else, is to take something apart and not be able to put it back together again.

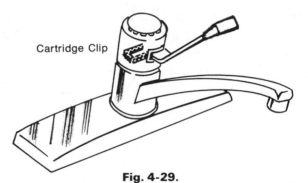

Fig. 4-29.

Position of internal cartridge retaining clip in cartridge-type faucet.

The cartridge for this type of faucet is held in place by a retaining clip. With some styles the clip is inside the faucet; with others it is outside. The clip is a U-shaped bit of metal. Fig. 4-29 shows a cartridge with an internal clip.

How to Repair a Swing Spout Leak

Water can leak and drip not only from the spout of your noncompression faucet, but from other parts of the faucet assembly as well. If you have a faucet with a swing spout, it is possible for the swing spout to leak around its base. You will see this as drops of water, or sometimes as a tiny rivulet in the case of a bad leak, running down the fixture and into the sink.

Before doing this repair, close the valve controlling water flow to the faucet. Check to make sure it's closed by turning the faucet handle to its open position.

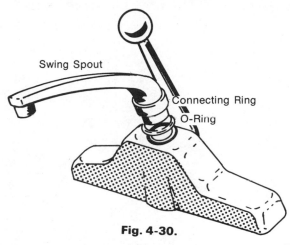

Fig. 4-30.

Swing spout sometimes develops a leak at its base.

Rotate the connecting ring counterclockwise (Fig. 4-30). You can use a wrench for this, but channel-lock pliers will be better and easier to work with. To keep from marring the finish of the fixture, put a strip of adhesive tape around the connecting ring.

After you have loosened the connecting ring sufficiently, you will be able to remove the swing spout just by lifting it. At the base of the swing spout you will find an O-ring. Get a new O-ring but make sure it is the same size as the old one. Coat the new O-ring with some heat-resistant grease and then reassemble your faucet.

How to Install a Convenience Faucet

If you have your own home, you may want to install a convenience faucet. You can connect the faucet to any water pipe, whether iron or copper, and you need not make any changes in the existing plumbing to do so.

The Saddle Faucet

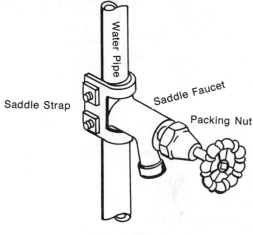

Fig. 4-31.

Appearance of saddle-type convenience faucet.

Fig. 4-31 illustrates how one type of convenience faucet, known as a saddle faucet, looks when installed. This faucet is operated by a ring-type handle and is a compression-type similar to compression faucets you may have in your kitchen and bathroom.

As a start, turn off the valve controlling water flow through the pipe. Select the part of the pipe where you plan to install the convenience outlet. Clean the pipe area that will accommodate the faucet with a cloth and then sand it lightly to remove any rust, dirt, or corrosion.

The saddle faucet comes equipped with a saddle strap and a pair of retainer bolts. Remove the bolts and put the faucet at the selected location. Then put the bolts back into place, attach the nuts, and tighten. You now have the faucet in place, except that there is no way for water to get into the faucet.

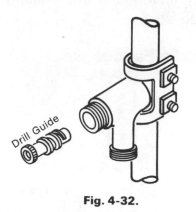

Fig. 4-32.

Use a drill guide to help bit make a hole in the water pipe.

Loosen the packing nut by rotating it counterclockwise with a wrench. You will now be able to remove the handle, the packing nut, and the stem of the faucet. Insert a drill guide, shown in Fig. 4-32, and drill a hole into the pipe, using a ¼-inch bit. Don't try drilling without the drill guide since the bit will "walk" all over the curved surface of the pipe. After you have finished drilling, remove the guide and as many metal chips as you can reach.

Reinsert the stem and tighten the packing nut. Close the faucet by turning its handle clockwise. Open the valve controlling water flow to the faucet. Open the handle of the faucet slowly to check for water movement out of it.

The Saddle-Type Tee Connector

The saddle-type tee connector is still another type of convenience faucet. Like the saddle faucet, you can use it with any kind of threaded pipe fitting. Fig. 4-33

shows the saddle type tee mounted on a pipe before the faucet has been threaded in. Remove the two nuts, disassemble the "tee" and then reassemble it on the pipe you've selected. Before tightening the nuts, clean the pipe thoroughly, preferably sanding it to remove any rough spots or dirt. Turn off the water supply.

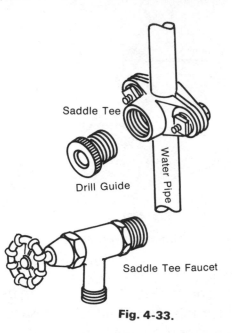

Fig. 4-33.

After you have done this, insert a drill guide and use a drill with a ¼-inch bit. After making a hole in the pipe, remove the drill guide and any metal burrs that may have collected inside the tee. You can then thread on the faucet, turn on the water valve, and then the faucet handle as a check.

How to Replace a Hose Faucet

If you have a private home you may have one or two outside faucets for a hose or for convenience. Replacing such a faucet is easy (Fig. 4-34). Turn off the water supply supply to the faucet and then rotate the faucet handle counterclockwise to let all the water drain out.

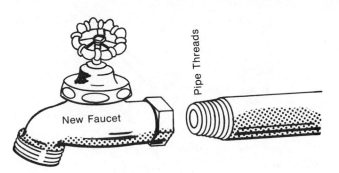

Fig. 4-34.
Replacing an outside faucet.

You will need two wrenches. Fasten one wrench to the pipe from which the old faucet is to be removed. The purpose here is to keep the pipe from turning as you rotate the faucet.

Using another wrench, turn the entire faucet counterclockwise. Keep turning until the faucet comes off. Coat the pipe threads with pipe joint compound and put on the new faucet. Make sure the beginning threads engage smoothly and easily. They must engage properly or you will cross thread the faucet and pipe. After you have made several clockwise turns of the new faucet by hand, use your wrench to make it completely tight. Turn on the water supply and note if any water leaks from the region between the pipe and the faucet. If it does, turn off the water supply, remove the faucet, and wrap the pipe threads with some lightweight string. Add more pipe joint compound and then replace the faucet. Make sure to put the faucet on as tightly as you can. Turn on the water supply, and then test the faucet by rotating its handle clockwise.

Lavatory Faucets

Like laundry and pantry faucets, lavatory faucets have their hot and cold

faucet centers separated by 4 inches. Lavatory faucets do have one feature not found in the other types and that is a pop-up. This is a rod located right behind the spout. Its purpose is to open or close the opening in the sink. Pull up on it and the opening is automatically closed. Push down and the water can flow down the drain.

Fig. 4-35.
Typical lavatory faucets. (Melard Mfg. Co.)

The handles can be plastic, such as Lucite, or metal. While a common spout is used for both hot and cold water, the spout is fixed in position, unlike kitchen, laundry, and pantry faucets. Some lavatory faucets are elaborately designed and can be the most expensive of all those you have in your home. A few are shown in Fig. 4-35.

Clogged Drains

There is one type of repair that is even more common than washer replacement and that is the clogged pipe. Everything goes into the average sink, ranging from food scraps to hair and hairpins. Some substances are soluble—that is, we can manage to dissolve them somehow. Others, such as bits of steel wool used for scouring the sink, bits of bone, or hairpins, must be removed physically. Clogging can happen with any sink you have in the house and applies to bathtubs as well.

There are a number of ways of removing the obstruction. The first method is probably the easiest and is certainly the least expensive.

Your initial step is to remove as much of the waste water accumulated in the sink as you possibly can. Use a glass or cup and pour the contents into a different sink or into the toilet bowl. This will remove most of the water. Take a sponge and mop up the balance of the water you are unable to scoop up with the glass.

It is unlikely that the clog will not allow any water to get through. Wait about an hour or so for the water that is in the pipe to seep past the clog. Now pour boiling water—not just hot, but energetically boiling—into the drain hole of the sink. Most clogs are made up of a gluelike combination of food forming a greasy ball. Boiling water dissolves grease and that is the technique used here.

Watch the water level in the pipe leading from the drain hole in the sink. As it lowers, pour in more boiling water. While the method described here doesn't always work, it is worth a try.

Fig. 4-36.

Plungers for clearing kitchen drains (Chicago Specialty)

If that method doesn't clear the clog, your next step is to try a drain plunger, often called the "plumber's helper" or the "plumber's friend." This tool (Fig. 4-36) is inexpensive, and you should have one in your house or apartment. It consists of a wooden handle and a flexible rubber suction cup at one end. There are two types: one for clearing sinks, the other for toilets.

Remove the sink drain. Plug the overflow opening of the sink with a damp cloth, otherwise you will simply be pushing water up through the opening. Let enough water into the sink to cover it to a depth of 2 or 3 inches. Coat the rubber lip of the plunger with petroleum jelly and put the rubber cup over the drain hole. Hold the wooden handle near the end away from the rubber cup and push down on the handle. Repeat your performance a half-dozen times. Remove the plunger, and if the water now drains out of the sink, you have cleared the clog.

Let hot water from the faucet run through your sink for about three minutes. Also wash the rubber cup of the plunger thoroughly, preferably with hot water, to clear it of any food debris. The action of the plunger may have brought up some of the clog material, which may be contaminated, from the pipe. There's no sense in storing a health hazard around your home.

If the first half dozen or so movements of the plunger did not clear the clog, repeat several more times. Make sure the entire circumference of the rubber cup touches the sink to prevent air from leaking in. When you push on the handle, push down all the way. Make your strokes energetic ones. Push sharply, not gently. When you push down on the plunger, you exert a pushing force on the water standing above the clog. You compress it, or at least you try to. The water pushes the clogging material and, hopefully, gets it on its way.

If you have a double sink you will need some help. Cover the second drain hole with a rubber stopper and have someone hold it in position. Otherwise, the pressure created by the plunger will simply push the water up through the second drain and there will be no force pushing on the clog. And when using the plunger, always make sure you have enough water in the sink to cover the rubber suction cup.

And now, after repeated efforts, using the plumber's helper has apparently done no good, for you still have about 3 inches of scummy water floating around your sink. It's about time to try another technique.

As a first step, remove as much water from the sink as you possibly can. A good method is to use a sponge and a pail. Remember, later, to wash the sponge thoroughly with soap and clean

water and to clean out the inside of the pail. Look beneath the sink and you will see a pipe leading away from the drain hole. If your sink is covered by a cabinet you'll find it useful to have a flashlight. Connected to the drain pipe you will see a trap. Fig. 4-37 shows a few of the different types.

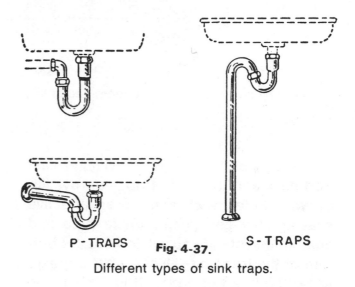

P - TRAPS   **Fig. 4-37.**   S - TRAPS

Different types of sink traps.

The purpose of a trap is to let water and waste flow through while preventing the backup of sewer gas through the pipe and on into your kitchen. Plumbing systems—and this applies to all of them—produce gas from the decomposition of food, soap, and excreta. These gases may not be toxic, but they do have an unsufferable odor. The trap also prevents insects such as water bugs and cockroaches from getting into your kitchen via the inside of the drain pipe.

Although there are different kinds of traps, basically they all consist of a downward loop in the piping. Traps are given different names, such as P traps and S traps, because of their fancied resemblance to these letters.

113

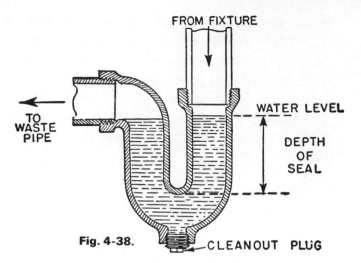

FROM FIXTURE

TO WASTE PIPE

WATER LEVEL

DEPTH OF SEAL

Fig. 4-38.

CLEANOUT PLUG

Cleanout plug is located at the bottom end of the trap.

Fig. 4-38 is a commonly used cast iron threaded trap. The trap is always filled with water, wich acts as an effective seal against gas in the waste pipe and against insects. If you will look at the bottom of the trap you will see what appears to be the head of a bolt. It is. This is the cleanout plug. The easiest way to remove the cleanout plug is to use a wrench.

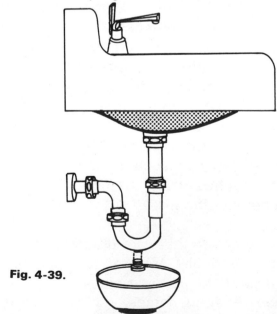

Fig. 4-39.

Hold a basin under the removable plug to catch the water and dirt that will come out of the trap.

Put a basin beneath the trap (Fig. 4-39) to catch the water in the trap, plus the accumulated debris; otherwise, you will have water and slop all over your floor or the bottom of the sink cabinet. Now turn the cleanout plug with your wrench. Rotate the tool counterclockwise to loosen the nut portion of the plug. As you do so, you may note some water beginning to seep into the basin. It may dribble a bit and then stop. Wait till it stops before continuing to loosen the nut. The whole idea is to let the trap water come out gradually and not splash you.

Once you have the plug removed, you will need some way of getting the solid waste out of the pipe. You can use a homemade tool for this purpose. Take a wire clothes hanger and bend the handle back and forth until it breaks off. What you want is a straight length of metal about 10 inches long. If the metal isn't straight, you can make it that way with a pair of pliers. Now, using the pliers, form a small U at either end of the wire. Push the U end of the wire into the pipe and work it back and forth. The U will catch on to the debris and pull it down through the pipe.

After you have removed as much crud as possible from inside the pipe, replace the cleanout plug. It would be helpful to smear the threads of the plug with pipe joint compound to make a more effective seal against water leakage. Make sure the cleanout plug is really tight and then turn on a faucet. At this time your sink should drain and no water should be coming out of the drain plug. If this is so, turn on the hot water faucet and let it run for about three minutes. This will help dissolve any remaining grease inside the pipe.

Not all sinks have a cleanout plug. In some, such as the P and S traps shown in Fig. 4-37, you will need to remove the entire trap. The entry and exit pipes leading to the trap are threaded and the trap is held on to the pipes by slip nuts (Fig. 4-40).

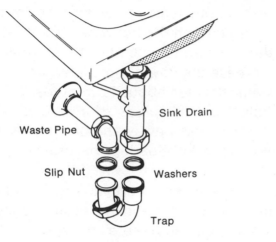

Fig. 4-40.
Trap that does not have a cleanout plug.

The advantage of this sort of trap is that it is much easier to clean than the one using a cleanout plug. The entrance through the cleanout plug is rather narrow, and so it is moderately difficult to get in and clean the drain pipe. But with a trap held on by slip nuts not only can you have access to the drain pipe, but, since you have the trap in your hands, you can take it to some other sink and wash it out thoroughly.

Chemical Trap Cleaners

There are other methods of cleaning sink drain pipes. One of these is to use ordinary household lye (caustic soda),

which is potent stuff. The directions on the label may suggest that your pour the lye, generally in powder or crystal form, directly into the drain. *Don't!*

One of the disadvantages of pouring lye directly into a drain is that the crystals may not dissolve. If you pour in more of the lye on the theory that "more is better," then the lye may form a solid, hard mass inside your drain pipe. Getting the lye out or trying to persuade it to dissolve can be either impossible or extremely time consuming. If you do get a lye buildup inside a pipe, keep at it with hot water. You may need to call a plumber, and if you do, be sure to let him know what has happened. Lye is dangerous to all human beings, and that includes plumbers.

Instead, put a tablespoonful in a glass of water. Before you do so, though, wash the glass with hot water. The purpose isn't to get the glass clean, but rather to raise the temperature of the glass. When you put the lye into a glass of water, there will be an exothermic reaction, just another way of saying that dissolving lye in water produces heat. Lots of it. If the glass is cold it may crack. If you have a glass swizzle stick, use it for stirring the lye/water combination and when the lye is completely dissolved, pour the liquid down the drain. Before you do so, however, try to remove as much water from the drain as possible, otherwise the lye water combation will spill over into the sink where it will do no good.

Lye doesn't dissolve the junk that is in your drain pipe. It combines with the fats which form the clog, resulting in a soft soap which you can then flush away with water. Let the lye remain in the drain overnight before washing it out. Lye will not harm iron, steel, brass, copper, or lead pipes, but it will damage aluminum, porcelain, and any enameled surfaces.

You may need to make a number of applications of lye and water before the clog is ready to let go. It might be an idea to dissolve a half-pound of lye in about two quarts of lukewarm water. Add the lye in small quantities and wear old clothing. If any of the liquid splatters on your hands or face, wash thoroughly and immediately. It's a good safety measure to wear safety goggles, although few people do so.

There are also various commercial cleaners you can use for drain cleaning. These are generally more expensive than lye. They are worth trying and will still cost you less than calling in a plumber.

A more professional method of using a drain cleaner would be to remove the stopper assembly, if you are working on a bathroom sink, or the sink strainer, if you are working on a kilchen sink. Using a funnel, pour a quantity of the liquid drain cleaner into the funnel. Make sure the liquid chemical does not rise enough to come into the sink. If you have a powder or crystal type of chemical, dissolve some of it in a glass container first. Do not pour solid chemicals into your drain.

Give the chemicals a chance to work. While there are claims made that such chemicals work and produce immediate results, this can also be a bit of advertising enthusiasm. It is better to let the chemical drain cleaner work overnight.

As a test, allow water from the faucet to flow into the drain. Turn the water on slowly and watch the drain. If the water rises in the drain and remains there, turn off the faucet, for the clog has not been cleared. If, however, the water does not do this, but seems to disappear down the drain, turn on the hot water faucet. Watch the drain and if you get no water backup, increase the flow of hot water. Let the hot water flow for about 15 minutes. This will help clear the pipes of any residue and will also wash away any of the chemicals you used for clearing the drain.

There are certain precautions to observe when handling drain cleaner. It would be advisable to wear rubber gloves. If you have glasses, wear them, or else put on safety goggles. Some drain cleaners are quite corrosive: Do not use the funnel for any other purpose, and wash it thoroughly after you are finished with it. Keep drain cleaner tightly closed, and put it where inquisitive little fingers can't reach or find it.

The Plumber's Snake

Still another method of clearing a trap is to use a plumber's snake (Fig. 4-41). This is a cleanout auger made of flexible spring metal and equipped with some sort of handle to let you rotate the tool. Drain augers are ¼-, ⅜-, and ½-inch types and range in length from 6 to 50 feet. For a kitchen sink a 6-foot auger is adequate. If your sink uses a cleanout plug, then a ¼-inch type is best.

Fig. 4-41.

Hand auger for cleaning kitchen or bathroom drains and traps. Remove strainer (kitchen sink) or stopper (bathroom sink) before using auger.

Some sinks have semicovered openings for the drain. The easiest way to clean is to put the auger down the drain from the top of the sink to clear the trap.

After you have the auger in position, you will need to rotate it. The reason for the reason for this is that one end of the auger is flared out to make better contact with the junk inside the pipe, to catch it and hold it. At the other end of the auger you will have a handle. As you turn the handle, the entire auger will turn, and with it, the "business" end. Always rotate the auger in the same direction, and at the same time push and pull it.

When you remove the auger, you will see that the flared end contains some of the material that was in the trap. Take the tool and dip the flared end in a pail of water to clean it. Then back to the sink

and repeat your performance until the auger no longer has evidence of clog material. You can then verify that the trap has been cleaned by turning on one of the faucets and watching the water disappear down the drain.

Clogged Horizontal Drain and Waste Pipes

If you have tried all the methods described so far and the clog still remains, then the obstruction is in the horizontal drain pipe leading away from the trap or in the vertical waste pipe to which this horizontal drain is connected. Your next step is to use the auger once again.

Remove the trap, but be careful not to get splashed by any of the chemical clog remover you have in the pipe. Put a basin under the trap to catch any water in the trap. After the trap is off, insert the cutting end of the auger into the horizontal drain pipe, as shown in Fig. 4-42. Insert the auger until you begin to feel some opposition. This might be the clog or it might be a bend in the pipe. Start turning the handle of the auger while pushing forward on it slightly. If you feel the auger penetrating more deeply into the drain pipe, feed more of it into the pipe. Then turn the handle about a dozen times and repeat.

The horizontal kitchen drain feeds into a vertical waste pipe, probably connected by a fitting that makes a 45° angle between the two pipes. Once you can get the auger past the fitting, the chances are very good that the clog in the horizontal drain has been removed or at least

117

broken. Keep working the auger back and forth until the auger moves very easily. Then replace the trap and test by turning on a faucet.

Fig. 4-42.
Clearing clog from horizontal drain for kitchen or bathroom sink.

If the clog is gone, turn on the hot water faucet for about 15 minutes. While the water is flowing, examine the trap to make sure no water is coming out of it. If the trap is inside a cabinet of some kind, you'll find it helpful to use a flashlight. Clean the auger in a pail of water containing some disinfectant. Always dry the auger thoroughly before storing it to keep it from rusting.

Prevention of Sink Clogging

You can avoid sink clogging in several ways. The first is to make sure you do not use the sink as a general garbage disposal unit. To prevent miscellaneous food wastes from wandering down the drain, use a strainer. There are many different types, a few of which are shown in Fig. 4-43. You have available a stainless steel basket strainer, a sink strainer cup, a sink strainer with a post that will let you control opening size, a flat drain guard, a pronged drain guard, and others.

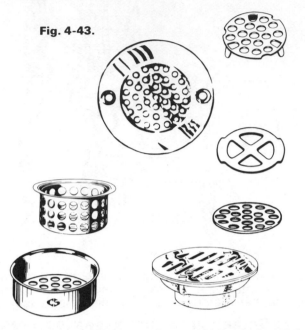

Fig. 4-43.

Various types of sink strainers. (Chicago Specialty)

From time to time, pour drain cleaner down your sink drain. This can be a commercial type or your own homemade stuff containing lye. And if you send hot water down the drain once a day you should be able to keep the drain clear indefinitely.

A dishwasher may contribute to your sink clogging problems. Clogging is caused by a film of grease forming on the inside wall of the drain pipe. This grease is a gluey substance, and food particles, such as coffee grounds, stick to it readily. Try to keep food out of the kitchen sink drain as much as possible.

There is another helpful little gadget you can use. This is a triangular garbage container that fits easily into a corner of the sink. Use it for parings and peelings. The container has holes to permit drainage of liquids. If you use such a container, empty it after each meal—not down the sink drain, but into your garbage pail. To prevent odors and possible food decay, clean the container daily.

How to Clear a Clogged Strainer

What we want from the water in our home plumbing system is the right amount from the right place at the right time. Problems arise when we get more water than we want, or not enough. But not only must we have water, we should be able to dispose of it as quickly as possible. We have a clog whenever we cannot make the water move into and through the drainage system. The clog can be complete, in which case no water goes through the drain, or it may be partial, with the water leaving the sink or tub or whatever with exasperating slowness.

Kitchen sinks are quite susceptible to clogging because of food waste and grease. The particles tend to form a compact mass and block the passage of water either partially or totally. As noted in the previous section, some sinks are equipped with strainers to prevent the passage of too large food particles into the drain. An excellent idea, but sometimes the strainer itself can become clogged. Poking through each individual hole of the strainer is an obvious solution, but not such a good one. By so doing you will be pushing food particles into the drain, something the strainer is trying to help you avoid. Besides, food and grease tend to accumulate beneath the strainer,

just where you cannot reach them while the strainer is in place.

The best thing to do is to take out the strainer and wipe it thoroughly with a cloth. After you have removed most of the clogging materials, you can wash both sides of the strainer with soap and water.

Some strainers simply rest in position in the sink drain, while others are held in by a pair of screws. If you have the latter, just use a screwdriver to remove the screws. Be careful not to drop them down the drain.

Clogged Bathroom Sink

The bathroom sink can clog because its drain connecting the sink to the trap doesn't allow water to get through. Unlike your kitchen sink, the bathroom type has a stopper which can be manipulated by a rod mounted on the rear of the spout. Pulling the rod up pulls the stopper down and closes the sink.

Fig. 4-44.

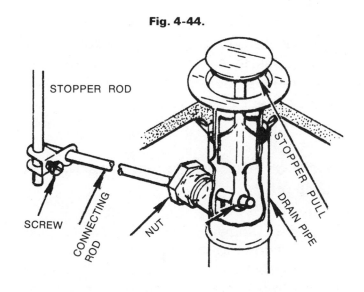

STOPPER ROD

SCREW

CONNECTING ROD

NUT

STOPPER PULL

DRAIN PIPE

Stopper assembly for a bathroom sink.

Fig. 4-44 shows the mechanism that operates the stopper. Some of these mechanisms are different from others, but they all have the same job to do and all work in much the same way.

The trouble isn't with the stopper itself, but the lower part of the stopper assembly, the part that always remains in the drain. It gets clogged with soap and hair and when the accumulation is large enough, water will either not drain out of the sink or will do so slowly.

To unclog the sink, remove the stopper assembly. If you examine Fig. 4-44, you will see a rod that connects the stopper assembly to the pull rod. Once you remove the connecting rod, you will be able to lift out the stopper and clean the drain. To do so, loosen the screw that holds the connecting rod to the vertical stopper pull rod. Undo the nut that holds the other end of the connecting rod. You will then be able to pull the connecting rod away from the drain and lift out the stopper assembly.

While you are at it, it would be a good idea to clean out the trap as well. This means your bathroom sink drainage will be clear as far as the drain pipe that connects to the exit side of the sink trap.

How to Stop a Shower Head From Dripping

The shower head of your shower corresponds to the spout of your kitchen or bathroom faucets. When the shower head leaks, the fault isn't in the shower head but in the shower faucet. The problem is due to a washer that needs to be replaced.

Fig. 4-45.

Shower head. Unit is often chrome plated and has a brass ball joint. The lever adjustment on the side permits adjustment of spray pattern from sharp needle to stream. (Chicago Specialty)

The faucet used to control the hot and cold water out of your shower head (Fig. 4-45) is essentially the same as your kitchen or bathroom faucets, except it is mounted horizontally. There are a number of different types and styles, but basically they work the same way.

To repair such a faucet, turn it to its on position and then close the valve that controls the water supply to this faucet. Wait a minute or two for the water to run out of the tub or stall.

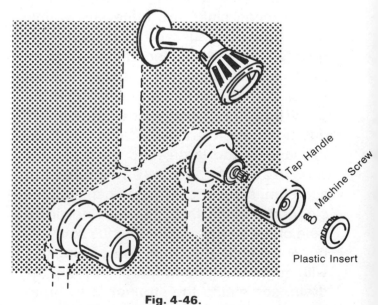

Tap Handle

Machine Screw

Plastic Insert

Fig. 4-46.

First steps in repairing a leaking wall-mounted shower faucet.

Fig. 4-46 shows the parts to be described and their physical relationship to each other:

On the front of the faucet is a plastic insert marked H, for hot, or C, for cold. The insert is usually a snap-in type, so you should have no trouble in getting it out. A small screwdriver will help.

Beneath the insert you will find a small machine screw. Remove this screw by turning it counterclockwise with a screwdriver. The screw holds a circular cover called a tap handle. The tap handle should now come off, but if it doesn't, just rock it back and forth.

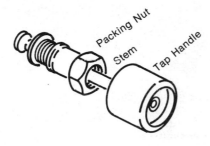

Fig. 4-47.
Basic parts of the stem assembly.

After you have removed the tap handle, you will see the stem assembly (Fig. 4-47). Closest to you will be a packing nut. Using a suitable tool, rotate the packing nut counterclockwise, and then the nut and the entire stem assembly will come out. Fig. 4-47 shows the result.

You can now replace the washer. Remove the machine screw at the end of the assembly, as illustrated in Fig. 4-48. If the screw looks damaged or worn, use a

brass replacement. Make sure the screw is an exact duplicate. Replace the washer held in by this screw and also the larger-diameter washer that fits over the stem.

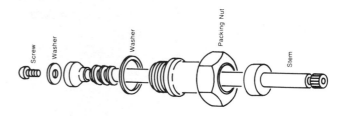

Fig. 4-48.
As a repair and trouble preventive, replace the washer holding screw, the faucet washer, and stem washer.

After you have mounted the replacement parts, reassemble. Turn the faucet to its off position and then turn the water control valve on.

Sometimes, when the water control valve is some distance away, turning the water on will result in banging in the pipes and very erratic flow of water out of the fixture. To prevent this from happening, turn the water control valve on just a little at a time. The reason for all the fuss is that you have drained the water supply pipe. The water rushing into the pipe is under pressure, and until the pipe is completely water filled, you will have some effects that can be frightening.

Shower Faucet Packing Leaks

If the shower leak does not come from the shower head but from the shower faucet, it is likely that the material under the packing nut needs replacement. Follow the same procedure just described and remove the packing nut and replace the packing material. But, as long as you are doing this much work, why not continue all the way and replace the faucet washer, its holding screw, and the larger stem washer?

How to Clear a Shower Drain

If you have a stall shower that has a clogging problem, you may be able to get rid of the clog by using water pressure. The floor of the shower has a strainer at its center, held in by two machine screws. Remove the screws and lift the strainer out.

Connect a garden hose to a water supply. Remove the nozzle from the end of the hose. Put this end into the shower drain and keep pushing the hose until it will move no further. Soak a number of rags in water and then pack them as tightly as possible in and around the nose so that the drain is sealed effectively. While you hold these rags firmly in place with your hands, have someone turn on the water and also ready to turn it off at your command. The water pouring out of the hose will exert pressure on the clog and may remove it.

If this doesn't work, you might try a plunger. And if that doesn't work, a chemical drain cleaner. As a last resort, call a plumber. If you do, remember to tell him what you did and call his attention to the fact that you did use a chemical drain cleaner. This will alert him to any possible risk from the cleaner.

The Bathtub Trap

Like your kitchen or bathroom sinks, your bathtub also has a trap, but unlike the sinks the trap isn't visible, and may not even be directly accessible.

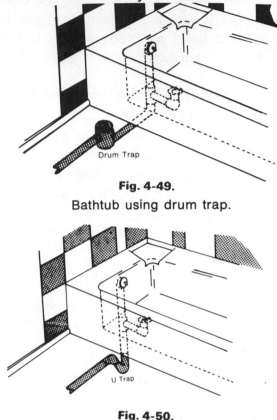

Fig. 4-49.
Bathtub using drum trap.

Fig. 4-50.
Bathtub using U trap.

There are two types of bathtub traps. One is the drum trap (Fig. 4-49), and the other is the U trap (Fig. 4-50). Bathtub traps are placed somewhere in walls or floors. In some houses the trap can be reached through a removable panel placed in a closet. Drum traps are generally near the bathtub drain. They may be located under the floor near the tub and may have a cover which can be removed so you can get at the drain.

Bathtub drains can and do get clogged because of hair and soap particles flowing down the waste water.

How to Clean a Drum Trap

Your first step is to empty the bathtub if it contains any water. By using a sponge and a pail you can manage to get rid of just about all the water that is in the tub due to the clogged drain.

The drum trap has a threaded cover with a nut head mounted on it. If you can get at the drum trap, you can remove the cover with a wrench. Turn the wrench counterclockwise. As you remove the drum trap cover you will see it has a large rubber gasket. If the gasket seems worn, or just about falls apart in your hands, get a replacement.

You will see two pipes coming into the drum trap, at opposite ends, with one pipe higher than the other. The lower pipe connects to the tub; the higher one to the drain. Because the drain is lower than the tub, water cannot return via the pipe connected to the tub. Instead, water will fill the trap up as far as the drain opening. This provides an effective water seal.

Cleaning the drum trap means just reaching in and getting rid of all the materials caught in the trap. Clean the trap thoroughly, using a bit of scrap cloth after you have removed all the gunk. If you feel squeamish about reaching in with your hand, then use an old teaspoon. Bend the spoon portion up a bit and then it can work for you like a miniature shovel that is bent out of shape.

After you have cleaned the trap, open the cold water faucet of the tub to let a small amount of water go down the drain. If, however, no water or very little water coming into the trap, then the clog exists in the drain pipe between the tub drain and the trap. Close the water and dry the tub.

To get rid of this clog, insert an auger into the drain pipe via the drum trap, and turn the auger slowly until the clog clears. The tub drain makes a right angle bend as it goes up into the tub and so this is a possible location of the clog. Keep turning the auger until you feel the clog giving way. Pull the auger out of the pipe, clean the auger head, and keep repeating the process until you can get no more material out of the pipe. Then turn on the water in the tub once again and watch the drum trap. This time the drum trap should fill with water and you should be able to see some of it going out of the drum into the exit pipe.

How to Clean a U Trap

If your bathtub has a U trap, you might try using a sink plunger to see if you can clear the clog. Fill the tub with water to a depth of about 2 or 3 inches. Above the tub faucets you will have a small handle for opening and closing the drain. Set the handle to its open position and then use the plunger.

If this method doesn't work, empty the tub using a sponge and a pail. Get as much of the water out as you can. Remove the strainer that covers the drain pipe and then pour in a chemical drain cleaner, following the same procedures as those described earlier in connection with sinks. Let the chemical remain in overnight and then check the following day to see if the clog has cleared.

As a final alternative call a plumber, but be sure to let him know you have a chemical drain cleaner in the pipes.

An Overheating Hot Water Tank

Two symptoms, coming singly or together, indicate that your hot water tank is overheating: a rumbling noise in the tank and or hot water coming out of a cold water faucet. The pressure caused by overheating can possibly cause the hot water tank to burst. The first thing to do is to shut off the burner for the hot water tank. If the heater is electrically operated, turn off the switch associated with the burner. If you cannot find this switch, go to your main fuse box and remove the fuse for the wiring for the hot water tank, or turn off the switch if you have a thermal reset type of box. The interior of the tank has corroded or rust may have accumulated. Call a plumber.

How to Take Care of Your Kitchen Sink

Kitchen sinks get more abuse than any of the other sinks in the house, for they are not only used more often but are affected by the composition of different foods. The easiest cleaning technique is to wash the sink immediately after every use.

You may have received a printed notice informing you that your brand-new sink is acid resistant. This does not mean it is impervious to food acids. Don't permit fruit or vegetable juices to remain on the sink surface for more than short periods of time. An acid resisting sink should be able to wilhstand all citrus fruits—orange, lemon, grapefruit juices—provided these are not allowed to remain on the sink surface indefinitely. Give yourself a time limit of one hour. That's reasonable enough.

If your sink has a regular enamel finish, you will find it helpful to cover the work area with a rubber mat. Such sinks are susceptible to acid damage, so if you have a fruit liquid spill, mop up and wash the sink immediately.

Wet tea bags and coffee grounds will stain enameled surfaces if allowed to remain for a long time. It may be your custom to take a long, despairing look at a sink after the party has gone home, but it is better to clean before you go to bed than in the morning. By morning you will have an assortment of stains you will not be able to clean away. Soap and water won't help. Cleanser won't help. Bleach won't help. And scrubbing won't help.

Don't use your kitchen sink for work in photography. The chemicals used for photographic development are potent and will damage the finish of a sink even more rapidly and more effectively than food stains.

If you use one of the triangular food scrap containers in your sink, mentioned earlier, make sure you empty it out after each meal. Wash the area beneath the container before replacing it. Washing doesn't mean flicking the surface just once with a sponge. Use soap and water and clean thoroughly. It is the only way to keep that section of your sink from becoming permanently discolored.

The best way to clean a sink is to use hot water and soap. It is easier and quicker to use powder cleansers but some of these are highly abrasive and their continued use will gradually remove the finish of the sink. Washing soda is also a bit too strong to use. If you are having a new sink installed, you may get washing instructions with it. If not, drop a note to the manufacturer and get his advice. The advice given to you by salesmen selling sinks may be good or bad, depending on how much they know about the subject.

A dripping faucet can stain a sink in a way which is almost unbelievable. That is one reason, and quite a good one, for getting rid of drips as quickly as you can. Water may look clean; it may look pure and crystal clear. But its appearance is no indication of its contents. It can easily contain dissolved minerals which can and will wear away the surface coating of your sink.

There are other ways in which sinks can be damaged, usually beyond repair. Don't drag pots or pans across the sink surfaces. If you do you will get scratch marks that cannot be washed away in any manner, no matter what you use. Don't chop ice on the drainboard. The sharp end of the ice pick can and will puncture the surface of the sink.

If, despite all your precautions, or possibly because of your failure to take precautions, you do get marks on your sink, you can buy a small bottle of porcelain touch-up. It's a toss-up, however, as to which is less offensive looking—a mark or scratch showing through the porcelain, or a touch-up that looks obvious.

How to Take Care of Bathroom Sinks

Bathroom sink surfaces generally outlast those of kitchen sinks because they aren't subjected to as much abuse. If you have a medicine cabinet mounted above the sink, as is common, just make sure that the glasses, bottles, and jars arranged inside the cabinet don't have a tendency to fall into the sink. Medicine cabinets are often overcrowded. Not uncommonly, bathroom sink stains are often due to contact with broken medicine bottles.

When a medicine bottle breaks, clean the sink immediately. Use some toilet tissue to get as much of the liquid out as you can and also make sure you remove all the glass particles. Tiny shards of glass are dangerous. They can cause severe finger cuts, and if they get into the sink drain can quickly produce a clog. And they will not dissolve no matter how much of El Magico drain cleaner you pour into the sink.

The best cleaner for a bathroom sink is hot water and soap. Or else use a non-abrasive cleanser. Wash the fixtures with a soap solution of water, rinse, dry, and then polish with a soft cloth. Dirt has a habit of accumulating around the various crevices of the hardware used on the sink. You can pick this out with a toothpick. Don't use a knife or hard-pointed instrument for cleaning dirt out of fixtures.

Bathroom sinks have a drain-hole

closing feature, so it is easy to use the sink to hold water for any purpose, possibly for washing hose or other garments. Don't allow the water to stand. Instead, let it flush away and then wash the sink. Body acids contained in clothing can attack the sink finish. Also, from a more practical point of view, it is much easier to clean a sink right after you have finished using it. Dirty water that is allowed to stand puts a scumlike finish on the sink surface that is often difficult to remove.

How to Take Care of Bathtubs

The best way to clean a bathtub is with hot water and soap. To make the job easier, use a soft bristle brush with a long, curved handle. If you must cope with a tub that has been neglected and is quite dirty, you may be able to get good results with the help of some naphtha base laundry soap. Use any kind of scraper you have and finely slice about half the bar of soap into a quart of hot water. If you don't have a scraper, try to cut the half-bar section into small pieces.

The idea behind all this scraping and cutting is to get the soap to dissolve quickly in the water. Using the solid bar will mean waiting around most of the day. After you have a solution of naphtha base laundry soap and hot water, add two tablespoons of kerosene. Use a large sponge and wash the tub surface area repeatedly. You may need to use a bit of muscle, but the results will be worth it. When you are finished, wash the tub with clear warm water.

When decorating the bathroom, always be sure to cover the sink, tub and toilet. You can get a plastic drop cloth for one-time use for very little money. The idea here is not only to protect the sink, toilet, and tub surfaces from paint, but from falling tools and plaster.

Don't ever stand on your sink to reach the ceiling. And if you must stand in the tub, take your shoes off. This may sound obvious, but it is a way in which tubs are often damaged.

How to Clear Clogged Toilets

Like sinks, toilets can become clogged, but for toilets the problem may be more difficult to solve. The first thing to do is to forget about using lye. Toilet bowls, made of vitreous china, can be cracked by the heat developed by the lye, and there's always the possibility that lye may damage the bowl directly.

A first start on a clogged toilet is to use a plunger. But before you do, it would be helpful to learn a bit more about toilets and how they work. When you flush a toilet the action of removal of water plus waste is a siphoning one. Fig. 4-51 shows the steps of the process.

Start with drawing 1. A represents the bowl, and B is the trap. If we pour water into the bowl at a slow rate, the trap will fill, and the remaining water will flow through C and D. This isn't a siphoning action.

The opposite action is to fill the bowl with water so rapidly that both trap B and pipe D contain water (drawing 2). As a result, the water level in bowl A will rise since trap B and pipe D will be unable to let water flow through them rapidly enough. The idea here is like a sink. If you turn both faucets on, the sink will fill with water since the water will not be able to escape through the drain so quickly.

Fig. 4-51.

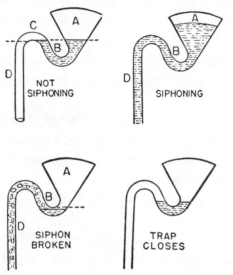

Siphoning action of a toilet bowl.

We now have pipes D and B filled. Pipe D, though, has a greater weight of water than trap B. But if at this time no more water flows into bowl A, the weight of the water in D will literally pull the water out of bowl A (drawing 3). It will continue to do so until the water level reaches the horizontal dashed line in drawing 3.

Not only water, but air in the bowl is also drawn into the trap and pipe D. Thus, the downward movement of water in pipe D literally sucks water and air, pulling both down. But this action cannot continue indefinitely since the water in pipe D escapes into a waste pipe. When this happens we no longer have water in pipe D, but there is a small amount of water in

the bowl (drawing 4). Water remains in the trap because there is no force being exerted on it. There are various kinds of toilet bowls (fig. 4-52), but they all work on the same basic principle.

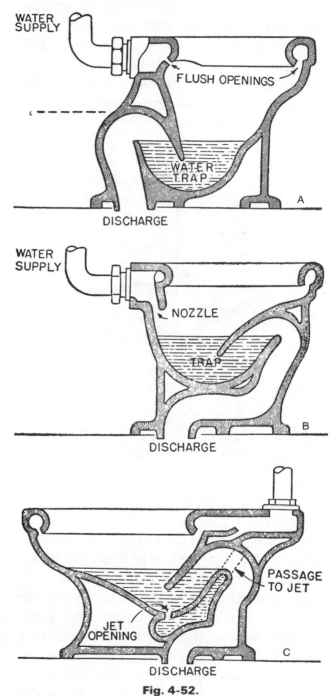

Fig. 4-52.
Various types of toilet bowls: (A) siphon bowl with reverse trap, (B) siphon washdown bowl, (C) siphon jet bowl.

127

Now that you are ready to clear the toilet bowl with your "plumber's friend," examine the rubber force cup on this tool. It should have a fold-out section, or lip. Lubricate the lip with petroleum jelly. The idea here is to have a snug fit on the flowout pipe of the bowl. Once you have the plunger in position, move the wooden handle back and forth rapidly about a dozen times. Try to keep the handle perpendicular to the drainage hole of the bowl (Fig. 4-53).

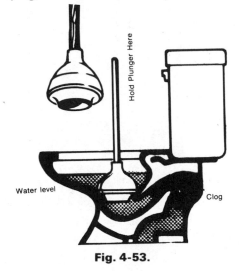

Hold Plunger Here

Water level

Clog

Fig. 4-53.

Smear lip of toilet plunger with petroleum jelly. Plunger must be vertical. Move handle up and down to dislodge clog. Water level in bowl must be above rubber cup of plunger.

Naturally, you will need to test to determine if you have managed to clear away the blocked passage. The easiest way, but not the best, is to flush the toilet. The problem here is that you may not have cleared the clog, so you will end up by having a flooded bathroom floor. Instead, take a large container, such as a pot, fill it with water and then pour the water into the bowl. If the clog has been removed, you will not be able to fill the bowl with water since part of it will keep escaping down the drain. You can then flush the drain in the usual way, with the expectation that the force of the drainage water will clear away any remaining debris.

It's possible that your initial efforts with the plunger will not clear the clog. This can happen when you use the toilet bowl as a diaper disposing unit. Diapers are absorbent but they just aren't designed to pass through the trap in a toilet.

For this next technique take a large pot or kettle and fill it with hot water from your sink faucet. Then put the pot or kettle on your stove and heat it. What you want isn't just hot, but boiling, water.

When the water boils, don't try to heat it any further. It will not get any hotter than it is and will just boil off. Pour the water into the toilet bowl. Don't flush the bowl. Now repeat this procedure about two or three times.

Once more, fill the pot or kettle and put it on the stove to boil. Take about three cups of liquid bleach and one cup of low-suds detergent powder and pour both into the toilet bowl. Now add the boiling water. The combination of hot water, detergent, and bleach will go to work on the clog, will soften it, and will at least get it into a condition where it can be moved. Wait about an hour to give your chemical preparation a chance do its work.

Bend out the lip of the plunger as shown in Fig. 4-53 and lubricate it with petroleum jelly. Insert the plunger and move it up and down. You may find it helpful to push the handle down slowly and pull it up rapidly. You'll know that the clog is dispersed by the response of the plunger. Once the clog has moved, the downward action of the plunger will feel much easier.

If the plumber's friend doesn't clear the bowl of its stoppage, you can use an auger. Get the type made for toilet use. Insert the business end of the auger into the drainage hole of the bowl and slowly turn the handle at the other end. You'll need to work by feel. Don't force the auger. If you feel that the auger is up against some obstruction, back off a bit, and then continue turning the auger.

There is no clog cleaning method that is infallible, and no one can guarantee you 100 percent success. It all depends on the composition of the clog. People throw all sorts of things into toilet bowls with the happy, but unwarranted assumption, that it is a universal drain—that anything you want to get rid of can flush down the toilet. Not so. Used razor blades, bits of cement from work done around the bathroom, floor sweepings—all these and more—can and do form a compact, hard mass. Then the only solution is either to call in a plumber or disassemble the toilet bowl.

You should be able to use toilet bowls for years without clogging. If clogging is a persistent problem, get a plumber because the clog material just won't go away by itself. In some cases the clog isn't a complete one—that is, the water flushes sluggishly. This means that some water is getting past the clog, but not enough to produce the siphoning action mentioned earlier. A clogged toilet is not only unsightly and odorous, it is downright unhealthy.

The auger, also known as a snake, is a spring steel coil. When you turn its handle you are capable of exerting quite a bit of force. Use it carefully because if you don't, it is possible to crack the toilet bowl. When you then call the plumber, he will not only hand you a large bill, but his voice or expression will say, "I told you so."

Repairing Toilets

While a clogged toilet is a common event, you can also have trouble with the flushing mechanism. But before your problems begin, it might be a good idea to lift the top off the toilet tank and examine the mechanism while it is still in good working order. Note the height of the water level. Measure from the top of the tank to the surface of the water to get some idea of how much water must be in the tank for proper flushing.

If possible, make some sort of scratch or other mark at the water level. Then, in the future, if the water is above or below the mark you will at least know that the toilet flushing mechanism isn't working the way it should. (Modern tanks have such a mark.) If there isn't enough water in the tank, the toilet will not flush properly and you may need to depress the flush leverl a number of times. This wastes water and is time consuming. If there is too much water in the tank, it will take longer to refill and also, once again, you will be wasting water. This is water you pay for and, over a period of a year, can amount to several thousand gallons.

Fig. 4-54.

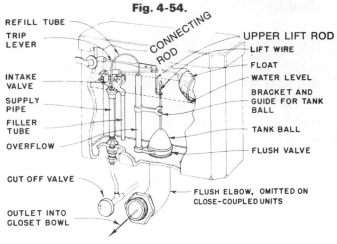

REFILL TUBE
TRIP LEVER
INTAKE VALVE
SUPPLY PIPE
FILLER TUBE
OVERFLOW
CUT OFF VALVE
OUTLET INTO CLOSET BOWL
CONNECTING ROD
UPPER LIFT ROD
LIFT WIRE
FLOAT
WATER LEVEL
BRACKET AND GUIDE FOR TANK BALL
TANK BALL
FLUSH VALVE
FLUSH ELBOW, OMITTED ON CLOSE-COUPLED UNITS

Details of a toilet tank.

Fig. 4-54 shows the parts inside the toilet flush tank. There are all sorts of mechanisms available, but the general idea is always the same. When you flush the tank by depressing a handle, usually located at the upper left on the outside of the tank, the action lifts a trip lever. This raises a connecting rod to which a lift rod is attached. The lift rod is screwed into a tank ball. In effect, the true purpose of the lever is to lift the tank ball. When the tank ball rises, the water in the tank escapes through the flush valve, goes down through the flush elbow and on into the toilet bowl.

When the water exits from the tank, the level is lowered. As the water level goes down, a float, made of copper or plastic, goes down with it. At this time the tank ball falls back into position over the flush valve, closing it and stopping the flow of water from the tank into the toilet bowl. Water now pours back into the tank from the supply pipe. As the water rises,

so does the float. The float, however, is attached to a rod, which, in turn is connected to the intake valve. When the water level becomes high enough, the float, through its extension arm closes the intake valve.

Fig. 4-55.

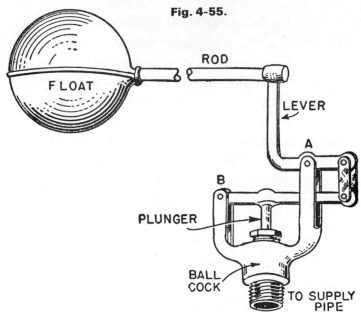

FLOAT
ROD
LEVER
A
B
PLUNGER
BALL COCK
TO SUPPLY PIPE

One type of water supply and shutoff mechanism for toilet tanks.

Fig. 4-55 shows the details of the float and the intake valve. This is just one type among many, but they all work along the same lines. If you can fix one, you should be able to repair them all. The float shown in the illustration is lightweight and hollow. It is removable and is threaded so you can screw it onto the connecting rod. The float is available in hardware/plumbing stores as a separate item, but you can buy the entire mechanism if necessary.

After a toilet has been flushed, the float will not be in the horizontal position shown in the drawing but will be much further down. As a result, the connecting rod, to which it is attached, will also be down, thus forcing the part marked "lever" down. The effect of this action is to raise the plunger, allowing water to come up through the supply pipe and to enter the tank. But as the float rises, due to the increasing volume of water in the tank, it will raise the lever, and the action will serve to push the plunger down, shutting off the flow of water coming in from the supply pipe.

Continuous Flow Into the Toilet Tank

When this problem occurs, you may hear the noise of water as it flows ceaselessly into the tank. You may also hear water rushing into the overflow tube, a safety feature designed to prevent the tank from overflowing. However, there is a limit to the amount of water that can be drained away by the overflow tube, so it is possible for water to rise in the tank, spill over, and flood the bathroom floor. The water must go somewhere; if the bathroom is on a second floor, the water will find its way downward, ruining the ceiling of the room below.

How to Replace a Float

All of this because of a defective float. It pays to listen to your toilet; it may be trying to tell you something. To determine if the float is defective flush the tank and then lift the rod connected to the float. This will shut off the flow of water into the tank.

Hold the rod with one hand to keep any water from coming in and, with the other, unscrew the float. Shake it. If you hear water sloshing around the inside or if water drips out of it while you are holding it, the float is defective. Tie the rod which was connected to the float to the trip lever or just attach a weight to the other end of a string and let it hang outside the tank. Use any method you wish to hold the float rod up so as to keep water from coming into the tank. Then buy a replacement float. Replacement is easy; just screw in the new float.

It is also possible there is nothing wrong with the float but that the connecting rod to which it is screwed is bent too far upward. When this happens, an extra amount of water must flow into the tank to have an effect on the float. The float, then, is too high and so does not shut off the plunger mechanism (refer to Fig. 4-55 again) soon enough. The additional water will flow through the overflow tube.

The cure is to bend the rod so it assumes the shape of a slightly inverted V. In short, bend the rod so the float is lower down in the tank. The rod is made of copper, threaded at both ends. Just flush the tank and then bend the rod. If this produces just a partial cure, then bend the rod just a bit more.

The deeper you make the bend, the less water you will have in the tank. But you need a certain amount of water in the tank to be able to flush it properly, so there is a limit to how far you can go with this repair technique.

If the plunger mechanism is defective, no amount of bending of the copper rod will help. You can check easily. Lift the rod so it is either horizontal or slightly higher. If water still comes into the tank, then the water-supply and shutoff mechanism shown in Fig. 4-55 is defective.

Toilet Doesn't Flush

There must be enough water in the tank above the toilet to produce a good flushing action. If the rod that supports the float is bent downward too sharply, the float will be too close to the bottom of the tank, so just a small amount of water in the tank will exert enough pressure on the float to shut off the intake valve. The cure is simple. Bend the rod holding the float so it is more horizontal and has less of a bend in it. Don't overdo it or you'll get more water into the tank than you bargained for.

How to Adjust Tank Water Level

After you have obtained a new float, you may find that the old connecting rod is no longer satisfactory. The threads for holding the float may be so worn that you can't fasten the float securely. Generally, when you buy a float, you get a connecting rod with it. If you compare your old rod with your new one, you will see that the new one is straight and the old one bent. Using the old rod as a guide, try to bend the new rod into the same shape. Use a pair of pliers and you should have no trouble.

One end of the connecting rod screws into the top end of the intake valve. The other end of the rod screws into the float.

Remember, it is always a good idea when you disassemble any plumbing fix-ture to make a note of the steps you followed. Replacing parts means following the same steps in reverse. You removed the float connecting rod and the float, so you should be able to replace these old parts with the new ones.

After you have the assembly completed, let the tank fill with water. If the water reaches the same level it did originally, the repair is completed. If the water level is too high, you will need to bend the rod in such a way that the float pushes down harder on the water.

If the water is too low, you will need to bend the rod so that the float is higher up. Experiment by bending the rod either back or forth until the tank fills to the level it should have.

As a general rule, the correct water level is about 1 inch below the top of the overflow tube.

The Float Connecting Rod

Sometimes a float will get just a little water inside it, so you, or a plumber, may bend the connecting rod to compensate for it. But if a little bit of water can get into a float, more can find its way in, so ultimately the bend in the rod assumes the shape of an inverted V. But the float is inexpensive; therefore, rather than getting involved in such plumbing shenanigans, replace it. It is much less work doing so than mopping up the floor.

If the float at the end of the rod is loose and no amount of turning will tighten it, you can make a temporary repair by wrapping some cotton thread around the end of the rod. This will hold the ball in place long enough to give you time to buy a new rod. This isn't a permanent repair. Change the rod; otherwise you will have to do so when you least expect it, and it is sure to be at a most inconvenient time.

Tank Ball Problems

Tank ball. (Chicago Specialty)

Fig. 4-56.

When the tank ball (Fig. 4-56) drops, it is supposed to go right into the opening of the flush valve (sometimes called a spud) and to do this so well that no more water escapes through the valve into the toilet bowl (refer back to Fig. 4-54). However, if the ball does not seat properly there will be water drainage from the tank into the bowl. You'll hear it, and it also represents a substantial waste of water.

There are several possible aspects to this problem. The first is that the tank ball may be worn or may no longer fit properly into the flush valve seat. The other is that the flush valve seat may be slimy or worn. Or a combination of the two.

Water Keeps Running into Toilet Bowl. Turn off the tank water supply valve and flush the toilet. Lift the tank ball and use some string to keep it up and out of

the way. Dry the valve seat thoroughly with a cloth. Put some rubbing alcohol on a cloth and wash the valve seat. Repeat the process a number of times. Now dry the tank ball and wash it with rubbing alcohol. Remove the string and let the tank ball fall into position in the valve seat. Turn on the water supply valve and examine the water in the toilet bowl. If you can see no traces of water flow, no bubbling, then the repair is completed. If water keeps flowing, try replacing the tank ball with a new one.

Lever Jiggling. Sometimes a toilet will be noisy and will not become quiet until you jiggle the flush lever. Then it will settle down and remain silent only until the next time someone uses the toilet. And once more, the cure—a temporary one—will be to jiggle the flush lever.

The problem here is that the tank ball doesn't fit properly into the drain hole in the toilet tank. Jiggling the lever makes the tank ball dance around a bit and the pressure of the water above the ball finally forces it into the correct position.

Fig. 4-57.

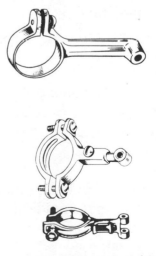

Various types of brackets and guides. (Chicago Specialty)

Fig. 4-58.

Lift rods: lower lift rod (left) and upper lift rod (right). (Chicago Specialty)

What you need to do is to adjust the bracket and guide (Fig. 4-57) so that the lower lift rod (Fig. 4-58) is able to move up and down easily. Loosen the screw that holds the bracket to the overflow pipe (again, refer back to Fig. 4-54). When it is sufficiently loose, empty the tank by flushing it and then try to position the bracket and guide so that the lift rod connected to the tank ball lets the ball fall into the correct spot. It does take some patience and experimentation, but after a bit of time you should be able to get the ball to drop in correctly.

Sometimes the tank ball will not drop into place because of friction between the lift rod and the bracket. The purpose of the bracket is not only to hold the lift rod in position but to act as a guide. If the rod seems to catch in the bracket, cover the rod with a very thin coating of petroleum jelly.

After you have finished, and as a check, flush the toilet several times. The toilet should be absolutely quiet and you should finally be relieved of your flush lever jiggling chore.

How to Replace the Tank Ball Assembly

The movement required of the tank ball assembly plus its total immersion in water at all times can finally wear the assembly enough so the only solution is replacement. You can buy a tank ball kit consisting of the tank ball, lift rod, and bracket. (See the following subsection: Tank Ball Assemblies.)

Turn off the water supply to the toilet tank and flush the tank to empty it. Remove the old tank ball assembly, but before you do take note of just how it is mounted. You will need to remove the refill tube that fits into the top end of the overflow tube. Just lift it up and out of the way. This will let you slide the loosened bracket and guide up and off the overflow tube.

As a first step, you will need to join the two lift rods, the lower and the upper. Just slide the lower lift rod through the eye section of the upper. Now take the lower lift rod and slide it through the guide section of the bracket. As a final assembly step, screw the tank ball onto the threaded end of the lower lift rod. This does sound complicated, but if you will go back to Fig. 4-54, you will see just how to do it.

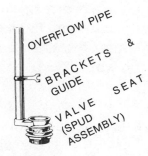

Fig. 4-59.

Bracket and guide mounted on overflow pipe. (Chicago Specialty)

Mount the bracket (Fig. 4-59) on the overflow tube and slide the bracket down until it occupies just about the same position as the old one. Tighten the bracket holding screw. Put the refill tube back into position at the top of the overflow tube. Connect the upper lift rod by inserting it in one of the holes at the end of the trip lever.

The assembly is now completed. This doesn't mean it will work right the first time. Open the water control valve and let the tank fill with water. Then flush the tank. You may need to adjust the position of the bracket and guide several times before the assembly works the way it should.

Tank Ball Assemblies

The tank ball must either fall directly into the center of the flush valve (somewhat like hitting a target dead center with each shot) or it must be nudged into position. If the tank ball does not fit the flush valve snugly, water will flow into the toilet, a noisy and water-wasting setup.

Any number of devices have been designed to overcome this difficulty. In some cases the tank ball replacement is precisely that—a ball—so no matter how it drops, it always presents the same round surface and closes the flush valve. In some cases, the lift rod is replaced by a flexible chain, so less restriction is put on the movement of the tank ball.

Fig. 4-60 illustrates one possible tank ball assembly. Known as a flapper, it

has no bracket or lift rods. Instead, the valve is closed by a flexible "stopper" mounted at the base of overflow tube. The drawing shows the two possible positions of the tank ball. As water flows out of the tank, it pulls on the flapper and the flapper falls into position right over the valve.

Fig. 4-60.

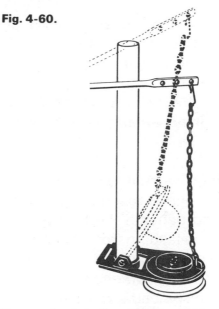

Flapper tank ball assembly. (Chicago Specialty)

Fig. 4-61.

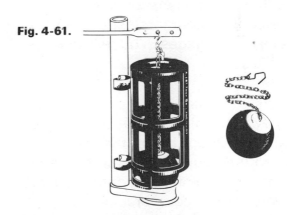

One type of tank ball assembly. (Chicago Specialty)

Another arrangement, and one that works quite well, is the assembly shown in Fig. 4-61. The unit consists of a plastic housing which clamps the overflow tube

UNION PUBLIC LIBRARY
TIVERTON, R. I.

in two places. The tank ball is a ball suspended by a chain. The housing guides the descent of the ball so that it must move into the correct position over the vale.

How to Replace the Flush Valve Seat

If the flush valve seat is worn or damaged, no type of ball assembly will keep water from flowing through the valve and into the toilet bowl. Close the water supply valve to the toilet and then flush. Mop any remaining water out of the tank with a sponge.

The flush valve seat is held in place by a very large coupler resembling a giant nut. It is located beneath the tank and is on the waste pipe leading from the tank. It is in an awkward spot, so you will need to get beneath the tank somehow to work it loose. You will also need a wrench whose jaws can open widely enough to accommodate the dimensions of the coupler. Turn the coupler counterclockwise until it completely disengages. You will then be able to lift out the seat.

Replacing what you have removed with a new assembly is just a matter of working in reverse. Insert the new seat and fasten the coupler beneath the tank. Put some pipe joint compound around the threads of the coupler.

With the tank ball in position, let some water—a small amount—flow into the tank. Look beneath the tank to make sure that you have no water seepage around the coupler. If you do see drops of water, wipe them away and look again. If

more water accumulates the coupler isn't tight enough.

Manually raise the lift wire. Note whether the tank ball seats easily and smoothly in the flush valve. As a further test, let more water flow into the tank until it is about one fourth full. Let the tank ball fall into its closing position. Examine the water in the toilet bowl. There should be no air bubbles coming into it, and you should not be able to see any water flowing into the bowl. As a final test, let the tank fill with water. The intake valve should shut off, no water should flow into the bowl, and the toilet should be completely quiet.

Of course, matters may not proceed as smoothly as you would like. They seldom do. You may need to move the bracket and guide for the tank ball around a bit. The lift wire may seem to stick. The tank ball may not drop properly. It is all a matter of adjusting the bracket and guide for the tank ball so that the tank ball drops unerringly into the flush valve and closes it securely.

It isn't always necessary to go to all this work. You can replace all the parts except the flush valve, since replacing the flush valve is the most difficult part. In that case, just remove the supply pipe, the bracket and guide for the tank ball, the tank ball, and its connecting rods. Dry the seat of the flush valve with a cloth. Take some household cleanser and clean out the valve seat thoroughly. Wash the valve seat to make sure no cleanser particles remain. Then connect the new assembly—the new supply pipe, tank ball, and bracket and guide for the tank ball. As before, you may need to do some experimenting to get the tank ball to drop precisely into position.

Toilet Is Noisy

Inadequate flushing can also be caused by the position of the float. During the flushing and refilling actions the float will move down and up. It must be free to do so, without scraping against the inside walls of the tank. If it does, there may be enough friction to keep the ball imprisoned at too low a level. The cure is to bend the copper support rod for the float so that the float is free of obstruction. Since the scraping is invariably against the back wall of the tank, bend the rod in a horizontal direction toward the front of the tank.

Tank Gurgles

Except when at work, a toilet tank should be quiet. If you hear a regular sort of gurling coming out of the tank, become suspicious. Lift the top of the tank and find out for yourself what is going on. Sometimes the water level in the tank is so high that water constantly runs down the overflow tube. The trouble is that the float is riding too high and as a result isn't activating the intake valve properly. Bend the copper rod holding the float in a downward direction. This means the water level will reach the bottom of the float that much sooner and will shut off the intake valve that much more quickly.

Bathroom Floor Around Toilet is Always Wet

Examine the underside of the toilet tank. Wipe it with a dry cloth. If you see drops of water collecting on the underneath flat portion of the tank, then you have a leak from the coupler. You may be able to seal the area around it with some kind of sealing compound, but the trouble is that the water will prevent the sealer from drying and making a permanent seal. The real cure is to remove the coupler. The coupler may have a larger washer, generally rubber. The washer may be inside the tank, or outside it, or both. Replace the washer or washers, and tighten the coupling. Naturally, you must do this work only after emptying the toilet tank and arranging to keep it empty while you are making the change.

Tank Sweats

If you live in a humid area or you have excessive humidity in the bathroom, the top of the toilet tank may sweat, that is, you will note a thin film of water or beads of water on it. The sides of the tank will also get wet, and in severe cases, drops or water may collect on the underside of the tank, ultimately falling to the floor and forming small puddles.

This water is due to condensation of the moisture in the air. The cold surface of the tank reduces the ability of the air around it to hold water vapor, and the vapor condenses on the tank. The various surfaces of the tank are cold due to the water inside the tank.

As a rule this should not happen. The water inside the tank should reach room temperature, and while the external surface of the tank may feel cool to the touch, it should also be at room temperature.

The sweating may be symptomatic of a small leak inside the tank. Water may be leaking out of the inlet valve and the excess may be flowing down the overflow tube. The amount may be small and so the action may be so quiet that you will not notice it. Yet this water current, small though it may be, helps keep the water temperature low enough to cool the tank surface.

The obvious cure is to remedy the leak. The tank ball and its connecting rod may not be exerting enough force on the shutoff valve. Bend the rod downward slightly so that the ball rides lower in the tank. If this does not cure the trouble, you may need to replace the shutoff valve assembly.

Another solution is to cover the inside of the tank with a liner, such as foam rubber padding. The purpose of the liner is to keep the water from making contact with the inner surface of the tank.

Fig. 4-62.
Tank cover set minimizes effects of sweating.

Finally, you can buy a toilet cover set (Fig. 4-62). This consists of a cloth material which fits over the top of the tank and also covers the remainder of the tank. The toilet cover set does not hinder lifting of the tank top. It insulates the tank from the air, and any condensation that does occur is absorbed by the cloth. In some homes a toilet cover set is used as decoration and not to get rid of the effects of condensation.

Water Keeps Running Inside the Toilet Tank

Water running constantly in the toilet tank not only can cause unsightly condensation but represents a serious waste of water. Further, since the overflow tank can take just so much water at any one time, the tank can overflow. Such an overflow can easily destroy a ceiling on a lower floor.

To test whether you need a new intake valve, lift the rod connected to the float. If you must exert considerable upward pressure to shut off the water flow, or if the water flow will not turn off no matter how hard you lift the rod, then you need an intake valve replacement.

As shown earlier, in Fig. 4-54, the water for the tank comes through a valve, flows up through a supply pipe inside the tank, and then through a valve into the tank. When this valve is closed, no more water passes into the tank. The valve is operated by the copper rod connected to the float. When the copper rod is lifted up, the valve is closed. In this position the tank ball if floating on the surface of the water somewhere near the upper part of the tank. When the toilet is flushed, the float moves down because of the flow of water out of the tank.

How to Replace the Intake Valve Assembly

To replace the valve means you must replace not only the valve but the entire assembly, consisting of the intake valve, the refill tube, and the supply pipe.

As a first step, close the cutoff valve. If the tank doesn't have a cutoff valve—not all of them do—then you must turn off the main water supply valve in your basement.

After you have turned off the water, flush the toilet. This will get rid of most of the water in the tank. The tank will not refill because you have shut off its water supply. Take a sponge, and mop up the remaining water in the tank. You can squeeze the wet sponge right into the toilet bowl.

You will see a bit of curved copper tubing coming out of the top of the intake valve. This tubing goes from the intake valve into the overflow tube. First, lift the tubing out of the overflow tube. The other end, the end that is fastened to the intake valve, is threaded. By turning it counterclockwise a few times, you can unscrew it from the intake valve.

Look beneath the tank and you will see that the filler tube is held in position by a large connector and that there is a substantial washer, made of rubber, right above the connector. Use a wrench and rotate the connector counterclockwise.

Keep turning it until you are able to remove the filler tube. After you get the filler tube out, you will see that it also has a large washer at the bottom.

Your replacement kit will consist of a new supply pipe at the top of which is mounted the new valve. You will also get a length of copper tubing which may be straight or curved. One end of the tubing is threaded and is designed to screw into an exit hole on the intake valve.

Mount one of the washers on the bottom end of the supply pipe before you put it in the tank. You will see that this washer has a V-shaped edge. Mount the washer so that the V fits in the cutout hole at the bottom of the tank. Now put the other washer on the water supply pipe leading from the cutoff valve. This washer also has a V shape. Mount it so that the V end fits into the hole at the bottom of the tank. However, as a first step, make sure there is a connector directly below the washer. You can either use the old connector or put in a new one.

The bottom end of the supply pipe is threaded. Rotate the connector so that it turns on the threads of the supply pipe. Once again, the best way to replace the supply pipe and its accompanying intake valve is to note carefully the steps you take in removing the old one.

After you have replaced the assembly, release the float and then turn the handle of the cutoff valve to allow some water—not too much—to flow into the tank. Look carefully to make sure no water drips from beneath the tank. If the area around the bottom end of the supply pipe looks dry, and remains that way, you can connect the copper tube—the tube that will connect the intake valve to the overflow tube—back into position. This copper tube is quite soft, and you should be able to bend it into place easily.

Turn the cutoff valve to let more water flow into the tank. Note the height of the water level. After the water has reached its correct level, flush the tank by depressing the trip lever. Repeat once or twice just to make sure everything is in working order.

There are variations of intake valve and supply pipe assemblies, so the best thing to do when you decide to make a replacement is to take the old unit with you when you visit your plumbing supply store.

How to Remove a Toilet Bowl

One serious toilet bowl problem is leakage around the bottom of the bowl. In some cases the leakage may have caused the title near the toilet bowl to have become so discolored that no amount of cleaning is of help. Finally, if the bowl has cracked, or if you want a more efficient type, replacement is necessary.

To remove the bowl, close the main water valve or the water valve near the tank. Flush the tank. You can remove the water from the bowl with the help of a rubber siphon. This consists of a rubber ball-like structure with two rubber pipes connected to it. Put one rubber pipe into a pail and the other into the toilet bowl. Squeezing the rubber ball will suction water out of the toilet bowl into the pail.

Disconnect all water pipes leading to the tank if the toilet is a one-piece unit. Disconnect the tank from the toilet bowl if the toilet is a two-piece unit.

Fig. 4-63.

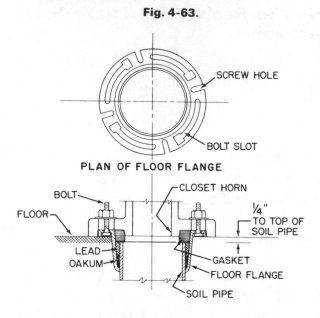

Views of connection of toilet to pipe.

Remove the seat and cover from the toilet bowl. Very carefully pry loose the bolt covers and remove the bolts holding the toilet bowl to the floor flange (Fig. 4-63). Rock the toilet bowl back and forth a bit to break the seal holding the toilet bowl to the floor. You should then be able to lift the bowl up and away.

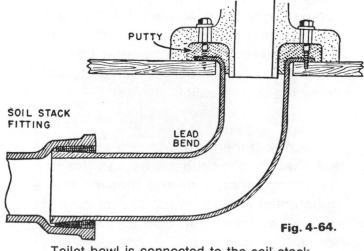

Fig. 4-64.

Toilet bowl is connected to the soil stack.

The opening of the pipe leading to the soil stack (Fig. 4-64) will now be exposed. Put a new wax seal around the toilet bowl base and press it into place. You can use either a wax seal, or your new toilet bowl may come equipped with a gasket.

Set the toilet bowl in position and use a level to make sure the bowl isn't tilted at an angle. Press down firmly and then install the bolts that hold it to the floor flange. Draw the bolts up snugly but not too tightly or the bowl may crack or break. Keep your carpenter's level on the bowl while working on the bolts. If the floor slopes, you may need to shim one side of the toilet bowl or the other to make sure it is level. Finally, install the toilet seat and cover.

Broken Toilet Seat

Rubber bumpers are used on the toilet seat cover so as to cushion the contact between the cover and seat. There are bumpers as well on the underside of the toilet seat to soften the contact between the seat and the toilet bowl. These bumpers corrode in time and also become extremely hard. You can buy bumper sets to replace them.

The toilet cover and seat, if cracked or split, can be dangerous. You can get a replacement and it is then just a matter of removing the existing hardware.

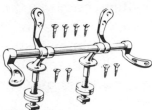

Fig. 4-65.
Hardware replacement kit for toilet bowl. (Chicago Specialty)

Sometimes the seat and cover are in good condition, but the associated hardware has become rusty and corroded. You can get a complete kit (Fig. 4-65) that will let you make a substitution. Toilet bowl hardware is sometimes difficult to remove since the screw threads often rust. If you cannot remove the hardware with a wrench, you may need to use a hacksaw.

Precautions against Pollution

It may seem strange that you must take precautions against water pollution in your own home, but pollution is a definite possibility. Consider that sewage gases do form in the pipelines that extend beyond the traps; that food and waste can accumulate in kitchen sinks, bathroom sinks, and toilet traps. Water that passes through these traps can become polluted.

Diseases such as typhoid fever and amoebic dysentery are carried by polluted water. What you may or may not do by yourself to the plumbing supply lines in your home is often governed by local plumbing laws. One of the purposes of these laws is to protect the health of the community. However, there are certain things you can do for your own protection and the protection of your family.

1. Make sure there are no leaks in drain pipes through which sewage or sewage gases can escape. If, as an example, your kitchen sink becomes clogged, and cleaning the sink trap and the pipe connecting the trap to the sink does not unclear the clog, then it is evident that the drain pipe leading down and away from the trap is stuffed. One way of clearing the

clog would be to drill a hole in the drain pipe and insert a snake, working it back and forth until the clog is removed. The drain pipe is generally in the basement and goes down at a slight slant toward the main drain pipe.

After you clear the drain pipe, you are left with a hole. It is through this hole that sewer gases can escape. Buy a plug, after measuring the diameter of the hole. If necessary, ream the hole larger to accommodate the plug. It is also a good idea to caulk around the plug just to make sure that you have a tight seal. Should you ever need to remove the plug again, you will be able to break the seal simply by turning the head of the plug with a wrench.

2. If, for some reason, you decide to alter the plumbing design in your home and connect one pipe to another, you must make sure that the water flow from one pipe cannot contaminate the water flow in the other.

3. Do not ever try to eliminate traps. A plumbing system will work without them, but they do prevent the backup of sewer gas into the home.

4. A toilet flushes, as explained earlier, because of the siphonage effect of the connecting drain pipe. Depending on how pipes are connected, and the amount of water in each, it is possible to get a siphonage effect from one pipe to another. Thus, it is possible to introduce waste from one pipe line to a pipe carrying usable water.

5. If you need to replace a length of

pipe in your home, possibly because the pipe has corroded beyond repair, do not buy secondhand pipe. Your local building code may not permit it. All piping in a new home must be new; all replacement piping for all homes, no matter how old, must also be new. The reason for this is that once a pipe has become polluted, it may never be free of it. Further, with secondhand piping you don't know the use to which it was put.

6. The number of shutoff valves in any home depends on the builder and the requirements of your local plumbing code. These requirements vary from one geographic location to another. Having a shutoff valve is like having insurance: You never know when you are going to have to depend on it. You should have shutoff valves for each cold and hot water sink faucet, and this includes kitchen sinks, bathroom sinks, and laundry or "mud room" sinks. You should have drain valves for water supply piping systems and for hot water storage tanks. And your hot water heater storage tank should have a pressure-relief valve to relieve pressure buildup in case of overheating.

7. Flushing a toilet removes waste, but a glistening appearance doesn't mean the interior of the bowl is hygenically clean. There are antiseptic preparations on the market that will help.

8. If you have someone in your home who is ill, call your local health department to learn if you may dispose of paper wastes in the toilet drain. Do not use the toilet for any products other than paper.

9. Let hot water flow through your

sinks—all of them—at least once a month not only to prevent clogs but to help clear waste caught in the traps.

10. Stall showers tend to accumulate mold in crevices, particularly along the base edges. Clean regularly with antiseptic solution. Also wash the stall shower floor with antiseptic solution. Cleaning with soap and water isn't enough.

Chapter V

You Can Plan a Bathroom

At one time bathrooms were strictly functional. But even before then the bathroom existed outdoors in the form of a privy, also known variously as a one holer or two holer, depending on the accommodations. The privy, a primitive type of toilet, was kept outdoors for a very practical reason. Since it wasn't equipped with a water supply, the ever present odor simply did not make it suitable as an in-house room.

Water has always been available, but not water under pressure. You must not only lead water to a pipe, you must force it through the pipe. It was when we achieved the machinery and realized it could be used for pumping water into our homes that the indoor toilet became a possibility.

The room was first called a toilet since that was its prime function. Later, as the need for cleanliness became a bit more obvious, a bathtub and sink were added. The sink was, and sometimes still is, called a lavatory. The word "toilet" was dropped in polite society and a toilet became a bathroom, a washroom, a WC (water closet), and a powder room. But however you may want to designate it, it is one of the more necessary rooms in a home. So much so that newer homes offer two or three bathrooms, or one or two bathrooms plus a half bathroom. A half bathroom contains a toilet and sink, but no tub or shower facilities.

The bathroom has also become a work of art. Originally using a bare wooden floor, later covered with linoleum, it is now tiled, covered with square or irregularly shaped mosaics, or is equipped with wall-to-wall carpeting or rugs. The walls, no longer bare white, now have special, and expensive, wallpapers specifically designed for bathroom use. The fixtures have become more ornate. Lighting has progressed from the single naked bulb operated by a pull string to soft, shielded, opulent ceiling and wall electric fixtures. A more recent addition has been the "medicine" cabinet, so-called since it was originally intended to hold just a few necessary medications, but which is now used as a catchall for everything but food.

At one time little, if any, attention was paid to the bathroom. A newly married couple would move into their new home, and it was not until they began raising a family that they first began to realize that more people meant more bathrooms or else more inconvenience. Adding another bathroom to a house, or even a half bathroom, is one of the prime reasons for remodeling.

Before You Start

Adding a sink, or a sink plus a toilet, or a complete bathroom, is a project, even for those who are determined on a do-it-yourself routine. Unless you have the tools, unless you know how your plumbing system works and have the aptitude, it is better to make use of the services of a plumber. But the more you know about plumbing, the more you will save, even if you do not so much as lift a section of pipe. If you can talk with your plumber in his "language," if you can show you know what a vent pipe is, or a fitting, or a fixture, if you can indicate your awareness of what the installation problems are, you should be able to negotiate a lower cost.

You should also shop, just as you would for any other high ticket item. You can get prices on all the fixtures, independently of the plumber. You can get some idea of how much piping will be needed and, with a little effort, learn just what such piping costs. Subtract all this from the bid and you will get some idea of the charge for labor.

When you come to an agreement on price, put it in writing. The agreement should include the total cost; a description, such as color and size of the various fixtures; and preferably the model numbers and name of the manufacturer. There should also be a statement that puts the liability for an unsatisfactory installation or damaged fixtures on the plumber. You should also get a warranty on fixtures and parts for a certain length of time, preferably at least a year. If the installation works well for a year, it will probably continue to do so after that.

Stay away from oral agreements. They aren't worth the air they take up. Most of us, including plumbers, remember only what we want to remember. Someone who installs your new bathroom, knowing you have his written statement and signature, may feel you have the means for compelling him to assume his responsibility fully—as indeed you have.

Your new installation must comply with your local plumbing codes and regulations. In some areas, the local government will insist on making an inspection of the finished job. Good. Plumbing inspectors have considerable experience and will have the expertise to point out flaws which should be corrected.

And in some areas you must get permission to connect your new bathroom to existing sewer lines. A sewer can carry just so much waste, so if the sewer in your area is at or near its maximum capacity, you may be denied a building permit. But whatever you do, don't start building a bathroom and then decide to apply for a permit later. If you do, you may have a bathroom that goes nowhere. No provision for fresh water in; no provision for waste going out. Perhaps a beautiful room; certainly a useless one.

Some Possible Bathroom Arrangements

You can locate your new bathroom in various ways. If you have a room you are not using, you might consider putting it to work. Or, you may take some space away from an existing room, partition it, and use the sectioned-off area as the bathroom. Finally, you may make more efficient use of the space you have, possibly not to include a full bathroom, but a half bathroom perhaps, or possibly just an additional sink.

Fig. 5-1 shows a number of possible bathroom arrangements. Before you even begin to plan the bathroom, you must decide whether it will have limited or liberal use. A limited arrangement is one in which the bathroom is essentially designed for one person alone or one person helping another, such as a child or an invalid.

All of the bathrooms in Fig. 5-1 have three fixtures: a toilet, a sink, and a bathtub. The view given in the drawings is as though we were located above the bathroom, looking down on it.

In considering a bathroom, remember you must have space in which to move around. Suggested room dimensions appear on each drawing. Regard them as minimum. If you can increase them, so much the better.

The bathrooms are divided into two categories: family bathrooms and one-person minimum bathrooms. If you have a space problems, the one-person minimum bathroom may be for you, even though it doesn't have the spaciousness of the others. Better a limited bathroom than none. However, do not install a minimum bathroom just with the idea of economizing. All of the bathrooms contain three fixtures, and that will represent a large part of what you will be paying for. Bear in mind the fact that the labor cost will be about the same in all cases.

For the minimum space arrangements, the doors can be 2 feet, 4 inches wide and are 2 feet, 8 inches wide for family bathrooms. The dimensions given for the fixtures are average. You may find some that are smaller, but with the room dimensions given in Fig. 5-1 you should consider the fixture dimensions as maximum. The location of the fixtures may be determined by the positioning of the pipes in the walls. While an experienced plumber would probably know just where the pipes are, a house plan (if you have one or can get one) would be extremely helpful in planning the connecting pipe layout.

The upper six drawings assume plumbing pipes in one wall. This wall would be the one opposite the door. If you will examine these six drawings, you will see that all the fixtures are essentially in the same place and are positioned to get the shortest run of piping between them and the pipes in the wall right behind them. The basic differences among the six drawings is either in the positioning of the door and the door dimensions or in the length and width dimensions of the proposed bathroom.

If you have plumbing pipes in two walls, you can allow yourself a little more variety in the placement of the fixtures as

Fig. 5-1.

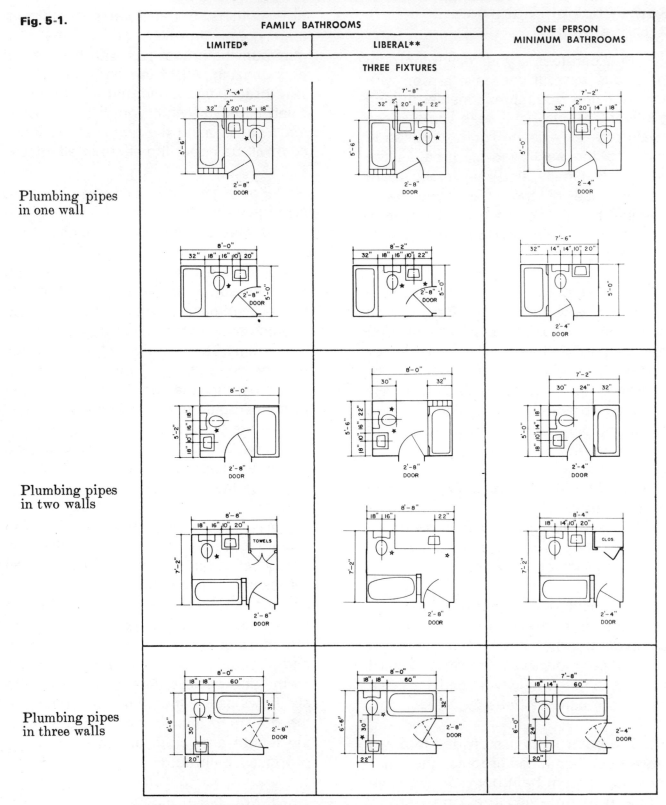

*Space provided at one location for adult to stand to help young child or elderly person.
**Space provided at two locations for adult to stand to help young child or elderly person.

Some possible bathroom arrangements. This is a
view looking down on the bathroom.

shown in the center group of six drawings. Note also that most of these rooms are a bit larger than the first six.

If you have available piping in three walls you can have the greatest flexibility in the arrangement of the fixtures, as shown in the lower three drawings. This doesn't mean that you must follow the positioning illustrated here, but rather that you can use almost any arrangement you want. A further advantage in the lower three drawings is that you can have the door opening from left or right, as indicated.

Bathroom Planning Techniques

One method of planning your bathroom, is to draw an outline of the exact size of the room. Draw it in proportion, using a scale of 1 inch equals 1 foot. A bathroom measuring 6 feet by 8 feet would then appear as a rectangle 6 inches by 8 inches.

Now draw your fixtures to the same scale and cut them out of the paper on which you have drawn them. Mark them so you know which is which and then move them around inside the drawing of the outline of the bathroom. On the bathroom outline drawing also indicate the position of the door. If the bathroom is to have a window, include that.

The fact that you have pipes in one wall doesn't necessarily restrict you to the upper six drawings shown in Feb. 5-1. However, you should understand that the closer the fixtures are to existing piping, the less the installation will cost. Thus, the toilet is usually connected practically directly to the soil stack. This means that the location of the soil stack will just about decide the location of the toilet. The bathtub and sink (lavatory) don't have such restrictions. This does not mean, however, that you cannot put the toilet just where you want. You should know there may be practical difficulties involved and that your installation cost may go up. If you can afford the extra piping and the labor involved, your plumber will soon be able to tell you if your proposed fixture positioning plan is practical.

Fig 5-2 shows plan drawings you can trace or redraw in doing your bathroom planning. By marking your bathroom floor plan with numbers you will be able to get some idea of the amount of "walking around" room you will have after the fixtures are in place. If you do decide to copy the drawings in Fig. 5-2, be sure to note that you have several groups. These in the lower right are at a scale of ¼ inch per foot; those at the lower left are a scale of ½ inch per foot.

Still more possible bathroom arrangements using three fixtures are shown in the upper six drawings in Fig. 5-3. Since the plumbing pipes are in three walls there is a much greater number of possible variations.

Compartmented Bathrooms

For a bathroom to be worthy of the name you must have a minimum of three fixtures: a sink, a toilet, and a tub. The tub may have provision for a shower head, but it is still a tub. The same room minus the tub, no matter how large the room might be, would properly be regarded as a half bathroom.

BATHROOM CUTOUTS

Fig. 5-2.

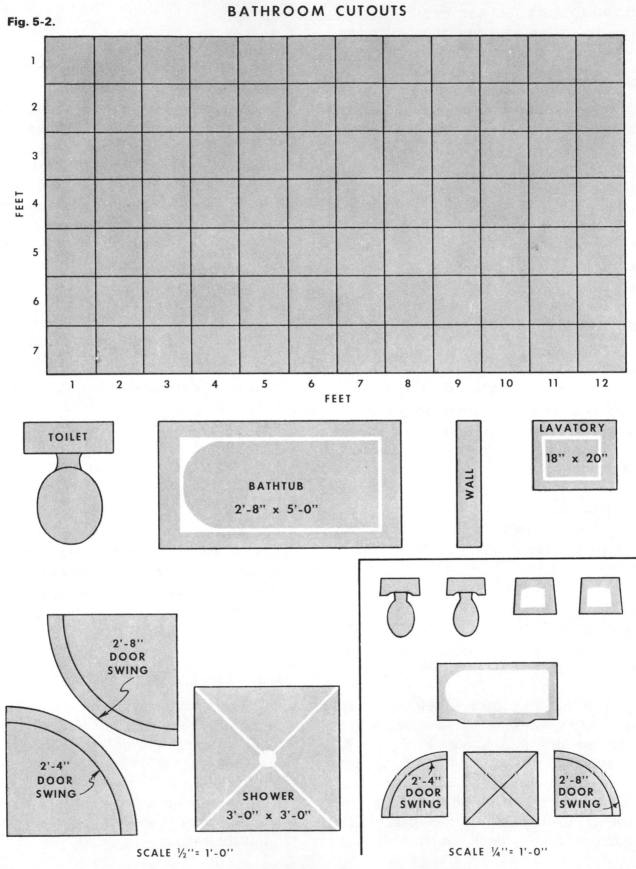

Cutouts you can use for planning a bathroom.

Fig. 5-3.

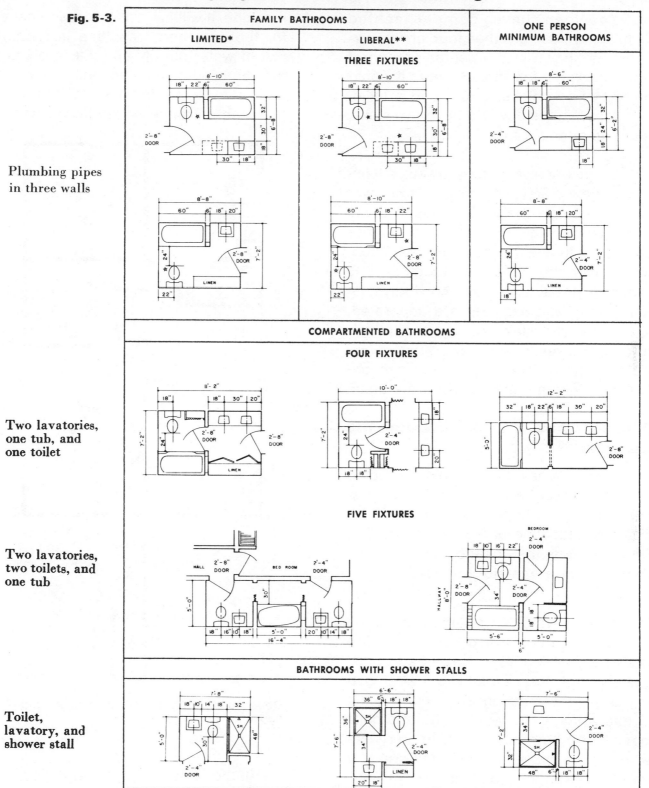

Plumbing pipes in three walls

Two lavatories, one tub, and one toilet

Two lavatories, two toilets, and one tub

Toilet, lavatory, and shower stall

Space provided at one location for adult to stand to help young child or elderly person.
**Space provided at two locations for adult to stand to help young child or elderly person.*

Additional bathroom arrangements.

You can have compartmented bathrooms having either four or five fixtures, as shown in the center portion of Fig. 5-3. With a four fixture setup it would consist of two sinks, a tub, and a toilet. With five fixtures it would have two sinks, two toilets, and a tub.

Some bathrooms have a sink, a toilet and a shower stall, as shown in the lower three drawings in Fig. 5-3. Usually, with bathrooms of this type there is another bathroom in the house that has a tub. Where two sinks are used together, it is common practice to have not individual sinks, that is, sinks that are separated, but rather two sinks having a common surface. However, in the drawings showing the use of five fixtures you can see that the sinks are indeed separate units.

Where Should You Locate the Bathroom?

If you are having a home constructed for you, it is quite likely that the builder will show you a floor plan, which will indicate the location of the bathroom. Fig. 5-4 indicates the location of a single bathroom in a one-story house.

There are several advantages to having the bathroom positioned here. It is close to and convenient to all three bedrooms. Since people use a bathroom after getting up in the morning and before going to bed at night, its location here is quite logical. The bathroom can also be reached from the kitchen without any need for walking through the living room. Still another advantage is that the bathroom is placed next to the utility room. Since this room contains a clothes washing machine, it will have all the piping needed for the bathroom, resulting in a shorter run of water supply and waste pipes for the bathroom connections. Since the bathroom is off the hall, it isn't visible from the entrance or the living room.

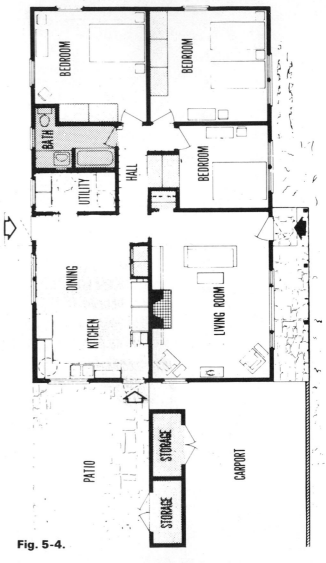

Fig. 5-4.

Good location for a bathroom in a single-story house

If the house is a split-level type or if it has two full floors, the bathroom is usually located on the second floor since this is also where you will have the bedrooms. In this case there is usually a half bathroom downstairs for convenience.

Fig. 5-5.

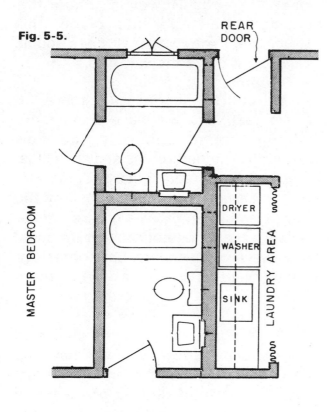

Master bathroom, main bathroom, and laundry area—an arrangement for economical piping.

Fig. 5-5 shows one possible placement for a bathroom adjacent to a master bedroom. This drawing shows two bathrooms, one with a hall entrance and the other with an entrance from the master bedroom. Both bathrooms are near the laundry area, so once again the piping arrangement can be short.

The master bathroom also has an entrance that enables it to be reached from the rear door. A double-door bathroom can be a convenience, but it can also be a nuisance. It means locking two doors to ensure privacy. It also means that bathroom wall space that could be used for shelving or some other purpose is no longer available.

The Bedroom Lavatory

If the house has a single bathroom, it is certainly desirable to install an extra sink somewhere nearby. Sometimes an extra lavatory can be put in a bedroom (Fig. 5-6). If possible, select a bedroom that immediately adjoins the existing bathroom, for in this way you may be able to connect directly into the bathroom piping.

Fig. 5-6.

You can install a convenience sink in a bedroom.

Covering the added lavatory with louvered swinging doors will hide the sink and will help maintain the decor of the bedroom. If the sink is enclosed by a cabinet, some of the area beanth the sink, often not utilized, can be used for holding towels or bathroom accessories. And even though the bedroom has its own lighting arrangement, it would be a good idea to have supplementary lighting installed above the sink. Adjacent to the sink there should be an electric outlet for the use of appliances such as electric shavers; plus a towel rack; and a mirror or medicine cabinet put above the sink. The area directly above the sink should be tiled or else the sink should be the type that has a splashback to protect the walls from water. Don't forget the convenience of having a toothbrush holder and a holder for a glass.

The Small Square Bathroom

Fig. 5-7.

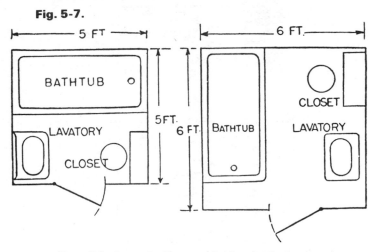

Possible layouts for small size bathrooms.

The smallest bathroom shown earlier (Fig. 5-1) occupies an area of about 35 square feet. But if you have a serious space problem, and just about all of us have, it is possible to get a bathroom into an area of only 25 square feet, as illustrated in Fig. 5-7. This is just about the minimum for a full bathroom containing three fixtures—a tub, sink, and toilet. If you decide to have such a "mini" put into your home, you will wonder, as the studs

and the rest of the wood framework go up, whether you aren't really building a closet instead. However, once the bathroom walls go into place, the bathroom will look larger. It does sound strange, but that's the way it is.

Of course, if you can spare 36 square feet, you will have a bit more walking-around space in the new bathroom. The bathrooms shown in Figs. 5-1 and 5-3 are rectangular, a somewhat more pleasing shape than that of the bathrooms in Fig. 5-7, which are square but while they may not present the most attractive layout, square bathrooms are an improvement over no extra bathroom at all.

If your available space happens to be long and narrow, you will have no great flexibility in positioning the fixtures. If you put all the fixtures along a single wall, the effect will be to make the room look even longer. Since the sink can be positioned almost anywhere, you might try putting it up against one of the shorter walls, although this is not indicated in any of the drawings in Fig. 5-8.

Drawing A shows two doors. Again, this can be an advantage and a nuisance. It will, however, make the single long wall on the right side of the room seem shorter.

Drawing B shows one possible rearrangement of the fixtures with a single door near the center of the long wall facing the fixtures.

The arrangement in drawing C is possibly the least desirable. The right wall is completely unbroken, making the room look longer than it is. Further, because of the narrowness of the room, it may not be practical to "break up" that wall with shelving.

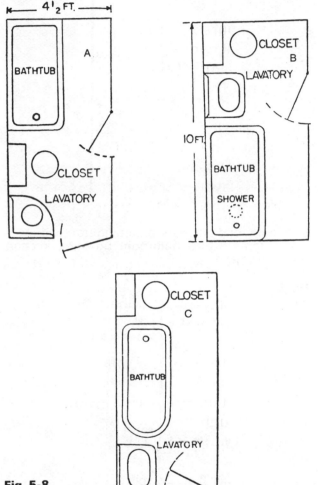

Fig. 5-8.

Some possible arrangements for a long, narrow bathroom.

The Bathroom for a Single-Story House

One of the advantages of a single-story home is that the simplest plumbing is usually adequate. The reason for this is that the soil stack can be erected near the bathroom, so very short pipes can be used from the bathroom to the stack.

Shorter pipe lines mean not only greater economy but less chance of trouble. And if trouble does come in the form of a clogged or leaking pipe, the repairs are easier to make. Further, the soil stack and its accompanying vent need not be so long. Venting for the single-story home is often accomplished by a single roof vent. But if the house is to be consistent with the modern trend toward more bathrooms, additional venting is needed.

Fig. 5-9.

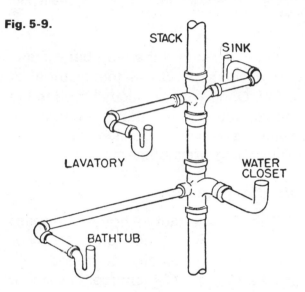

Bathroom fixture arrangement for single-story home.

Fig. 5-9 shows the plumbing needed for a one-story home. Like the plumbing setup shown in Fig. 5-3, this arrangement also uses four fixtures. The only difference is that the fixtures are positioned somewhat differently around the soil stack. The final location of the fixtures is sometimes determined by the door and bathroom window. The window isn't positioned above the bathrub, for example, for that would make it difficult to open or close the window or to clean it. The fixtures must also not interfere with the free opening and closing of the door.

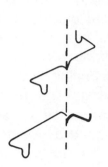

Fig. 5-10.

Plumber's symbolic drawing of the bathroom shown in Fig. 5-9.

Fig. 5-10 shows the plumber's drawing that corresponds to the pictorial of Fig. 5-9. Once you get accustomed to the symbols, you will find that the plumber's drawings give you a quicker concept of the plumbing arrangement.

Two-Story Layouts

The single-story home supplies maximum plumbing economy; the two-story house is usually equipped with more bathrooms. Of course, the more plumbing fixtures you have, the more piping you need, the costlier the installation, and the greater the possibility of future plumbing repairs.

Fig. 5-11 is a plumber's drawing with the bathroom on an upper floor and a kitchen sink on a lower. Once again, note that the water closet, or toilet, is the fixture closest to the oil stack. The bathtub and the upstairs bathroom lavatory, or sink, connect through a common, horizontal waste line to the stack. While the upper portion of the soil stack is used for venting, there are additional vents, as shown by the dashed lines. A large vent comes up from the downstairs sink, and

the upstairs sink also has its own vent. The entire venting system connects to a single roof vent, which is a continuation of the soil stack.

Fig. 5-11.

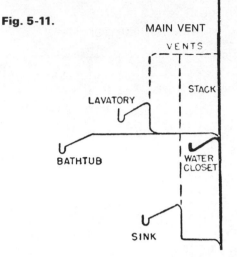

Bathroom and kitchen plumbing for two-story home: three-fixture bathroom upstairs, kitchen sink downstairs.

Fig. 5-12.

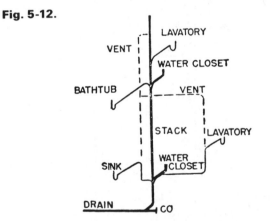

Bathroom upstairs, half bathroom downstairs.

In the next illustration, Fig. 5-12, we have a somewhat more elaborate arrangement for a two-story house. Upstairs we have a bathroom with a (lavatory,) a water closet, and a bathtub. Downstairs we have a half bathroom with a lavatory and water closet. Shown at the left is a sink for the kitchen. We have more fixtures now, so, as might be expected, we have a more elaborate venting system. The kitchen sink has its own vent pipe, with the downstairs bathroom sink also connecting to it. Both toilets, upstairs and down, vent through the soil stack. Also, both toilets are closer to the soil stack than are any of the other fixtures.

Apartment bathrooms

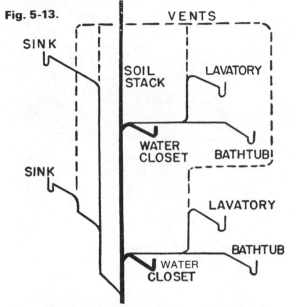

Fig. 5-13.

VENTS

SINK

SOIL STACK

LAVATORY

WATER CLOSET

BATHTUB

SINK

LAVATORY

BATHTUB

WATER CLOSET

Possible arrangement for three-fixture bathrooms in an apartment building.

Bathroom designs for apartment buildings (Fig. 5-13) follow the same plumbing principles as those used for private homes. The soil stack will have a larger diameter, but generally a bathroom on one floor will be located directly beneath the bathroom on the floor above. The physical arrangement of the fixtures in the bathrooms on all the floors will usually be the same, so the piping from the fixtures to the soil stack is repeated, floor after floor.

However, no apartment building depends on the soil stack alone for ven-

ting. The sinks and toilets have individual vent pipes which go from floor to floor. Kitchen sinks also have their own venting system. The toilets vent through the soil stack. In an apartment building you can expect to have a number of roof vent pipes. And the roof vents are generally much higher than those in private homes, where they may be just a foot or so above the roof level.

Duplex Drainage

A duplex is a two-family home with a common wall separating the living quarters for the families. Having one wall in common means lower construction cost. And since one wall is completely enclosed, the homes aren't so exposed to winter winds and therefore are less expensive to heat. There are also other economies, since the two homes can share a common soil stack, contained in the common wall.

Making Changes

Adding a sink, putting in new bathroom fixtures, installing a half or full bathroom are all easy to do if you have a private home, enough room, and a budget that's elastic enough to take care of the expense. In an apartment house the living quarters are someone else's property. A lease limits the changes that may be made by a tenant, and they usually exclude anything as drastic as revamping a bathroom or making an installation. This isn't pure arbitrariness on the part of the owner. Making changes can affect the plumbing system throughout the building. Further, just like the owner of a private home, the owner of an apartment house must adhere to the building and plumbing codes of his area.

Precautions In Piping Installations

Pipes aren't just put into a wall. They must be supported and cannot be allowed to sag. If you will examine the upper part of Fig. 5-14, showing the bathtub waste line, you will see that the joists, or wood, supports for the floor, are notched. Notching is required to keep the pipe from interfering with the floor. In addition, notches or holes are cut or drilled through the flooring to accommodate vertical piping. A hole is preferable to a notch, provided it can be made near the center of the board.

Fig. 5-14.

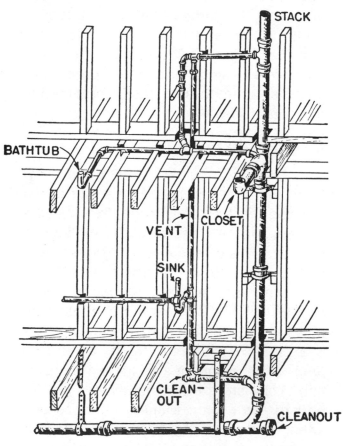

Vertical and horizontal joists must be notched or drilled to accommodate the pipe.

When a joist is notched it is weakened in proportion to the deapth of the cut. If you have a joist that measures 2 x 8 and notch it 4 inches, you have reduced the strength of that joist to the equivalent of a 2 x 4 piece. In other words, you have cut the strength of the joist by 50 percent. If, however, you cut only a 2-inch notch, the joist would have the strength of a 2 x 6.

Fig. 5-15.

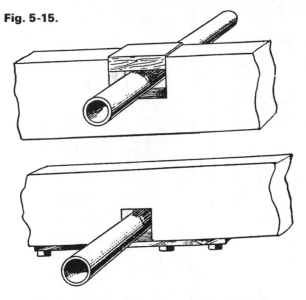

Methods of reinforcing notched joists.

The farther from its end supports a joist is notched, the weaker the joist becomes, But while it is necessary to notch joists, these structural members of the house can be reinforced. The notch in the upper drawing in Fig. 5-15 is reinforced by jamming a wood block into the open space above the pipe. Not only does this strengthen the joist, but the pressure of the block helps keep the pipe firmly in position. In the lower drawing the notch is strengthed by a metal plate or strap held in place by screws. Top notching, as exemplified by the upper drawing, is preferable to bottom notching.

What You Should Know about Plumbing Fixtures

A plumbing fixture is any container or receptable which receives fresh water, hot or cold, and which is capable of discharging that water, when used, into the drainage system. In some fixtures, as in a sink, the water is drained away by gravity. In a toilet it is siphoned out.

All fixtures have a smooth surface especially designed not to absorb water. The surface is deliberately made smooth to eliminate places where waste might lodge and accumulate. The surface shape and finish encourage cleanliness.

Fixtures are generally made of enameled cast iron, enameled pressed steel, or, for kitchen sinks, stainless steel. Some fixtures are also made of nickel silver, Monel Metal, or copper. You may come across some older sinks made of slate or soapstone, and sometimes even concrete is used to make sinks.

More recently, some fixtures have been made of fiberglass. The gloss and color of the coating appear similar to those of enameled or china finishes, and the coating resists ordinary household chemicals.

Toilets are always made of vitreous china, which is sometimes used for bathroom sinks as well. A man-made material, a sort of synthetic marble, is also used for bathroom sinks. You may sometimes see a sink made of real marble, although probably it is an antique

Bathtubs

Built-in tubs made of cast iron or enameled steel aren't completely self-supporting. You must secure them to the adjacent studs by 2 x 4 inch supports or by means of special hangers. If, after the tube is installed, a crack or larger opening appears between the tub and the wall, you will have a region where dirt can and will accumulate.

Free-Standing Bathtubs

Fig. 5-16.

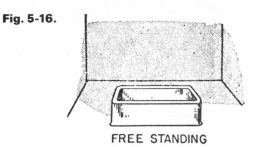

FREE STANDING

Free-standing tub is positioned away from all bathroom walls.

If, for some reason, it is impossible to anchor the tub to the studs, you can use the free-standing type shown in Fig. 5-16. The free-standing tub is built only onto the floor and is free of the wall on all sides. However, unless the free-standing tub is well away from the wall, you will have an area between the tub and the wall that will be difficult to clean. In some deluxe installations, the tub is positioned in the center of the bathroom and is made its dramatic centerpiece. A tub of this kind may be mounted on a concrete base and raised above the bathroom floor, with steps leading to the tub. A setup of this kind requires a bathroom of ample size and possibly the services of an interior decorator in addition to those of a plumber.

Fiberglass Bathtubs

Bathtubs have always been very

heavy. Cast iron and steel bathtubs are among the heaviest plumbing fixtures you can have in your home. However, you can now get tubs made of fiberglass. These are much lighter in construction and can be installed where the wood framework of the house will not support the usual tub. They are excellent for use in remodeling situations where the area assigned for the new bathroom does not have a wood framework intended for that purpose. The tub shown in Fig. 5-17 also has a shower arrangment.

Fig. 5-17.

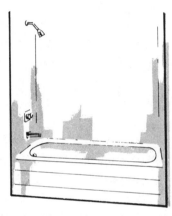

Fiberglass tub is lightweight and easier to install than heavier cast iron or steel tubs.

Recess and Corner Bathtubs

Fig. 5-18.

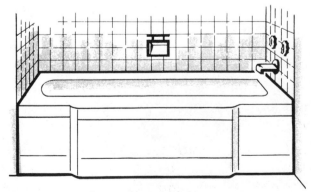

A

Recess tub.

B

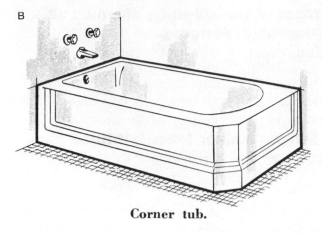

Corner tub.

Recess tub fits against three walls; corner tub against two.

A recess tub (Fig. 5-18A) is designed to fit between three walls, while a corner tub (Fig. 5-18B) is used in a corner between two walls. Such tubs come in sizes that start at 4 feet, but you can get them in 4½-, 5-, or 5½-foot lengths. The most common is the 5-foot length. The tub can have either a straight front or a wide rim. If the tub has a wide rim, as in drawing A, the overall width will be about 32 or 33 inches. A straight front tub is 30 or 31 inches wide.

A three-wall recess arrangement is ideal for use with a wall-attached shower. The three walls can be covered with tile, and a single, straight shower curtain pole plus a curtain will keep the water from the shower away from the bathroom floor. Just remember to keep the lower end of the curtain inside the tub.

Its suitability for use with a shower gives the recess tub an advantage over the corner tub. Because the corner tub is against only two walls, it requires a shower curtain rod that will curve to conform to the shape of the tub. While such rods are available, they are more difficult to install. They need to be supported from the ceiling. Further, the support, even if it is a single rod, interferes with the free movement of the shower curtain.

Single Wall or Pier Bathtubs

The pier tub, shown in Fig. 5-19, fits against one wall only. However, like other tubs, it must be anchored to the house frame. If you plan to install a pier tub, make sure there is ample room on both ends of the tub to permit cleaning. A pier tub arrangement is used when you want either a sink or a towel closet adjacent to the tub, or when the floor area does not permit a recess or corner installation.

Of the three arrangements—recess, corner, and pier—the pier is the poorest if the plan to include a shower. A shower isn't at all practical with the pier.

Fig. 5-19.

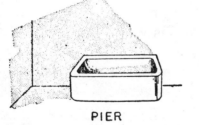

PIER

Pier tub fits against single wall only.

Corner Square Bathtubs

In corner square tubs (Fig.(Fig. 5-20) the interior, or bathing, portion is at an angle to the outer walls of the tub. Corner square tubs are suitable for recess or corner installation. Measuring about 4 feet by 3½ or 4 feet, they take up about the same bathroom floor area as the recess and corner tubs described

previously. They take up less wall room than those tubs but extend more into the bathroom area. You can use a tub of this kind where wall space is at a premium. They are also selected for decorative purposes since they look different from most bathtubs.

Corner square tubs have a built-in seat, and some have two such seats. While you can sit on the edge of a rectangular recess or corner tub, the width of the seat isn't really enough for comfort. The seat on a corner square tub is much larger.

A corner square tub is heavier than the rectangular recess or corner tubs, so before you invest in one, make sure that the framework to which it will be fastened can help support the weight. Sometimes, when a heavy tub is to be installed, the framework in the walls adjacent to the tub must be reinforced.

Fig. 5-20.

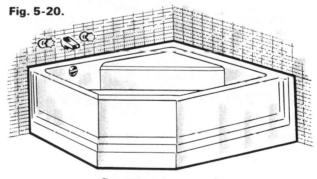

Corner square tub.

Corner square tub can have one or two seats.

Receptor Bathtubs

The receptor tub, illustrated in Fig. 5-21, is about 36 to 38 inches long, 39 to 42 inches wide, and 1 foot high. It is well suited for use as a wall-type shower installation. Because it isn't so high above the bathroom floor as other tubs, it is excellent for bathing children or adults who need assistance. The receptor tub also has a seat in one corner, which make it ideal for use in bathing feet for medical purposes.

Fig. 5-21.

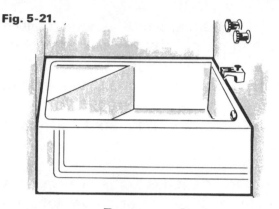

Receptor tub.

Receptor tub is closer to bathroom floor and so is well suited for bathing children.

Bathroom Sinks (Lavatories)

At one time tubs and sinks for bathrooms were always in white. The walls were also painted white, and the floor used white tiles. The whole effect was quite antiseptic and a constant reminder about the need for cleanliness. That wasn't such a bad idea, even if the overall decorative effect was somewhat depressing.

Today bathrooms are available in a variety of colors, from solids to pastels to murals. But whatever your color scheme, the three fixtures—the tub, sink, and toilet—should either have the same color or should be color coordinated.

Bathroom sinks can be wall-hung types or set in or on cabinets. The advan-

tage of the cabinet is that it comes equipped with doors which open onto shelves. The shelves provide additional storage space, always so urgently needed in nearly every home. The cabinets also conceal the trap and its associated drain pipes, and because the area around the sink is enclosed, there is less opportunity for dirt to collect under the sink. All in all, cabinet arrangements are desirable. They are also more expensive than sinks without cabinets.

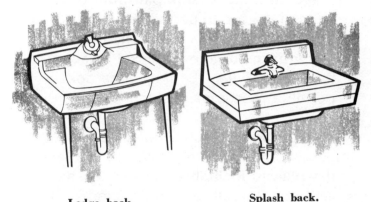

| Ledge back. | Splash back. |

| Shelf back. |

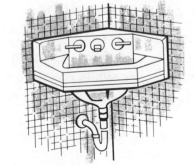

Slab with china leg.

Fig. 5-22.

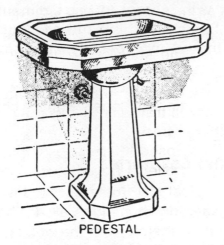

PEDESTAL

Various types of exposed bathroom sinks.

Fig. 5-22 illustrates a number of different styles of lavatories without cabinets. These are by no means the only ones available, but they will give you some idea of styles.

Pedestal Lavatories

A pedestal lavatory is built around a china base that successfully hides most of the plumbing. It is a rather old-fashioned style but is not unattractive. However, its structure makes it difficult to get near the trap, plumbing repairs are awkward. The pedestal is made of the same material as the sink and is easily cleaned with a damp cloth.

All of the sinks shown in Fig. 5-22 (except the pedestal type) are wall-hung, being supported by special brackets or hangers, sometimes supplemented by one or two legs. Some sinks, made of china, are literally works of art. They may be equipped with elaborately designed faucets in gold and highly ornamented. Some are made of simulated marble. But when you do get a sink, get cleaning instructions. Some cleaning agents are

abrasive and it doesn't take too long for the sink coating to wear away, exposing the rough metal below. Porcelain touch-up kits are available, but it is often difficult to match the sink color, so what you will get will be a very obvious patch. And this applies to white sinks as well as to those in color. An occasional wax polish on chrome-finished faucets will help protect them against water.

When buying a sink, remember that water will accumulate around the various upper surfaces surrounding the basin. Ideally, these surfaces should have a slight downward slant toward the basin so that excess water will have a chance to drain away.

Ledge Back Lavatories

These come in a width of 19 inches and 17 inches front to back and are also available with a 24-inch width and 20 inch front-to-back dimension. They are supported against the wall and have two legs, which are at the front end of the sink. Sometimes these legs are chrome plated, and while they may glisten in the showroom, they do require regular polishing. And if the chrome wears away, the base metal beneath will be exposed and will look more like a dirt mark than anything else. The trap beneath the sink is readily accessible for repairs.

Splash Back Lavatories

The splash back sink is available in three sizes: 19 inches wide and 17 inches deep, front to back; or 20 inches wide and 18 inches deep; or 24 inches wide and 20 inches deep. What you get in the way of a sink will sometimes be determined by how much wall space you can allow. A bigger sink may seem better; a sink with smaller dimensions may not make the bathroom look so crowded.

The splash back is so called because it has an extension at the back of the sink that prevents water from reaching the back wall. Unlike the ledge back, it also has a surface area large enough to hold a soap dish and a glass.

Slab Lavatories

This is a highly functional type of sink. It doesn't look very attractive in Fig. 5-22 because it isn't. It has a flat surface area surrounding the basin itself for soap dish or glass. The sink is supported by a single china leg coming down from the center. Since the leg is right in front of the trap, it makes removing the trap a nuisance. The solitary leg interferes with the free movement of a wrench necessary for removing the trap. The ideal trap to use with this kind of sink is the one that has a bottom plug. The china leg, because of its finish, is easier to keep clean than the chromium-plated legs of the ledge back.

Shelf Back Lavatories

Like slab sinks, you'll be able to get shelf back sinks in three commonly available sizes: 19 inches wide by 17 inches deep, front to back; 20 inches wide by 14 inches deep; and 22 inches wide by either 18 or 19 inches deep.

If you are looking for a narrow sink, that is, one that doesn't extend too far away from the wall, consider the shelf back with a front-to-back dimension of only 14 inches. This is three to four inches less than other types of bathroom sinks.

The shelf back is supported by two front-positioned legs. Either china or metal.

Corner Lavatories

Typical size for a corner lavatory is 17 inches on both sides along the walls, with an extension from the wall of 19½ inches. The sink is supported by the wall on two sides and doesn't normally come equipped with legs. This sink, as do most of the others illustrated in Fig. 5-22, has exposed piping.

The height of the sinks above the bathroom floor should be comfortable for you and the other members of your family. There is no fixed height, but the average is about 33 to 36 inches from the floor. For junior members of the family who can't quite reach, a step stool having rubber feet is a convenience. It also gets them accustomed to using the sink.

Cabinet Sinks

Sink cabinets for bathrooms are generally made of particle board or wood, and plastic in some cases. Some are straightforward cabinets, others have elaborate scrollwork. You can get them in a variety of colors. Obviously, the color should match that of the sink it will enclose or at least be in harmony with it. Lavatories may be set in or on the cabinets.

Three types of cabinet sinks are shown in Fig. 5-23. Drawing A shows a lavatory with a rolled rim basin. The purpose of the rolled rim, in the front part of the sink, is to keep water that has accumulated on the top of the sink away from you. Sometimes, when using a bathroom sink, you must stand very close to it. Getting water from the sink top all over your clothing can be a nuisance.

Fig. 5-23.

A

Lavatory-counter top with rolled rim basin.

B

Lavatory-counter top set on cabinet.

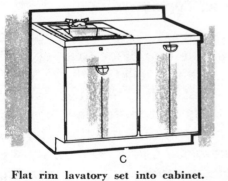

C

Flat rim lavatory set into cabinet.

Sinks with cabinet enclosures.

Rolled rim sinks are available in these sizes: 20 inches wide and 18 inches front-to-back; 21 inches wide and 17 inches front to back; and 27 inches wide and 20 inches front to back.

Drawing B shows a lavatory counter top set on an enclosing cabinet, while the drawing C is that of a flat rim lavatory set into the cabinet. The sink can be positioned in the top center of the cabinet, or off to one side. One of the great advantages of a sink cabinet, in addition to those mentioned earlier, is the greater surface area supplied by these cabinets. There is ample room for a glass, bottles of medication, or a place on which to rest a razor or hairbrush. Not all cabinet type sinks are square; some are round and others have rectangularly curved shapes.

Lavatory cabinets are usually available in two heights—31 inches and 34 inches. The bottom part of the cabinet is recessed, an advantage in letting you stand closer to the sink. These cabinets can be made higher by increasing the height of the toe space.

Toilets

Toilets are classified in several ways. One is by the way they work, that is, by their type of water action. The three most common are the siphon jet, reverse trap, and the washdown.

Siphon Jet Toilet Bowl

While this is the most costly type, it is also the quietest. The trapway is located at the rear of the bowl. The water surface is extra large for maximum cleanliness. And because the water seal is deep, the toilet supplies maximum protection from water gases generated in the drain pipe and soil stack. Fig. 5-24 is a cross section view of a siphon jet toilet bowl.

Fig. 5-24.

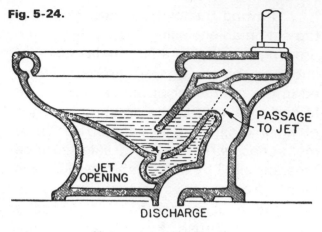

Siphon jet toilet bowl.

Reverse Trap Toilet Bowl

Fig. 5-25.

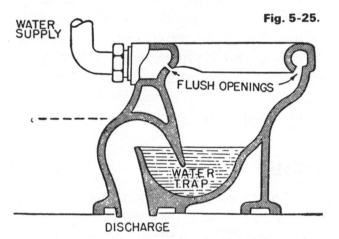

Siphon toilet bowl with reverse trap.

The reverse trap toilet bowl supplies the same water action as a siphon jet, but the trapway is smaller. Also, there is less water surface and the water seal is not so deep. Fig. 5-25 is an illustration of a siphon closet bowl with a reverse trap.

Washdown Toilet Bowl

The washdown type (Fig. 5-26) is the least costly of the three types, However, it also is the noisiest type, its water surface

is the smallest, and its water seal is the least deep.

Fig. 5-26.

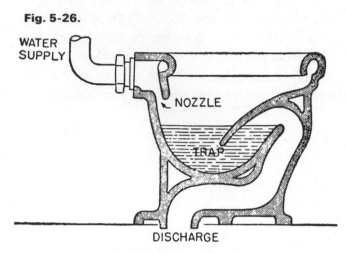

Washdown toilet bowl.

All three bowls work by siphoning action. Toilet bowls make some sound because you have the movement of a large amount of water. When you buy a toilet bowl, keep its possible noise-producing characteristics in mind, as well as its color.

Toilet Bowl Types

Toilets are available as one- or two-piece units. The one-piece toilet consists of a rear tank and a toilet, both made as a single, integral unit. The advantage of such a toilet is that the connecting pipe between the tank and the toilet bowl is hidden. One-piece toilets are also easy to clean. They are more expensive than two-piece models.

The tank of either type of toilet, is supported on the wall by means of tank brackets. However, the one-piece tank gets added support from the toilet section because it is made as a single unit.

Fig. 5-27.

	Tank		Extension of fixture into room (*inches*)
	Height (*inches*)	Width (*inches*)	
One-piece toilet	18½ to 25	26¾ to 29¼	26¾ to 29¼.
Close coupled tank and bowl	28½ to 30⅞	20⅝ to 22¼	27½ to 31⅜.
Wall-hung toilet	27 to 29½	21 to 22¼	26 to 27½ (concealed tank 22).
Wall-hung tank	32 to 38	17¾ to 22	26½ to 29½.
Corner toilet	28¾	19¼	31.

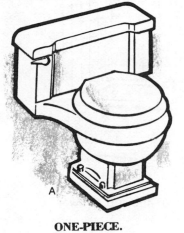

ONE-PIECE.
One-piece toilets are neat in appearance and easily cleaned, but are more expensive than two-piece models.

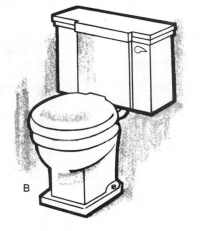

CLOSE-COUPLED TANK AND BOWL
The tank, a separate unit, is attached to the bowl.

TWO-PIECE WITH WALL-HUNG TANK.

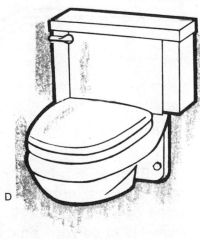

WALL-HUNG.
Completely wall-hung toilets make it possible to clean the floor under and around the toilet.

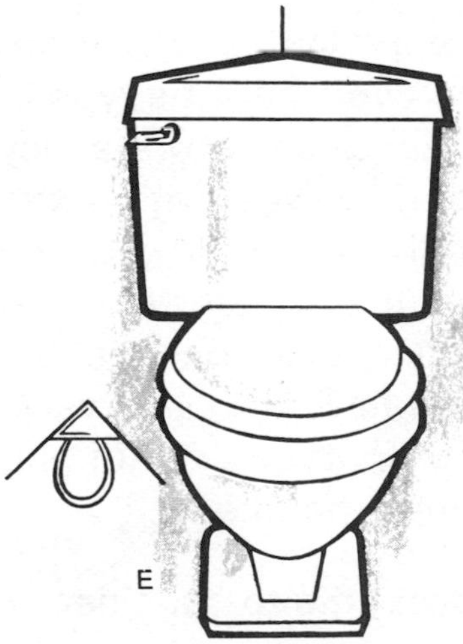

CORNER.
The corner toilet is a space saver. Note the triangular tank.

Toilets and their approximate dimensions.

In the two-piece unit the tank may be fairly close to the bowl, as in drawing B in Fig. 5-27, or it may be further away, as in drawing C.

The wall-hung toilet (D) has the advantage of greater cleanliness, since it is possible to clean the floor under and around the bowl. However, a bowl of this kind must be strongly supported, and it may be necessary to reinforce the wall behind the toilet.

Where bathroom space is at a premium, it is possible to use a corner toilet(E). The tank, instead of being rectangular in shape, as with most toilets in the home, is triangular. The tank is supported by both walls.

The chart at the top of the drawings supplies the height and width of the toilet tanks and also the extension of the fixture into the room, measured in inches.

Showers

The most generally used shower arrangement is the over-the-tube type illustrated in Fig. 5-28. Such showers may use the tub supply valves with extra valves to transfer the water flow to the shower head, or they may use two separate valves connected only to the shower head. Some have a mixing valve that changes the proportions of hot and cold water by a single handle.

Ideally, the best time to consider an over-the-tub shower is when the bathroom is being installed. In that way the pipes can be concealed in the wall. Alternatively, you can have part of the wall knocked out, if your intentions are

simply to add a shower, and then have the wall repaired and refinished. The most economical and easiest way is to install a shower fixture with the pipes exposed. However, you must still make a connection to the water supply, and this will involve knocking out a small part of the wall.

Fig. 5-28.

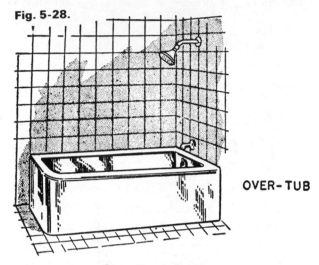

OVER-TUB

Over-the-tub shower.

Shower Heads

FLANGE

HEAD

Fig. 5-29.

Shower head and flange. (Hancock-Gross)

Shower heads are made of chrome-plated brass, chrome-plated plastic, or white cycolac (Fig. 5-29). The head has a swivel joint so you can direct the spray as you wish. Some are equipped with a face plate to let you get almost any kind of water spray pattern you want. Some heads have a water volume control so you can shut off the spray at the shower head.

The pipe connecting the head to the water supply pipe in the wall is known as a flange. It is threaded at both ends so as to make an easy connection to a fitting in the water supply pipe and also to the head. Some models have both volume and spray regulators.

The shower head should be at least 6 feet 2 inches above the floor of the tub. If you decide to use a tub shower, you should have a shower curtain to keep water from the shower off the floor. For some tubs you can also get a sliding door glass enclosure. However, these enclosures aren't available for every tub style, so if you intend having a shower and want a glass enclosure you may find yourself limited in your choice of tub selection. When installing a rod for a shower curtain, make sure the rod is about 4 inches above the shower head.

Shower Stalls

You can make a shower stall of masonry or tile, or you can get one that is prefabricated. If you have no available space in the house you might consider having one put in the basement. Prefabricated stalls are available in porcelain enameled steel or fiberglass. They range in height from about 74 to 80 inches and have a floor area of 30 x 30 inches to 36 x 36 inches or 34 x 48 inches. Fig. 5-30 shows two types of showers. One is a recessed stall and may come equipped with a shower curtain, although in new homes you will find a glass door used instead. The door doesn't cover the entire stall. An open area near the top of the door is used to provide ventilation and to prevent the stall from steaming up.

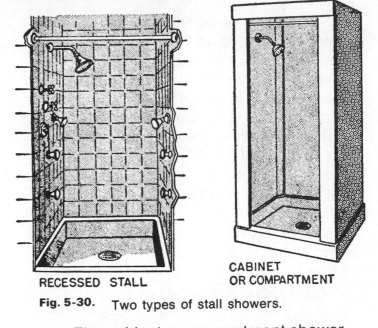

RECESSED STALL   CABINET OR COMPARTMENT

Fig. 5-30. Two types of stall showers.

The cabinet or compartment shower is used when the shower must be located in an area other than the bathroom. A shower curtain is used instead of a glass door as an economy measure.

Portable Shower

Showers for Built-In and Leg-Type Tubs

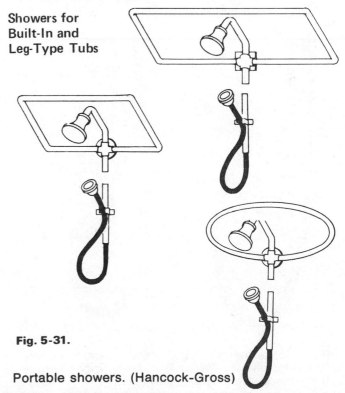

Fig. 5-31.

Portable showers. (Hancock-Gross)

If you have no shower facility and want to add one at the lowest possible cost, you can use the type shown in Fig. 5-31. The shower has a hose, or tubing, which connects directly over the water nozzle in the tub. The volume of water and its temperature are controlled by the tub's regular faucets. A rod around the shower is for a curtain. The curtain bars are chrome-plated and measure 24 x 30 inches or 24 x 42 inches. The ring type, shown at the right, has a diameter of 24 inches.

Personal Shower

Fig. 5-32.

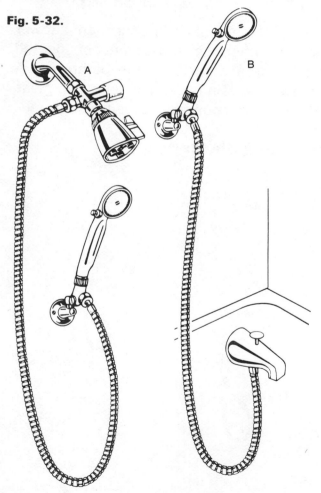

Personal showers. Unit A gets its water supply from the shower head. B gets its water supply from the bathtub spout (Keystone)

Still another type is the "telephone type" personal shower illustrated in Fig. 5-32. The shower head is attached to chrome-plated flexible tubing so you can easily direct the water spray to any part of your body. Some have a diverter valve that lets you switch easily from the hand-held shower to the built-in shower head. Unlike the portable shower, the personal shower must be permanently attached to the water supply. The connection can be made to an existing shower head or to the tub faucet. The personal shower doesn't replace the regular shower but simply supplments it.

Safety in the Bathroom

For elderly persons, invalids, or the physically handicapped, you can have support bars installed alongside toilets or safety rails for the bathtub. The bathtub safety rail, chrome plated, can be adjusted to fit the tub.

Safety bars, better known as grab bars, should be sturdy. And when you install them make sure they are firmly anchored. Some are held in by cement, but you can get a much better support by fastening them to the wood frame behind the wall.

Safety bars are available in various lengths and you can install them vertically or horizontally. A better arrangement is the angled grab bar (Fig. 5-33) suitable for either a tub or stall shower. The angled grab bar, extending both horizontally and vertically, supplies a greater opportunity to get a firm grip.

You can also get a wedge-type bathtub seat that is adjustable for all sizes

Fig. 5-33.

Angle bar for bathtub or shower.

and shapes of tubs. The seat is suitable as a support for those who are physically unable to make use of the tub. It is also ideal for foot soaking.

Fig. 5-34.

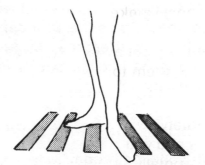

Safety treads for tub or shower. These are available in kit form so you can install them yourself. Some come in attractive decorative patterns. (Hancock-Gross)

Safety treads, Fig. 5-34, insure against slipping and falling in bathtubs and showers. And alongside the tub it is

always a good idea to have a non-skid bath mat. Tile floors are slippery when wet. If you want to use some sort of rug instead of a bath mat, make sure that the floor side of the rug has a non-skid backing.

Safety treads, Fig. 5-34, insure against slipping and falling in bathtubs and showers. And alongside the tub it is always a good idea to have a non-skid bath mat. Tile floors are slippery when wet. If you want to use some sort of rug instead of a bath mat, make sure that the floor side of the rug has a non-skid backing.

Never keep appliances that are operated from the house electricity near a tub or shower. This includes radio sets which are plugged into outlets, electric heaters, electric hair dryers. Never—but positively never—put an electric appliance that is power line operated on the edge of a tub while you are taking a bath. It could well be your last one. Electricity and water make a dangerous combination.

Bathroom Accessories

There are a number of accessories you can use to let you get greater convenience from your bathroom. An accessory may be nothing more than an extra towel bar, or towel ring, or a holder for a glass, and so on.

Towel Rods

You'll need towel rods for towels and washcloths, and if you make a practice of having guests, it would be a good idea to have a separate rod for separate towels.

To hang a bath towel and washcloth folded once lengthwise requires 21 inches. A better arrangement is to have a 28-inch rod so that the washcloth can be hung unfolded for quick drying.

Keep the children in mind. To teach them the fundamentals of cleanliness, put up towel rods on the side of the bathroom at a convenient height. A towel pole provides for extra towels in a minimum of space. You can also get towel rods that are swing-out types, supported at one end only.

Toilet Paper Holder

Toilet paper holders, made of china or metal, are usually recessed in the wall. Some paper holders are made to be fastened directly to the wall. The recessed type is better since it doesn't protrude as much into the bathroom and is a more secure holder. To install a holder of this kind you will need to knock out a small area of the wall that will accommodate the paper holder. Just make sure you do not cut so that you run into a building stud. Place the paper holder so its bar is about 30 inches from the floor, and if on a sidewall, about 6 to 8 inches beyond the front edge of the toilet. Some paper holders play a musical tune when the paper is unrolled, but then, there is no accounting for taste.

Soap Holders

You can have two types of soap holders in the bathroom and most bathrooms do use both. One is the plastic soap holder generally put somewhere on the surface of the bathroom sink. The other soapholder, made of vitreous china or metal and used for bathtubs and showers, is recessed in the wall. For the tub, put the soap holder at about the middle of the wall beside the tub and within easy reach from a sitting position.

However, for a shower still you would want to install the soap holder at about shoulder height. Plumbers normally center the holder, and while such positioning makes it look more attractive, it can also fill more easily with water from the shower. It is better to have the soapholder close to the wall opposite the shower head and sufficiently high so that normal water spray will not reach it, yet not so high that getting at the soap is awkward. You can also install a corner shelf in the shower stall for soaps, shampoos, and rinses.

Clothes Hanger

You will find it a convenience to put a metal hook on the inside of the bathroom door for holding garments such as bathrobes. Use a nonrusting hook and mount it about 2 inches below the top edge of the door so the door can be closed without interference. In any event, always put the hooks above eye level to prevent accidents.

Toothbrush and Glass Holder

If your bathroom doesn't already have these accessories, you can get them for easy mounting right up against a wall. They are made of metal or plastic. Metal is much more durable, requires more cleaning, but may rust where the plating wears off. Plastic is available in colors, is easier to clean, but is usually not so strong as metal types.

Unless a fly or mosquito or other insect never sees the inside of your bathroom, or is ever given an opportunity to do so, hanging toothbrushes on an exposed holder isn't such a good idea. Having the toothbrush in a holder is more convenient; storing it in a container, usually made of plastic, that can be closed and put inside a medicine cabinet, is much more sanitary.

Tumblers made of glass or plastic are also exposed to insects but can be washed thoroughly before and after using. A plastic tumbler is better than a glass since it won't fracture if it drops on the hard surface of a sink or tiled bathroom floor. Get plastic tumblers that are machine washable just so you can give them a really through scrubbing once in a while.

Drying Lines and Racks

The rod that supports the shower curtain also works as a clothesline in many homes. Ultimately, water from wet clothing manages to get through the plating of the rod and rust begins. Rods also collect dust on their hard-to-see upper surfaces, so every time you use the rod as a clothesline you are putting dirt right back onto a surface from which you just worked so hard to remove it.

As an alternative:

1. Use hooks on either side of the bathtub for holding a short length of honest-to-goodness clothesline. Put a knot at both ends so you can easily disengage the clothesline when not in use. You can store the line on any convenient bathroom shelf. If you can't get into the walls with hooks, or would prefer not to, you can get the kind that fasten on by suction cups.

2. You can also get a telescoping rod that comes equipped with suction cups. If you mount the rod high enough above the tub you can leave it in place, or you can remove it after each use. Why such a rod and not the curtain rod? Simple. You can get a plastic rod which will never rust. And you can remove the rod and get it out of sight whenever you want. You can also remove the rod to give it a quick wipe with a cloth before you use it.

3. You can get a drying rack. Get the kind that opens to supply maximum "clothesline" effect. To store it, fold it and keep it against the bathroom wall, or if you're lucky enough to have closet space, use it.

4. Some clothes lines are made to curl up inside a retractable holder. the holder has a hook so you can fasten it to any wall you wish. One end of the clothesline also has a hook. There is a spring inside the holder that will help roll up the line inside the holder when you are finished with it.

Medicine Cabinets

There are two basic types: those with sliding doors and those with doors that are hinged and swing open. Both types have mirrors. Medicine cabinets come in just about all sizes, shapes, styles, and colors. Measure your available wall space before you buy. If the cabinet has a swinging door, make sure it can open fully and freely without interference. Some

173

medicine cabinets have fluorescent lights across the top and sides. And these lights are either naked bulbs or may be shielded behind frosted glass or plastic. Some cabinets come equipped with convenience outlets to let you use an electric toothbrush or shaver.

A recess mounting is best although you can get medicine cabinets that are wall-mount types. When cutting a space in the wall for the medicine cabinets, avoid the studs. If the cabinet is to fit into the space between studs, then this will represent the maximum width of the cabinet. As an alternative, you can always use a wall-mount medicine cabinet, but these do protrude into the room.

Put the medicine cabinet at a convenient height. The top of the mirror should be about 69 to 74 inches above the floor. If you measure a distance of 48 to 54 inches from the floor to the bottom of the mirror, you will position the cabinet satisfactorily for the average person.

Towel Cabinets

When planning your bathroom, be sure to install a closet if you have the space for it. You can use the closet for storing all the bathroom supplies: soap; cleaning powders or liquids, toilet bowl cleaner, mop for the bathroom, toilet paper, tissues, and miscellaneous items that won't fit into your overcrowded medicine cabinet.

Regular-size bath towels folded in thirds lengthwise fit on a shelf that is 12 inches deep; folded in half they fit on a shelf 16 inches deep.

Fig. 5-35.

Limited storage using shelves that are 12 inches deep x 18 inches wide.

Fig. 5-35 shows the spacing arrangement you can use for storing a limited supply of towels and washcloths. Arrange the shelves so they are 12 inches apart. The shelves will be 12 inches deep by 18 inches wide. You can store the same amount of towels and washcloths by using shelves 18 inches wide by 16 inches deep, separated by just 10 inches, as shown in Fig. 5-36.

Fig. 5-36.

Limited storage using shelves that are 16 inches deep and 18 inches wide.

A more generous storage arrangement is one that has three shelves 16 inches deep x 18 inches wide (Fig. 5-37) or 12 inches deep x 26 inches wide (Fig. 5-38).

Fig. 5-37.

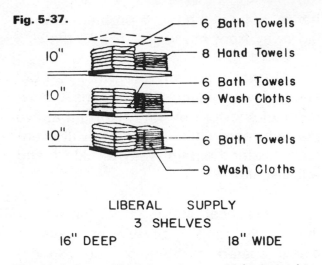

— 6 Bath Towels
— 8 Hand Towels
— 6 Bath Towels
— 9 Wash Cloths
— 6 Bath Towels
— 9 Wash Cloths

10"
10"
10"

LIBERAL SUPPLY
3 SHELVES
16" DEEP   18" WIDE

Three shelves, 16 inches deep x 18 inches wide, will take care of a family of two adults and two children.

Fig. 5-38.

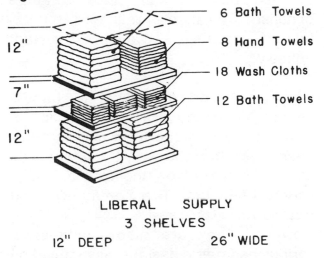

— 6 Bath Towels
— 8 Hand Towels
— 18 Wash Cloths
— 12 Bath Towels

12"
7"
12"

LIBERAL SUPPLY
3 SHELVES
12" DEEP   26" WIDE

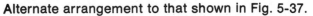

Alternate arrangement to that shown in Fig. 5-37.

You can also use a free standing cabinet that will give you all the shelf room you want. The trouble is that these not only take up a lot of bathroom space, but spoil the general appearance. You can get wall-hung shelves that will take care of at least part of your towel and washcloth problem. Or you can get the type that consists of metal-pole-supported shelves. These are easy to install and give you much more towel space than wall-hung shelving.

Hampers

The only thing you can do with a hamper is to keep moving it around until you find a place where it will interfere least with "walking around" room. If you are having a new bathroom constructed, give some thought to the possibility of having an in-wall hamper added. Hampers are more of a decorating, not a plumbing, problem.

Bathroom Ventilation

Every bathroom must have either a window or an exhaust fan. This is a requirement of your local plumbing code. Some bathrooms are also equipped with a heat lamp, which is ceiling connected and operated by a timer near the light switch. In some installations, the exhaust fan will come on when the bathroom light is turned on. Since the bathroom will not have a window, this means you will get automatic vent fan operation.

Try to avoid having the bathtub positioned directly below the window. This will make it very difficult to clean the window, or to open or close it, as needed. If you have no alternative but to have your tub located this way, get a window that can be opened or closed by turning a crank handle.

Lighting

You should have two sources of light for your bathroom. One will be a central, ceiling type and the other will be a supplementary light, probably associated with your medicine cabinet. The light should be wall-switch, not pull-chain operated. Make sure the wall plate that

175

covers the bathroom switch is plastic, not metal. *Do not* bring portable electric lamps into the bathroom. They can be killers!

Wall Finishes

There is a remarkable variety of wall finishes you can use for your bathroom, including paint, ceramic or plastic tile, plastic-coated hardboard, plastic laminates, wall paper, vinyl, cloth, fabric, fabric-backed wallpapers. Some finishes are practical; others are less so. A lot also depends on family use. If you have small children, you can logically expect dirty hands to touch clean walls, so a prime consideration should be ease of cleaning—or replacement, if cleaning is no longer feasible.

Paint is one of the more economical coverings to use. A latex-based paint is easy to apply and will dry quickly. It usually has a nonreflective surface and so eliminates bathroom glare. Some latex-based paints are washable. Whether they can be scrubbed without removing some of the finish is another matter.

You can use a gloss paint having an oil base. The trouble with such paint is that if air and/or water get beneath it, it tends to curl and pull away from the wall. When it does you have a problem, for the rest of the paint remains. Stripping down to the bare surface is hard work. Painting over a patch that has peeled away sometimes emphasizes the patch. A gloss paint has a highly reflective surface, so you may get an unpleasant glare, depending on the amount and kind of lighting you have. A semigloss paint is

better, but it still has the problem of pulling away from the wall.

Do not paint any area that can get sprayed with water. This means the interior of showers or the area right above the bathroom sink. The water will eventually blister the paint, may wrinkle it, and will discolor it.

A practical, although not too attractive covering for bathroom walls is plastic-coated hardboard. You can get these in many colors and some even have a simulated wood grain. Or you can use a vinyl-type wallpaper. This paper is water repellent, but such wall coverings can be expensive. Washable wallpaper is practical if you use a moisture-resistant adhesive.

Probably one of the best coverings is ceramic tile or the less costly plastic tile. Ceramic tile is made from clay that has been given the hot-oven treatment. You can get it glazed or unglazed and in a variety of colors. The commonly used bathroom size is 4¼ x 4¼ inches. However, they are also available in various geometric designs, assembled on cloth mesh or paper so you can fasten about a square foot at a time. You can tile a bathroom yourself, following the manufacturer's instructions, available when you purchase the tile.

Plastic tile is less expensive and is quite easy to install. Special adhesives are made for such tile. Not only is the cost an advantage, but the tile can be cut more easily to fit around pipes. You can cut ceramic tile with a special tool you can rent from the store where you buy the tile.

How to Repair Cracks Around Tubs and Showers

As a house ages, it moves. And when it moves it takes walls with it. Tubs and showers attached to the walls may not go along with the idea of such transportation and so a crack develops between these units and the wall. Also, as grout and tile sealer get older, they may harden and crack naturally. From a plumbing viewpoint, no harm is done. Water enters the tub and/or shower properly and leaves, also properly. But the trouble is that water can enter the crack, particularly in a shower, and even in a tub if the occupant splashes about.

After the water enters the crack it must go somewhere. It will run along beams and studs, may reach ceilings and stain them, or worse, weaken them. Such stains are very difficult to paint over and often "bleed" through several coats of paint—that is, the discoloration is almost impossible to cover. Finally, all cracks between tubs, showers, and walls are unsightly and are dirt catchers.

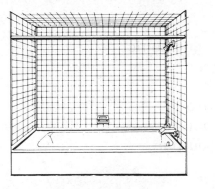

Fig. 5-39.

As a first step in repairing a bathroom crack, buy waterproof grout or plastic sealer.

To eliminate a crack you need a waterproof crack filler. You can get either waterproof grout, or plastic sealer (Fig. 5-39). The advantage of grout is that it costs less, but isn't so easy to use as plastic sealer. Grout is available in powder form, and you can get it in different colors. To use the grout, mix a small quantity with water and stir until it forms a smooth paste. Use too much water and the grout will run rather than stick in the crack. Use too little and you will get a lumpy paste that won't let you make a smooth repair. You'll need to experiment a bit to get it right.

Plastic sealer comes in a tube, just like toothpaste. Squeeze the tube from the bottom and keep the tube cap on when not using the sealer. Squeeze out just enough to do a little of the job at a time.

Fig. 5-40.

Use a painter's spatula or putty knife for removing the old, partially loose grout.

As a start, remove the old crack filler. You can use a painter's spatula or putty knife for this (Fig. 5-40) obtainable in hardware or paint stores. Work out all the old grout. Don't use a screwdriver for this job. The blade is too thick and not wide enough to cover much surface area. Don't let any of the grout get into the tub or shower drain or you'll have more work than you counted on.

Before you go ahead with the actual

work, spread newspapers over the floor of the tub or shower and make sure the papers cover the drain. The purpose here is twofold: to keep your shoes from scratching the tile surface of the shower or the porcelain finish of the tub, and to keep grout from getting into the drain.

Cleanliness is the next step after you remove all the old grout. Use sponge and a pail of water containing some detergent or any one of the commercial cleaners to wash the grout area thoroughly. Move the sponge back and forth as shown in Fig. 5-41. If, in the process, you discover some old grout you overlooked, get busy with the putty knife again.

Fig. 5-41.

Clean the crack thoroughly with a detergent solution. Work the sponge back and forth.

Fig. 5-42.

Dry the surface thoroughly before making any repairs.

After a thorough cleaning, do a thorough drying job (Fig. 5-42). Grout or plastic sealer do not get along well with wet surfaces. Use clean rags for drying the crack, and if the rag won't fit in, wrap it around the blade of the putty knife or

spatula and work it in. It might also be a good idea to wait an hour or so to give evaporation a chance. Keep the bathroom door open and if possible, open a window, to get some air circulation.

Fig. 5-43.

Pour some grout into a bowl containing water and mix thoroughly.

If you've decided to use grout, pour a small amount of it into a bowl (Fig. 5-43). Add cold water to the powder while stirring the mixture with the putty knife. The idea here is to mix thoroughly and to add water until you have a thick paste. Don't make the mixture too watery. Then, using the putty knife, force the grout into the crack (Fig. 5-44). Examine the entire length of the crack to make sure you haven't overlooked any spot. Slide the blade of the knife over the grout, making it as uniformly smooth as possible, and then remove any excess (Fig. 5-95). Don't try to save any grout—it just can't be done.

Fig. 5-44.

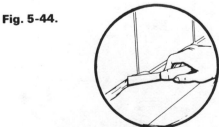

Apply grout with a putty knife.

Clean the putty knife immediately and also the bowl containing the remainder of the grout. A good method is to use a pail of water. Do not use a sink for cleaning either the knife or the bowl. Do not empty the contents of the cleaning pail into either a sink or a toilet. Instead, pour it into the nearest sewer opening. Don't postpone the cleaning job, for grout dries hard. Remove the newspapers from the tub or shower and make sure that you get all grout particles out.

Fig. 5-45.

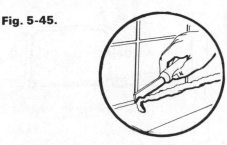

Wipe away excess grout with the putty knife.

The advantage of the plastic sealer is that it is premixed. You can apply it directly from the tube in the form of a ribbon along the crack (Fig. 5-46). With a putty knife or spatula, force the plastic sealer into the crack and then run the knife or spatula over the surface to make it smooth. Work fast since the plastic sealer dries in a few minutes. Always keep the cap on the tube when it isn't in use; otherwise the plastic will harden at the opening and possibly inside the tube as well.

Fig. 5-46.

Apply plastic sealer directly from the tube.

How to Make Bathroom Wall Repairs

One of the big problems in the bathroom stems from what also makes the bathroom possible—water. With the bathroom window closed, with no other access to ventilation, water vapor and steam do more than just cloud the surface of mirrors. They condense on wall surfaces as well. If the wall has been painted with an oil base point, in time the water will get beneath the paint and then cause it to curl out and away.

The cure is to remove all the paint, or to remove as much of the flaking paint as possible with a putty knife. Then apply a mixture of spackle and plaster in the ratio of about one part spackle to three parts of plaster. You can measure the spackle and plaster with a cup. Mix the two thoroughly and add cold water until the mixture forms a smooth paste, without lumps.

Cover the exposed areas of the wall with the spackle-plaster combination and try to get as smooth a surface as possible. After the spackle-plaster has dried thoroughly—allow at least five hours—sand the finish with a coarse grade of sandpaper to bring the surface flat with the painted wall. Use a fine grade of sandpaper to get a smooth finish. You can then repaint the entire wall. You may need to apply several coats to keep the repaired section from having a different color from the rest of the wall.

The advantage of spackle is that it keeps the plaster from drying too rapidly and also helps supply a smoother working surface.

Replacing Flexible Tile

Fig. 5-47.

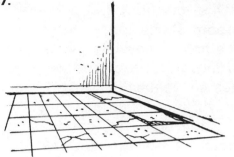

Cracked, worn or broken floor or wall tiles make the bathroom a depressing place.

Flexible tile used for bathroom floors can become nicked or gouged, or severely discolored from accidentally dropped medication (Fig. 5-47). You can replace such tiles, but you will have two problems. The first is to be able to match the existing tiles, but if you have some pieces left over from the original installation, or if it is a very popular type of tile, then your first problem is solved. The second is a bit more difficult. As tile is exposed to light and to wear, it changes color. It may have darkened. And so the replacement tile will be quite obvious. However, even if you don't have a perfect match, it will be better than tile that is damaged.

As a first step you will need to remove the loose or damaged tile. You can use an electric iron to help soften the adhesive. Put a section of rag between the tile and the faceplate of the iron to avoid damaging the surface of the iron. If the iron has a steam setting, turn it off.

Try lifting one corner of the tile with a putty knife (see the tools shown in Fig. 5-48). If you can get the knife into position

beneath the tile, keep working it back and forth, and at the same time keeping the hot iron directly above it. It takes a little maneuvering and if you can get someone to help you, so much the better.

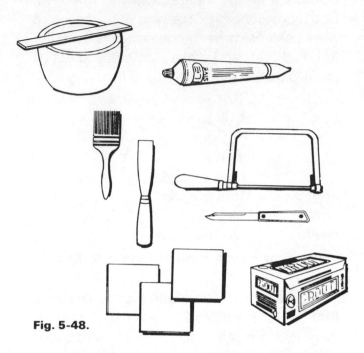

Fig. 5-48.

Assortment of things you will need for replacing flexible, plastic, or ceramic tiles in a bathroom.

Not all of the original adhesive will come off with the tile. Some will still be on the floor. Scrape away the adhesive using a floor scraper. You may need to use coarse sandpaper to remove some stubborn spots. Keep the sandpaper away from the adjoining tiles to keep from damaging them.

Now fit a sample tile into the space you have just provided. If the replacement tile is a bit too large you can trim it with a knife or shears. As tile gets older it tends to become brittle. If you warm the tile before cutting, it will have less of a tendency to break.

Fig. 5-49.

Spread adhesive with a brush or putty knife (left). After the flexible tile is in position, use a rolling pin to push it into its proper place.

Once you are certain the replacement tile will fit, spread adhesive on the floor or wall with a putty knife (Fig. 5-49). Make sure you cover the entire surface area of the exposed section of wall or floor. Wait about five minutes to give the adhesive a chance to begin setting; then put the tile down and press it into position firmly. Remove any adhesive that may squeeze out of the edges. Continue pressing down on the tile, and when you are sure no more adhesive will push out, press it more firmly into place by using a wooden rolling pin. If you have no roller, cover the tile with a sheet of newspaper and then step down on the tile. Move your foot so as to be sure to cover every section of the tile. Afterward, remove the newspaper and examine the tile carefully to make sure it is uniformly flat.

Just one precaution: The surface to receive the tile must be absolutely flat. If there are any nail heads in the floor, or any bumps of any kind, or any tiny lumps of old adhesive, the result will be a bump in the new tile. And as you step on it, the new tile will crack or break right in the area of that bump.

Replacing Ceramic or Plastic Tile

Usually a replacement is needed here since the ceramic or plastic tile has fallen out. If the old tile is till in place, you

will need to pry it away from the wall (Fig. 5-50). Don't try to use the hot iron technique with ceramic or plastic tile. After the old tile is removed, prepare the surface for a replacement by cleaning away all the old adhesive. You can use a scraper or a putty knife, or coarse sandpaper.

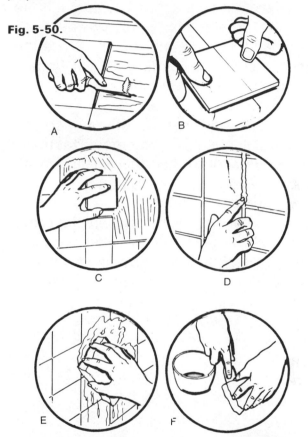

Fig. 5-50.

Steps in replacement of ceramic tile. Remove old tile with putty knife (A). You can cut the tile by scoring it on back surface and pressing down on table surface (B). After applying adhesive, put tile into position (C). Remove grout with finger (D). Wash tiles (F), and remove excess grout from tile surface with putty knife.

Check to make sure the new tile will fit. If the tile is plastic, you can cut it with a saw. If the tile is ceramic, you can rent a cutting tool from a store that sells tiles.

Put the tile into position temporarily to make sure it will fit and will not be above the surface of the other tiles. Then remove it, spread adhesive on the wall or floor, and also on the back of the tile. Press the tile firmly into position. Remove any adhesive that squeezes out of the edges of the tile.

If you have just replaced a ceramic tile, there will be a space between this tile and the others. Mix grout powder with water and make a stiff paste. Press the grout into the tile joints with your fingers and then make it smooth.

Grout is available in different colors, but while is the most common. Naturally, you will want to match the existing grout color.

Remove any excess grout *before it dries.* Wash the tiles to make sure all grout on any surface is cleaned away.

After you are finished and are engaged in a cleanup campaign, put all waste—leftover plaster, pieces of grout, newspapers, bits of adhesive, scrap plastic or ceramic—into a bag for removal to a garbage pail. Do not, under any circumstances, put any of these items into the toilet bowl; if you do, you may have an unexpected, and difficult, plumbing job on your hands.

One of the advantages of ceramic over flexible tile is that it does not discolor as it gets older, nor does it become more brittle. This means your replacement tile will supply a better match. However, the grout will be conspicious, for grout does get grayish as it gets dirty. You can get a grout cleaner to restore the grout to its original color.

Chapter VI

Quick-Fix Plumbing

What you can do in the way of plumbing in your home depends mostly on your abilities and your mental attitude. But even without prior skills there are many plumbing jobs you can do. If you are tired of being wholly dependent on someone else, you will soon learn there is a tremendous satisfaction in independence. This doesn't mean you can graduate immediately to the complicated job of installing a complete bathroom, but there are numerous lesser jobs you can tackle.

The important thing in plumbing is to know when you need a plumber, and when you don't. There will be times when you must give in; but now there will be an increasing number of times when you will have the soul and spirit of a determined do it yourselfer. And that's good.

How to Add An Aerator

The purpose of an aerator is to add air bubbles to water coming out of your faucet. Air contains oxygen, among other gases. Oxygen is a good cleaning agent and so is a no-cost additive for dishwashing chores. Some people prefer the taste of oxygenated water. Finally, aerated water, because it reduces splashing when the faucet is wide open, supplies another advantage.

It's easy to add an aerator. Examine the spout of your faucet. It may have threads on the outside, or on the inside, or it may have no threads at all. No matter. Whatever type of faucet you have, you can add an aerator.

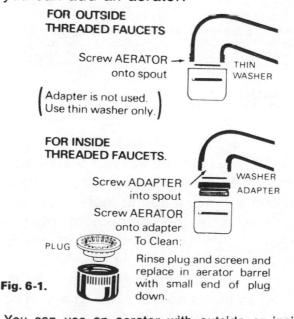

FOR OUTSIDE THREADED FAUCETS

Screw AERATOR onto spout

THIN WASHER

(Adapter is not used. Use thin washer only.)

FOR INSIDE THREADED FAUCETS.

Screw ADAPTER into spout

WASHER
ADAPTER

Screw AERATOR onto adapter

PLUG

To Clean:
Rinse plug and screen and replace in aerator barrel with small end of plug down.

Fig. 6-1.

You can use an aerator with outside or inside threaded faucets. (Melard Mfg. Corp.)

If the faucet spout is outside-threaded (see Fig. 6-1) all you need do is to screw the aerator right onto the spout. It should go on easily and smoothly. If it doesn't, don't try to force it. the idea is to have the threads of the aerator engage the threads of the spout. Once the beginning threads make contact, you should be able to turn the aerator so it screws onto the spout. Rotate the aerator counter-clockwise to mount it; clockwise to remove it.

If the spout is inside-threaded, just follow the manufacturer's directions, which come with the aerator. If the spout has large threads—15/16 inch—unscrew the slotted shaft and screw the flange into the spout, using a flat rubber washer.

FOR UNTHREADED AND ODD-SIZE FAUCETS

1. If opening has a spring insert, remove it with a bent pin or clip.
2. Insert adapter into spout as far as possible, and turn slotted shaft to the left with a coin until tight. If ADAPTER fits loosely, unscrew SLOTTED SHAFT and replace black collar with large BLUE collar. If ADAPTER will not fit, replace black collar with smaller RED collar OMITTING the BRASS WASHER.

Clean AERATOR occasionally by removing and rinsing parts.

Fig. 6-2.
Use adapter for unthreaded or odd-size faucets. (Melard Mfg. Corp.)

For unthreaded and odd-size faucets (Fig. 6-2) use the adapter that comes with the aerator. The opening to your faucet may have a spring insert. This will interfere with the placement of the aerator, so remove it with a bent pin or clip. Insert the adapter into the spout as far as possible. Turn the slotted shaft to the left as far as possible. using a coin or small screwdriver. Turn until it is tight. It is

possible that the adapter may fit a bit too loosely. In that case you will find that the manufacturer has supplied you with a special collar that will make the adapter fit.

While the aerator, when installed, becomes part of your fresh water supply, the mesh screen portion of the aerator will need occasional cleaning. Just remove the aerator, turn it upside down, and let water from the faucet pass through it. Dry the aerator and hold it up to a light bulb. You should be able to see if all particles have been removed. If not, repeat the washing process.

How to Stop Packing Leaks

A worn washer is the most common cause of leaks from faucets and valves. However, you can also get leaks from these fittings, and from traps and shower heads as well, due to worn packing. The leak from a trap or valve may be out of sight, but it can cause water damage and it can add a surprising amount to your water bill.

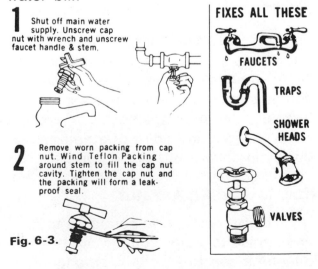

1. Shut off main water supply. Unscrew cap nut with wrench and unscrew faucet handle & stem.

2. Remove worn packing from cap nut. Wind Teflon Packing around stem to fill the cap nut cavity. Tighten the cap nut and the packing will form a leak-proof seal.

Fig. 6-3.

FIXES ALL THESE

FAUCETS

TRAPS

SHOWER HEADS

VALVES

Defective packing can cause leaks in faucets, traps, shower heads, and valves. (Melard Mfg. Corp.)

You will find Teflon packing an ideal and long-lasting remedy for such simple plumbing repairs. Shut off the main water supply, unscrew the cap nut with a wrench (Fig. 6-3), and remove the faucet handle and stem assembly by hand.

You can now remove the worn packing from the cap nut. Wind the Teflon packing around the stem to fill the cap nut cavity. Now replace the faucet handle and stem assembly and tighten the cap nut. Here is where you must exercise some discretion. There is such a thing as making the packing nut much too tight. If you do, you may find it difficult to turn the faucet or valve handle. If that is the case, just turn the packing nut back a bit and try the handle again. You want the packing nut as tight as possible, of course, but not so tight that the handle is difficult to turn. You need have no such consideration when you replace the packing for a trap, for this part does not have a handle.

If the old packing consists of a rubber seal that is doughnut shaped, you might also try using an O-ring seal.

How to Install a New Sink Spray

All sorts of things can happen to a sink spray. It may leak, adding to your water bill. It may dribble water instead of supplying it with some force. It may spit out tiny bits of rubber with the water. It may work when it feels like working—not at all a good situation and exasperating when you want to finish with the dishes.

It's easy to put in a new spray. The first step is to remove the old one (See Fig. 6-4). First, turn off the faucet. The spray head is held in place by a plastic collar. This collar is ribbed so you can hold it more firmly. Hold the collar with one hand and turn the spray head with the other, and the spray head will then come off in your hand. Put the spray head aside and examine the end of the rubber hose to which the collar is attached. On top of the collar assembly you will find a rubber washer. Remove it. Note: On some models the plastic collar is an elongated handle that screws directly into the spray head. If a brass fitting holds the hose to the head, unscrew this fitting.

Now that you have removed the rubber washer, you will be able to see a retaining clip. This clip holds the collar in position. You can force the retaining clip off with a flat blade screwdriver, but be careful you don't jab the palm of your hand when doing so.

Once you have the retaining clip removed, you will find the plastic collar will come right off. Put a pan or a bucket on the floor and put the free end of the hose into it. The idea here is to let any water remaining in the hose dribble out.

You are now ready to work on the other end of the hose. Unscrew it with a wrench or pliers. It may be difficut to use an ordinary wrench or pliers, depending on the way your faucet was installed. You may find it much better and easier to use a basin cock wrench, specifically designed for such work and an ideal tool for this purpose. You can also use this tool for removing and installing new faucets in your home. You should now have the entire sink spray hose removed and are ready to install a new unit.

Fig. 6-4.

1. TO REMOVE OLD SPRAY

A. Turn off faucet.

B. Unscrew spray head from plastic collar, and remove washer.*
*On some models the plastic collar is an elongated handle that screws directly into the spray head. If a brass fitting holds the hose to the head, unscrew this fitting.

C. Pry off clip, remove plastic collar and lower hose through hole into a pan to collect the water remaining in hose.

D. Unscrew hose with a wrench or pliers. (A basin cock wrench is an ideal tool for this purpose. It can also be used when removing and installing a faucet).

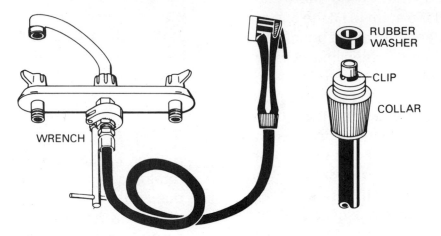

2. TO INSTALL NEW UNIT

A. Unscrew spray head and remove washer.

B. Faucets with female thread.   Faucets with male thread.

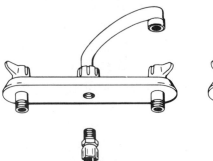
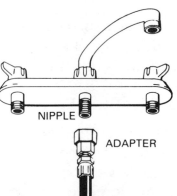

Wrap hose fitting with pipe tape supplied and screw hose directly into the faucet. (The adapter is not used)

Attach adapter to hose and screw onto faucet nipple. Tighten adapter and hose securely.

C. Pry off clip and remove plastic collar. Insert hose through hole and replace plastic collar, clip and washer. Use new clip supplied. Screw spray head onto plastic collar.

How to install a replacement sink spray. (Melard Mfg. Corp.)

By now you will know whether your faucet is equipped with an internal (or female) thread or has a nipple with an outside (or male) thread. If you examine your new sink spray replacement, you will find it comes equipped with an adapter. You won't need this if your faucet has a female thread, so just put it aside. Don't throw it away; you may find it useful for some other plumbing job.

Wrap the hose fitting with pipe tape and then screw the hose directly into the faucet. If you omit using the pipe tape you will have a water leak at the area where the fitting goes into the female thread.

If your faucet has a male-threaded nipple, attach the adapter to the hose and then screw it onto the faucet nipple. Be sure to put some pipe tape around the nipple before you do so. Now tighten the adapter securely.

All you need do now is to work on the other end of the hose. The steps you take will be the same as those you used in removing the spray head, but in reverse order. Slip the plastic collar over the free end of the hose. Mount the new retaining clip that holds the plastic collar in place. Mount the rubber washer and as a last step, screw the spray head onto the threaded end of the plastic collar.

Turn on the cold water faucet and try the spray. With the spray on, examine the connections at both ends of the spray hose. There should be no dripping. Further, you should have complete control over the spray hose.

Don't throw away the old hose or any plumbing hardware. It's a good idea to keep this sort of stuff in an empty carton. An old grocery carton is just fine for this purpose. Granted you may never use any of the hardware you collect, but then again, there may be times when you will find the hardware useful for some miscellaneous plumbing repair.

Leaking Faucet

This plumbing problem was discussed previously, but there are still a number of small difficulties you should know about. It is sometimes hard to remove the faucet handle. The handle may be a type that is a force-fit. It is held into place by forcing it onto a fluted stem. Sometimes the only way to remove such a handle is through the use of a special handle removing tool. If the handle is made of cast metal, trying to pry it loose with a hammer may cause it to fracture. Try working the handle loose with a tool, using the tool beneath the handle to give you leverage.

Do not assume, because you cannot immediately see a holding screw, that the faucet handle is a force-fit type. In some faucets the holding screw is cleverly concealed, so first make sure your faucet handle isn't this type. The screw may be mounted on top of the handle or somewhere along the side. If on the top it may be concealed by a plastic insert.

Fig. 6-5 shows the position of the screw with reference to the handle in one type of faucet.

After you shut off the water supply, remove the screw. This doesn't mean the faucet handle will automatically lift off. Through its design and continued use, the handle may still be firmly in place and so you may still need to pry it upward. Once you've managed that, you can unscrew the bonnet nut with a wrench and then remove the stem assembly.

Fig. 6-5.

Tools required: wrench & screwdriver.

A. Shut off water supply.

B. Remove screw from handle and lift or pry off handle; and unscrew bonnet nut with wrench. Remove bonnet and stem assembly.

C. Loosen screw and remove old washer. Select a new washer that fits snug into stem recess and tighten screw. Replace screw if necessary. Install washer with smooth side exposed.

If your faucet continues to leak, the faucet seat is rough and worn. To smooth out rough seats, purchase a FAUCET FIXER Reseating Tool

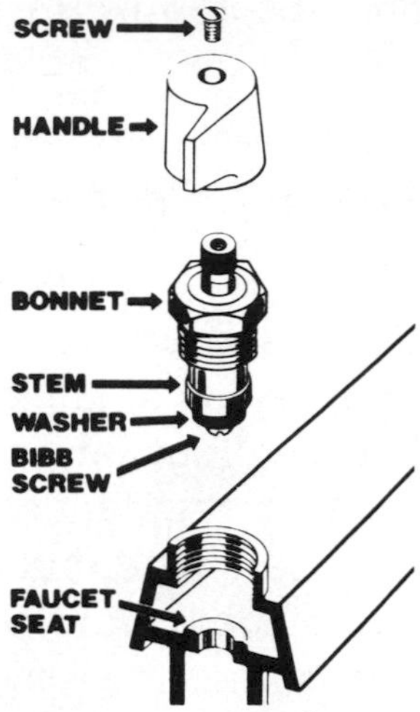

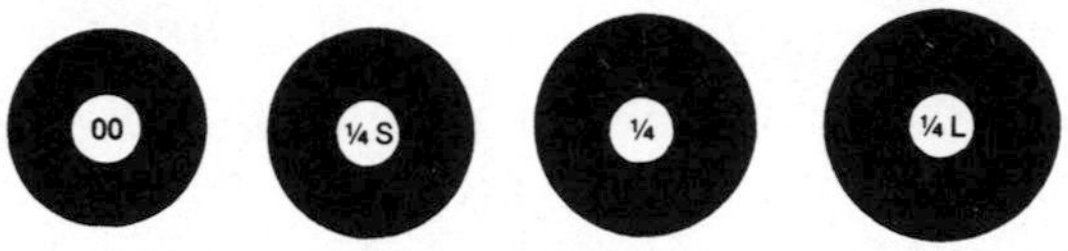

If the head of the bibb screw is too large, the faucet will continue to drip. (Melard Mfg. Corp.) Some faucet handles are held in place by three set screws. (Melard Mfg. Corp.)

The washer is held in place by a bibb screw. Since this screw is in contact with water and air so regularly, it has every reason to rust—and it will rust unless you use a nonrusting type, such as a brass screw. The head of the screw must have the right diameter. If the diameter of the bibb screwhead is too large, the washer will not be able to fit the faucet seat and no amount of pressure on the handle will stop the dripping of the water. Further, if you try to put pressure on the handle when the screwhead is too large, you may easily damage the faucet seat. Then, what

was a small plumbing job originally becomes a much larger one.

Before you replace a washer, examine it. If it is the flat type, mount it so the smooth side is exposed. If it is the beveled type, mount it so the bevel side is out.

The easiest, but not the most economical way of buying washers is to get a box of the so-called assorted sizes. This will supply washers in all sorts of diameters, but since you can use one size only for your particular faucet, you are really paying for washers you may never need or use. Learn your washer size. There are many different types and the lower part of Fig. 6-5 shows just a few of the more common ones. The best way to do it is to remove your old washer, take it with you to the plumbing store, and ask them to identify the size for you. Put this information on a card and then tack the card to the inside of your kitchen cabinet.

Finding the location of the screw (or screws) that hold your handle in position is just the first step. Removing or loosening the screw is the next. Some handles are held in by three set screws, as shown in Fig. 6-6. For these you will need a set screw wrench.

How to Install a Snap-In Washer

Not all faucet washers are held in by screws. Some are snap-in types, such as the one shown in Fig. 6-7. To use such a washer, remove the old one. Select a snap-in washer that is the same size or slightly smaller than the old one. Put a spacer on top of the washer and then push the metal extension of the washer into the space formerly occupied by the washer screw. The spacer is supplied with the washer and is nonmetallic.

TO REMOVE OLD HANDLE:
Unscrew holding screw to remove old handle. (Pry off button if necessary.) Tap handle upward if tight.

TO INSTALL NEW HANDLE:
1. Slip adapter onto stem and tighten set-screw with wrench included in package.

2. Slip handle on the adapter and tighten old center screw with screwdriver.

SET-SCREW

3 point vise grip — won't slip off

For all faucets — installs in seconds

REPLACE OLD CROSS HANDLES, LEVER OR CANOPY HANDLES

Fig. 6-6.

After you have installed the new washer, turn on the water supply and make a test. There should be no dripping and the flow of water should be in full force when the faucet handle is fully open. If not, try a thinner spacer. If you find the faucet continues to leak, the valve seat (faucet seat) is worn and must be smoothed with a seat dressing tool. Washers of the kind shown in Fig. 6-7 are designed to give years of trouble-free service. They cost a little more than the usual faucet washers but are well worth it because they save time and reduce annoyance.

How to Stop Leaks at Faucet Spout

You can have a leaky faucet without being aware of it. If the leak is at the handle or the spout, the water will follow a path that is almost unnoticeable down into the sink. The same amount of water coming out of the spout would be deemed a nuisance, but because handle and spout leaks are quiet, they are often ignored. The problem is that such leaks do add to your water bill; they waste a lot of water, and in some cases they can result in sink staining.

This trouble is caused by a defective O-ring seal. All you need do is to replace the ring and the problem is solved, and it is quite easy to do.

To put in a new O-ring, follow almost the same procedure as you would use in replacing a faulty washer. Shut off the water supply and then remove the screw holding the faucet handle in place. Unscrew the bonnet nut with a wrench, and after you lift out the bonnet, unscrew the stem. The O-ring is part of the stem assembly. Take off the worn O-ring and replace it with one that is identical in size. If you buy an assortment of O-rings you should be able to find one that fits. See Fig. 6-8 for details.

Fig. 6-7.

TOOLS REQUIRED:
Wrench and Screwdriver

A. Shut off water supply.

B. Remove screw from handle and lift or pry off handle; and unscrew bonnet nut with wrench. Remove bonnet and stem assembly. Loosen screw and remove old washer.

C. Select the "5 YEAR WASHER" that is the same size, or slightly smaller than the old washer. Place washer on flat surface and push stem onto washer.

D. Install stem, nut and handle assembly into faucet. Tighten nut and try faucet. If full flow is not obtained, remove the small washer, and file off the tip of the stem if necessary.

If your faucet continues to leak, the faucet is rough and worn, and must be smoothed. We recommend using our FAUCET FIXER Reseating Tool. When properly installed, the "5 YEAR FAUCET WASHER" will give you years of service on a smooth seat.

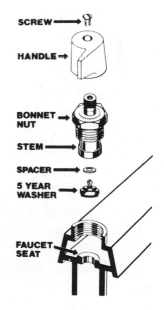

SCREW

HANDLE

BONNET NUT

STEM

SPACER

5 YEAR WASHER

FAUCET SEAT

Snap-in faucet washer is designed for years of trouble-free service. (Melard Mfg. Corp.)

Fig. 6-8.

TOOLS REQUIRED:
Wrench and Screwdriver
TO REPAIR LEAK AT HANDLE

1. Shut off water supply.

2. Remove screw from handle and lift or pry off handle; and unscrew bonnet nut with wrench. Remove bonnet assembly and unscrew stem from bonnet.

3. Remove worn 'O'-Ring from stem and replace with identical size 'O'-Ring from assortment. Replace and tighten bonnet.

TO REPAIR LEAK AT SPOUT

1. Unscrew spout nut to remove spout.

2. Remove worn 'O'-Ring and replace with identical size 'O'-Ring from assortment. Replace spout nut and spout.

Replace O-rings to stop leaks at faucet spout and faucet handles. (Melard Mfg. Corp.)

Fig. 6-8 also shows how to repair a leak at the spout. Unscrew the spout nut and then lift the spout up and out. When you do, you will see the worn O-ring. Remove it and replace it with one of the correct size. All you need do is to replace the spout nut and the spout.

The Time It Takes to Make a Repair

Don't be impatient with yourself if it takes more time to make a repair than you expected. After all, you are doing work that isn't familiar, using parts that are new or strange, and you may not have quite the amount of confidence you should have. No matter; in time you will be able to do a plumbing repair in just a matter of minutes that originally required an hour or more. You will also wonder why you ever thought such jobs were difficult.

Just one precaution. If you have someone else doing the work for you, possibly a friend or neighbor, don't be

satisified to watch. Participate. There's a world of difference between looking and doing.

How to Install a Flapper Tank Ball

If you must jiggle the flush lever to make your toilet more quiet, or if you notice water constantly running into your toilet bowl, then it's time to replace the tank ball. But while you are doing so, why not move ahead a step and install a tank ball whose construction forces it to make a positive fit in the valve seat and which will end your toilet lever jiggling once and for all.

REPLACEMENT FOR ALL OLD STYLE TANK BALLS

A. TO REMOVE OLD TANK BALL:

1. Move refill tube and spring out of the way
2. Pull up lift wire and unscrew old tank ball
3. Unhook upper lift wire from lever and remove both lift wires
4. Loosen guide screw and slide guide off overflow tube

B. TO INSTALL NEW FLAPPER TANK BALL:

1. Slide expanding collar onto overflow tube until it bottoms. Spring must be on the outside, with "L" shaped arms at the bottom.
2. Align plastic collar with bulb centered in seat. Hook chain onto lever with minimum slack when in closed position.
3. Replace refill tube and spring in the overflow tube. If bulb of flapper hits front of valve, raise collar slightly until it clears and falls flat. **Fig. 6-9.**

Flapper tank ball supplies positive valve-closing action. (Melard Mfg. Corp.)

Fig. 6-9 shows the setup. Your first step is to remove the old tank ball. Coming into the overflow tube is a soft copper tube bent almost in the form of a semicircle. Lift this and move it out of the way. If you also have a spring clip at the top of the overflow tube, move that out of the way as well. Now pull up the lift wire. The bottom end of the lift wire is attached to the tank ball. Unscrew the tank ball by turning it counterclockwise.

There are two lift wires. One is the wire you disconnected from the tank ball, and the other is the upper lift wire. The upper lift wire is loosely connected to the lever arm. Remove both lift wires. Connected somewhere near the lower part of the overflow tube you will find a guide. The purpose of this guide is to hold the lower lift wire in position, but now that you have removed the lower lift wire you no longer need the guide. The guide is fastened to the overflow tube by means of a screw. Loosen this screw and then you will be able to slide the guide up and off the overflow tube. You are now ready to install the new flapper tank ball.

In your flapper tank ball kit you will find a collar. Slide this collar onto the overflow tube right down to the bottom. The spring must be on the outside, with the L-shaped arms at the bottom. Align the plastic collar with the bulb centered in the seat. Hook the chain onto the lever. With the tank ball in its closed position—that is, with the tank ball sitting firmly down in the valve seat—the chain (actually working as a lift wire) should have no slack.

Now before you do anything else, try working the flush lever on the toilet tank. As you do, watch the action of the tank ball. It should lift easily and drop back directly into the center of the valve seat. If the bulb of the flapper hits the front of the valve, all you need do is to raise the collar slightly until the tank ball clears and falls flat. It's all just a matter of getting the collar in the correct position.

By using the flush lever, lifting the tank ball and watching it drop, you should be able to position the collar until you get absolutely correct tank ball action. Tighten the collar screw and your days of listening to constant toilet tank gurglings are over.

How to Install a New Trap

Older type traps have a nut on the bottom to permit access to the trap. This arrangement has the great advantage of convenience. To get at the inside of the trap, all you need do is to rotate this stop nut couterclockwise. The problem, though, is that the access hole covered by the nut is small. This means that while you can get at the inside of the trap, it isn't easy to do so. It is also difficult to get at the drain pipe leading away from the trap.

Fig. 6-10.

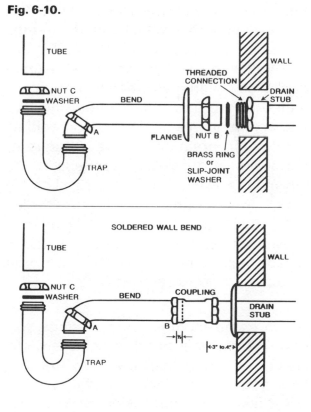

How to install a more modern trap. (Melard Mfg. Corp.)

191

A much better type of trap is the one that is held in place by a pair of slip nuts. Fig. 6-10 shows this type of trap. It is a 1¼-inch p-type to replace the trap you will need a 10-inch adjustable wrench, or channel-lock pliers, or a slip-joint wrench. As a start, put a pan or pail under the trap. If the old trap is the type that has a nut (plug) at the bottom of the trap, unscrew this nut to let accumulated water out of the trap.

Now turn the nuts that hold the trap in place until you can feel the trap becoming loose. Hold the trap with one hand and also loosen the nuts by hand. You should be able to do so once the tool you have been using has loosened the nuts sufficiently. The reason for working by hand this way is to give you better control over the water that will fall out of the trap.

You should also replace the drain pipe (also called a wall bend) that is connected to the trap. Quite often, the trap and wall bend are packaged and sold as a unit. If this drain pipe or wall bend is attached to a threaded connection, as shown in Drawing A in Fig. 6-10, slide the flage back and unscrew slip nut B. Also make sure nut A is completely off and away from the trap. With nuts A and B pulled back onto the drain pipe, you should be able to remove it.

In some plumbing installations you may find the wall bend is soldered into position. Using a hacksaw, saw the wall bend about 3 or 4 inches away from the wall. Make life a bit easier for yourself. You will be cutting while working in a cramped position so use a new blade in the hacksaw. After you are finished, slide the flange over the stub—the remaining bit of pipe sticking out from the wall.

To install the new trap, slide a new nut (A), the flange and old nut B, and the brass ring over the wall bend. If there is no brass ring you will find a slip-joint washer instead. If you sawed off the old wall bend, use a slip coupling of the type shown in drawing B. You may find, however, that your new wall bend is a bit too long, so you may have to saw off the excess length. In any event, allow for ½ inch to enter the new coupling.

Now put the wall bend into the drain stub, or the coupling, and screw on nut B loosely. Slide nut C and the washer onto the tube. Place the trap into position and then tighten all nuts.

When you tighten the slip nuts start the tightening process by hand. In this way you will be able to feel when the nut engages the threads. As you continue to turn the nuts by hand you will find it gradually becomes harder to do so. You can then finish the job by shifting to a tool.

After you've installed the trap and the wall bend, turn on a faucet and check for leaks. If the trap is in an area that is dark, as in a sink enclosure, use a flashlight. If you see any evidence of leakage, tighten the slip nuts a bit more.

How to Install a Personal Shower

The trouble with a shower head is that it sprays the upper part of the body only. However, there is no reason why you cannot modify your existing shower arrangement with a personal shower. The personal shower removes the limitation of the shower head. It is idea for people who, for therapeutic reasons, need the stimulation of a water stream on their legs or other parts of the body, or for those who want the thorough cleansing action.

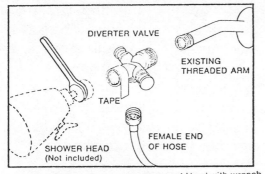

1. To remove Shower Head, grasp the top of Head with wrench and turn counter clockwise, while holding shower arm with pliers. To protect chrome, wrap masking tape or rag around shower arm, or use a Strap Wrench (Melard #1307.)

NOTE:
If shower arm has a ball end, replace it with a shower arm threaded on both ends. Obtain a threaded arm at your local store.

2a. Wrap white sealing tape (enclosed in package) tightly clockwise around threads of diverter valve and shower arm as indicated.

b. Screw shower head onto diverter valve <u>by hand</u> until tight. Turn shower head for an additional 1/2 turn with pliers, carefully. Do not use Wrench.

c. Screw diverter valve with shower head attached onto shower arm <u>by hand</u> until end of shower arm seals against washer in diverter, and hose thread faces down. Do not use Wrench.

3. Screw female end of hose onto diverter valve <u>by hand</u>.

4. Remove screw from hang-up bracket and snap bracket over metal hose in desired location. Tighten screw.

Fig. 6-11.

How to install a more modern trap. (Melard Mfg. Corp.)

Fig. 6-11 shows the steps to take for easy installation of a personal shower. As a first step, remove the existing shower head. To do this grasp the top of the shower head with a wrench and turn counterclockwise, while holding the shower arm with pliers. You'll want to protect the chrome finish so wrap it with masking tape or else use some rags. Your shower may be the type that has a shower arm with a ball end. Replace it with a

shower arm that is threaded at both ends. You can get such an arm at a plumbing supply store.

As a first step toward installation of the personal shower, you will need a diverter valve. You will find this included with the personal shower kit when you get it. Tightly wrap some sealing tape clockwise around the threads of the diverter valve and the existing shower arm. The shower arm is the length of pipe that extends from the wall and is the pipe to which the shower head was fastened originally.

Screw the shower head onto the diverter valve by hand until it is as tight as you can make it. Once you have done that, turn the shower head for an additional half turn with pliers, carefully. Do not use a wrench.

You now have the shower head screwed onto the diverter valve. Screw the diverter valve onto the shower arm by hand until the end of the shower arm seals against the washer in the diverter. The hose end of the diverter valve must face downward. Again, do not use a wrench.

At this time you can screw the female end of the personal shower hose onto the diverter valve. Do this by hand. Finally, move the hang-up bracket that is on the metal part of the shower hose until it is in the location you want. Tighten the screw.

Don't depend on the shower head for turning off the water supply if the shower head is equipped with a shutoff valve. You can use this shutoff valve to turn off the flow of water from the shower head when you use the personal shower attachment. When you are through showering, always turn off water flow with the tub's faucet handles.

Toilet Problems

Because it is used so much and because the water level in the toilet tank must be correct if the flushing action of the toilet is to be effective, and because there are so many parts that can get out of order, the toilet can be a nuisance. Not only a nuisance, but a noisy one, and a water waster as well. Once the valve that controls the flow of water into the toilet tank becomes defective, the only solution is to replace it. While it looks like a tough job, it is not all that difficult, and you should be able to handle it without calling for help.

Start with Fig. 6-12. this is the assembly you are going to replace. Fig. 6-12 also shows a cutaway view of the entire toilet tank setup, with all parts numbered.

As a first step shut off the water supply to the toilet. If you have a valve directly beneath the toilet, use it; otherwise turn off the main water valve. Flush the toilet to drain the tank and then sponge out any water remaining in the tank.

Now unscrew the coupling nut (2) and lock nut (5). These are beneath the toilet tank. After you have done this you should be able to lift out the entire ballcock assembly, shown in drawing A in Fig. 6-12. Remove all old parts from the fresh water supply pipe. However, if this pipe has an enlarged end, don't bother removing the old coupling nut (2).

Fig. 6-12.

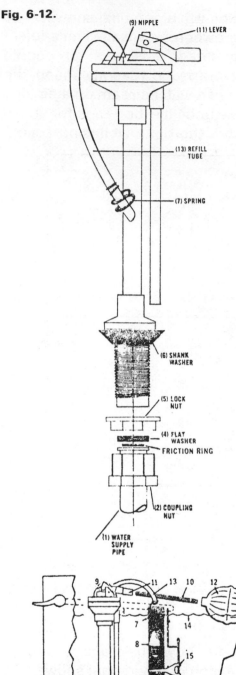

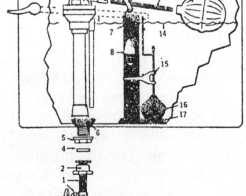

Steps in replacing toilet valve (ballcock) assembly. (Melard Mfg. Corp.)

194

Examine the new ballcock assembly you purchased and you will see that it is remarkably similar to or probly identical to the old one you just removed. At the bottom of the new ballcock assembly you will find a coupling nut (2), a locknut (5), and a washer (4). Remove these and put them over the water supply pipe (1). Insert the new ballcock. Screw on the lock nut, but don't tighten it.

You must now determine the type of water supply pipe you have. If it has a flat end, use a friction ring and flat washer and screw up the old coupling nut. If it has a conical end, screw up the old coupling nut. You can discard the friction ring, flat washer, and coupling nut.

Now follow these steps in order. Clip the spring (7) to overflow tube (8). Push the flexible refill tube (13) onto the nipple (9). The refill tube tip inside the spring must be slightly above the top of the overflow tube (8). If the refill tube is too long, cut off the excess length.

Screw float rod (10) into the ballcock lever (11) and screw the float (12) onto the float rod (10). The float must not touch either side of the tank. If it does, adjust the position of the ballcock. Tighten locknut (5) and coupling nut (2).

Turn on the water supply and let the toilet tank fill. Check the alignment of the tank ball and guide. Adjust the water level (14) to within 1½ inches of the top of the overflow tube by bending the float rod.

Now here are some problems you may encounter:

Valve Will Not Close

The end of the refill tube is set in overflow below tank water level (14). Water level should be about 1½ inches below the top of the overflow tube (8). Bend the float rod (10) down and this will lower the level of the water.

Rubbing Float

Any rubbing will prevent proper action of the toilet. You can correct this condition by turning the float valve or bending the float rod. If necessary, loosen the float valve to turn it.

Float Leaks

If the float (12) has water in it, replace it. Unscrew the float and shake it near your ear to determine if it has water in it. If you can hear water sloshing around inside, or if you can feel the water movement, the float is a leaky one.

Toilet Tank Won't Fill

Check to see that the water supply valve (1) is open. Check if the tank ball (16) is seating properly. Improper seating can be caused by misalignment of the guide (15). Check the guide to be sure it is located so that the tank ball falls directly into the seat (17). Relocate, if necessary, by loosening the screw on the guide.

Tank Doesn't Flush Sufficiently

If the tank doesn't flush sufficiently, the tank ball may be seating too soon. Check the position of the valve guide (15). If set too low, it will not allow the tank ball to lift high enough. Correct this by raising the guide.

Snap Action

If the snap action on closing is very strong and your tank fills too rapidly, that is, in less than 40 seconds, you probably live in an area where the water pressure is very high. Under these circumstances you can regulate water flow and reduce snap action by partially closing the water supply valve (1).

Frozen Water Pipes

Cold weather can create havoc with the piping part of a plumbing system under certain conditions. Pipes that are in the ground outside your home should be laid below the frost line. Pipes in crawl spaces beneath your home or in outside walls or in an unheated basement can also contain water that will freeze.

When water freezes it expands. If the pipe can expand with the water, then it is less likely to burst. Iron pipe and steel pipe will not expand very much. Copper pipe will stretch to a limited degree, but after it does so it does not go back to its original dimensions. And if you let copper pipes freeze repeatedly, they will ultimately crack. Flexible plastic tubing can tolerate repeated freezing, but again, this isn't the sort of treatment pipes should be expected to take.

There are various ways of preventing freezing. Maintain your home temperature at not less than 40° F. This includes the basement, as well as upper rooms and the attic. If you have thermostatically controlled heat and you must leave your home for several or more days, set the thermostat to maintain a minimum of 40°.

You can also insulate those pipes you can reach, but while this may slow the freezing process, it cannot stop it. All that insulation can do is delay the loss of heat from pipes. Ultimately, the cold air in the house will get through the insulation and will reach the water inside the pipe. Metal pipes are better conductors than plastic, so the water inside the metal pipes is subjected to freezing temperatures much more quickly.

Don't try to thaw a frozen pipe with a blowtorch. Because the torch supplies tremendous heat to a restricted section of the pipe, the water in that area can quickly turn to steam, even while the rest of the pipe is still clogged with ice. The steam can generate enough pressure to burst the pipe, scalding anyone within reach.

If you cannot have a heating system turned on while you are away, you should drain the pipes. Shut off the main water valve—the valve that controls the flow of fresh water to all pipes. Then open all faucets, starting with those on the top floor of the home. Don't close any faucets, even if there is no more water flowing out of them.

As a next step, remove all water in traps. If the traps have a drainage plug, open it. If the traps don't have such a plug, loosen the slip nuts that hold the trap in place, and remove the entire trap. Flush the toilet and then, using a sponge, remove all the water from the toilet bowl.

Now replace all the traps you have removed and pour some antifreeze into the sink drains. Use the same antifreeze you have in the radiator of your car. You will need to pour in just enough to fill the trap.

If you have a separate hot water tank, drain it. And if your oil burner isn't an automatic type, but is one to which you must add water for a hot water system, drain it also.

Finally, call in a plumber and have him check what you have done. This will be a lot cheaper than replacing the house piping.

Chapter VII

Septic Tanks

The trouble with a plumbing system is that most of it is invisible. Yes, you can see the fixtures and even some of the pipes. But, for the most part, the fresh water supply and the drain setup are out of sight, in the walls, or hugging the walls and ceiling in the basement. Most people, particularly those who are about to buy or build a home, think of plumbing in terms of number of bathrooms.

But every bathroom, and every sink, shower, and lavatory, must ultimately connect with a sewer. Urban communities have public sewers but as you get out into the suburbs, you may reach the end of an existing sewer system. This means, then, that in such areas, sewage disposal—which is taken for granted in urban communities—because the homeowner's problem.

There is no question that public sewage disposal is the best method. The system is installed, maintained, and operated by the local government, and while you pay for its use in the form of tax-es, you are only responsible for the plumbing system in your home—not outside it. But if you decide to buy, build, or rent in an area not serviced by a public sewage disposal system, you have no alternative but to set up your own. This alternative is a septic tank installation, a private sewage system.

The Septic Process

There are two steps in the septic process. In the first the sewage is allowed to pass into a container known as a septic tank. The sewage is kept in this tank until it becomes as decomposed as possible, a process that is aided by enzymes, bacteria, and fungi. These agents help disintegrate the solid material, both animal and vegetable, into liquid form. In the second step, the liquid, sometimes referred to as effluent, moves from the septic tank through perforated drain tiles to a filter bed or to a drainage field, sometimes referred to as a septic tank absorption field. Here the liquid is given an opportunity to make contact with the air.

The Basic Septic Tank System

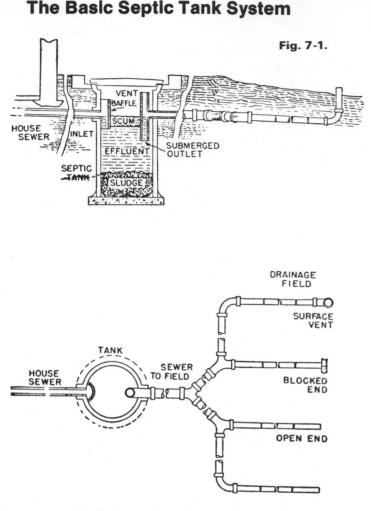

Fig. 7-1.

Basic type of septic tank installation.

There are various possible septic tank arrangements. Fig. 7-1 shows just one type. Drawing A in Fig. 7-1 is a side view of the septic tank system; drawing B is a top view. The house sewer empties into the septic tank. The sewage consists of a mixture of solid matter and liquid, and so the heavier portions settle down to form a sludge at the bottom of the tank. Grease and lighter substances rise and form a scum, while liquid fills the space between the sludge and the scum. Bacteria of types which need no air or oxygen decompose or putrefy much of the sludge within about 24 hours. Various

gases develop, agitating the contents of the tank, and so hasten the action.

The liquid (or effluent) between the scum and the sludge can flow out of the tank though a pipe or submerged outlet positioned to avoid both the sludge and the scum. The effluent is health hazardous and therefore must not be allowed to contaminate any fresh water source. It is important to keep it away from wells or springs.

The overflow of effluent from the tank is then dispersed over a fairly wide area through drain tile or perforated pipe. The tile or pipe is laid in trenches or in a seepage bed and is covered with soil; the soil is planted to grass and no part of the system is visible. With other types of installation, the filtration takes place in specially prepared beds of broken stone, screened gravel, coarse sand or coke, retained by embankmets or by masonry enclosures.

In some spetic tank setups, the effluent is brought into one or more distribution boxes before moving to the absorption field. The purpose of the distribution box is to control the flow into the drain tiles so that there is more unfiorm movement of the effluent. One of the other advantages of the distribution box is that it permits examination of the effluent to make sure that sludge isn't being carried along with it.

There are certain requirements for any septic tank arrangement: The connection between the house sewer and the septic tank must be tight jointed. There should be no chance for sewage to go anywhere except into the septic tank. The same condition applies to the effluent leaving the septic tank. It must flow to the distribution box, drainage field, or filtration bed, and nowhere else. The septic tank system of Fig. 7-1 should work well for many years, provided it is properly installed and maintained and that the soil in the disposal area is suitable.

In a conventional septic tank absorption field, as shown in Fig. 7-2, drain tile is laid out in trenches. Both the tank and the tile are covered with soil with the area planted in grass. Fig. 7-3 shows that the septic system is covered and is invisible. The effluent from the septic tank is carried through the drain tile to all points of the absorption field, where it is absorbed and by the surrounding soil.

Nonuniform Effluent Distribution

The functioning of the septic tank shown in Fig. 7-1 depends on the use of plumbing facilities in the home. As liquid wastes come into the septic tank from the home, an equivalent amount of effluent will rise in the submerged outlet inside the septic tank, and so the effluent level inside the septic tank will remain at a substantially constant height. Actually, the rate of flow from the house into the tank is just a few gallons at a time, and so the discharge from the septic tank is also just a few gallons. Because this is a rather slow rate, most of the discharge will seep into the earth from the first few feet of drain tile. The result is that the absorption field (also called a discharge field) isn't used uniformly. That part of the field near the tank will tend to become saturated and very foul, while the remainder of the field will be unused. The overall effect is

the same as using an inadequate field. To avoid that problem, a better arrangement than that of Fig. 7-1 is used.

Septic Tank Siphon Arrangement

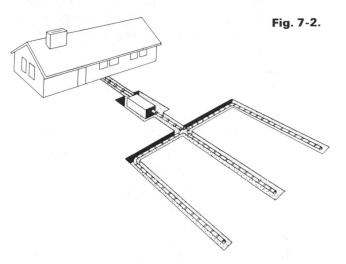

Fig. 7-2.

The drain tile is buried in trenches.

That better arrangement is illustrated in Fig. 7-4. With this setup the effluent is now distributed more uniformly through the absorption field. Instead of a single septic tank, two tanks are used. The tank connected to the house sewer is referred to as a septic tank or sometimes as a settling tank. This tank is connected to another called the siphon tank.

Like the basic septic tank, the settling tank has a submerged outlet, and, as a matter of fact, the settling tank works in the same way as the basic tank. As the liquid effluent in the settling tank rises, it will discharge through the submerged outlet when its level is high enough. The effluent then flows into the siphon tank instead of directly into drain tiles.

Note that the siphon tank is equipped with a trap. The higher the level of liquid in the tank, the more compressed the air becomes in the region above the liquid. The effluent will continue to rise, however, until it reaches the level indicated as "high water line" in the drawing. By now the air above the effluent is highly compressed and exerts enough pressure on the surface of the liquid to force the liquid through the trap.

The action is just as though you had flushed a toilet. There is now a rapid flow of effluent through the drain tiles to the drainage field, but because the effluent flows with considerable velocity, it reaches all parts of the field. The pressure of the air above the effluent exerts a force similar to that of a pump, but once the flow of water has started through the trap, the continuing action is like that of a siphon. In other words, air pressure starts the movement of effluent through the trap, and siphonage continues it.

Note the cap placed above the drain pipe leading to the trap in Fig. 7-4. The flow of effluent will continue until the level of effluent reaches the edge of the cap, and then it will stop. No further effluent will go out to the drainage field, and once again the siphon tank will start filling until it reaches the high water line.

Drain Tile Capacity

The total volume of the drain tiles, or its capacity, is often made equal to the volume of one complete discharge. This means that during a single discharge from the siphon tank, the drain tile system is completely filled, and so the effluent escapes into all parts of the absorption field. The absorption field is thus used to its maximum capability. There is little chance of backup into the siphon tank,

even though some effluent may be coming into it from the septic tank. Actually, there may be a long time before the siphon tank discharges again. During this period, oxygen in the air penetrates the earth or the filtration bed. The effluent is given an opportunity to evaporate.

The siphon tank is equipped with a vent. (see Fig. 7-4). The purpose of this vent, unlike that of the venting systems used inside the home, is to permit the escape of liquid effluent if the siphon should become clogged.

A siphon system can be added to an existing septic tank installation. There are various types of siphon systems. Whether you need a siphon tank depends on the extent to which fixtures in the home are used. When a home is used for year-round living and has a number of occupants, a siphon tank might be necessary; weekend or summer homes, it might not.

There are other factors to consider. The house might be situated on a high level and so the drain tiles could have a pitch or slope that would ensure good distribution of the effluent to all parts of the absorption field, something not possible where the ground is flat. Or the drain tiles might discharge into an already polluted stream or into salt water. In some cases, two or three septic tanks are used, with one discharging into another. All these septic tanks are of the same size and construction.

Septic Tank Design and Construction

A septic tank is a storage unit that is

completely enclosed. It isn't vented to the outside air, nor is there any reason why it should be, because the bacterial action does not require oxygen. Any vent pipe that is included is simply for the purpose of relieving effluent pressure on drain tiles.

The cubic content of the tank should be proportional to the volume of sewage per day. Septic action is usually satisfactory if the tank can hold the volume of sewage produced in a 24-hour period. But this varies, of course, with the number of persons in the household. A typical allowance would be from 25 to 50 gallons of sewage per person per day. Thus, for a family of five, the capacity of the septic tank could be anything between 125 and 250 gallons. To allow adequate space for installing a septic tank consider that a gallon occupies 231 cubic inches of space or 0.134 cubic foot. A 200gallon tank, then, would take up 200 x 231 or 46,200 cubic inches, or 200 x 0.134 or approximately 27 cubic feet.

It is considered that 12 hours between discharges from the septic tank is enough to keep the absorption field in good condition. If the capacity of the settling tank is that required to hold sewage for 24 hours, the capacity of the siphon tank between the high-water line and the low-level line should be about half the capacity of the settling tank.

A septic tank is nothing more than a large watertight container. It is sometimes called a settling tank, since solid matter gradually settles to the lower part of the tank. Here the solid matter is gradually decomposed into fine particle form by enzyme and bacterial action.

Septic tanks can be made of almost any material that is watertight and will remain that way without rotting. If steel is used, it is coated with asphalt. Septic tanks can also be made of concrete, concrete block, brick, or clay tile. Septic tanks made of precast concrete are delivered to the site by the manufacturer.

The top and bottom of a septic tank should be concrete. The top of the tank usually has a pipe extending from it, with a screw-on plug cap. The plug can be removed for measurement of the sludge layer at the bottom of the tank, or for removal of the sludge when it buids up to too high a level. Septic tanks also have baffle plates for controlling the flow of waste into and out of the tank.

According to the U.S. Public Health Service, the minimum tank capacity for a two-bedroom home should be a 750 gallons. They suggest 900-gallon tanks for three-bedroom homes and 1000 gallon units for four bedroom homes.

Clean, coarse sand or gravel	200	12	20
Light loam or fine sand	330	20	32
Fine sand with some loam or clay	500	30	50
Loam with some sand and clay	830	50	82
Clay with some sand or gravel	350	80	136

The gas developed in the septic tank is noxious. If you plan to inspect the septic tank, possibly to make a measurement of the sludge depth, remember that the fumes that escape are extremely unhealthy. Keep the cap off for an hour or so to give the gases a chance to escape. The gases are also explosive, so follow a no smoking rule when the screw-on plug at the top of the septic tank pipe is off. Methane is one of the gases generated inside the tank.

A septic tank can also be made of 24-inch-diameter vitrified sewer pipe with bottoms of 4-inch-think concrete. The inside of the bottom can be protected with a heavy coating of asphalt cement, such as that used for roofing. The purpose is to make all joints inside the septic tank absolutely watertight so as to prevent seepage into the earth surrounding the tank.

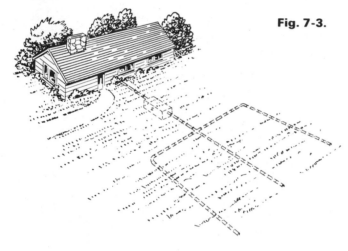

Fig. 7-3.

The septic tank and drain tiles are covered with earth.

Fig. 7-5 shows a vertical cross section through a concrete settling tank and a siphon tank built as a single unit. It works in the same way as separate tanks. The vertical walls are usually made 6 to 8 inches thick while the bottoms and tops are 4 to 6 inches thick. The tops are made of reinforced construction with heavy gauge wire mesh or with steel rods embedded in the concrete. The built-in connection shown between the two tanks is formed in the concrete wall by inserting any light-gauge sheet metal pipe in the forms before the concrete is poured.

The depth of liquid to the high-water line in the siphon tank depends on the type and size of siphon used, since it is the depth here that determines air pressure in the siphon and how the device acts. For a given capacity in the siphon tank, its length and width will have to satisfy the fixed depth to be used. Since the outer walls are ordinarily straight and continuous for the two tanks, the width of the settling tank will be the same as that of the siphon tank, so the depth and length of the settling tank will have to suit the required capacity.

Effects of Temperature

Bacterial action in the septic tank moves along more quickly when the contents of the tank aren't too cold, so in areas where winter temperatures fall to low levels, the top of the tank should be about 1 or 2 feet below ground level and should be tightly covered.

The Absorption Field

The idea of the drainage field is to let the oxygen in the air work on the thinly spread effluent liquid and the finely divided substances carried along with it. In planning a septic tank sewage disposal system, you must first learn if the soil can absorb the liquid sewage that flows from the septic tank. You cannot assume that earth is earth and that all soils absorb equally well and equally rapidly.

The best drainage field is made up of clean, corase sand or gravel, or any other substances which the air can penetrate easily. Further, the drainage field should not have a tendency to become waterlogged or to remain soggy. Distribution tile is sometimes put down on a bed of gravel, slag, coarse cinders, coke, or broken stone and is then covered lightly. Instead of being laid in such a specially prepared field, the tile can be buried in anylight soil that is porous and well drained.

Absorption Capacity

Installing a septic tank, with or without a siphon tank, is no guarantee the system will work well. How long and how well it will work depends largely on the absorption capacity of the soil. Two things must happen: The effluent must be absorbed by the soil, and it must be filtered by the soil. If unfiltered effluent reaches the surface it may contaminate ground water. Further, unfiltered sewage that manages to reach the surface has a bad odor and attracts flies and other insects, which may use the region for breeding. Such insects can be disease carriers.

Effects of Sunlight

The effluent must evaporate while any residue, generally consisting of small particles, must be oxidized. Oxidation is done by the oxygen in the air, with a considerable assist from sunlight. For this reason the drainage field should be free of trees or shrubs. There is a further reason for having the drainage field clear of trees. Tree roots could penetrate the open joints or perforations of the drainage tiles and this would result in clogging. This does not mean the surface cover of the absorption field should be barren. If it is, erosion by wind and rain could expose the tiles. You can prevent erosion by growing any thick, coarse grass.

Drain Tile Depth

In cold regions, bury the tiles no deeper than necessary to protect them against frost, and in warmer climates, bury them just enough to allow for a few inches of top covering. Ideally, you should try to get the tiles as close to the earth's surface as possible. Drainage tiles near the surface can be more easily reached by air. For this reason, before installing drain tile, the earth in the absorption field should be plowed or broken up, to make it more porous.

Knowing the absorption capacity of the soil will help determine the size of the absorption field you need. The slower the absorption rate, the larger the required field. The slower the absorption rate, the larger the required field. If you own a lot which has a very slow rate of absorption, it is possible you may require an absorption field larger than your property. Your local plumbing codes may prevent you from installing a septic tank sewage system. This, in turn, may make it impossible to construct a home on the site.

Conversely, if you are planning to buy ground on which to build a home, it would be a good idea, before making any purchase, to learn if you can connect your intended home to an existing sewer system. If not, you should learn whether the soil has an absorption capacity that is adequate for the kind of home you want to build.

Sometimes, because a lot cannot provide sewage facilities, its price will be depressed substantially below true market value. What seems to be a bargain may not be such a bargain after

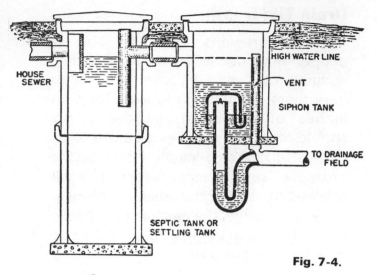

Fig. 7-4.

Separate septic and siphon tanks.

all. Some soils, regardless of the size of the lot, are just not suitable for use as septic tank absorption fields.

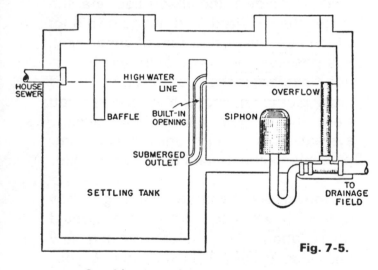

Fig. 7-5.

Combined septic and siphon tanks.

Amount of Tile Required

The total length of open-joint or perforated tile needed for a septive tank system depends on the volume of effluent, and that, in turn, depends on the number of people in the household and their habits. It also depends on the characteristics of the drainage field. If the field is light and not compacted, you could have good distribution of the effluent with fairly short lengths of tile, while a different kind of drainage field might call for longer lengths of tile having a smaller diameter. The following tabulation indicates the type of field, the total field area required per person, and the total length of tile in 3-inch and 4-inch diameters.

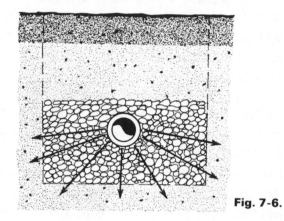

Fig. 7-6.

With the right type of loosely compacted soil, the effluent moves out easily and readily.

Fig. 7-6 shows how the effluent reaches all points of the absorption field from the drain tile, with the effluent being absorbed and filtered by the surrounding soil. However, the effluent moves very slowly into compact soils, which consist largely of clay with some sand or gravel (Fig. 7-7). Clay-type soil takes almost seven times as much field area to function as does clean coarse sand or gravel. Examined another way, it requires the use of about seven times as much tile of a given diameter for a clay field as it does for a coarse sand or gravel field. Further, it is quite possible for a sewage absorption field to fail to work properly when the field is either poorly drained or so compact that the absorption rate is very slow.

Fig. 7-7.

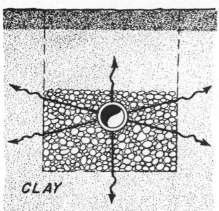

With a clay type or highly compacted soil, the effluent moves out relatively slowly.

One of the problems when the soil is poorly drained is that it becomes saturated with water during wet weather and may remain saturated for a long time after heavy rains. The result if there is no space left for sewage effluent. An absorption field of this kind may work well only during dry weather.

With soil that has a slow absorption rate, the effluent may rise to the surface, even during dry weather, while in wet weather the only way to describe the absorption field is "a boggy mess."

An absorption field can also fail for a number of other reasons:

1. The land may be too steep.
2. There may be a seasonable high-water table.
3. The soil may be very shallow and layered over bedrock.
4. The soil adjacent to and immediately below the drain tiles may be extremely compact.
5. The absorption field may be subject to flooding from time to time.

6. The total area of the absorption field may be too small to accommodate the number of persons using the plumbing facilities.

Where the soil consists of heavy clay or other substances through which air can penetrate only with difficulty, it will be necessary to break up the soil much more than with other soil types. If the soil is highly compacted, it may be necessary to put in underdrains, as shown in Fig. 7-8. An underdrain consists of open-joint tiles buried twice as deep as the drainage tile and preferably midway between the drainage lines. The underdrain can lead to an outlet at a still lower level, since the purpose of the underdrain is to prevent saturation of the drainage area.

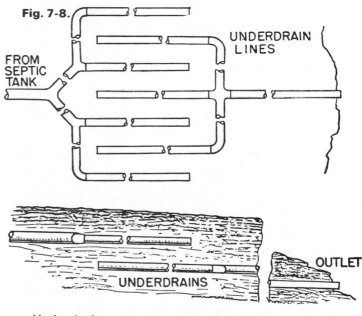

Underdrain used to supplement drain tiles.

Installation of Drain Tiles

Install open-joint or perforated drain tiles with a slight downward slope of about 1 foot in 100 feet. The idea is not to get the effluent to the end of the drainage tile in a hurry, but rather to have it disperse uniformly. At the same time the effluent is not going to flow uphill, nor do you want it collecting along a length of horizontal pipe. You can make the final 15 or 20 feet of each line level with a slight upward slope so you do not get a large puddle or pool of effluent at the ends. As shown earlier (fig. 7-1B), the ends of the perforated tile can be closed off with brick or stone, or they can simply be left open. One of the advantages of having the tiles come above the surface is that it lets air enter them, with the result that there is better oxidation and evaporation of the effluent.

If you have drain tiles running in parallel, make them at least 6 feet apart, but there is no particular advantage in having the separation greater than this.

Drainage on a Steep Slope

When the drainage field has a steep slope the lines of drain tile can be laid along the contours according to a plan such as that shown in Fig. 7-9. As much as possible keep the pitch of the drain tiles at about 1 foot in a 100 feet. You can have a sharp drop in the connections between the tiles. In this way you will have a succession of tiles with a normal slope, with a very steep drop of the connecting tiles, bringing them down to successively lower levels. The only requirement is that each portion of the absorption field should receive a proportionate quantity of effluent.

The fittings where the tile lines diverge can be of the V-branch type, so that the movement of effluent is approximately equal in both directions. Do not use a fit-

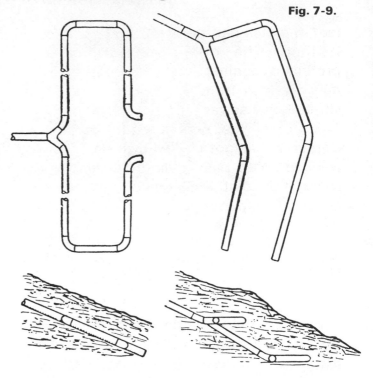

Fig. 7-9.

Layout of drainage tiles on steep slopes.

ting which has a straight-through section and a branch off to one side. With this type of fitting most of the effluent will continue along a straight line, with very little effluent going through the branch. With a V-fitting the effluent has no choice but to divide into two paths.

To make sure there is no chance of polluting a fresh water supply, the first open joint or perforated drainage tile should be at least 300 feet from any well or spring that supplies drinking water. The slope of the land between the well or spring should be downward toward the drainage tiles.

Laying Tile

When you install drainage tile, butt joint the first few tiles together at their ends, but gradually increase the separation along the line. During the last 15 or 20 feet, the tiles can be separated by about ½ inch. The open joints must be protected against dirt or pebbles that may wash in from the top. If the tile is vitrified clay sewer pipe, as shown in Fig. 7-10, point the socket ends downhill. Center the spigot end with three or four wedges. With plain cylindrical tile, surround the joint with broken stone and cover the top portion of the tile with a piece of board. A better method is to put short lengths of large-diameter clay gutter beneath and on top of the open joints.

With tiles made especially for drainage, having perforations along the side to be laid at the bottom, the joints between lengths are made with slipover sleeves and no other special protection is needed. Your local plumbing code may have something to say about tile placement, and you will probably find you are required to have it at least 10 or more feet away from buildings and neighboring property lines.

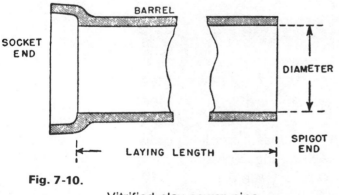

Fig. 7-10.

Vitrified clay sewer pipe.

Sewer Lines

The pipe connecting your house sewage to the septic tank is called the house sewer or house sewer line. It is often made of 4-inch extra-heavy cast iron soil pipe or else 5-inch or 6-inch vitrified sewer pipe. Since it will not be a single length of pipe, the joints must be made tight for the entire length between the house and the input to the septic tank. The septic tank should be a minimum of 50 feet, preferably at least 100 feet, from your home, with the connecting sewer pipe buried deeply enough to protect it from frost. The minimum slope per 100 feet of run for the sewer pipe should be 2 feet for 4-inch pipe, 1½ feet for 5-inch pipe, and 1 foot for 6-inch pipe.

Clogging and Cleaning

Grease is possibly the most frequent reason for clogging of the drain field tile and other parts of the system, so it is advisable to install a grease trap at the kitchen sink. Fig. 7-11 shows a typical grease trap. Greasy water comes through the inlet to the upper part of the trap. The grease floats on top of the contents of the trap. The remaining waste water goes into a space partitioned as shown in the drawing. The grease trap has a removable

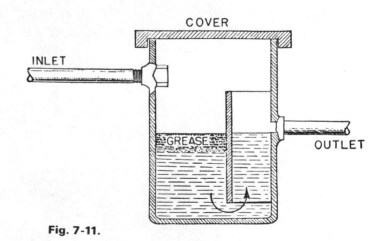

Fig. 7-11.

Grease trap.

cover so that accumulated grease can be removed. If this isn't done, the grease may form a scum thick enough to clog the trap and prevent liquid from reaching the outlet.

Soil Surveys

If you want to know more about the soil of the area you intend using as an absorption field, a published soil survey of your county will help. This includes a description of the soil and interpretations for soil use and shows the location and extent of each kind of soil. Soil surveys are published by the Soil Conservation Service (SCS), Washington, D.C. Local or

county offices of the SCS in your district or your state agricultural experiment station can tell you if a soil survey of your county has been published, and if so, where you can get a copy.

A soil map, such as the one shown in Fig. 7-12, will have letter symbols to indicate the various kinds of soils. In Fig. 7-12, Dakota soils are identified as **De**, clyde soils as Cg.

Soils

Dakota soils are dark colored and are found in sandy or gravelly material under

Fig. 7-12.

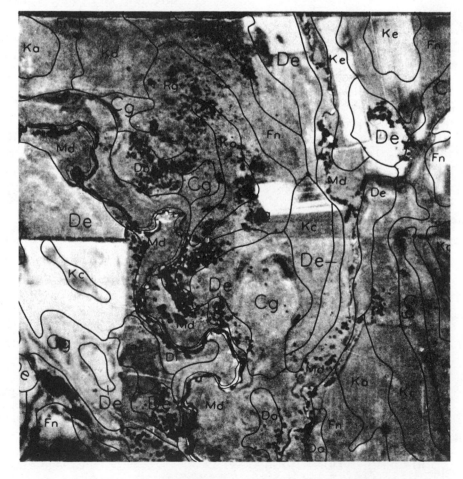

Portion of a soil map.

210

prairie grasses. The usual range of slope is from 0 to 17 percent. Dakota soils may be Dakota loams or Dakota sandy loams. Dakota loams have a finer textured surface layer and subsoil than Dakota sandy loams. Dakota loams are well drained while the sandy loams are somewhat excessively drained. With Dakota loam, runoff is medium and internal drainage is medium to rapid. This soil is easy to work and can be plowed throughout a wide range of moisture content.

Clyde soils are dark colored and occur in very poorly drained depressions. The black color and organic matter content are the result of the decay of sedges and rank sloughgrass.

Clyde soils are found in low-lying areas that are periodically flooded, especially after heavy rains. Except during dry periods the water table is generally very high and the soils are excessively moist. In some areas, the soil is saturated most of the time.

Clyde silty clay loam is a soil that is very dark-gray plastic high in organic matter. It extends from a depth of 12 to 20 inches. Beneath it is sand and gravel in varying amounts. In some places there are numerous boulders on the surface.

This soil is fertile but because of its heavy texture and wetness is difficult to work.

Dakota loam has slight limitations for use as a septic tank absorption field. It is well drained and has medium to rapid permeability. Clyde silty clay loam has severe limitations for use as a septic tank absorption field. When wet it absorbs septic tank effluent very slowly.

Septic tank disposal systems work very well in deep, permeable soils. Layout and construction problems may be encountered on slopes of more than 15 percent. Flood plains are not suitable for absorption fields. See Fig. 7-13.

Soil Factors

Whether a septic tank disposal system will work well depends not only on how the tank works, but also on the rate at which effluent moves into and through the soil. This, in turn, depends on soil permeability.

However, soil permeability, while important, isn't the only characteristic that will affect performance. Other factors are ground water level, soil depth, underlying material, the slope of the absorption field, and nearness to bodies of water such as streams, lakes, or wells.

Soil permeability is that characteristic of soil that lets water and air move through it. Permeability is determined by the soil type—the amount of gravel, sand, silt, and clay in the soil. Not all clays are alike and so permeability is also affected by the type of clay. Water moves faster through soils that are sandy or which have a high gravel content than through clay.

Some kinds of clay expand little when wet; others are so-called plastic types and expand so much when wet that the pores of the soil swell and become closed to water absorption. This behavior of

Fig. 7-13.

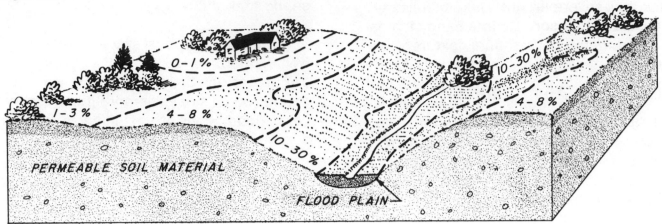

Slope variations in percents. A flood plain isn't suitable for a drainage field.

plastic clay-type soils means that such soil has less capacity to absorb septic tank effluent.

Effect of Ground Water Level

In some soils the ground water level is just a foot or so beneath the surface of the ground, not just following a heavy rain, but all year. In some areas, the ground water level may be high in winter and in early spring. There are also areas where the water level will rise quite high during prolonged rains. Regions where the water level can reach the surface or a point just below the surface are unsatisfactory for use as an absorption field.

Once the ground water level rises to or near the surface, the soil will be so wet, so saturated with water, that it will be unable to absorb effluent. As a consequence, the effluent, instead of being absorbed by the earth or being given an opportunity to oxidize or evaporate, will rise to the surface. The absorption field will stink and will constitute an unhealthy condition (Fig. 7-14).

Fig. 7-14.

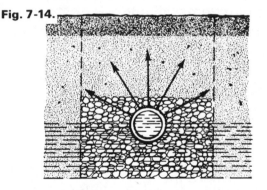

High water table at tile level forces the effluent upward to the surface.

Depth to Rock, Sand or Gravel

There should be at least 4 feet of soil material between the bottom of the trenches or seepage bed and any rock formation. Fig. 7-15 shows a representative area that might be considered for an absorption field. The deep soil over limestone, at the left, has moderate limitations for use as a septic tank absorption field. On the steeper slopes, given in percentages, layout and construction may be difficult. The soil that is 10 to 20 feet thick, at the extreme right, may not be suitable for absorption fields if the water supply is to come from a well.

The shallow soil, shown as 2 to 4 feet thick, has severe limitations. If this region is used as an absorption field, the stream at the bottom of the hill may become polluted.

Slope of the Absorption Field

If an absorption field is placed on a steep slope where there is a layer of dense clay, rock, or other impervious material near the surface, the effluent will flow above the impervious layer to the surface and will then run unfiltered down the hillside (Fig. 7-16). However, slopes of less than 15 percent usually do not create serious problems in either construction or maintenance, provided the soil is satisfactory.

In constructing a septic tank sewage disposal system on sloping land (Fig. 7-17), the tile lines are laid on the contour. Serial distribution, as shown in the drawing, it is necessary on most sloping fields or in fields where there is a change in soil type.

Fig. 7-16.

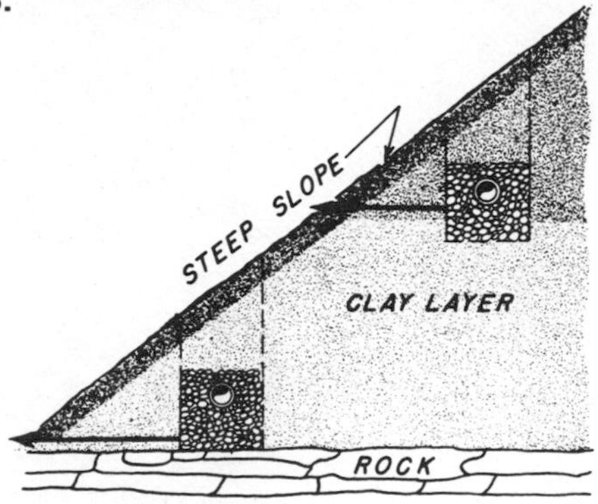

With steep slopes, effluent may run off.

Percolation Tests

Percolation tests are used to determine the absorption capacity of the soil and the size of the absorption field. Your local plumbing code may specify that such tests be performed by trained people, usually from a local health department. The tests are generally done when the soil moisture is at or near its capacity—in other words, under the worst possible conditions. If with such conditions the soil can absorb effluent, then there will be no problems when the soil is dry.

Fig. 7-15.

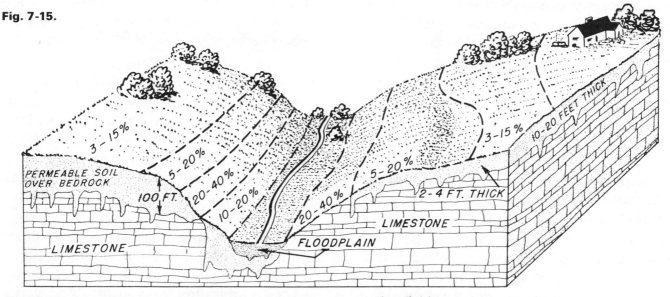

Typical problems encountered in the location of an absorption field.

Fig. 7-17.

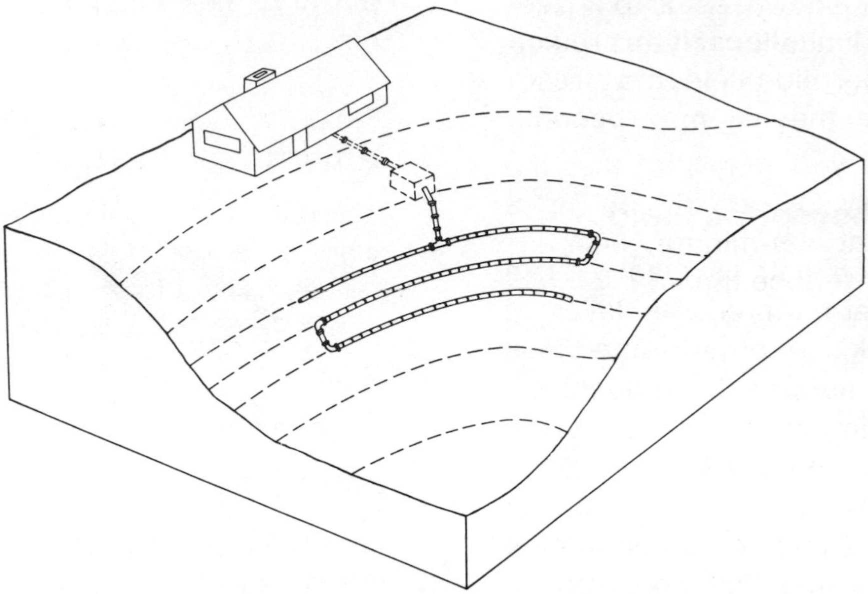

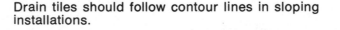

Drain tiles should follow contour lines in sloping installations.

Percolation tests require digging six or more test holes (Fig. 7-18) 4 to 12 inches in diameter and about as deep as the proposed trenches for the drain tiles. The holes, which are spaced uniformly over the proposed absorption field, have their sides roughened to remove any slick that might interfere with water entering the soil. Loose dirt at the bottom of the holes is removed and 2 inches of sand or fine gravel are then added to prevent sealing of the holes.

The next step is to pour at least 12 inches of water into each hole, with water added as needed to keep the water level 12 inches above the gravel for at least 4 hours, or preferably overnight during dry periods. If tests are made during a dry season, the holes should be thoroughly moistened to simulate wet weather conditions.

If the water is to remain in the test holes overnight, adjust the water level to about 6 inches above the gravel. Measure the drop in water level over a 30-minute period. Multiply that by 2 to get the inches per hour. The number of inches that the water level drops in the holes is the percolation rate.

The percolation rate will vary from one hole to the next. Take all of the percolation figures you have calculated and add them. Then divide by the total number of holes on which you have made your tests. This will give you an average percolation rate.

If no water remains in the test holes overnight, add water to bring the depth to 6 inches. Measure the drop in water level every 30 minutes for 4 hours. Add water as often as needed to keep it at the 6-inch level. Use the drop in water level that occurs during the final 30 minutes to calculate the percolation rate.

In sandy soils you may find that the water seeps away too rapidly to make measurements at 30-minute intervals feasible. Instead, reduce the time interval between measurements to 10 minutes and then run the test for only 1 hour. Use the drop that occurs during the final 10 minutes to calculate the percolation rate.

How to Calculate the Size of the Absorption Field

Most public health agencies set standards for the size of absorption fields on the basis of the number of bedrooms in a house, which probably gives the best estimate of the number of occupants.

Fig. 7-18.

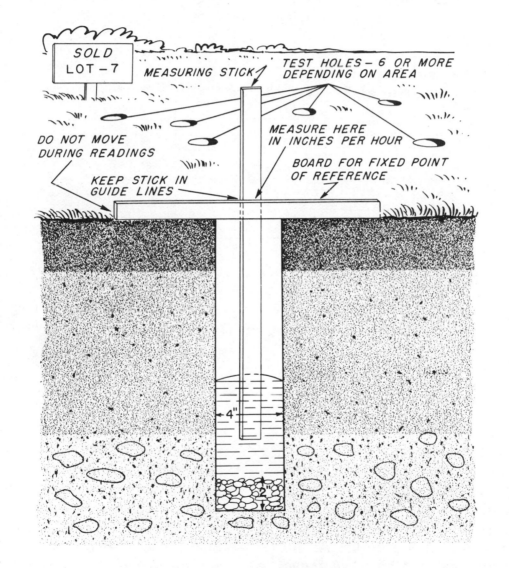

A percolation test hole with measuring stick is shown in the foreground; other test holes, properly distributed, are in the background.

Fig. 7-19.

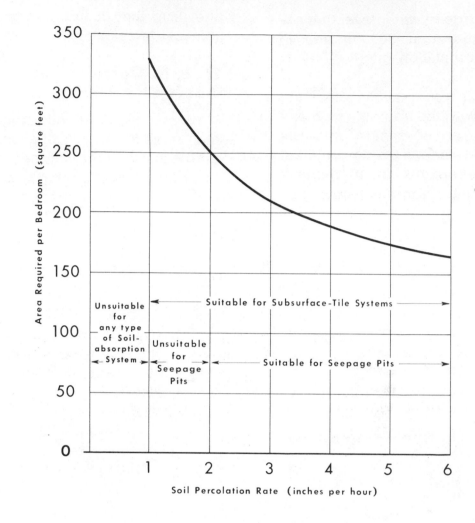

Graph for calculating size of absorption field.

To calculate the size of the absorption field, use the chart shown in Fig. 7-19. If you look along the bottom part of the chart, you will see it is calibrated in terms of soil percolation rate in inches per hour. Select your percolation rate, and then move upward toward the curve. At the point where you intersect the curve, move your finger to the left and you will find the area required per bedroom in square feet.

As an example, assume your percolation rate is 3 inches per hour. Put your finger on the number 3 and move directly upward until you reach the curved line. Then move horizontally to the left and you will intersect slightly above 200. The number will be about 210. This is 210 square feet per bedroom. If your house has three bedrooms, then you will require 3 x 210 or 630 square feet for your absorption field.

Count only the bottoms of the trenches as the effective absorption area. To find out how long the trenches should be and how much drain tile or perforated pipe you will need, divide the square feet of absorption area need by the width, in feet, of the trenches. This will give you the total trench length.

The trenches should be spaced 6 to 8 feet apart. Multiply the total trench length by the distance between trench center lines to get the total area, in square feet, to be occupied by the absorption field.

As an example, assume you have a two-bedroom house and that the trenches are to be 2 feet wide, and that the soil percolation rate is 2 inches per hour. Locate the digit 2 on the bottom of the chart and move upward to the graph. Move to the left and locate the number 250. For two bedrooms the absorption area required will be 2 x 250 = 500 feet. Dividing 500 square feet by 2 feet (this is the total length of trench and tile or pipe required.

For this system the best layout would be four trenches, each about 62 feet long. But three trenches, each about 84 feet long, would also make a good layout. Trenches should not be more than 100 feet.

Choosing a Septic Tank Absorption Field

1. If you plan to buy land for the purpose of building a house on it, learn beforehand whether the soil will accommodate a septic tank system for the number of bedrooms you plan to have.

2. Before you plan a sewage disposal system, get in touch with the health department of the community. They may be familiar with septic tank problems of the land.

3. Learn the laws governing sewage disposal in the community, what permits are required before installing a septic tank, the inspection requirements, and the penalties for violations. If your septic tank installation doesn't work properly, you may not only take a loss on your investment but also receive a penalty.

4. The soil permeability of the land you intend buying should be moderate to rapid. Try to obtain percolation data about the property. It should be at least 1 inch per hour.

5. The ground water level during the wettest season should be at least 4 feet below the bottom of the trenches in a subsurface tile absorption field and 4 feet below the pit floor in a field using seepage pits.

6. If the soil is rocky, or if boulders must be moved, consider the added expense of installing a septic tank system in such an area. Rock formations or other impervious layers should be more than 4 feet below the bottom of trenches, seepage bed floor, or pit floor.

7. Does the land slope very steeply? Trenches and seepage beds are difficult to lay out and construct on slopes that have a pitch of more than 15 percent.

8. Don't select as an absorption field any area that is within 50 feet of a stream or any other body of water that may be used as a fresh water source. Never install a sewage disposal system on a flood plain or any area that is subject to flooding.

9. You may have problems if the proposed absorption field consists of a

variety of soils which vary in their absorption capacity.

Seepage Pits or Beds

Instead of being dispersed through subsurface tile in an absorption field, you can dispose of the effluent by having it move from the septic tank into a seepage pit. This is a covered pit (Fig. 7-20) with a porous lining through which the effluent seeps into the surrounding soil.

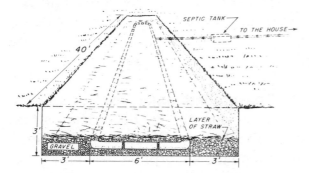

Construction details of a seepage pit or bed.

Before you decide that a seepage pit is a preferred arrangement, check with your local health authorities. It is quite possible such an installation is prohibited.

Cesspools

A cesspool is a tank that contains the sewage produced in the home. Cesspools, like septic tanks, are buried in the earth. Unlike a septic tank, the cesspool is constructed so that the sewage can seep into the ground surrounding it.

One of the advantages of a septic tank over a cesspool is that the perforated tile of the septic tank system spreads the effluent over a large area, giving both earth and air an opportunity to work on the effluent. Because cesspools are limited in this respect, they can produce serious health hazards and so are prohibited in many areas.

Sometimes a cesspool arrangement will use two tanks. The effluent flows into one tank, which is completely watertight. This first tank retains solid waste, but permits liquid matter to flow into a second tank. This second tank, known as a leaching tank, is constructed so that the liquid waste can seep into the earth. The leaching tank walls are porous.

This arrangement overcomes one of the most serious problems of the single-tank cesspool. In the single-tank cesspool, the walls must be porous enough to let the effluent escape. But the liquid contains particles of solid matter and these tend to clog the "pores" of the tank walls. When this happens, the effluent has no way to escape, so it overflows from the tank.

How to Take Care of Your Septic Tank System

The chemical action that takes place in a septic tank is sometimes referred to as "digestion." Enzymes and bacteria work on the solid matter, reducing it to finely divided particles suspended in liquid.

However, there are certain materials that either are not affected by septic tank action or require an exceptionally long time. Certain substances take so long to decompose they can properly be described as being non-biodegradable. Solid materials such as rags, heavy cardboard, plastic, china, and metals (razorblades, spoons, knives, and the like) shouldn't be allowed to move into the septic tank.

However, accidents do happen, so in some septic tank setups the submerged outlet of the septic tank or settling tank is fitted with a wire screen of about ¼ inch mesh to catch substances that can't be decomposed and to keep them out of the siphon or the drainage tile.

The sludge that accumulates in the bottom of the septic tank or the settling tank must be removed about once a year, or else it will pass through the drainage field, clogging the perforated tile and making it necessary to dig up and clean the whole filtration system. Sludge is usually removed by bailing or pumping. It's a messy job which is best left to commercial companies that specialize in septic tank maintenance.

In locations where there is a nearby slope extending below the bottom of the tank it is possible to install a drain pipe from a valve placed in the tank bottom, then to drain and flush out the sludge through this outlet. The removed sludge can be taken out in barrels or tanks to a place where it may be buried with safety.

Scum that forms at the top of the liquid in the septic tank must be removed before it becomes so deep that it may pass through the tank outlet.

Various chemicals* are available for dissolving the sludge into liquid form. These can be poured into a toilet in the home and then flushed into the septic tank. Some homeowners believe that adding yeast to the flush water of a toilet helps the process of decomposition of the

*Bac-Tivaror, FX4, Enzivator, Roebic Formula K37, Sanzyme, Septic-Kleen, Septicare, and others.

sludge. Some chemicals that are offered to septic tank owners are designed to encourage enzyme action in the tank, thus hastening the natural process that takes place.

If you plan to use yeast, you might try about a half-pound of brewer's yeast powder in about a gallon or two of hot water. Stir the yeast thoroughly until it is completely dissolved. Pour the yeast-water combination into the toilet bowl closest to the septic tank. The water you pour into the toilet bowl will tend to flush the bowl, and so the liquid will flow from the house sewer line into the septic tank.

The Double Septic Tank System

In some installations, two septic tanks are used. One tank takes care of all toilet waste, while the other handles liquid waste only, such as that from sinks, showers, tubs and washing machines. One of the problems which might arise here is due to phosphates used in washing powders, bleaches, and detergents. These substances can inhibit the bacterial action in the septic tank, and so the action of enzymes and bacteria on the sludge becomes much slower. The result is a much more rapid accumulation of slude and the need for more frequent cleaning.

Still another problem is the fact that washing machines are capable of dumping large quantities of water into the septic tank at a rather rapid rate. The velocity of the discharge into the tank is such that the sludge is stirred up and manages to flow out with the effluent. There are two factors here, both bad. The first is that his escaping sludge has not been acted upon by bacteria and so is really untreated sewage. The other is that this sewage is capable of blocking the "pores" of the drain tile, preventing the free flow of effluent into the drainage field. Keep in mind that the septic tank does not purify sewage; it simply prepares it for that step. Purification is taken care of by the soil (which acts as a filter) and by the air (which acts as an oxidizing agent).

Puddling

Puddling is the term applied to pools of effluent which reach the surface around some part of the area using drain tiles. Puddling can be due to drain tiles which are broken or which have been forced out of place. It's a good idea to keep cars or trucks from moving across any absorption field. The pressure caused by the vehicle on the earth can crack the drain tiles or push them out of position.

Excessive use of a device such as a washing machine can also cause puddling. Don't run one wash load after another. Instead, try to space your wash loads to give the earth a chance to absorb the effluent.

Chapter *VIII*

Plumbing Data

Table 1. Decimal equivalents for fractional parts of an inch.

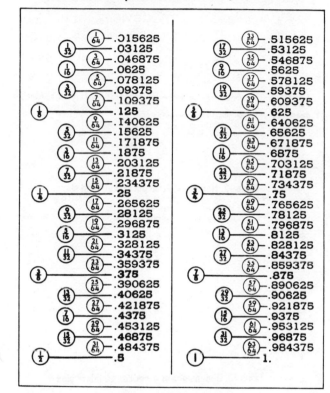

1/64	.015625	33/64	.515625
1/32	.03125	17/32	.53125
3/64	.046875	35/64	.546875
1/16	.0625	9/16	.5625
5/64	.078125	37/64	.578125
3/32	.09375	19/32	.59375
7/64	.109375	39/64	.609375
1/8	.125	5/8	.625
9/64	.140625	41/64	.640625
5/32	.15625	21/32	.65625
11/64	.171875	43/64	.671875
3/16	.1875	11/16	.6875
13/64	.203125	45/64	.703125
7/32	.21875	23/32	.71875
15/64	.234375	47/64	.734375
1/4	.25	3/4	.75
17/64	.265625	49/64	.765625
9/32	.28125	25/32	.78125
19/64	.296875	51/64	.796875
5/16	.3125	13/16	.8125
21/64	.328125	53/64	.828125
11/32	.34375	27/32	.84375
23/64	.359375	55/64	.859375
3/8	.375	7/8	.875
25/64	.390625	57/64	.890625
13/32	.40625	29/32	.90625
27/64	.421875	59/64	.921875
7/16	.4375	15/16	.9375
29/64	.453125	61/64	.953125
15/32	.46875	31/32	.96875
31/64	.484375	63/64	.984375
1/2	.5	1	1.

Table 2. Metric Conversion Guide.

INCHES TO MILLIMETERS

To find milimeters use this formula:
Inches x 15.4

To find inches use this formula:
Millimeters x .03937

⅛" —	3.175	2" —	50.8
¼" —	6.35	2½" —	63.5
⅜" —	9.525	3" —	76.2
½" —	12.7	3½" —	88.9
¾" —	19.05	4" —	101.6
1" —	25.4	4½" —	114.3
1¼" —	31.75	5" —	127
1½" —	38.1	6" —	152.4

Table 3. Weight of Cast Iron Soil Pipe.

Pounds Per 5-foot Length

DIAMETER Inches	STANDARD	EXTRA HEAVY Single Hub	EXTRA HEAVY Double Hub
2	18	25	26
3	26	45	47
4	35	60	63
5	45	75	78
6	52	95	100
8		150	157

Table 4. Storm Drains and Leaders

Maximum Drained Area, Sq. Ft.

PIPE DIAMETER	DRAINS	LEADERS
1¼	130	
1½	210	
2	350-440	500
2½	670-790	960
3	1050-1250	1500
4	2150-2650	3100
5	3600-4700	5400
6	6000-7500	8400
8	12000-16000	17400

Table 5. Horizontal branch capacities in fixture units.

WASTE PIPE Diameter	MAXIMUM UNITS PER BRANCH	SOIL PIPE Diameter	MAXIMUM UNITS PER BRANCH
1¼	1	3	20
1½	3	4	160
2	6	5	360
3	32	6	640
		8	1200

Table 6. Diameters and maximum lengths of vent stacks.

STACK DIAM. Inches	FIXTURE UNITS	1¼	1½	2	2½	3	4	5	6	8
¼	1 max.	45								
1½	8 max.	35	60							
2	18 max.	30	50	90						
2½	36 max.	25	45	75	105					
	12		34	120	180	212				
	18		18	70	180	212				
	24		12	50	130	212				
3	36		8	35	93	212				
	48		7	32	80	212				
	72		6	25	65	212				
	24			25	110	200	300	340		
	48			16	65	115	300	340		
	96			12	45	84	300	340		
4	144			9	36	72	300	340		
	192			8	30	64	282	340		
	264			7	20	56	245	340		
	384			5	18	47	206	340		
	72				40	65	250	390	440	
	144				30	47	180	390	440	
	288				20	32	124	390	440	
5	432				16	24	94	320	440	
	720				10	16	70	225	440	
	1020				8	13	58	180	440	
	144					27	108	340	510	
	288					15	70	220	510	630
	576					10	43	150	425	630
6	864					7	33	125	320	630
	1296					6	25	92	240	630
	2070					4	21	75	186	630
	320						42	144	400	750
	640						30	86	260	750
	960						22	60	190	750
8	1600						16	40	120	525
	2500						12	28	90	370
	4160						7	22	62	252

Table 7. Stack capacities—Total fixture units

STACK DIAM. Inches	TOTAL LENGTH FEET (Max.)	MAXIMUM With Only Y-fittings	FIXTURE UNITS With Sanitary tees
1¼	50	1	1
1½	65	12	8
2	85	36	16
3	212	72	48
4	300	384	256
5	390	1020	680
6	510	2070	1380
8	750	5400	3600

Table 8. Stack capacity per branch interval.

STACK DIAM. Inches	MAXIMUM FIXTURE UNITS IN ONE INTERVAL—8 FT. LENGTH With Only Y-fittings	With Sanitary Tees
1¼	1	1
1½	4	2
2	15	9
3	45	24
4	240	144
5	540	324
6	1120	670
8	3480	2088

Table 10. Elbow and tee equivalents in feet of straight vent pipe.

ELBOW OR TEE Diameter	PIPE LENGTH	ELBOW OR TEE Diameter	PIPE LENGTH
1¼	2½	3½	11
1½	3	4	13
2	5	5	19
2½	7	6	24
3	9	8	35

Table 9. Equivalent lengths of vent pipe.

Number of Feet for Equal Resistances

SMALLER PIPE DIA.	LARGER PIPE DIAMETER 1½	2	2½	3	3½	4	5	6	8
1¼	2.3	10	26	87	192	375			
1½		4.1	11	36	80	170	529		
2			2.6	8.7	19	36	130	242	
2½				3.3	7.3	14	46	128	530
3					2.2	4.4	14.5	38	160
3½						2.0	6.6	17.5	72
4							3.3	8.7	36
5								2.6	13
6									4.1

Table 11. Dimensions of copper tubing for water service.

Nominal Size	Actual O.D.	Wall Thickness Type K	Type L	Type M
¼	⅜	.035	.030	.025
⅜	½	.049	.035	.025
½	⅝	.049	.040	.028
⅝	¾	.049	.042	.030
1¼	⅞	.065	.045	.032
1	1⅛	.065	.050	.035
1⅛	1⅜	.065	.055	.042
1½	1⅝	.072	.060	.049
2	2⅛	.083	.070	.058
2½	2⅝	.095	.080	.065
3	3⅛	.109	.090	.072
3½	3⅝	.120	.100	.083
4	4⅛	.134	.110	.095
5	5⅛	.160	.125	.109
6	6⅛	.192	.140	.122
8	8⅛	.271	.200	.170

Type "K"—For underground service, general plumbing and heating purposes, gas-steam and lines.
Type "L"—For general plumbing and heating purposes.
Type "M"—For general plumbing purposes with solder fittings only.
NOT for underground services.

Table 12. Horizontal drain pipe length and slope.

PIPE SIZE Inches	Minimum (inches)	LENGTH Maximum (feet)	FALL IN INCHES Minimum	Maximum
1¼	2½	5	1¼	1¼
1½	3	6	1½	1½
2	4	8	2	2
2½	5	10	1¼	1½
3	6	12	1½	3
3½	7	14	1¾	3½
4	8	16	2	4
5	10	20	1¼	5
6	12	24	1½	6
8	16	32	2	8

Table 13. Dimensions of American standard pipe.

Nominal Size	I.D.	O.D.	Wall Thickness	Threads per Inch
⅛"	0.269	0.405	.068	27
¼"	0.364	0.540	.088	18
⅜"	0.493	0.675	.091	18
½"	0.622	0.840	.109	14
¾"	0.824	1.050	.113	14
1"	1.049	1.315	.133	11½
1¼"	1.380	1.660	.140	11½
1½"	1.610	1.900	.145	11½

Nominal Size	I.D.	O.D.	Wall Thickness	Threads per Inch
2"	2.067	2.375	.154	11½
2½"	2.469	2.875	.203	8
3"	3.068	3.500	.216	8
3½"	3.548	4.000	.226	8
4"	4.026	4.500	.237	8
4½"	4.506	5.000	.247	8
5"	5.047	5.563	.258	8
6"	6.065	6.625	.280	8

Table 14. Plumbing symbols.

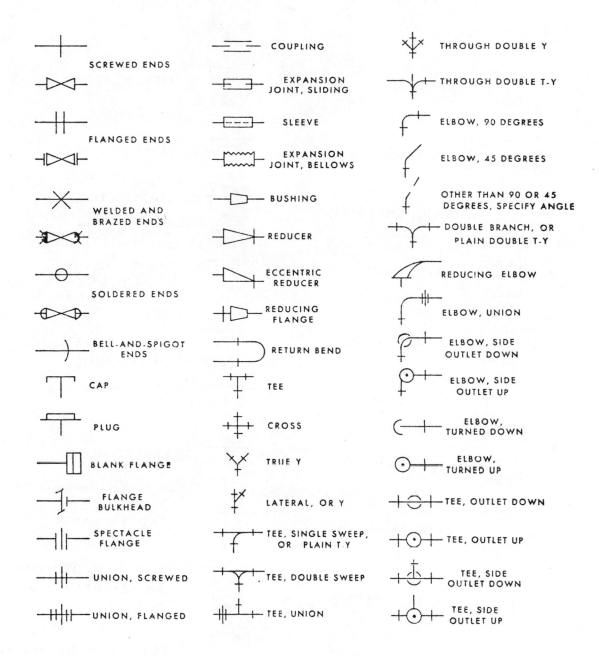

BATH. ANGLE TUB

BATH, SITZ
SB

BATH, ARM
AB

BIBB, HOSE
HB

BATH, CORNER

BIDET
B

BATH, EMERGENCY
EB

WATER CLOSET,
LOW TANK
LT

BATH, FOOT
FB

WATER, CLOSET,
NO TANK

BATH, HUBBARD
HB

WATER CLOSET,
WALL-HUNG
WH

BATH, INFANTS
IB

DISHWASHER
DW

BATH, LEG
LB

FAUCET, HOSE
HF

BATH, PRENATAL
PB

FAUCET, LAWN
LF

BATH, RECESSED

FOUNTAIN, DRINKING
AND ELECTRIC WATER
COOLER
EWC

FOUNTAIN, DRINKING,
PEDESTAL
DF

BATH, ROLL RIM

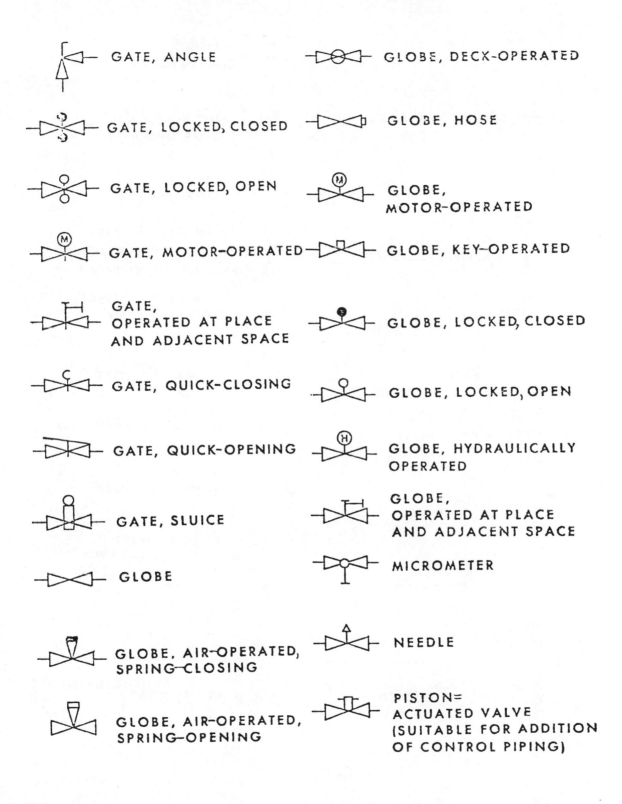

GATE, ANGLE

GLOBE, DECK-OPERATED

GATE, LOCKED, CLOSED

GLOBE, HOSE

GATE, LOCKED, OPEN

GLOBE, MOTOR-OPERATED

GATE, MOTOR-OPERATED

GLOBE, KEY-OPERATED

GATE, OPERATED AT PLACE AND ADJACENT SPACE

GLOBE, LOCKED, CLOSED

GATE, QUICK-CLOSING

GLOBE, LOCKED, OPEN

GATE, QUICK-OPENING

GLOBE, HYDRAULICALLY OPERATED

GATE, SLUICE

GLOBE, OPERATED AT PLACE AND ADJACENT SPACE

GLOBE

MICROMETER

GLOBE, AIR-OPERATED, SPRING-CLOSING

NEEDLE

GLOBE, AIR-OPERATED, SPRING-OPENING

PISTON= ACTUATED VALVE (SUITABLE FOR ADDITION OF CONTROL PIPING)

The Encyclopedia of Household Plumbing

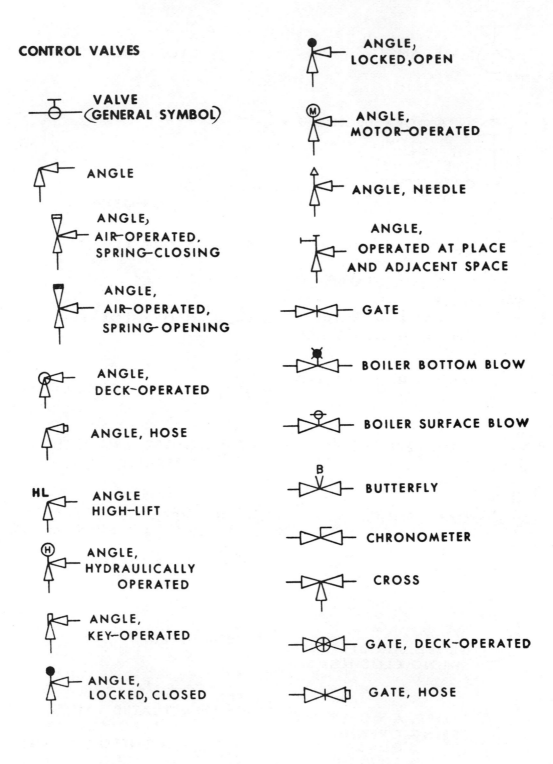

CONTROL VALVES

VALVE (GENERAL SYMBOL)

ANGLE

ANGLE, AIR-OPERATED, SPRING-CLOSING

ANGLE, AIR-OPERATED, SPRING-OPENING

ANGLE, DECK-OPERATED

ANGLE, HOSE

ANGLE HIGH-LIFT

ANGLE, HYDRAULICALLY OPERATED

ANGLE, KEY-OPERATED

ANGLE, LOCKED, CLOSED

ANGLE, LOCKED, OPEN

ANGLE, MOTOR-OPERATED

ANGLE, NEEDLE

ANGLE, OPERATED AT PLACE AND ADJACENT SPACE

GATE

BOILER BOTTOM BLOW

BOILER SURFACE BLOW

BUTTERFLY

CHRONOMETER

CROSS

GATE, DECK-OPERATED

GATE, HOSE

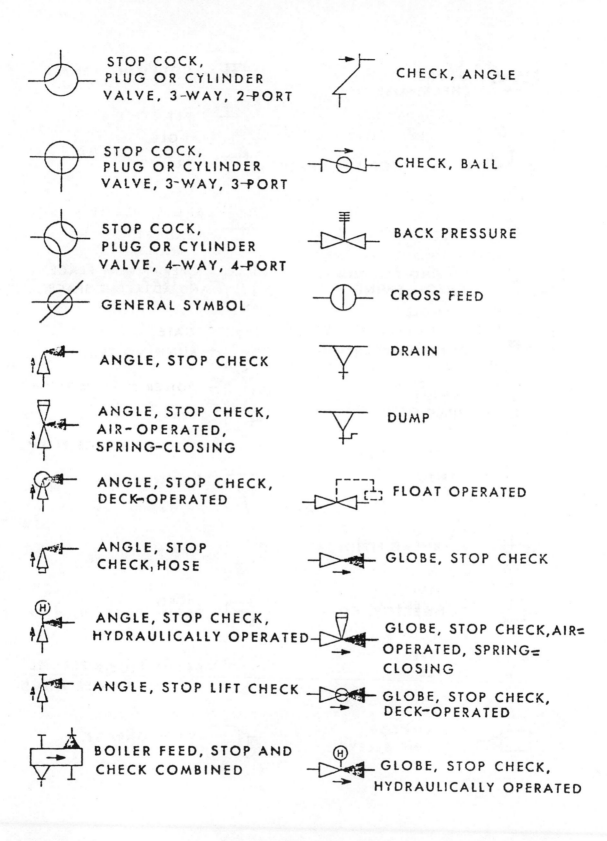

STOP COCK, PLUG OR CYLINDER VALVE, 3-WAY, 2-PORT

STOP COCK, PLUG OR CYLINDER VALVE, 3-WAY, 3-PORT

STOP COCK, PLUG OR CYLINDER VALVE, 4-WAY, 4-PORT

GENERAL SYMBOL

ANGLE, STOP CHECK

ANGLE, STOP CHECK, AIR-OPERATED, SPRING-CLOSING

ANGLE, STOP CHECK, DECK-OPERATED

ANGLE, STOP CHECK, HOSE

ANGLE, STOP CHECK, HYDRAULICALLY OPERATED

ANGLE, STOP LIFT CHECK

BOILER FEED, STOP AND CHECK COMBINED

CHECK, ANGLE

CHECK, BALL

BACK PRESSURE

CROSS FEED

DRAIN

DUMP

FLOAT OPERATED

GLOBE, STOP CHECK

GLOBE, STOP CHECK, AIR-OPERATED, SPRING-CLOSING

GLOBE, STOP CHECK, DECK-OPERATED

GLOBE, STOP CHECK, HYDRAULICALLY OPERATED

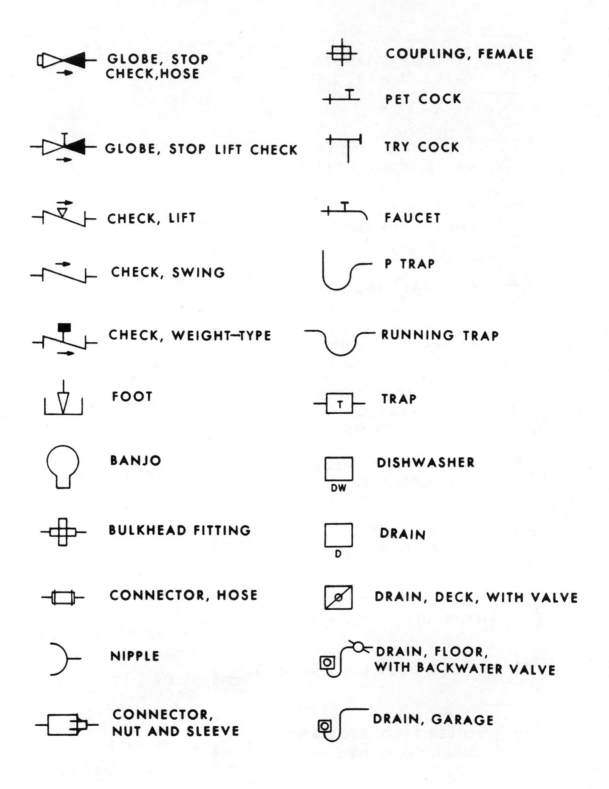

GLOBE, STOP
CHECK, HOSE

GLOBE, STOP LIFT CHECK

CHECK, LIFT

CHECK, SWING

CHECK, WEIGHT—TYPE

FOOT

BANJO

BULKHEAD FITTING

CONNECTOR, HOSE

NIPPLE

CONNECTOR,
NUT AND SLEEVE

COUPLING, FEMALE

PET COCK

TRY COCK

FAUCET

P TRAP

RUNNING TRAP

TRAP

DISHWASHER

DRAIN

DRAIN, DECK, WITH VALVE

DRAIN, FLOOR,
WITH BACKWATER VALVE

DRAIN, GARAGE

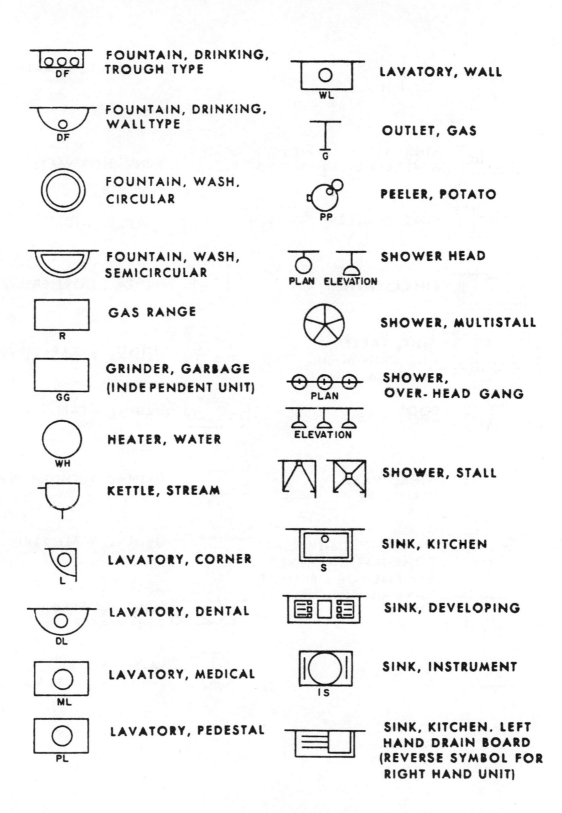

FOUNTAIN, DRINKING, TROUGH TYPE
DF

FOUNTAIN, DRINKING, WALL TYPE
DF

FOUNTAIN, WASH, CIRCULAR

FOUNTAIN, WASH, SEMICIRCULAR

GAS RANGE
R

GRINDER, GARBAGE (INDEPENDENT UNIT)
GG

HEATER, WATER
WH

KETTLE, STREAM

LAVATORY, CORNER
L

LAVATORY, DENTAL
DL

LAVATORY, MEDICAL
ML

LAVATORY, PEDESTAL
PL

LAVATORY, WALL
WL

OUTLET, GAS
G

PEELER, POTATO
PP

SHOWER HEAD
PLAN   ELEVATION

SHOWER, MULTISTALL

SHOWER, OVER-HEAD GANG
PLAN
ELEVATION

SHOWER, STALL

SINK, KITCHEN
S

SINK, DEVELOPING

SINK, INSTRUMENT
IS

SINK, KITCHEN. LEFT HAND DRAIN BOARD (REVERSE SYMBOL FOR RIGHT HAND UNIT)

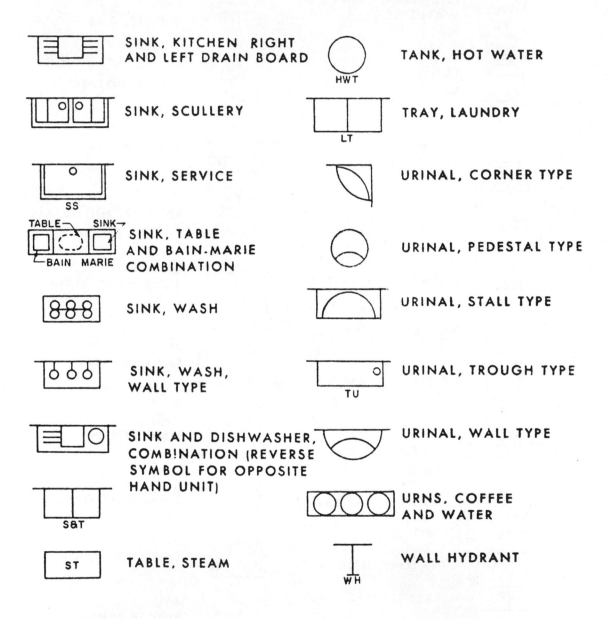

SINK, KITCHEN RIGHT AND LEFT DRAIN BOARD

TANK, HOT WATER

SINK, SCULLERY

TRAY, LAUNDRY

SINK, SERVICE

URINAL, CORNER TYPE

SINK, TABLE AND BAIN-MARIE COMBINATION

URINAL, PEDESTAL TYPE

SINK, WASH

URINAL, STALL TYPE

SINK, WASH, WALL TYPE

URINAL, TROUGH TYPE

SINK AND DISHWASHER, COMBINATION (REVERSE SYMBOL FOR OPPOSITE HAND UNIT)

URINAL, WALL TYPE

URNS, COFFEE AND WATER

TABLE, STEAM

WALL HYDRANT

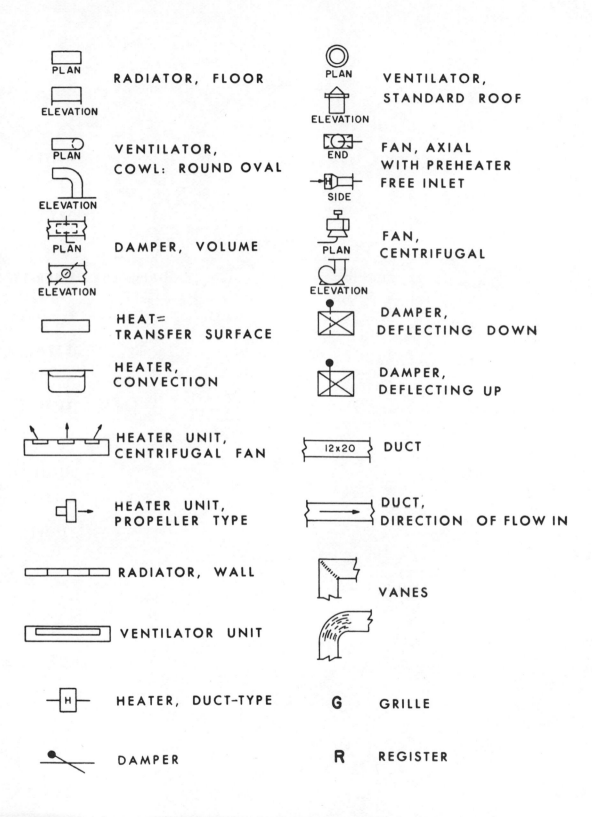

RADIATOR, FLOOR	VENTILATOR, STANDARD ROOF
VENTILATOR, COWL: ROUND OVAL	FAN, AXIAL WITH PREHEATER FREE INLET
DAMPER, VOLUME	FAN, CENTRIFUGAL
HEAT= TRANSFER SURFACE	DAMPER, DEFLECTING DOWN
HEATER, CONVECTION	DAMPER, DEFLECTING UP
HEATER UNIT, CENTRIFUGAL FAN	DUCT
HEATER UNIT, PROPELLER TYPE	DUCT, DIRECTION OF FLOW IN
RADIATOR, WALL	VANES
VENTILATOR UNIT	
HEATER, DUCT-TYPE	GRILLE
DAMPER	REGISTER

Glossary

A

ABRASIVE CLOTH
Specially processed cloth for cleaning copper tubing and fittings prior to soldering. Available in rolls 1½ inches x 10 yards.

ABS
Acrylonitrils-butadiene-styrene plastic pipe.

ADAPTER
(1) A fitting for joining pipes of the same size but made of different materials. (2) A device for connecting steel pipe to plastic pipe. (3) A fitting for connecting pipes of the same material but different diameters.

AERATOR
Device for oxygenating water, filling water flow with air bubbles. Available for all types of faucets as screw-on or snap-on types.

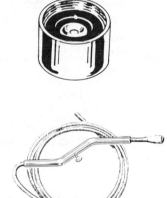

AIR CHAMBER
Capped section of short length of pipe, supplying an air cushion to prevent water hammer.

AUGER
Tool for clearing clogs from pipes.

B

BACK VENT
(1) A branch vent installed for purpose of protecting fixture traps against siphoning. (2) Any vent which lets air enter a waste pipe to prevent siphoning of water out of traps.

BACKFLOW
See *cross connection.*

BALLCOCK
Assembly used inside toilet tank for bringing water into tank. An automatic valve controlled by position of float.

BAR HANGER
Hanger for supporting a sink against a wall.

BASIN WRENCH
Tool for installing or removing headed bolts from hard-to-reach places.

BASKET
Type of strainer that fits into disposal opening of sink, extending down into it. Has deep body compared to flat strainer.

BRACKET HANGER
Hanger for supporting sink against a wall.

BRANCH
Any pipe connected to a fixture.

BRANCH VENT
Vent pipe connecting from a branch in the drainage system to the vent stack.

BUSHING
Device used when a pipe, a fitting, a faucet, or a valve is to be connected to a threaded opening of larger size. Bushings have female (internal) threads and male (external) threads.

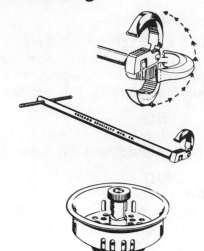

C
CALK
Material used to seal joints, particularly in drainage cast iron pipes.

CAP
Device used to close the end of a pipe.

CAULK
To seal, generally at pipe joints, to prevent escape of water or to provide water-tight seal.

CHAIN WRENCH
Tool that will handle pipe up to 4 inches IPS outside diameter. Ideal for use with large pipe or where ordinary wrenches cannot reach.

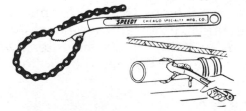

CLAMP STRAPS
Straps for holding and/or supporting pipes.

CLEANOUT, or CLEANOUT PLUG
Plug which can be removed to permit access to pipe for cleaning.

CLOSE NIPPLE
A short nipple. See also *nipple.*

CLOSED END NUT
A nut having a closed cap. A type of cap nut.

CLOSET
Synonym for "toilet."

CLOSET BEND
Pipe connecting toilet waste exit of toilet bowl to fitting of soil stack.

CLOSET SPUD
Connector or coupling between water supply pipe and bottom part of ballcock assembly in toilet tank.

CLOSET SPUD WRENCH
Tool for opening toilet (closet) spuds, strainers, and trap nuts.

COLD WATER MAIN
Piping for cold water system.

COMBINATION LOCK NUT WRENCH
Tool with one end sized for use on large strainer lock nuts, and opposite end sized for 1½-inch and oversized 1½-inch slip nuts.

COMPOUND
See *pipe joint compound*.

CORNER TUB
Tub that fits into corner of bathroom. Two corner walls butt against tub.

COUPLING
Fitting used for connecting or joining two or more pipes, or a pipe and a fixture.

CROSS CONNECTION
Link between fresh water and contaminated water or sewage. Also backflow.

CPVC
Chlorinated polyvinyl chloride plastic pipe.

D

DIAMETER OF STEEL PIPE
Size of pipe is its ID (inside diameter). For example, ¾-inch steel pipe is pipe having an ID of ¾-inch.

DIE
Also known as pipe die. Used for cutting threads on outside of pipe. A tool for cutting male threads.

DIE STOCK
Handle and holder for a die.

DISPOSAL FIELD
Portion of a septic tank system. Used to permit absorption of liquid waste into the earth.

DIVERTER
Valve for changing flow of water from one faucet to another. Commonly used for diverting water from tub faucet to shower head.

DIVERTER SPOUT
Spout with attachment for diverting water to another faucet or shower spray head.

DRAIN
(1) Length of drain pipe. (2) Pipe in sewage portion of plumbing system. (3) Any pipe that carries waste.

DRAIN FLANGE
Flange that covers drain hole of sink. The flange has a pipelike extension that is threaded.

DRUM TRAP COVER
Cover used for bathtub trap.

DRUM TRAP WRENCH
Tool for opening drum traps.

DRY VENT
Vent which never carries water or mixture of waste and water.

DWV
(1) Abbreviation for drainage, waste, and vent system. (2) A type of very thin rigid copper pipe.

E
EIGHTH BEND
Fitting bent at an angle so that connecting pipes are at a 45° angle to each other.

ELBOW
Fitting that is internally threaded at both ends.

ELL
Abbreviation for elbow. A fitting for connecting pipes at an angle.

ESCUTCHEON
Ornamental plate used for covering small section of pipe, particularly at area where pipe enters wall.

F

FAUCET
A valve, generally used with a fixture, such as a sink, for controlling the flow of water.

FAUCET FOUNTAIN
Turns any faucet into a fountain. Eliminates use of cups. Supplies aerated faucet stream.

FEMALE THREADS
Internal threads.

FIELD
See *disposal field*.

FINISH PLUMBING
Plumbing that is visible, hence must present an attractive appearance or "finish."

FITTING
Device for joining two or more pipes or for connecting pipe to a fixture.

FITTING GAIN
Amount of space inside a fitting required by a pipe.

FITTINGS FOR COPPER TUBING
Used for connecting copper tubing to tubing, pipe, or fixtures. Made of cast bronze, bronze, wrought copper, or brass.

FIXTURE DRAIN
Drain that includes a trap and is connected to a branch waste pipe.

FIXTURE SUPPLY PIPE
Part of branch line connected to a fixture.

FIXTURE UNIT
Term used to designate the flow of 1 cubic foot of water per minute.

FLANGE
Protruding rib, rim, edge, or collar used at one end of pipe shaft to supply support and finished appearance. May come with screw holes to accommodate screws for holding to wall.

FLANGE NUT
Nut used for connecting flared copper pipe to a threaded (flared) fitting.

FLANGE UNION
Union held together with nuts and bolts. See also *union.*

FLARE
End of copper pipe bent outward in circular form.

FLOAT
Metal or plastic ball used in toilet tanks. Float is attached to threaded rod known as the float arm.

FLOAT ROD
Copper rod, threaded at both ends, with one end screwed into valve of ballcock assembly and other to the float. A connecting rod used in toilet tanks.

FLOOR AND CEILING PLATES
For supplying decorative finish at floor or ceiling for pipes going through room.

FLOOR FLANGE
Flange, made of brass, positioned beneath drain hole of toilet.

FLUSH BALL
Part of toilet tank assembly. Fits into flush valve seat. When lifted, lets water flow into toilet bowl, flushing it.

FLUSH VALVE SEAT
Part of toilet tank assembly. Flush ball fits into flush valve seat to close flow of water into toilet bowl.

FORCE CUP
Also known as plunger or plumber's friend. For clearing clogs from toilets and drains. Similar to type used for clearing sink clogs.

FPT
Abbreviation for "female pipe thread."

FREE STANDING TUB
Tub that is free of walls on all sides.

G
GASKET
Large, circular washer used for providing watertight seal.

GATE VALVE
Valve that doesn't control amount of water flowing through it. Water either flows at maximum or is completely off. Uses a gatelike disc.

GLOBE VALVE
Valve that controls amount of water flow.

GREASE TRAP
Trap for separating grease from other kitchen waste.

GROUP VENT
Branch vent that provides venting for two or more fixture traps.

H
HANDLE PULLER
Tool for removing all hooded type and all cross and lever handles.

HANGER
Support for pipe.

HARD WATER
Water that contains dissolved minerals such as calcium or magnesium sulfate or bicarbonate.

HORIZONTAL BRANCH
Also known as a lateral. Pipe that extends horizontally at a slight pitch from soil stack or waste stack and takes discharges from fixtures not connected directly to soil stack.

HOT WATER MAIN
Piping for hot water system.

HUBLESS PIPE
Pipe that has smooth ends, without spigot or hub.

K
K TYPE
Heavy, rigid copper pipe.

KNOCK CHAMBER
Short length of pipe with cap at one end, used for prevention of water hammer. Also known as air chamber and antiknock chamber.

L
L TYPE
Medium-weight rigid copper pipe.

LAVATORY
Material used to seal joints in drainage cast iron pipes. A calking material.

LIP UNION
Special type of union. See also *union.*

LONG QUARTER BEND
Quarter bend fitting with one section of the fitting much longer than the other. See also *quarter bend.*

LOWER LIFT WIRE
Threaded solid wire connected at lower end to flush ball and at upper end to upper lift wire. A part of the toilet tank assembly.

M
M TYPE
Also known as M. Lightest version of rigid copper pipe.

MAIN
Principal pipe to which are connected drain and waste pipes, either directly or through branches.

MAIN DRAIN
See *soil stack.*

MAIN HOUSE DRAIN
Pipe connected to the main house sewer. A pipe joined by all waste and drain pipes in the plumbing system.

MAKEUP
Length of pipe that goes into a fitting.

MALE THREADS
External threads.

MITER BOX
Box made of extremely hard wood or metal. Slotted for cutting pipe, usually at 45° or 90° angles.

MIXING FAUCET
Separate faucets with a common spout. Adjustment of handles permits control of temperature and amount of water flow.

MPT
Abbreviation for "male pipe thread."

N
NIPPLE
Small length of pipe, either wholly or partially threaded externally. Number of threads per inch can vary with different nipples.

O
OFFSET
(1) To run at an angle. The offset arm of a fitting is at an angle to the rest of the fitting. An offset pipe is at an angle to the remainder of the pipe run. (2) A combination of elbows, bends or special fittings which carry one section of a stack to one side of the original line, then allow it to continue on a line parallel to the original direction.

OPEN END NUT
Nut that has a through hole. A type of cap nut.

OUTLET OPENING
Opening in a tee which is at an angle to the other two openings of this fitting.

OVERFLOW PIPE
Part of toilet tank assembly. Used to prevent excessive buildup of water in toilet tank.

OVERFLOW TUBE
Tube positioned vertically in toilet tank. Used for draining excess water from tank.

P
PACKING
Material used to prevent leakage from a nut, such as a packing nut.

PACKING NUT
Part of the hardware of a faucet. Used for holding spindle of faucet in position.

PIER TUB
Bathtub built into floor with single wall at its back.

PIPE DIE
See *die*.

PIPE JOINT COMPOUND
Sealing material put on threads of pipes and fittings. Used for lubrication and prevention of leaks at joints.

PIPE TAP
Tool for cutting internal threads in pipe. Taps are available for pipes ranging from ⅛-inch to 2-inches IPS.

PIPE VISE
Vise especially designed to hold pipe.

PITCH
Slope of a drain pipe.

PLUMBER'S FRIEND
Also known as force cup or plunger. A rubber suction device equipped with a handle, used for removing clogs.

POP-UP VALVE
Device for opening and closing sink drains.

PVC
Polyvinyl chloride plastic pipe.

Q
QUARTER BEND
Fitting bent at an angle so that connecting pipes are at 90° angle to each other.

R

RADIATOR NIPPLE WRENCH

Capacity ½, ¾, 1¼, 1½, and 2 inches. Small end is inserted into nipple of radiator until proper size is reached. Pipe wrench is then used to turn tool and loosen or tighten nipple.

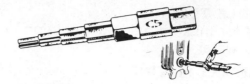

REAMER

See *tapered reamer.*

RECESSED TUB

Tub that has walls against three of its four sides.

REDUCER

Fitting used to join two pipes having different diameters.

REDUCING TEE

Fitting for connecting three pipes. Can have one opening larger or smaller than the other two, or may have three different sizes for the three openings.

REFILL TUBE

Copper tube connecting toilet valve assembly to overflow pipe. Part of toilet tank assembly.

RELIEF VALVE

Valve fitted onto hot water heater to prevent excessive temperature or pressure.

RELIEF VENT

Pipe connected between a branch from the vent stack and the soil stack or a waste stack, primarily to let air circulate between the two stacks.

REVENT

Pipe used only for venting purposes.

RISER

Pipe that is part of a main or a branch that goes up through the walls.

RUN OPENING

Pair of openings in a tee which are in line. Openings in a tee which lead directly into each other without bends.

S

SADDLE TEE
Used for making quick connection to existing water line.

SANITARY FITTING
Fitting used in a drainage system.

SELF-TAPPING REPAIR PLUG
Hardened steel, tapered screw with bolt head, used for repairing leaks in boilers, tanks, and pipes. Has neoprene washer.

SERVICE ENTRANCE LINE
Pipe connected between outside water main and water meter.

SERVICE TEE—See *street tee.*

SHOWER CURTAIN RODS
Rods mounted above tub that has a shower attachment or stall shower. May be straight or angled or corner-type. Available with or without hooks for shower curtain. Made of chrome-plated brass or anodized aluminum.

SHOWER FRAME
Rectangular frame, brass, chrome plated, 26 x 45 inches. Has ceiling support.

SHOWER HEAD
Connects to shower arm. May have adjustable spray feature. ½-inch IPS connection. When in plastic, is available in colors. Also made of solid brass, chrome plated.

SHOWER HEAD VOLUME CONTROL
Device for regulating flow of water from shower. Internally and extrenally threaded and connects between shower head and shower arm.

SHUTOFF VALVE
Used for turning off water supply to fixture or pipe. Also see *valve.*

SIDE VENT
Vent that connects to drain pipe through a 45° y fitting.

SINGLE-LEVER FAUCET
Faucet that uses spring pressure for shutting off water supply.

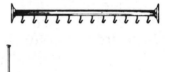

SLEEVE
Device—made of rubber, plastic, neoprene, asbestos, or other substances—designed to fit or slip over a section of pipe.

SLIP NUT
Internally threaded nut, generally complete with washer.

SLIP TEE
See *three-way slip tee.*

SNAKE
An auger. Long flexible cable for cleaning out clogs.

SOFT WATER
Water that has little or no dissolved minerals such as calcium or magnesium sulfate or bicarbonate.

SOIL STACK
(1) A drain that receives waste from toilets and branch waste pipes. Also known as a main drain. (2) The vertical main that receives waste from all fixtures.

SPEEDEE
Chrome-plated copper tubing having ⅜-inch diameter. Easy to bend.

SPINDLE
Part of faucet that turns with handle and is equipped with washer at one end.

SPLINE
Vertical projections on a shaft that fit into slots on a corresponding shaft, enabling both to rotate together.

SPOUT
Part of a faucet. Terminal of pipe through which water flows. Usually solid brass or die cast, chromium plated. Internally threaded for connection to pipe.

SPOUT WITH TWIN ELL
Spout with built-in fitting for connection to hot and cold water pipes.

SPUD
See *closet spud.*

STACK
See *vent stack* and *soil stack.*

STEM
Portion of faucet assembly. Holds washer at one end.

STRAIGHT CROSS
Fitting which will accommodate four pipes having the same diameters.

STRAIGHT TEE
Fitting for connecting three pipes of the same diameter.

STRAINER
Cover for disposal opening in sinks and tubs.

STRAINER LOCK NUT WRENCH
Tool for opening strainer lock nuts.

STRAP WRENCH
Tool for turning pipes. Has heavy malleable body and latex-treated nylon web for use on chrome-plated pipes.

STREET TEE
Also known as a service tee. Has one run opening with a female thread, the other with a male thread, and outlet opening with female thread.

SWEAT SOLDERING
Soldering with a torch, used for connecting copper pipes.

SWEATING
Condensation. Accumulation of moisture on outside of toilet tanks or pipes.

T
TAPERED REAMER
Tool for deburring and cleaning inside end of pipe.

TEE
Fitting resembling the letter *T*. Has three openings for pipes. See also *three-way slip tee*.

TEE HANDLE
Handle for faucet with connecting hole in center or at one end. Hole is splined so no screw fastener is needed.

THREE-WAY SLIP TEE
Fitting equipped with slip nuts and used for connecting three pipes.

TOILET AUGER
Also known as closet auger. Special type of auger for clearing clogs from toilets.

TOILET TANK BALL
Seals across top of flush valve in toilet tank, permitting water shutoff from tank into toilet bowl.

TRAP
Device which permits flow of water and sewage through it while blocking passage of air and sewer gas in the reverse direction.

TRIP HANDLE
Handle on outside of upper left side of toilet tank. Used for flushing toilet.

TUB TRAP
Trap for a bathtub.

U
UNION
Fitting that joins pipes but which can be opened to allow for easier disassembly of piping system.

UPPER LIFT WIRE
Part of toilet tank assembly. Bottom end is connected to lower lift wire; upper end to trip lever.

V
VALVE
Device for controlling the flow of water. Valves can be inserted directly in pipeline or may be used as terminals at end of pipes, as faucets.

VENT
Upper part of the soil stack. Pipe connecting soil stack to pipe that extends above roof level.

VENT INCREASER
Section of pipe, narrow at one end, wider at the other. Fits on roof end of vent.

VENT STACK
Vertical vent pipe.

VISE
See *pipe vise.*

W

WATER CLOSET
See *closet*.

WALL-HUNG TOILET
Toilet completely supported by a wall.

WC
Water closet or toilet.

WET VENT
Waste pipe that also acts as a vent for other fixtures on the same line.

WYE BRANCH
Fitting with entry for pipe to come in at an angle.

Y-BRANCH
Fitting generally used in soil stack, linking two vertical sections of soil stack and having a branch to a drain pipe.

696   N.F.3099

Clifford, Martin
Household Plumbing
Installation & Repair

UNION PUBLIC LIBRARY
TIVERTON, R. I.

Rock-a-bye fuzzy,
Don't squirm like a bug.
Here comes a great big
Orangutan hug.

MMMMMM-UMM!

Rock-a-bye young one,
Lie by me and stay,
So I can kiss you
The elephant way.

TIC-TIC-TICKLE!

Rock-a-bye bear cub,
Come closer now, scootch
So Mama can land
a Panda bear smooch.

MWWWWAH!

Rock-a-bye kit cat,
Stop with the hisses
So I can give you
Whiskery kisses.

WHISK! WHISK!

Come now, my trunkling,
My dear big-eared dumpling,
Tomorrow you'll run,
You'll trumpet and spray.

WAIT...

Come now, my redhead,
My tree-for-a-bed head,
Tomorrow you'll hoot,
You'll swing and you'll play.

Come now, my bear cub,
My soft woolly-hair cub,
Tomorrow you'll roll,
You'll climb and you'll chase.

Come now, my leopard,
All spotted and peppered,
Tomorrow you'll pounce,
You'll roar and you'll race.

STOMP, STOMP!

STOMP, STOMP,

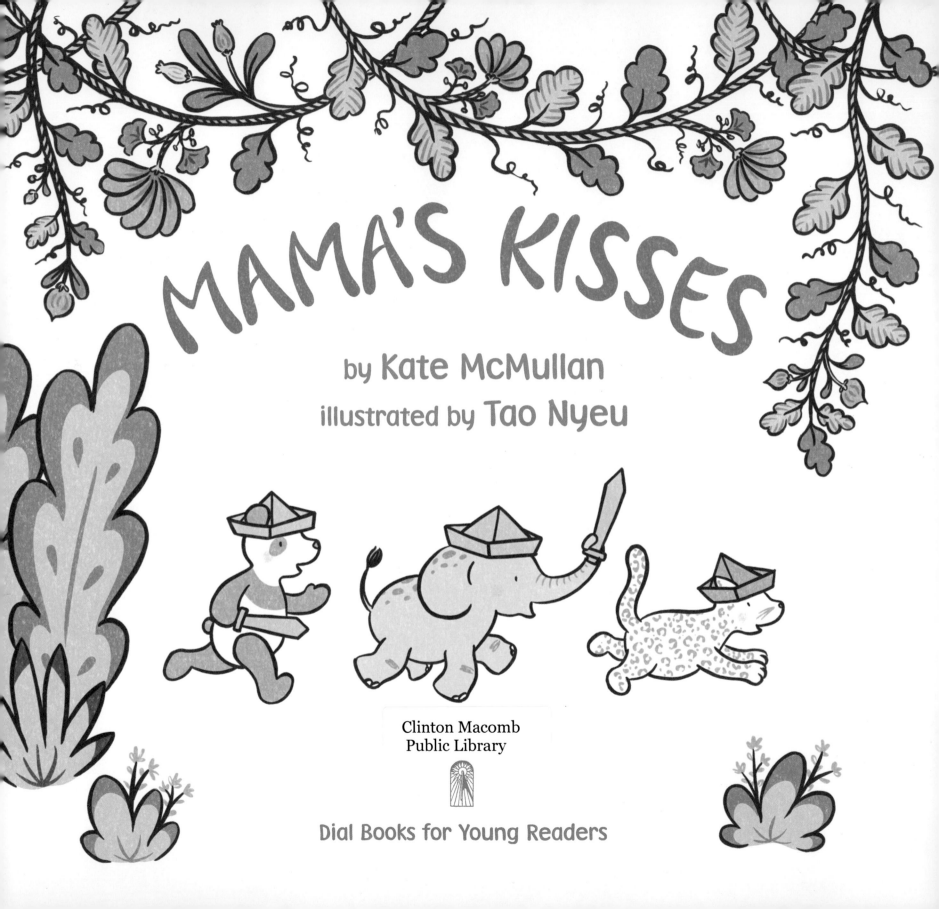

MAMA'S KISSES

by Kate McMullan

illustrated by Tao Nyeu

Clinton Macomb
Public Library

Dial Books for Young Readers

For Arthur and his mama, mwwwwah! —KM

For my babies, all one, two, and three. —TN

Dial Books for Young Readers
Penguin Young Readers Group
An imprint of Penguin Random House LLC
375 Hudson Street
New York, NY 10014

Text copyright © 2017 by Kate McMullan
Illustrations copyright © 2017 by Tao Nyeu

Penguin supports copyright. Copyright fuels creativity, encourages diverse voices, promotes free speech,
and creates a vibrant culture. Thank you for buying an authorized edition of this book and for complying
with copyright laws by not reproducing, scanning, or distributing any part of it in any form without permission.
You are supporting writers and allowing Penguin to continue to publish books for every reader.

Library of Congress Cataloging-in-Publication Data • Names: McMullan, Kate, author. | Nyeu, Tao, illustrator. • Title: Mama's
kisses / Kate McMullan ; Illustrated by Tao Nyeu. • Description: New York : Dial Books for Young Readers, [2017] | Summary:
"A mother panda bear, elephant, leopard and orangutan follow their rambunctious little ones through the jungle as they
try to corral them for bedtime"— Provided by publisher. • Identifiers: LCCN 2015049504 | ISBN 9780525428329 (hardcover)
Subjects: | CYAC: Bedtime—Fiction. | Jungle animals—Fiction. | Mother and child—Fiction. | Stories in rhyme.
Classification: LCC PZ8.3.M238 Mam 2017 | DDC [E]—dc23 LC record available at https://lccn.loc.gov/2015049504

Printed in China • 10 9 8 7 6 5 4 3 2 1

Design by Lily Malcom • Text set in Fontoon

The artwork was created using ink, colored pencils, and Photoshop.

Give YOUR baby animal kisses!

Leopard kiss = rub cheeks   Elephant kiss = pull hand inside sleeve, tickle
Panda kiss = tummy smooch   Orangutan hug = BIG hug

APR 1 4 2017

W9-BSI-171